RIVERBOAT

MISSISSIPPI
PIRATES

Also by Douglas Hirt
in Large Print:

Devil's Wind
Colorado Gold
Riverboat
A Passage of Seasons
Able Gate

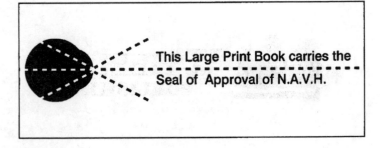

RIVERBOAT

MISSISSIPPI PIRATES

Douglas Hirt

WHEELER
PUBLISHING

Copyright © 1995 by Douglas Hirt.
Riverboat Series #2.

Published in 2005 by arrangement with
Cherry Weiner Literary Agency.

Wheeler Large Print Western.

The text of this Large Print edition is unabridged.
Other aspects of the book may vary from the original edition.

Set in 16 pt. Plantin by Minnie B. Raven.

Printed in the United States on permanent paper.

Library of Congress Cataloging-in-Publication Data

Hirt, Douglas.
    Riverboat Mississippi pirates / by Douglas Hirt.
        p. cm. — (Wheeler Publishing large print western)
    ISBN 1-59722-126-0 (lg. print : sc : alk. paper)
    1. Ship captains — Fiction.   2. Pirates — Fiction.
    3. River boats — Fiction.   4. Mississippi River — Fiction.
    5. Large type books.   I. Title.   II. Wheeler large print
    western series.
    PS3558.I727R583 2005
    813'.6—dc22   2005021760

In memory of
GLENN CARTER

As the Founder/CEO of NAVH, the only national health agency solely devoted to those who, although not totally blind, have an eye disease which could lead to serious visual impairment, I am pleased to recognize Thorndike Press* as one of the leading publishers in the large print field.

Founded in 1954 in San Francisco to prepare large print textbooks for partially seeing children, NAVH became the pioneer and standard setting agency in the preparation of large type.

Today, those publishers who meet our standards carry the prestigious "Seal of Approval" indicating high quality large print. We are delighted that Thorndike Press is one of the publishers whose titles meet these standards. We are also pleased to recognize the significant contribution Thorndike Press is making in this important and growing field.

Lorraine H. Marchi, L.H.D.
Founder/CEO
NAVH

* Thorndike Press encompasses the following imprints: Thorndike, Wheeler, Walker and Large Print Press.

All Aboard the *Tempest Queen!*

THE CAPTAIN: William Hamilton was a veteran of thirty years on the river. Now, he had his own boat — and as far as he was concerned, the *Tempest Queen* was the finest and fastest packet on the Mississippi.

THE GAMBLER: The astute Dexter McKay knew every trick that was in the book — and some that weren't. Urged on by his curiosity and his loyalty, he often found out things he wasn't supposed to know . . .

THE LAND OWNER: Clifton Stewart came from a rich family and could have been living a life of luxury and ease. But his love for a mulatto kept him working on the *Tempest Queen* and searching for her at every port.

THE OFFICER: Lieutenant Sherman Dempsey was responsible for delivering gold and supplies to the Army stationed at Fort Leavenworth. A man who took his duty seriously, Dempsey would see to it that all his orders were fulfilled.

THE LADY: Miss Cora Mills was bringing her nephew to Fort Leavenworth to see his father. But when the river pirates took over, she learned that the ship was no place for a child — or a lady.

THE SERGEANT: Sergeant Philip Carr was a very able soldier, and second-in-command to Lieutenant Dempsey. But there was something about the man that McKay didn't trust . . .

THE DOCTOR: Reuben Samuel was a kindhearted man traveling in Missouri with his wife and his stepsons, Frank and Jesse. When they found an unconscious man in the river, Reuben knew they had no choice but to care for him.

THE PIRATE: Deke Saunders was one of the most bloodthirsty river pirates in the land. He dressed like a preacher and answered to "Reverend Saunders," but inside was a soul as diabolical as the Devil himself.

THE STRANGER: To most of those who met him, Charles Hart was nobody special. But a few knew and feared him by his real name, William Clarke Quantrill . . .

THE KID: Frank James was a responsible boy at age sixteen, keeping his little brother Jesse out of trouble and discouraging his dreams of piracy and banditry. But the older brother had a well-concealed desire for action and adventure . . .

Prelude

A late afternoon sun bludgeoned its way through the hot, misty air and penetrated the green cover of oak and poplar leaves with lances of golden light, mottling the grassy clearing beneath the trees in bright splotches. The trees seemed to hold little power to protect the land from the August heat or from the humidity that settled like a wet blanket in the swampy ravine — and upon the three men languishing there, near the side of the road.

Against the moss-covered, slanted side of a tree stump, Deke Saunders lay gasping as if on his deathbed — as if the heavy air pressing down upon him no longer bore enough oxygen to supply his meager needs. His discarded black frock coat lay in a crumpled pile nearby on the coarse grass where presently a green snake was finding its way through the folds and onto more profitable hunting grounds. Saunders's black slouch hat had landed a few feet away in a different direction. He had unbuttoned his black shirt, laying bare his sunken chest, slick with sweat, to the gentle hand of any passing breeze. His right arm was flung across his eyes, shutting the sun out, his left dangled as if of a dead man's, grasping the clerical collar in the hook of his fingers where they curled naturally.

Mosquitoes and clouds of black flies hovered about him, but Saunders had grown weary of swatting them and had agreed to suffer their torment in silence, occasionally rising to the challenge of a buzz in his ear or a sting to his cheek where the tangled gray beard did little to protect it. But beyond this minor defense, the heat of the afternoon had sapped all of Deke Saunders's strength to defend himself.

On the other side of the lane that wound through the swamp, Deke's nephew, Harold Madden, had similarly given himself over to the tortures of the afternoon heat, and the bugs. With his back propped against the bark of an oak tree and his knees drawn up, Harold Madden stared at the ground between his feet as if in a daze, killing the time by extinguishing ants and beetles with a whack of his bowie; the steady *whomp . . . whomp . . .* was slowly digging nails into Deke Saunders's nerves. Harold wore a straw hat and no shoes. His sleeves ended in frayed edges just below his elbows, as did his trouser legs several inches above the ankles.

Sitting off by himself, the third fellow, Jason, seemed little affected by the heat, although sweat streamed from his half-naked body and glistened like water over an ebony stone in the shafts of sunlight coming through the leafy cover overhead. He wore a tattered straw hat, half a shirt, and shredded trousers that ended in threads at mid-thigh. Jason's back was a patchwork of scars — like livid worms all crawling off in different directions. Jason was used to rough conditions and attended them with a quiet resolve the other two men could not quite muster. There was no telling what Jason thought about his present situation or the oppressive heat, for he never spoke except when confronted with a direct question.

And there they sat: the three of them withering in a sweltering silence broken only by the croak of frogs, the buzz of mosquitoes, the chirp of a tanager, and the occasional *whomp . . . whomp . . .* of Harold Madden's broad-blade bowie crashing down upon some insect.

"Will you put that damn knife away, Madden!" Deke Saunders finally erupted, unable to contain his mounting irritation any further. He sat up straight, his bare, scarecrow chest heaving, his bushy eyebrows contracted. "You is about to drive me crazy!" He slashed viciously at an attacking fly and stood. Saunders was a lanky man, more bone than flesh, with sunken eyes and a scattering of gray hairs — thinned by the years — flying from his scalp in all directions.

"Su— sure thing, Deke. I di— didn't mean to bother y— y— you," Madden said.

Saunders shifted his view up the two-rut lane, buttoning his shirt and lifting an arm through his suspenders. He walked off a few paces and stopped, suddenly cocking an ear at the road where it made a bend ahead. The trees and low growth all about the clearing were so thick that a man would have had a hard time moving more than a dozen feet in any direction — except along the almost motionless water of the swamp behind him. Its water was a light green, covered over entirely with duckweed and lily pads. Once in a while a frog would leap and make a hole and a ripple in the floating mass, and then slowly the green would flow back to repair the damage.

Saunders listened a moment longer, his head cocked, and then he glanced over at the younger man. "You hear anything, Harold?"

Madden strained against the soft background noise of the swamp and shook his head. "No. Don't — don't hear nothin', Deke."

Saunders scowled and continued to listen. Slowly, the scowl deepened. "Well, I sure do hear something. There's a rider a coming." Saunders wheeled about to the black man. "Here, Jason, you best get out of sight!"

"Yes, suh." Jason scurried down to the water's edge, and in an instant the dense vegetation completely hid him. Deke lifted his other arm through the suspender and fixed the clerical collar back in place around his neck. In another moment he had the frock coat on and was brushing out the creases. Madden came across the road and grabbed a long squirrel gun from the rank grass, blowing on its lock where a bit of debris had gathered.

Saunders glanced at the rifle. "Put that down till we know who it is."

Madden leaned it against the bole of a

tree within easy reach.

The hoofbeats were louder now, just around the bend in the road. Saunders retrieved his hat from the grass and was settling it in place upon his head when the rider appeared.

Deke gave a tight grin, his rotted teeth made a fleeting appearance, and then were hidden once again by his thin lips. "There, you see, Harold, it is only Grady."

"You nev— never know, Deke. Might have bee— been the patrollers."

The rider drew up and swung off his horse. Saunders strode out to meet him. "What took you so long, boy? You was suppose to be back hours ago."

"Sorry, Pa. I meant to but —"

"Here, what's that I smell on you, boy?" Saunders leaned closer and sniffed. "You been drinkin'?"

"Only one drink, Pa. Honest."

Saunders's fist shot out, and the next moment Grady was picking himself off the road, rubbing his chin. "Aw, Pa, what you do that fer?"

"When I send you into town to do a job for me, I don't expect you to come back drunk."

"I ain't drunk." Grady Saunders stood.

Deke took the boy's chin in his fingers

and studied it. "And I'll wager you was carousing with them women as well. You ain't hurt, none." He released Grady's chin. "I should have hit you harder. Now tell me what you found out."

Near the water's edge, Jason emerged from cover. Grady watched the black man go back to his place in the shade, then shifted his eyes to his father.

"Carr ain't in St. Louie, Pa. I asked around fer him on the wharf."

"He was suppose to be there two days ago."

Grady shrugged his narrow shoulders. At twenty-five, he was already a younger image of his father; slender as a rail, gaunt of cheek and chest — although not quite as tall and still carrying a bit more hair on top. "The wharfmaster says the *Lulla Belle* ain't even come into her berth yet."

"Hum. There must have been trouble upriver then."

"That's would be my guess, Pa." Grady scratched himself and waited as his father pondered this news.

"Well, I reckon we'll have to hang around here a little while longer then," Deke said finally. "There is no way a boatload of Federal troops is going to stop in St. Louis without us knowing 'bout it."

17

Grady looked at him, suddenly concerned. "You think that Carr might try a double cross on us, Pa?"

Saunders's eyes narrowed at his son. "I don't trust nobody. I sometimes don't even trust you, boy."

Grady grinned and chuckled a little nervously, unable to hide his uneasiness in the presence of this fierce, old man. Then Grady's expression changed, and he lowered his voice. "We got us another problem, Pa," and his view shifted back to the runaway slave sitting a little distance away.

Deke caught the urgency in his son's voice, took Grady's sleeve, and stepped off a few paces. "What kind of problem?" he said, lowering his voice.

"There is a warrant out for that runaway. His picture is posted all over St. Louie."

"So? A warrant is good. That just means we got legal possession of him — again." Deke grinned. "Leastwise till we sell him . . . again."

"This time they got a description of the men who sold him last, Pa, and it sounds real close to me and you." Grady pulled a folded paper from his pocket.

"What? Here, lemme see that." Deke opened the poster. The picture on it was

Jason's, all right, and the warning at the bottom described Deke and Grady in detail. The old man frowned.

"What we gonna do about it, Pa? They catch us with that nigger now, and it's a lynch rope around our necks fer sure."

Saunders's cold gray eyes shifted. He considered the black man across the clearing and then said softly, "Well, Grady, we've netted three thousand dollars off of him so far. I reckon the time has finally come to send Jason North like we had promised him we would do."

Grady chuckled.

Deke wadded the poster up and stuffed it into his coat pocket. "I reckon it is time to break the good news to Jason."

Grady followed at his father's heels.

"Jason."

"Yes, suh, Reverend Saunders?" The black man looked up at him.

"Jason, stand up here."

Jason arose.

"Grady here has just been to town. He says the patrollers have gotten wind of where you is, so I reckon it's time I give you your due and send you North like we agreed."

At once a spark of excitement animated Jason's tired face. "Yo' gonna send me Nort'?"

"You ready to go, Jason?"

"Yes, suh, Reverend Saunders!"

"Good. Now first I need to square with you." Saunders pulled a wad of money from his pocket and counted out five hundred dollars in bank notes. When he put it in Jason's big, calloused hand, the black man only stared.

"Something wrong, Jason? It is what we agreed on."

"No, suh! Ain't nothin's wrong. This here is more money den I's ever sees in a lifetime!"

Saunders grinned. "Well, you earned it. And the rest of this money will go to helping other poor slaves get to freedom, just like I promised."

"Yo's doin' a grand task, Reverend Saunders, and us colored folks sure do bless yo'!"

Deke Saunders's grin eased into a wide, benevolent smile — a mighty chore for the old man's flint-hard face. "Hearing you say that, Jason, is the only reward a man like me asks for. Now, before I send you on your way, I think we ought to take a walk down by the water and say a powerful prayer for safe deliverance on your journey." Deke took the runaway slave by the arm and led him to the edge of the swamp. "Now, you just kneel down here, and I'll start, Jason."

When the black man was on his knees, Deke Saunders raised his voice plaintively, "Dear Lord, you got yourself a good nigger here, and Jason deserves the rest that freedom offers. Into your mighty hands we commend his journey which is about to begin right now."

As he prayed, Deke Saunders walked behind Jason, whose head was bowed, and reached under his coat.

The boom of the big Colt's revolver reverberated across the swamp. Birds rose in frenzied flight, circling overhead, and a half dozen small splashes sounded out in the overgrown swamp as smaller critters took cover beneath the green water.

"Amen!" Deke stood over Jason's body, holstered his revolver, and removed the money from the lifeless, black fingers.

Grady came up alongside him. "You sent him on his way, Pa, like you promised."

"I always keep a sacred trust, Son."

Grady turned Jason's body over with the toe of his boot. The top of the black man's head had been blown away but leaving staring eyes to gaze up at the two men. "He do look peaceful now, Pa."

Harold Madden showed up and looked

down at the dead man. Deke shoved the five hundred dollars into his pocket and put out a hand. Madden placed his bowie in it. The preacher slit the body from belly to brisket, cut out his entrails, and tossed them far into the swamp. Madden found a rock to put into the glistening, pink cavity, and Deke stuffed the poster in with it. Madden and Grady heaved the body into the swamp. It sunk immediately, and slowly the floating duckweed flowed back to cover over the place where Jason had gone under.

Deke washed his hands and went back out onto the road to wait for Carr's arrival.

Chapter One

Captain William Hamilton studied the cards that had just come across the table to him. He was sixty-two years old, stout but not fat, with gray hair thinning on top and a closely trimmed gray beard that he gently tugged at now, contemplatively. Hamilton was master of the riverboat *Tempest Queen*: the finest and most elegant packet to ply the Mississippi — or so he was quick to point out to anyone who asked. But at the moment, her grand main cabin, with its stained-glass skylights, crystal chandeliers, gleaming parquet-tiled floors, and huge gilded mirror at the far end in the ladies' salon, was quite empty — except for three people: a workman on a stepladder some distance away, painting the ceiling scrollwork, and Captain Hamilton and the man across the table from him, who was dealing out the cards with the smoothness of a well-oiled machine.

The *Tempest Queen* had been at the St. Louis boat docks for the last twelve days, getting new paint, much needed engine maintenance, and repaired and new paddle-boards. The sugar and cotton businesses had had a booming year, passenger traffic had been brisk throughout the spring and early summer, and now in the wake of an August nearly spent — the dull season, as it was called along the river — Hamilton had put in for repairs and a well-needed sprucing up. The cotton trade would begin again soon, and the *Tempest Queen* would be ready for it . . . all two hundred and eighty-seven feet of her from bow to stern.

The final card came across the table to Hamilton and when he had collected it, he lifted an eyebrow and fitted the card in to its proper place.

"There! You did it again!"

Hamilton's eyes shot up. The man across the table was glaring at him in exasperation.

Dexter McKay snatched his cigar from the ashtray, puffed mightily three times, and returned it. He was a handsome man, at present wearing a slightly soiled ruffled shirt with the top two buttons unlatched. The stiff paper collar and tie had been deposited on the edge of the table in deference to the August heat. His usual checked vest, brown frock coat, and tall beaver hat had been left in his cabin. McKay was somewhere in his late thirties, although he had never mentioned his exact age. He had allowed his hair to become slightly long since coming aboard the *Tempest Queen* as a more or less permanent passenger that spring, but he kept it greased and combed straight back. He cultivated bushy side whiskers, a carefully clipped mustache, and like Hamilton, a neatly trimmed imperial beard.

"What did I do wrong this time?" Hamilton tried to hide his annoyance. After all, this was for his own good. After a near disaster with three determined gamblers earlier that spring, Captain Hamilton was determined to master the game of poker, or like an alcoholic who finally swears off whiskey, he was going to give up cards forever — if he could.

McKay said, "I just dealt you your third king, and what did you do?"

"I don't know."

"You lifted an eyebrow! You always lift an eyebrow when you get a hoped-for card, Captain."

"Humm." Hamilton's eyes narrowed suddenly. "How did you know I had been dealt three kings?"

McKay cleared his throat. "Err, never mind."

"I do mind, Mr. McKay. When I agreed to let you stay on the *Tempest Queen*, it was with the injunction that you do not cheat at cards."

"I wasn't cheating, Captain," soothed McKay's silky voice, a carefully trained tool that could almost convince a pot of boiling water it was in fact an iceberg. "But I had to know what cards I was dealing you, so I could properly break you of your confounded habit of raising an eyebrow! Any gambler along the river would pick up on that in an instant. It's the reason those scoundrels, the retired general and his cronies, were nearly successful in cheating you out of the *Tempest Queen*, and almost stealing it for good!"

"Humm. Well, all right — I suppose." Hamilton could never forget the incident or the way Dexter McKay had stepped in at the last moment to win his precious riverboat back for him. "But by-the-devil, how am I ever going to beat you if you know what's in my hand?"

McKay grinned innocently and shrugged his shoulders, drawing again on his cigar. "It is not important that you beat me, Captain, for in fact, you can never beat me unless I allow it. What is important is that you learn to control yourself, to rightly think through the cards dealt to you, to learn when to call and when to fold, and most importantly, to learn when someone is leading you on. In an honest game there are just so many hands you can reasonably expect to win. When you discover that you have beaten the odds for too long, then it is time to find a new game, for as sure as this mighty river flows south to the Gulf, Captain Hamilton, you are being set up!"

"Humm. . . ." *Confounded man has the audacity of a riverboat pilot.*

"Captain Hamilton!"

The old riverboat master rotated in his seat. At the front of the main cabin, four lead-glass doors opened out onto the promenade and beyond that the wide, curving staircase, which descended to the main deck. Hamilton's chief engineer, Edward Lansing, had poked his head through the doorway.

"Some gentlemen to see you, Captain." Lansing stepped aside as three men strode in. The first two were military men, a lieutenant and his sergeant by the insignias on their uniforms; the third, a civilian. The lieutenant led the way to Hamilton's table.

The riverboat captain put his cards upon the white, starched tablecloth as they approached. "What can I do for you, Lieutenant?" Although Hamilton was an easy mark where cards were concerned, when it came to the river trade, he was a shrewd player, and he could see that these men had pressing business on their minds. But what sort of business might the military have with him?

"You are Captain William Hamilton, master of the *Tempest Queen*?"

"I am."

The army lieutenant stuck out a hand, and Hamilton took it. "I'm Lieutenant Sherman Dempsey. This is my sergeant, Philip Carr. And Mr. Eric Jupp." He paused to let his view wander about the long, main cabin, a feast for the eye of any man who had not before been aboard a craft such as the *Tempest Queen*. "I am happy to make your acquaintance, Captain. You've got a fine-looking vessel here."

"Thank you. What is it I can do for you, Lieutenant Dempsey?"

The army officer's view came back. He smiled and nodded his head at Dexter McKay before returning his full attention on Hamilton. "I was informed by the wharfmaster that your fine vessel is currently undergoing repairs but will be ready for the river trade again in two days. As far as he knew, you had not yet taken on any obligations either up the river or down."

Hamilton would not confirm his current schedule but said merely, "The wharf-master is not privy to my manifest, sir. Perhaps if you speak plainly what is upon your mind?"

"Of course. I am in charge of transporting replacement troops, matériel, and a paymaster to Fort Leavenworth. Three days ago our contract boat, the *Lulla Belle*, burst a seam in her boiler. Fortunately, no one was injured, but we've been stranded ever since and have only just arrived in St. Louis with the aid of a towboat. Now I am stuck here with forty men, twenty-five tons of supplies, and a paymaster whose presence in Fort Leavenworth had been sorely missed for over five months." Lieutenant Dempsey smiled thinly. "You know how slow the budgeting process has been in Washington. Congress as usual, leaves military financing until the very last."

Hamilton's bushy eyebrows dipped. "You want to engage the *Tempest Queen* to complete the journey to Fort Leavenworth?"

"Precisely, sir."

"Impossible."

Lieutenant Dempsey was momentarily taken aback by Hamilton's flat refusal.

"But, Captain, I implore you to reconsider. Yours is the only available boat, and I am in a bit of a dilemma here. Certainly in two days when you are ready to steam away you could take on this mission. If not to help out your country, then at least consider the payment I am authorized to make."

Hamilton waited for the lieutenant to continue.

"I am authorized to pay your going rate for cargo and passengers — deck passage, of course — and a premium on top of that of ten thousand dollars."

"Ten thousand dollars is a hefty premium, sir. Are you talking about government script or hard cash?"

Lieutenant Dempsey seemed indifferent about the sum. Apparently requisitioning transportation for the army was a thing he was used to doing, and he knew any lesser amount would be meaningless to Hamilton, who could easily triple that amount on a single trip down to Baton Rouge. "Hard cash, sir. The paymaster carries gold this trip. You see I am serious about my needs and am willing to pay a fair price for your services. And, of course, you may take on whatever freight and passengers you can attract for the trip as well. Our needs are small and will not possibly task the capacity of your boat."

"Humm. You make a fair offer. I wish I could oblige you, Lieutenant Dempsey."

The army lieutenant was not easily put off. He rested a hand on the pommel of his saber and smiled as if he suddenly understood. "I see. Well, Captain Hamilton, what price would make you reconsider?"

"Sir, I do not quibble over money."

"Then what do you want?" Genuine confusion came to Dempsey's brown eyes.

"Lieutenant Dempsey, the *Tempest Queen* is a deep-draft Mississippi vessel. She was never designed to ply the waters of the Missouri River, and unless my recollection is faulty, or the government has suddenly moved its location, Fort Leavenworth sits on the Missouri. The Missouri requires a smaller boat, shallower draft, stern wheel. Everything the *Tempest Queen* is not."

"You are mistaken, Captain." This was the civilian, Eric Jupp. "The Missouri River, as far west as Fort Leavenworth, is wide enough and deep enough for a boat this size." He spoke with authority on the matter. Captain Hamilton glanced over and noted for the first time Jupp's quiet arrogance, his aloofness, and his general air

31

of boredom with these negotiations. The man said no more, as if nothing else needed to be said.

Hamilton shifted his view back. "Even if the *Tempest Queen* could navigate the Missouri as far west as Fort Leavenworth, Lieutenant Dempsey, I still could not possibly transport you and your men. Like I said, we are a Mississippi boat. My pilot is a Mississippi pilot. He is not licensed for the Missouri River. I doubt I could find a competent Missouri riverboat pilot with proper papers on such a short notice, and if I did, Missouri pilots don't come cheap — even those that only work the lower river draw twice the pay of a Mississippi pilot."

Dexter McKay, a ghost of a smile on his lips, was quietly observing the negotiations and drawing casually on his cigar. Hamilton wondered briefly what the gambler was thinking, for he knew that hardly any small detail escaped McKay's notice. McKay put down the cigar and spread three cards upon the table: a pair of deuces and a queen. Turning them faces down, he began to shuffle them about, as if merely passing the time. This caught the eye of the sergeant, who inched nearer, his curiosity piqued.

"Monte?" Hamilton heard the sergeant inquire softly of McKay.

"Care to place a wager?"

The sergeant shook his head. "I have nothing of value with me to wager."

McKay glanced at the heavy gold ring upon the man's finger. The sergeant caught that and grinned and shook his head again. "Couldn't possibly, sir. It is the family crest."

The army lieutenant cleared his throat. Sergeant Carr stepped quickly back to his place at his superior's side. Dempsey tried again to make inroads with Captain Hamilton. "I am sure the trip will take no more than three and one half days there, a day to unload, and another three and one half back. You would be on the Mississippi again in a week and a day."

Hamilton pursed his lips. "You seem to forget the problem of a pilot, sir."

"If that is the only obstacle, then rest at ease. I have solved it."

Hamilton scowled warily.

"Mr. Jupp here *is* a Missouri riverboat pilot."

Hamilton chided himself for not having guessed as much. Jupp had the same insufferable self-confidence about him as Hamilton's own two pilots — Patton Sinclair and Jethro Pierce — and nearly every other pilot of his acquaintance. He considered the lanky civilian narrowly. "You have got your papers, Mr. Jupp?"

Jupp removed an envelope from his inside vest pocket and handed it over. "I've taken riverboats as far north as Fort Benton, Captain Hamilton." He said it as if the feat was no more exacting than a Sunday excursion to Jefferson City. "As you can see, I'm certified clear up to the Great Falls. I've worked with Shreve and La Barge. Most recently I have piloted the stern-wheeler *Omaha Express* between St. Charles and Yankton."

"Humm." Hamilton handed the papers back. "This certificate seems all right. You ever pilot a side-wheeler?"

"The *Excursion*, sir. Three years at her helm in the trade between St. Louis and St. Joseph."

Lieutenant Dempsey said, "The army hired Mr. Jupp because of his reputation on the Missouri River and because he came highly recommended by no less than Captain Joseph La Barge. I can confidently recommend him to you, Captain. The *Tempest Queen* could be in no finer hands. So, you see your need of a riverboat pilot is already answered, and as for the

34

question of Mr. Jupp's fee, the army has already paid him for his services."

Hamilton had been outmaneuvered, his arguments easily dismantled by Lieutenant Dempsey's logic and Eric Jupp's fine reputation. Considering the proposal now, he could think of no good reason not to take Lieutenant Dempsey and his supplies up to Fort Leavenworth. "Very well. I will transport you and your men, sir.

Dempsey was obviously pleased, but he did not gloat on this victory or allow even a smile to disrupt his self-controlled professionalism. "Thank you, Captain Hamilton. I shall have my men begin transferring the matériel immediately. You determine the army's charges, and I will have the funds transferred to you, in gold, before we depart in — two days?"

"Two days will be fine, Lieutenant Dempsey. Oh, and tell your men to be careful aboard. Everything has just been painted, and I do not wish to begin my regular trade in cotton and sugar with a boat that is not in top shape."

"Of course, Captain Hamilton. A week from now you will not know we have been aboard at all."

"Humm . . ." Somehow, Hamilton had his doubts.

Dempsey and his entourage turned to leave.

"Lieutenant."

Dempsey wheeled back, military straight, with the snap of a well-trained soldier. "Sir?"

"You have no animals with you, I hope?"

"No. No horses or animals of any species, sir."

"Very good. Good day, sir."

When the three men had left, Hamilton turned back to McKay. "Well, what did you make of them?"

McKay shrugged his shoulders and put the monte cards aside. "The lieutenant is very professional. The pilot very confident."

Hamilton grunted. He would have used a different word to describe Jupp. "And the young sergeant?"

"He is quite well-to-do — or a least has aspirations in that direction."

"Oh? How do you deduce that?"

"He was wearing an expensive ring with a family crest."

"That denotes pride, not wealth."

"True." McKay smiled and took up his cards once more. "But his boots, although of military design, were not military issue. They were custom-made to his measurements, and of a finer leather than those Dempsey was wearing. His blouse was tailored as well. His bearing is that of a man of means, and his curiosity in cards suggests he is a gambler. . . . I'd wager it would be no trouble coaxing him into a friendly game of monte."

Hamilton huffed. "You read all that in a brief few minutes?"

"I read most of that in the first few seconds. The rest of the time I spent trying to determine why he was so nervous."

Hamilton shot him a curious look. "The sergeant was nervous?"

"Absolutely."

Hamilton laughed. "You amaze me, Mr. McKay. I think your imagination has overcome you this time."

McKay merely smiled back.

Hamilton stood. "Well, we shall have to continue this lesson in cards some other time. Suddenly I find I have things to do."

"It should be an interesting trip."

"How's that?"

"Different scenery."

"Humm. There will be that and more — more snags and bars as well. The Missouri is running low this time of the year. I only pray that Mr. Jupp is the first-rate pilot Lieutenant Dempsey makes him out to be." Hamilton departed the main cabin through the ladies' salon and out the back through one of the two doors on either side of the wall-size gilded mirror. He took a ladder up to the hurricane deck and went to his quarters, which were at the head of the texas. Inside, he hung his cap on a hook and sat behind the desk, drawing out a sheet of foolscap and uncapping the ink-well.

He spent a few moments consulting a book of charts, then dipping his pen, he wrote:

Independent packet — for Lexington, Independence, Westport Landing, Fort Leavenworth.
Steamer TEMPEST QUEEN — William Hamilton, master.
Will leave for above and intermediate ports on Thursday
August 25th at 10 A.M.
For freight or passage apply on board.

Hamilton pressed a blotter to the ink, and as he gave it a moment to fully dry, he glanced at the faded daguerreotype in the ancient brass frame. The frame had once been gilded, but time, and the moisture that comes with living on the Mississippi

River, had removed mostly all of the gold, leaving the dull yellow of the brass beneath and the green of verdigris growing along the seams where the pieces of the frame had been joined together. From it, Cynthia smiled out at him, forever young, forever happy, exactly as she had looked on their honeymoon in Paris, France. How he had loved her, and how he had grieved when the river had poured over the land that calamitous, lightning-rent night when their levee crevassed. . . .

For years afterward, her death had come back to haunt him whenever spring brought its violent storms. He had despaired of ever getting over the tragedy of losing his wife and their two young children, but even that seemed distant now, and put neatly away. Storms no longer haunted him. He had conquered that one last ghost the very night McKay had won his boat back from the retired general. Odd how life had changed for him in only a few brief months.

"Well, my dear, we shall be traveling up the Missouri this trip. What do you think of that? Humm? I suppose it will be a break in the monotony, although I do dislike leaving the Mississippi. The Missouri does seem such a reckless and wild river."

Hamilton turned back to his sheet of paper, the ink dry now, and folded it into thirds and put away his writing instruments.

Chapter Two

This summer has been insufferable! Clifton Stewart lamented as he stole quickly along the larboard promenade and scurried up a ladder, glancing about to make sure that infernal slave driver, Edward Lansing, had not seen him make his escape from the heat of the boilers down on the main deck. Stewart had never before imagined that his body could hurt in so many places, or so badly . . . and Lansing didn't seem to take any notice of his pain in the least. He just drove him on and on until he dropped, working him sixteen hours a day, as if he were one of the black firemen or deckhands! And now Lansing wanted to fire up those infernal boilers! On a day when the mercury was topping one hundred degrees!

Stewart peeked up onto the hurricane deck, saw that it was deserted, scrambled up the last few steps of the ladder, and made a dash for the great curving swell of the larboard paddle box where he fell against the engine-room skylights into a bit of shade and slumped slowly to the deck, sleeving the sweat from his forehead that poured as if his skin had sprung a thousand leaks.

It was times like this that made Clifton Stewart seriously reconsider his decision to leave the comforts of his father's plantation — and his own property that he had forsaken a mere week before his twenty-fourth birthday, the day it would have passed into his hands! He wilted in the heat, recalling the tall, shady oaks, the perfectly groomed grounds, a cool lemonade and juleps that Lila or Jullene would fetch for him from the springhouse on hot days like these.

Stewart moaned softly to himself and rotated a stiff arm. He wondered why, after four months of this, he hadn't finally gotten used to it. He could never remember hurting so completely; never remember ending the day so bone weary as to fall into bed and be asleep before hitting the pillow. He never hurt so much! — except perhaps on that rare occasion at the Merryville races when he rode all five of his father's fine Thoroughbreds in a single afternoon. But then that ache was a pleasant sort, usually localized in a different part of his body.

Even here in the shade of the paddle box, the heat of the afternoon was suffocating. He closed his eyes and lolled his head back. He could end this misery in an instant, he knew. All he had to do was return home and admit his foolishness. . . . But then Clifton Stewart recalled the object of his quest, the reason he had left home and fortune to take the lowliest job aboard a riverboat. Mystie Waters! That raven-haired, olive-skinned beauty with the dark, mysterious eyes . . . and an amateur ornithologist more than his equal! In the brief span of a week he had fallen hopelessly in love with the beautiful chambermaid, and in a minute of thoughtlessness, he had lost her — perhaps forever. So now he rode the riverboat, inquiring in every port after her. About all he knew for certain was that her mother and father still lived in Cairo, Illinois, and that when she had carried her luggage off the *Tempest Queen* that night four months ago in Natchez-Under-The-Hill, Mystie had been determined to stay on the Mississippi River and find work on another riverboat.

The *Tempest Queen* had not been able to put into Cairo on this last trip up the river, but Captain Hamilton had accepted a contract to haul farm implements from

Cairo down to Vadalia on his return trip, and he had already given Clifton permission to disembark for a couple of hours and call on Mystie's parents. At least with them he could leave the letter. He had composed it weeks ago, and even now it lay safely under his pillow on his cot in the crowded deckhand quarters under the main deck.

He recalled Mystie's musical laugh, her keen wit, her telescopic eye for birds . . . and his eyes stung. He had loved her from first sight, but it was only after that gorgeous spring afternoon in Vicksburg that he decided he must have her always in his life.

A boot swung out of his consciousness and gave him a swift kick as he remembered his last words to her; words of rejection, blurted out in haste when he had discovered the "taint" in her blood.

I can not see you any further . . .

He had said it not out of any forethought, but from an automatic reaction; the result of a lifetime of training. Thinking back on it now, moisture gathered in his eyes.

How could I have been so foolish?

"I thought that was you scurrying about like a stowaway rat in the pantry," a voice said at Stewart's left.

Clifton's eyes shot open. For an instant he thought Chief Mate Lansing had caught up with him, but then he relaxed. It was only the gambler, Dexter McKay. Stewart and McKay had come aboard the *Tempest Queen* about the same time, and through a number of circumstances, they had become close friends. McKay was a font of knowledge on all that was worldly — all that Clifton had never learned living beneath the umbrella of his father's wealth. Even though McKay was a Northerner, he had become a mentor of sorts to the younger man.

"I was only trying to find some rest from that maniac down below."

"Lansing?"

"Who else?"

McKay shrugged his shoulders and leaned casually upon his ebony walking stick with the silver horse-head grip. He glanced around the freshly painted hurricane deck, unscuffed yet by the feet of crew and passengers. Not a dozen feet away was the texas deck where the officers and other members of the crew lived. "You have chosen a rather prominent place to hide in," McKay observed.

Clifton frowned. "I guess I wasn't

thinking. I just wanted someplace shady, and away from those furnaces. This was about as far away as I could get — short of leaving the boat. I tell you, Mr. McKay, it is inhuman to make a man work in this heat from sunup to sundown!"

McKay said nothing but his sagacious smile made Stewart take pause and then say, "All right. I know what you are thinking."

"You do? What am I thinking?"

"You are thinking that the colored people we have working our plantation feel the same way as I do about this heat, and the work. But I tell you, Mr. McKay, it just is not true. Like most other Northerners, you don't understand at all."

McKay sat in the shade next to the young, wealthy planter, recently turned fireman, deckhand, night watchman . . . and every other lowly job available on a riverboat. As Captain Hamilton had said when he had agreed to take Stewart on — more out of pity than actual need — that he had no jobs available, but he could surely find something for the man to do. And Hamilton had been true to his word.

McKay gripped his walking stick, rested his forearms upon his knees, and smiled indulgently. "Why don't you explain it to me?"

46

Clifton thought a moment, then said, "I suppose the easiest way to explain it is that the Negro is not as advanced a species as you or I, Mr. McKay. Heat and hard work do not affect him as they do the white man. Darwin has just proved that."

"Darwin?"

"Certainly you are aware of his momentous paper just published by the Linnaean Society of London?"

McKay shook his head, vaguely bewildered. "Since you are the amateur naturalist, suppose you explain it to me."

"Essentially, Darwin has discovered that certain species are more advanced than others. It is obvious the Negro is of a less advanced order. In time the colored race would have died out completely if not for the benevolent hand extended to him by the white man."

"Why should he die out?"

"It is due to things like competition and environmental pressures and —" He paused and stared at McKay. "I have lost you, haven't I?"

"Who is saying all of this?"

"Charles Darwin."

"And who is he?"

"Why, sir, he is a famous English naturalist."

"I'll wager the man's a crackpot," Mc-Kay said beneath his breath but loud enough for Stewart to hear.

Stewart frowned. "That just shows how little you understand of science."

"Perhaps I do not understand science" — McKay grinned — "but I do understand fine Scotch, and I have just recently acquired a bottle of that Glen-what's-it-called that you admire so much. It is in my stateroom, and if you would care to come along, I can guarantee it a more genial place to escape Mr. Lansing's railings than sitting up here against the paddle box where all can see you."

"Glenlivet?"

"Now, how come I can never remember that?"

"I'll be happy to share a drink with you, Mr. McKay." Stewart stood at once. The two men made for the ladder to the deck below, but at that moment Captain Hamilton came out on the little porch in front of his cabin and spied them.

"Mr. Stewart."

Clifton drew up stiffly. "Caught!" he whispered to McKay, and turned about. The captain beckoned with an arm. "Please come here a moment."

Stewart shuffled over like a truant

schoolboy caught sneaking off with a cane pole and bucket of worms. "Sir?"

"Are you engaged at the moment? Has Mr. Lansing sent you on some task up here?"

"Ah, no, sir. I . . . I was just passing by when Mr. McKay stopped to talk."

"Well, good. Then it is a stroke of luck that I happened to step out just now. I need you to run into town on an errand for me."

"Into town?" Stewart's face brightened. "You want me to run into town for you? Certainly, Captain, I would be most happy to run your errand." Indeed, Clifton would have done most anything for a chance to get off the boat and set his feet on solid ground again. Especially since it put him that much farther out of reach of Lansing — at least for a little while. But more important, in the past twelve days at dock, he'd not had a moment to himself except at night when he was too tired to do anything but sleep. This errand would give him an opportunity to inquire around St. Louis about Mystie. As with every landfall the *Tempest Queen* made where Stewart was able to disembark, he put out the word that he was searching for the beautiful young mulatto. He had posted notices in the shops where a woman working on riverboats might visit. St. Louis, a hub of river trade, was an ideal place to put out his feelers.

"I have an advertisement here," Hamilton went on, placing the folded paper in Clifton's hand. "I want it taken to every newspaper in town; place it under departures on the Missouri River. Here is enough money to cover the expense." He dropped a handful of coins into Stewart's palm.

"The Missouri River, sir?"

"Yes, we will be taking a run up to Fort Leavenworth and back. It will be a change for the *Tempest Queen*, I know, but we shan't be gone but a day over a week."

Stewart put the paper and the money into his shirt pocket and fastened the button. "I shall see that the advertisement gets properly placed, sir."

"Thank you, Mr. Stewart." Hamilton returned to his cabin, and Stewart to McKay's side.

"We are going up the Missouri River, Mr. McKay!"

"So I have heard."

Stewart looked suddenly apprehensive. "You don't suppose we will encounter any wild Indians, do you?"

McKay grinned. "I doubt that we will be going far enough west for that. Only as far as to Fort Leavenworth, I believe."

Stewart seemed relieved. "Thank goodness for that. I am afraid I am going to have to pass on that drink. Perhaps later. The captain wants me to deliver an advertisement to the newspapers."

Together they went down to the boiler deck where the main cabin and the passenger staterooms were located. McKay veered off along the promenade toward his own cabin while Stewart hurried down the wide, newly varnished stairway to the main deck.

"Where the blazes have you been, Mr. Stewart?" Lansing's voice lashed out at him like a hot poker. "Get your lazy hind quarters over here and start hefting wood into these furnaces. Mr. Seegar wants a head of steam up to check them new pipes, and I need every hand I can get hold of, even worthless, pampered, useless, whining, feather pillows like you who thinks they are too good for honest, hard work!"

Stewart drew himself up stiffly, suppressing a tremble of fear, and approached Lansing as if the man had horns and a tail. "Ah, sir — ah, Captain Hamilton has asked me to run an errand for him, ah —

in town, sir." Clifton's voice was suddenly weak, and he avoided the chief mate's eyes, studying the deck at his feet instead — as he'd seen the black firemen do when under Lansing's guns — as the slaves on his father's plantation did when brought before the overseer or his father after being caught stealing from the truck patch or slacking off in the hayloft above the harness shed.

"Errand? What sort of errand the captain got you doing?"

"Ah, err, well, he wants me to place this advertisement." Stewart fumbled the paper from his pocket.

Lansing snatched it away and studied it a moment, then handed it back. "The Missouri, heh? What in blazes are we doing going up that muddy stream?"

"By my word, I don't know, sir. I did not ask."

"Well, all right. Be on your way about the captain's errand, then. But as soon as you are through with it I want you back here where I can use you. Is that clear?"

"Yes, sir!"

Stewart hurried off the *Tempest Queen*. When he made dry ground he breathed a sigh, and as he started into town he felt a weight equal to that of a hogshead lift from his shoulders.

★ ★ ★

When they left the *Tempest Queen*,
Lieutenant Sherman Dempsey waved
down a hire-carriage. As the two-horse rig
pulled to a stop, Sergeant Carr said, "If
you don't mind, sir, I have a few things I'd
like to pick up before I go back to the boat
— while we are on this end of town."

Dempsey paused with a boot on the iron
step-up and grinned. "You can be frank,
Sergeant. What you're really after is someplace that serves cold beer."

Carr grinned. "Well, that was not fore-
most on my mind, but the notion had occurred to me."

Dempsey nodded his head. "Go do your
shopping, Phil. I'll return to the *Lulla Belle*
and arrange for a towboat to pull her to a
berth near the *Tempest Queen*."

"Thank you, sir."

Dempsey stepped up into the carriage.
"Pickin's Boatyard," he directed the driver,
and closed the door behind him. "See you
later, Sergeant," he said through the
window as the carriage rattled away over
the cobblestone wharf road that paralleled
the new railroad tracks.

With Lieutenant Dempsey gone, the
smile slipped from Carr's face and was replaced by fixed determination reflected in

his brisk, unswerving stride. He passed a row of brick shops with hardly a glance at them or the goods displayed behind their plate glass windows, and continued along the busy street until he found what he was looking for.

At Turner's Livery he obtained a saddle horse, and inside half an hour of his bidding Lieutenant Dempsey farewell, Sergeant Philip Carr was urging his mount into a gallop, in a rising column of fine dust leaving St. Louis behind him.

"Blasted varmints!" Deke Saunders withdrew his hand from the back of his neck and studied the smear of blood across his palm. "They'll eat you alive if'n you let 'em."

"Ma— maybe we ought t— to go alookin' fer him again, Deke?"

The preacher slung his black coat over a shoulder and came up the road, squinting at the speckled leaves overhead and into the glaring sun burning down. "Not yet. Something must have happened to delay him, that's all."

Down by the edge of the swamp near the unmoving, green water that smelled like rotting cabbage, Grady looked up from the huge catfish he was turning on a spit over a small fire. "It's been years since we've seen Carr, Pa. He might have changed. Besides, he ain't never done anything like this before. He's mighty proud of that uniform, from what I hear. It might be it's givin' him second thoughts."

"Giving who second thoughts?"

The three of them turned as one, startled by the voice that had suddenly spoken behind them. Harold Madden had instinctively reached for his squirrel gun, and Deke for his revolver, when they recognized the rider astride the breathless horse.

"Carr!" Deke could not hide his surprise. "How the hell you come up behind us like that and me not hearing you, and on a winded horse to boot?"

Philip Carr swung out of the saddle and led the horse into camp. "I drew up a few hundred yards back. I figured that if you were still waiting here for me you'd be on pins and needles by now. Didn't want to get a bullet in me from three jittery fellows. I walked up to the bend in the road. When I come around it, you three had your backs to me." He grinned. "Wondered just how long it would take for you to discover me. Good to see you, Deke. It has been a long time."

Deke said, "We was beginning to wonder

if you didn't have a double cross in mind."

"Me double-cross you? Now why would I do that? You and my old man are friends, practically part of the family the way I recall him talking about it." Carr strolled to the fire, hunkered down, and eyed the fish on the spit. "That's one impressive catfish, Grady. Catch it here?"

"Right over there aways, Phil. They grow 'em big around here. Must have lots o' meat to scavenge on." Grady's gaunt face broke into a wide grin, and he pushed a hand through his tangled, thinning yellow hair.

Harold Madden chuckled at their private joke.

Deke's mouth thinned in amusement, and he said, "Ain't seen your pa in years, boy. Heard he retired and is livin' in a big, fancy house, with slaves to do all the work for him now, and barrels of pirated rum in the cellar. He was smart, your old man. He stuck to a trade he know'd well."

"You could have, too, Deke."

The old man shook his head. "Beaver went out of fashion, and them trappers stopped comin'. Keelboats gave way to steam, and it got mighty hard to bait one of 'em and hauling 'em ashore. Weren't enough traffic on the Missouri to support us all. Nope, some of us had to go on to different things. I ain't seen your pa in nigh onto fifteen years, I reckon. In fact, I hardly recognize you in the fancy blue suit."

Carr stood. "The army's been good to me. Taught me a thing or two, but it could never teach me the things you did, Deke."

"Such as?"

"Oh, things like when to know you're being skinned and when you're not." Carr looked at the third man standing there. "Who's that?"

"It —t —t it's me, Ph— Phil."

"Harold? Harold Madden?" Carr was suddenly grinning and stuck out a hand. "Well, talk about a fellow changing. You must have put on twenty pounds. Here, let me look at you. You handsomed up considerably as well. Ole Deke can't call you the cattail any more, that's for certain."

Madden looked confused. "D— Deke called me that?"

"Well, never mind. It was a long time ago."

"All this reminiscing is warming to the heart," Deke said, "but let's get down to business. Where have you been, Carr?"

"Our transportation blew a boiler. We were laid up above Clarksville until we could find a towboat to bring us down to St. Louis. Just got in this morning. Spent the day hunting up another boat to complete the trip. I would have got away sooner, but I had a lieutenant stuck to me like a leech. Finally broke away from him about an hour and a half ago, and here I am."

Deke said, "Figured it was something like that. Grady, he thought you might be weaseling out on us because of some misguided loyalty to that uniform you're wearing."

"Grady has always had a suspicious streak in him."

Deke tossed his coat across the rotting stump and started along the road with Philip Carr at his side. "Tell me what you're carryin', and how many men are a guardin' it. Your letter was kinda vague."

"I didn't know all the details when I wrote you. Since then, I have helped load it all. If we can pull this off, none of us is ever going to have to work again. And if I play my cards right, I will end up in Washington, and you, my friend, can hang up that phony preacher's garb and settle down to a right comfortable life."

Passion burned suddenly in Deke's eyes, but he smothered it before Carr noticed.

"You're talking in circles, boy. Just say it right out."

"I don't have a written inventory on me, Deke. But I can tell you it's a job for more than just the four of us here."

"I got men all up and down the Missouri what would come in on this on a moment's word — if it's worth their while."

Carr gave the old man a smug smile. "You tell me if it's worth it. There are two hundred barrels of gunpowder, one hundred new Springfield rifles, four three-inch ordnance rifles, seventy of Colt's revolvers, ten thousand caps, and enough balls to hold off the entire Federal army for a month. . . ."

"That sounds like mighty heavy stuff to be hauling away," Deke observed, scowling.

"That's just the army's hard supplies. I didn't mention the thousands of small things it purchases to keep a fort like Leavenworth up and running. The weapons alone would fetch a handsome price if hauled out to the Territories and sold to Indian traders."

Deke hadn't thought of that. He nodded his head, pondering it from this new angle. Carr continued, "The sutler has all his supplies on board as well: crates of canned fruit, tobacco twists, and fifty barrels of whiskey and beer, to name just a fraction of what's there."

This perked Deke up. "Fifty barrels you say?"

"At the very least. I didn't count them, I just helped load them."

"Well, that would bring a fair price without risking your neck dealing with the Indians."

Carr laughed. "What are you talking about, Deke? You ain't thinking straight. The Indians would steal anything for you to pay for a barrel of whiskey. You'd clear twice what a white man would pay. You freight the whiskey and the guns out into the Territories, make a deal with some of the more important chiefs, and come back a wealthy man."

"Indians don't have no money."

"They have ways of getting it. You and I both know that."

Deke stifled a grin and put on his best poker face. "I don't know about that. I'd have to pay an awful lot o' men to carry this off. Is there enough there to cover it?"

"Hell, Deke, make it easy on yourself. Give it all to your men. That should make them happy."

Deke glared at the sergeant as if he had

suddenly gone mad. "What's this you say, boy?"

"You give it all away to your men. Let them worry about splitting it up and hauling it out to the Indians, or wherever else they care to. Instead, you walk off with the payroll."

Deke's eyes rounded. "There is a paymaster aboard as well?"

"There is, indeed, and what he is carrying is all that I'm interested in." Carr paused to let that sink in, then said, "He's transporting over three hundred thousand dollars. Not government script, mind you, but hard cash. Gold."

It took Deke a moment to recover from that. Three hundred thousand dollars could make a man rich a dozen times over.

They had walked up the road a way, and now Deke turned and they started back toward camp. The old man was grinning. "Three hundred thousand split four ways, that's —"

"Seventy-five thousand each. I've already figured it out."

Deke whistled softly. "You said you had to hire a new boat. What's its name?"

"The *Tempest Queen.* She's a big Mississippi side-wheeler. Still in the boatyard getting a new coat of paint, but she'll be under steam in two days."

"We could put a dozen men aboard her —" Deke stopped abruptly and looked at Carr. "How many men does the army got?"

"Forty troops, four sergeants, including myself, and Lieutenant Dempsey, who is in charge of transporting matériel for the army. It's about all he does now. He's with the quartermaster department out of division headquarters, in Chicago."

"Good man?"

Carr shrugged his shoulders. "I get along okay with him. He's solid, by-the-book military. Spent some time down in Texas before the trouble with Mexico. That's about all I know about him."

"Well, now there's the rub. How do we steal a riverboat what's being guarded by that many soldiers?"

Carr laughed. "That's your problem."

Saunders shot him a narrow look.

"And here is another problem for you, Deke." Carr drew up and eyed the older man. "I don't want just seventy-five thousand dollars out of this deal."

The old man's view narrowed further.

"I want a hundred and twenty-five thousand dollars. The way I figure it, if it weren't for me pulling strings back in Chicago to get myself transferred to Fort Leavenworth, and more strings to get on the boat with the paymaster, and then to do the snooping around that you wanted done, you wouldn't get anything at all."

Deke didn't speak right away, and then a slow grin moved across his face. He shifted his view to Grady and Harold by the cook fire. "Let's move off a little way and discuss this where them two can't hear." Deke took a path through the tangled growth and came to the edge of the green water where the black flies hovered like clouds above their heads. "I don't suppose I can talk you out of this, boy?" Deke said when he had craned his neck to make sure the other two men couldn't hear.

"I don't think so, Deke. I figure I've got more to lose than you. Since I'm taking the bigger risk, I deserve the bigger cut."

"I see." Deke scratched his unshaved chin a moment. "What will I tell the boys?"

"Tell them whatever you want. It isn't my problem, Deke."

"No, I reckon it's not. Reckon it's my problem." Deke's view dropped to the rank grass at their boots, and then all at once he pointed. "What is that there? Why, it sure do look like someone dropped a gold piece out of their pocket."

"Where?"

"Why, right there." Deke pointed.

Carr stepped forward and bent for a closer look.

Deke drew his revolver, and the big weapon bucked in his hand, the roar of it driving the wildlife into a sudden frenzy. Carr lurched forward, landing at the water's edge. And slowly the green of the floating duckweed gave way to a spreading red tinge.

"Reckon it ain't my problem no more," Deke said softly to himself, and the next moment Grady and Harold came crashing through the tangled growth.

"What the hell happened —" Grady began, and then he saw Carr's body sprawled there, what was left of his head lying in the water. "You kilt him, Pa?"

"Reckon you was right 'bout him, son. He was goin' t' double-cross us. A greedy sonuvabitch, just like his own pa." Deke put out a hand, and Harold placed the bowie in it. "Turn him over, search him good, take his revolver and boots."

Grady removed the items, unbuttoned the blue blouse, and dragged the saber from beneath him. Deke tried on the boots, cursed when they didn't fit, and gave them to Grady. They didn't fit him either. Grinning, Harold Madden found himself with a new pair of handmade army boots.

"I — I ain't never had no— nothin' this fancy before, Deke," he said pulling them on.

"I want the sword, Pa."

"What are you goin' to do with that, boy?" Deke grabbed it up and tossed it far out into the swamp. "It will only draw a lot o' questions if someone takes notice to it." He tucked Carr's revolver in his belt, spied the gold ring and twisted it off Carr's finger, dropped it into his pocket, and moved over the dead sergeant with Harold's big knife. When he had finished, they heaved the body out into the swamp and watched it sink immediately.

Grady grinned. "You are determined to make this prime catfish water, Pa. Crawdads, too."

"All God's creatures got to eat, boy," Deke said flatly.

The men laughed and went back out to the road. Deke put the revolver with his coat and said, "When we finish up with dinner, Grady, you and me will go into St. Louis and find us a riverboat what's named *Tempest Queen*. Harold, you take the horses and hightail it out along the river and pass the word to any of our boys what want a cut in this deal. Tell them it's all the guns and whiskey they can carry off — that should get them interested. Tell 'em to board the *Tempest Queen* along the way, and not too many at once. We don't want the army getting suspicious. And tell 'em I'll be watching to see which ones throw in with us, and which ones don't — and I will remember them what don't later on. I want at least twenty men handy when I'm ready to make my move. We'll have forty troops to deal with, and we'll have to keep sharp. You understand all that, Harold?"

"I — I go— got it, Deke."

"Good. Now, let's eat."

Chapter Three

The St. Louis wharf was over a mile long and every inch of its length packed tight with puffing steamboats taking on cargo and passengers or disgorging themselves of the same. The hot, high sun was permanently obscured by a black, tumbling ceiling of smoke, seemingly supported on black pillars arising from the decks of busy steamboats. Beyond the wharf was the road, crammed with carriages and drays, and men scurrying everywhere, about the business of the river. Past the road lay a railroad spur with strings of flatcars and a small puffing engine doing its part to add to the soot flying overhead.

The buildings — brick and wood — were stained soot-black, every one of them. They consisted of a few supply stores, but mostly saloons. A full seventy-five percent saloons, Clifton Stewart mused as he strolled along a sidewalk that would eventually carry him into the heart of St. Louis where the city's newspapers were housed. He strictly avoided the saloons, even though a cool drink of something would be most refreshing now. He had heard rumors of the St. Louis bars and billiard rooms, and Captain Hamilton had warned his crew upon their arrival that if they wanted to avoid trouble, they best avoid the riverfront saloons.

Dexter McKay had made several forays to the local watering holes in the last dozen days and had returned to the *Tempest Queen* with his pockets full of steamboatmen's hard-earned pay. He, too, had advised Clifton that the rivermen's hangouts were not the place to go poking one's nose unless he had sharp wits, a fast fist, and a derringer or revolver hidden where he could reach it in a hurry.

Always a prudent man, Clifton heeded McKay's and Hamilton's advice, strictly avoided the saloons, and continued on his way, sidestepping and dodging the heavy foot traffic on the sidewalk. The road climbed away from the river, but even after he had gone several blocks, the smoky air had not cleared, and the yellow ball of the sun remained only an outline in the dingy sky. Soot seemed to settle on everything. St. Louis was a dirty place, Clifton decided, somewhat startled at the discovery, for he'd only known the towns of the lower

Mississippi River; much smaller places. Only New Orleans came close in size to St. Louis, but in that great city the air was not vicious as it was here. It did not sting one's eyes or burn one's lungs.

He spent the afternoon visiting the newspaper businesses — all that he could locate, including the two major presses. Afterward, when he had felt he'd discharged his obligation to Captain Hamilton satisfactorily — and certainly with more proficiency than could be expected from the lower-class rivermen of his brief acquaintance — Clifton Stewart decided he had earned the time to pursue his own interests — the sole reason he remained on the river: to find his lost love, Mystie Waters. The devil with Mr. Lansing's command that he return straight back to the *Tempest Queen.*

He slowly made his way back to the river, stopping at millinery shops and ladies' boutiques with pretty scarves and baubles in the windows. At each place he inquired after the lovely chambermaid, and to each inquiry he received the same reply. No one had seen the woman he described. He tried an apothecary, recalling that Mystie had visited a pharmacopoeia once while in Vicksburg; the answer was the same.

As he neared the river, his hopes climbed. Boats did not linger long at dock, he had learned, and if Mystie had any shopping to do, she would likely keep it as near as possible to the boat to which she was employed.

Still, no one could remember seeing a young lady with raven hair, a perfect smile, shining eyes, smooth olive skin as clear as rainwater. . . .

He wondered after a while if perhaps he were not describing her accurately or if his memory of her had become somewhat distorted. No, he decided firmly. Mystie was all of that, and more . . . and he would find her if it meant the rest of his life searching the backwaters of the Mississippi River!

Along the riverfront he discovered a ship chandler, a business that advertised tared rope, canvas, and machine parts; a busy place, filled with men wearing captain's coats and the haughty fellows in bowler hats and ties who, Stewart recognized right off, must be pilots. They filed in and out and hung like flies around the open doors, talking about the river and boats in a language still nearly as foreign to him as Chinese, although he was beginning to pick up some of it, but four months had not been enough time to master it. He knew the more common words, like *hawser* — a nautical name for a plain old rope — and he could properly identify *starboard* from *larboard,* it's true. But most of the words that assailed his ears as he stepped through the double doors into the shadowed warehouse-size building were still obscure and had a ring to them of adventures waiting to happen — adventures that Clifton Stewart wasn't sure he wanted any part of.

It was a riverfront business. He'd been warned to stay clear of them all, but here, as far as he could tell, gathered mostly captains and officers, and Clifton felt safe in their company. Besides, who best to know the whereabouts of Mystie than a captain who might have hired her. He stepped up to the counter, a long heavily planked, grease-stained affair that had seen years of boat supplies change hands over its top. On the other side of the counter, an immensely fat man in brown trousers and a tight, collarless, short-sleeved shirt with broad orange stripes running across it turned heavily from a back ledge. His belly dragged the material of the shirt down over his belt — if he wore one at all. Clifton was not certain. The man obviously was not wearing suspenders.

"What kin' I do fer you, lad?" The

counterman narrowed an eye at him, and Clifton was certain he'd met him before — perhaps in the pages of some adventure yarn or in the chronicles of Captain James Cook.

"Sir, I am looking for someone, a woman —"

The fat man laughed, his belly swayed dangerously close to a tier of cans nearby, and at once Clifton knew he had ill-phrased his problem. "Well, we don't sell none o' them here, lad, but if you find one, let me know 'cause I'm alookin', too."

Clifton grinned and allowed the man to have his humor, and when it had subsided, Clifton amended the statement. "I should say I am looking for my sister." It was a lie of course, but he had learned early on in his effort to locate Mystie Waters that folks were more apt to take you seriously if they thought you were seeking a lost member of the family. "She disappeared some months ago, but I have good reason to believe she is working on the river, perhaps aboard a steamer. Perhaps even one here at the wharf."

The man wiped his eyes and grinned affably. " 'Fraid I don't know too many women, lad. Ain't none what ever come in here. But maybe one of the captains know of her? What's her name?"

"It is very distinctive and I'm sure if you heard it you'd remember it. Mystie. Mystie Waters. Err — our mother was fond of the sound of it."

The man raised his voice. "Anyone here know of a gal by the name of Mystie Waters? This here feller is looking for her. It's his sister."

There was a moment of quiet as the chatter died down and the men thought, frowned, wagged their heads in the negative, and went back to their conversations. An older man with a gimp leg and carved walking stick came across the room. He wore a blue, box-cut coat with gold braids on the cuffs and a gold star. His face was nut brown and cut deeply in valleys and ridges. He hobbled up to the counter, and when he spoke, Clifton had to strain to hear the soft words.

"What did you say her name was?"

"Mystie. Her last name is Waters."

He pursed his lips and seemed to be raking through the rubble of long-forgotten thoughts.

"Waters, you say? Now, she wouldn't be from Kay-row, on the Illinois side, would she?"

"Yes! Yes, that would be her. Her . . . our

mother and father still live in Cairo! Do you know where she is?"

The old captain patted the air in front of Clifton's face as if to settle his sudden burst of energy. "Now just let me think a moment. Hum . . . yes I seem to recall the lass now. She works a steamer — now what's the name — ?"

"The *Tempest Queen!*"

"Yes . . . yes, that's it. *Tempest Queen.* Her master is Captain William Hamilton?"

"The very one!"

"Well, then that's where she be. I'm certain of it."

Clifton's hopes crashed. "But she left the *Tempest Queen* four months ago. She got off at Natchez. I have been searching for her ever since."

The old captain removed his blue cap and scratched the sparse gray hair beneath. "Well, then I guess I cain't help you no more, son."

Crestfallen, Clifton nodded his head, accepting the disappointment that had become all too common in his life. "Well, I thank you just the same, sir." Clifton started for the doors when the soft words behind him said: "Have you asked Bill Thorpe?"

"Who?" Clifton turned back.

"Old Billy Thorpe, the owner of Billy's Dock, up this road a piece. Billy knows more about the comings and goings along the wharf than any ten men combined," the ancient river captain said. "You go ask him. If your sister has been here, he'll know about it or my name isn't Captain Jack Fink."

"Thank you. I will." Stewart dove for the door but drew up suddenly as the name sank in. "Fink?" He turned back. "You aren't related to — ?" But the old captain had hobbled away and apparently did not hear him. Clifton shrugged his shoulders and stepped out of the dark store where the sunlight, even obscured as it was by the smoke of a hundred steamboats, made him blink.

Billy's Dock was a quarter mile up the road, exactly where Captain Fink had said it would be. Clifton hesitated at the bat-wing doors, peering over them into the gloom where drinking boatmen cussed and blustered and the click of ivory billiard balls made a constant din in the back-ground. His enthusiasm shriveled as his heart crept up into his throat. Was this one of *those* places that McKay and Hamilton had warned him about?

He regrouped his nerve and stood tall.

Well, so what if it was. The river had hardened him, and under Dexter McKay's tutelage he had learned a thing or two about self-defense. Not the sort of gentlemanly fisticuffs he'd been taught in college, but the down and dirty eye-gouging, backstabbing fighting they seemed to prefer in the saloons and billiard rooms that attracted the flotsam and jetsam of the river. Clifton squared his shoulders, marshaled his determination, and pushed the doors boldly aside.

No one paid much notice to him as he made his way to the bar — a long, scuffed thing that may have been varnished a long time ago, but it was hard to be certain now. He found a place between two muscle-bound boatmen, probably stevedores by the looks and smell of them. They made room for him grudgingly. Clifton gulped and buried his trepidation behind a brave face.

The bartender came over; a portly gent with thick, black hair, wearing a dirty apron around his middle. A ship's anchor was tattooed to his right forearm, and a most disgusting picture upon his left. Fortunately the thick black hair there covered most of it — except for the breasts, which constituted a great part of the illustration.

"What'll be, mister?" His voice boomed, as if it had come from the bottom of a barrel . . . as if his vocal cords had somehow been damaged at one time.

No doubt by a fist or an andiron.

Clifton cleared his throat, although it didn't need it, and try as he might to sound bold, his voice came out a timid squeak compared to that of the man behind the bar. "I am looking for Mr. William Thorpe."

The bartender rumbled with laughter. The two stevedores on either side glanced at each other and grinned into their beer mugs. "Mr. William Thorpe? Ain't nobody calls me William — at least not twice. I'm Bill Thorpe, or Billy if you want. What is it you want?"

"I . . . I was told you might be able to help me —"

"I don't help nobody what don't buy a drink in my place. Now run along, kid, before you get your head busted."

The stevedores were nodding and looking suddenly eager — a little too eager, Clifton thought. He cleared his throat again; this time he needed to. "Well, all right. I will have a glass of Glenlivet."

"A glass of what?" Billy scowled. "I serve beer and I serve whiskey. What'll it be?"

"Whiskey," Clifton yelped.

Billy poured a generous serving and pushed it across the bar. Clifton pushed across one of Captain Hamilton's coins in return. He'd pay him back later. He took a deep pull at the glass and winced as the raw whiskey burned his tongue. Certainly not what he was used to!

"Now" — Billy smiled amiably — "how can I help you?"

"I'm looking for a" — he almost made the same mistake — "my sister who disappeared some months back. I have good reason to believe she is working as a chambermaid aboard a steamer. Captain Jack Fink says you know more about the comings and goings here on the St. Louis wharves than any other ten men." He repeated Fink's assertion almost word for word, more out of nervousness than any lack of creativity. The lie about Mystie being his sister flowed more smoothly this time, no doubt due to a bit of Dexter McKay's influence rubbing off on him, he chided himself.

"Jack Fink says that? The old river rat." Billy shook his head, but he was grinning. "Well, all right then. Fink's a good man. Tell me about your sister."

Clifton went into a precise description,

and when he'd finished, there was an uneasy hush on the other side of the bar and on either side of him. After a moment Billy said, "I ain't never heard of nobody describing a sister like that. 'Skin clear as rainwater'?"

Perhaps he *had* overdone it this time.

"Did I say that?" He flashed a nervous smile. "I guess I'm just overwrought. I've been looking for months, you understand."

Billy was nodding his head. "I understand. I understand better than you think."

The boatman to his left gave a short, husky laugh; about as vulgar an expression a man can make without using words. "Sounds to me like he's describing a lover, Billy." He glanced at Clifton. "Just how fetchin' are you with your *sister?*"

Clifton stiffened. "Sir, you are impertinent."

"Im-pert'nent?" The boatman looked mildly amused.

"To suggest that there is anything indiscreet between my sister and myself —"

"I ain't suggesting you've been indiscreet. Only a little incestuous." The two boatmen laughed, along with Billy and some other fellows farther down the bar

79

who had been drawn to the conversation by the rise in their voices.

Billy said, "Leave the poor lad alone, now. Can't you see he's getting nervous."

Clifton felt the eyes about the barroom upon him, and stole a glance at the bat-wing doors, which suddenly seemed far away and unreachable. He steeled himself and pretended their jeering did not affect him. "I see that you cannot help me after all, Mr. Thorpe. I am sorry to have bothered you with it. Good day, sir." He turned to leave, and one of the boatmen stretched out a leg.

Clifton tripped, sailed forward across a table, and sent it crashing to the floor and its occupants scurrying aside.

The husky stevedore stood off the bar stool. "Oh, pardon me, *sir.*"

"You ruined our card game!" one of the men who had been at the table said, glowering down at Clifton.

Someone kicked him in the spine. "Git outa my way. You're blocking traffic."

Clifton got to his knees and eyed the lusty fellows suddenly standing about. He gulped down a lump in his throat and stood. The boatman who had tripped him advanced now, and Clifton saw in the man's hard eyes that no good was going to come of this. He shot a glance at the door again, but there was no way he could reach it with all the men standing about. Oh, how he wished he had not entered this place, and he longed to see Dexter McKay step through those batwings just now. The gambler always had a habit of showing up in the nick of time, and Clifton was convinced that *now* would be a good time.

The boatman put his face into Clifton's, and the young planter was surprised to discover that the man was in fact an inch or two shorter than himself. The massive expanse of his chest and shoulders, and the mountainous terrain of his arms, had made him appear much larger when he had been sitting on the bar stool. Clifton smelled the man's foul, whiskey breath when he spoke. "I'm gonna keep my weather eye sharp for that sister of yours, I think. And you know what I'd like to do to her once I find her?"

Clifton perceived the course of the boatman's thinking, and before the words came out he said, "You lay your vile hands upon Mystie and you will answer to me, personally!" His boldness startled him, and at once Clifton regretted the rash statement. The boatman's grin turned to ice. Clifton's thoughts raced ahead. What was he to do now? What was it McKay had told him — ? *Oh, yes, when your back is against the wall and there is no way out but fists and brawn, your best bet is to throw the first punch, and make it count for something. And there was something else, too . . . ? Yes, that was it! Always do the unexpected.*

Clifton kicked the boatman in the shin.

He howled and hobbled back and grabbed up his leg in both arms, hopping a circle in the middle of the floor. Clifton dove in with both fists flying. The boatman managed to block one. The other struck the point of his square chin, and Clifton's knuckles instantly went numb. He winced, drawing back, and shook his hand as if he'd just punched a leather sack filled with bricks.

The boatman plunged forward. Without breaking stride, he brought his fist up from somewhere down low. The blow lifted Stewart from the floor, driving the wind from him. He crashed down and contracted into a ball on the dirty floor. A boot sailed out. He tried to dodge, caught the toe on the forearm — a stinging blow that instantly set his arm on fire.

With a moan, Clifton rolled over and tried to protect himself. A boot drove into his back. His rib cage seemed to burst, and instantly pain exploded to all parts of his body, radiating electric sparks out into his fingers and toes. His head reeled, about to splinter. Drawing on some untapped reserve of strength, Clifton managed to get his knee beneath him. His eyes cleared momentarily, long enough to see the rage burning in the boatman's eyes, the crazed look of a man who had lost all control.

Clifton tried to speak, but the pain in his back had paralyzed his throat. Blood was choking him. Then all at once horror shaped his face. The boatman had grabbed a bottle off the bar, and putting all his muscle behind it, he swung out.

Clifton tried to protect his head, but his arm wouldn't move. His eyes rounded, then bulged as the bottle streaked closer. . . .

The stevedore stood there staring at the bottle in his fist as his rage seeped away. In a moment his vision cleared, and only then was he aware of the men standing about staring and the dead silence that hung like a morning fog in the air. He glanced at the whiskey bottle in his fingers, then down at the man on the floor with his head lying in a pool of blood near a cuspidor. As if pricked suddenly with a needle, he dropped the bottle and stepped back, wiping his hands on his shirt. Someone ventured forward and turned the young man over.

"I think he's dead," he said, lifting a lifeless eyelid with a finger.

"Oh, glory, no!" Billy Thorpe groaned and came quickly from behind the bar. He shifted his view from the floor to the burly man who seemed not quite recovered yet. "Just what I need, another killin' in my place."

"Well, the kid started it. Kicked me in the shin."

"You badgered him into it," a voice in the crowd rang out.

"Did not. It was a fair fight!"

Some agreed, some didn't. No one wanted to get too close to the matter. Billy marched back behind the bar and began polishing the mirror furiously. "I don't see nothing, understand. There's a wagon out back, and when I get finished here, I expect you to be out of here, and that kid gone with you."

The boatman nodded his head. "I understand." He lifted the body off the floor as if it weighed no more than a lady's suitcase, lightly packed, and slung it over a shoulder. Someone opened the backdoor for him.

In the alley behind the saloon, the boatman dumped his cargo into the back of a wagon and drew a sheet of canvas over it. He leaped into the seat, gave a snap to the reins, and got the horse moving. Once out of the gloom of the alley, the nervous boatman drove far beyond the end of the landside of wharf where thick trees grew up along the crumbling bank of the Mississippi River. Behind him he had left the long string of steamboats. He pulled up to the bank's edge, which dropped away a dozen feet. Below, the river had washed ashore a tangled mat of branches, logs, boards, crates, and a smashed chicken coop.

The boatman glanced around, and when he was certain no one was watching, threw back the canvas, slung the body over his shoulders, and at the edge heaved it far out. He heard it crash through the branches, and he thought he heard a splash from below. When he peered over, gripping a sapling to keep from falling himself, he did not see any trace of the young man who had come inquiring after his missing sister. Satisfied that no one had seen and that the body would not soon be discovered, he drove the wagon back behind Billy's Dock, left it there, and hurried away to his boat, which was scheduled to depart that afternoon.

Chapter Four

The disabled army transport boat *Lulla Belle* had been towed to a berth near the *Tempest Queen* the evening before, and now, with the sun still low in the morning sky and red behind the sooty air, Lieutenant Sherman Dempsey gave the orders to begin off-loading and transferring matériel. The replacement troops heading for Fort Leavenworth, fresh from division headquarters, snapped to; Dempsey assigned each of his sergeants a task to accomplish and enough men to see that it got done. He had Sergeant Carr down for overseeing the transfer of the artillery pieces, but the young officer hadn't showed up for reveille that morning, and when Dempsey had gone to investigate the missing sergeant, he had discovered that none of the officers or troops had seen him since the previous day.

Dempsey left a man in charge of the work aboard the *Lulla Belle*, and putting the truant sergeant temporarily out of mind, he strode out onto the wharf with the boat's manifest tucked under his arm. Already the air had grown hot and humid. Dempsey unbuttoned his blue, wool blouse as he crossed the *Tempest Queen*'s gangplank, and by the time he had located Captain Hamilton aboard the big packet's main deck, the jacket was slung over an arm and his shirt open at the throat.

They exchanged formalities, and Hamilton introduced the lieutenant to his chief mate. "This is Mr. Lansing. You two met briefly yesterday. He'll be directing your men where to place the cargo aboard the *Tempest Queen*."

"Very good. I've hired drays locally, but my men will do all the moving. You have an impressive boat, Captain Hamilton. I suspect our little lot won't take up but a fraction of the deck space you have available."

"I hope to be taking on more cargo and passengers," Hamilton said, and he patted the newspaper under his arm. "I've placed an advertisement. I would like to make the most of this diversion from our regular schedule."

"I understand." Dempsey let his view run along the bustling wharf not far from the boatyard where the *Tempest Queen* was getting her new coat of paint. "In a busy place like St. Louis I should think you would have no trouble taking on a full load."

"Perhaps so, but with only two days notice. . . ." Hamilton's voice dropped off, and he shrugged his shoulders. Like the army lieutenant, Hamilton had abandoned the formality of his uniform jacket and was in shirtsleeves and suspenders. The dog days of summer on the Mississippi River were a great equalizer; in shirtsleeves it was hard to tell a general from a private — a riverboat captain from a mud clerk.

The first of the mule-drawn drays pulled up in the boatyard, and as Dempsey's men began hauling the army's supplies aboard, Dexter McKay came down the wide, formal staircase, his ebony walking stick tapping the steps lightly. His mouth compressed into a tight line of concern as he approached them, his hooded eyes heavy with worry.

"Good day, Captain Hamilton, Lieutenant Dempsey," he said briefly. "I see you have begun bringing your supplies aboard."

Dempsey nodded his head. "The transfer should be completed by this afternoon." He lifted the manifest and grinned. "Got it all right here. I've done this so many times I could probably do it while asleep, and barring a mishap — or another missing man — it should all go as clockwork."

Hamilton lifted a bushy eyebrow. "Speaking of missing men" — he glanced at McKay — "have you located young Mr. Stewart yet?"

McKay shook his head, and the frown upon his face deepened. "I've just been from stern to bow again, and no one has seen him."

"You've misplaced a man as well?"

Hamilton said, "I sent Mr. Stewart into town yesterday on an errand, and he has yet to return."

"That is very much like what happened to Sergeant Carr. He went into town as well. No one saw him return, and he was not at reveille this morning."

"Humm." Hamilton pulled thoughtfully at his neatly trimmed gray beard.

McKay said, "I'm going ashore to look for him. It is not like Mr. Stewart to stay out all night."

"No, not at all," Hamilton agreed.

Lieutenant Dempsey had only known Sergeant Philip Carr a short while, but in that little time he'd come to learn that Carr had big ambitions and a growing career. Dempsey had had men under his command desert before, and considering the dangerous work, long hours, and meager pay, desertion was almost understandable. But he didn't think Carr would ever leave the army, not with his sights set on an appointment to Washington. Thinking it over, what he had dismissed earlier as a mere inconvenience, he was now beginning to regard with concern.

"Mr. McKay, if you can wait for a few minutes while I get this loading started, I'd like to join you. My missing man may be in trouble, as I suspect you now believe yours to be."

"I'd be happy for the company, Lieutenant Dempsey."

A half an hour later the two men were making their way up the wharf road, checking in at the businesses along the way, peddling their inquiries at every occasion. Of the first dozen places they stopped, two people remembered the young man inquiring after a woman with a remarkable name . . . but that was all. They had no idea where he had gone after leaving. Finally they found a man who did know; a corpulent fellow behind a greasy counter in a ship chandler's establishment.

"I remember the fellow you're lookin'

fer," he told McKay. "Seemed a nice lad, but very worried. He was searching fer his sister, he was; a gal named Mystie. I wouldn't rightly forget a name like that, now would I? But as fer your missing sergeant, Lieutenant Dempsey, I can't help you there."

"His sister?" McKay seemed to stifle a grin. "Do you know where he went afterwards?"

"As a matter of fact, I do. He was heading down to Billy Thorpe's place."

"Why did he go there?" McKay asked, grabbing hold of this first real lead.

The fat man behind the counter gave an indifferent shrug of his wide shoulders. "Captain Fink said Billy would know if his sister had been on the wharves — and by the way, who are you?"

"A friend. Where is this Billy Thorpe's place?"

"He owns Billy's Dock, a saloon and a billiard parlor up the road a piece."

McKay left at once, and when Lieutenant Dempsey caught up with him, he said, "You suspect something is wrong now, don't you?"

McKay strode ahead briskly, his walking stick swinging forward at each step with machinelike precision, making precisely timed clicks upon the pavement as he went. "I am afraid that Mr. Stewart has lived a somewhat overprotected life, Lieutenant. I have been schooling him in the fine art of keeping one's neck out of trouble; however, he is a long way from earning his diploma."

Dempsey noted the concern etched in McKay's handsome, neatly barbered face, shaded beneath the brim of his carefully brushed beaver hat. He wore a newly laundered shirt with ruffled front, a stiff paper collar, and a brown, silk cravat. His five-button vest was unfastened at the moment, held together only by the heavy gold watch chain dipping from pocket to pocket with a diamond-studded fob flopping madly as his long legs carried him quickly up the busy road.

At Billy's Dock, McKay's rapid pace never faltered, and he pushed the swinging doors apart and marched immediately inside. His abrupt arrival brought startled faces up out of beer mugs and whiskey glasses.

"These gentlemen are at their drinking early," Dempsey noted quietly at McKay's side. His view shifted warily around the saloon, lingering a moment at the two billiard tables — one currently in use. The place had an unhealthy air about it, and unconsciously Dempsey's hand fell to the hilt of his saber.

McKay was taking in the place in a careful manner or so it appeared to the army lieutenant. McKay studied a card game with particularly keen interest; then all at once his gray eyes flicked up, and when they located the bartender, he made straight for the man. Dempsey hung back, his army training and his instincts constraining him to keep a guard in reserve. He stepped over to the far end of the bar where he could keep an eye on McKay and also watch the narrow saloon that stretched before him.

"I'm looking for Billy Thorpe."

"I'm Billy Thorpe," the man behind the bar said, polishing a chipped mug with a dirty towel, not bothering to look over.

"I was told a young man by the name of Clifton Stewart was in here yesterday to see you," McKay said without the formality of an introduction. Dempsey heard the control in McKay's voice that spoke of a man who possessed the utmost confidence in himself.

The man behind the bar proceeded to fill the mug with beer and pass it down the bar to a waiting customer. Only then did he look at McKay. "Lots of young men come in here, mister. The river is filled with them. I don't know their names — don't want to."

"He would have been inquiring after a woman by the name of Mystie Waters — err, his sister."

"Can't help you." The bartender turned his back to McKay and began pyramiding whiskey glasses against the polished mirror.

Out the corner of his eye, Dempsey saw McKay's hand dip into a vest pocket. Five gold coins appeared, and he dropped them noisily, one by one, to the top of the bar, each landing precisely on top of the previous one, making a neat stack. The black-haired bartender glanced over at the sound. From another pocket McKay produced a deck of playing cards and set them upon the bar, too.

"Say, mister, what are you doing?"

McKay grinned disarmingly. "Merely trying to jog your memory, sir. Here is one hundred dollars. If you can remember the young man whom I am looking for and tell me where he might be now, I will cut you for that stack of coins."

"Cut me?" The barkeep's eyes narrowed suspiciously as he glanced at the cards. He considered the offer a moment, then asked, "I get to shuffle them cards first?"

"Oh, absolutely! As many times as you like."

"Well," he hesitated, an eye — as it appeared from Dempsey's point of view — fixed upon the stack of coins. "Now that I think back, I kinda do recall a fellow in here yesterday. But he didn't say his name, you see, that's why I didn't remember him right off."

"Of course. A perfectly understandable oversight."

"Yeah, right. You seem a sensible fellow," the bartender grinned and went on. "Well, he was in here asking after a gal, and I think he did say she was his sister. I recognized her name and told him that I'd heard his sister was working a boat down on the wharf. Yeah, that's what I told him."

"And?" McKay urged.

"Let's see — oh, yeah. I heard she was working on the *City of Alton*. That boat was docked here yesterday. He went off to find her, and last I heard, the *City of Alton* pulled out about four o'clock in the afternoon."

"Is that all?"

The bartender nodded his head. "Yep. That's all. Now let's cut them cards."

Frowning, McKay pushed the deck across the bar to him. Billy took it up, shuffled it, and set it down between them.

"Go ahead," McKay said.

Billy parted the deck, and his face broke into a grin as he showed McKay the king of diamonds that he'd cut.

"That will be hard to beat," McKay said easily, almost bored, Dempsey thought. He was becoming quite curious of the outcome now — and of this man who seemed to handle life as easily as some men handle breakfast. McKay made his own cut immediately and held up the card for Billy to see, and it was almost as if he knew exactly what it would be, for he'd not even bothered to look at it himself.

"An ace! Damnation all to hell!" Billy roared and tossed his cards to the bar. McKay gathered them up, put the coins back in his pocket, and went outside.

On the sidewalk he waited for Lieutenant Dempsey to join him. "An impossible lead to follow — at least for now" — McKay glanced over at Dempsey — "and we still have made absolutely no headway at finding your missing man."

"You knew you were going to cut an ace, didn't you?"

"Hum? Oh, I was just lucky."

"Lucky? My big toe!" Dempsey said, and he caught the faint glimmer that came momentarily to McKay's eyes and the slight lift at the corner of his mouth. "He's lying, you know. He knows more than he wants to let on."

"Yes, I know. That's why he told a story I couldn't possibly check up on."

A man staggered out of the saloon with red, droopy eyes, and as he passed, he gave them a look and a nod of his head. Dempsey glanced at McKay. As if instantly understanding each other's thoughts, they fell in step behind the man. He ducked into the first alleyway he came to and fell against the building, suddenly shaking. When the tremors passed he peered hard into McKay's face and said, "I know what happened to your friend, the one what was in here yesterday."

Dempsey said, "Tell us where he is." There was the ring of authority in his voice, as if he was used to giving orders and having them obeyed.

The man fought down another tremor and ignored the army officer, keeping his runny eyes on McKay. "I . . . I might tell you . . . if you want?"

"Might! Speak up, man," Dempsey said, growing impatient.

McKay put up a hand to silence the lieutenant. "Perhaps our friend here would like one of these to help loosen his tongue?" He picked a gold coin out of his pocket. The man's eyes cleared, but when he grabbed for the coin, McKay moved it just out of his reach.

"Your friend, he was in here yesterday. I seen him. He come looking for his sister just like you said. Billy, he lied to you, mister. Downright lied." The drunk licked dried lips and kept an eye on the coin as if it were a target at the end of a rifle sight.

"And?" McKay prompted. "Where is he now? Where did he go?"

The man blinked and shook his head. "I don't know where he went, mister. If he was a God-fearing man, well then I reckon he went to Glory, for sure as I is standing here, your friend went and got himself kilt."

McKay's eyes narrowed. "Killed? Are you certain?"

"Yes, sir. Billy, he knows all about it. Reckon that's why he lied to you like he done."

McKay frowned, pushed the coin into the man's shaking hand, and strode out of the alleyway. Dempsey leaped after him. McKay was going to need a rear guard, he was certain, if he'd read rightly the determination he had just seen in the man's face.

McKay burst through the batwings, and Dempsey stopped just inside and glanced around the dark interior. Every eye was on McKay as he strode tall and purposefully back to the bar.

Billy Thorpe came down the bar as if to meet this challenge head on. Dempsey moved along the wall, unobserved; everyone seemed curious about what the handsome stranger was about to do.

The bartender said, "Did you forget something, mister?"

In a voice as calm as water in a bowl, McKay said, "Yes, I forgot to buy myself a drink."

"I can fix you right up."

"Whiskey."

Billy Thorpe filled a glass and set it on the bar. McKay snapped a coin on the wood next to the glass, but when Billy went to pick it up, the ebony walking stick flashed and cracked upon the bar, pinning the bartender's hand beneath it. Before Billy could move, McKay had grabbed up a fistful of filthy shirt and yanked the man hard across the bar.

The calm in McKay's voice became a keen edge, sharp enough to cut steel. "You forgot to tell me that Mr. Stewart was killed. You lied to me, Mr. Thorpe, and now I want to know exactly what happened and who is responsible."

"I don't know what the hell you're talking about, mister."

McKay twisted the material until it drew tight around the bartender's throat.

Where he stood at the end of the bar, Dempsey watched two men stand away from their table. The army lieutenant caught the eye of one of them, and when he put a hand on the revolver at his side, both men reconsidered and sat back down.

Thorpe gagged, sputtered, and finally croaked, "All right, all right, I'll tell you!"

McKay released Thorpe with a shove that sent him back against the mirror, and a half dozen neatly stacked glasses crashed to the floor.

The bartender rubbed his throat, hate glaring in his eyes. Dempsey had all he could manage keeping tabs on what was happening with McKay and what might be happening out on the saloon floor. A man at the billiard table was watching with pointed interest, patting the palm of his hand with a cue stick. Dempsey inched along the bar, nearer to McKay and Thorpe.

"All right, your friend didn't go off looking for that woman on another boat like I said. He never walked out of here. He got himself into a fight with a boatman, and when it was all over the boatman had busted in his head, and your friend was dead."

"Where is he now?" Dempsey heard a catch in McKay's voice.

"I dunno. The fellow what bashed in his brains took him out the back way. He used my wagon. I ain't never seen him before, and I ain't seen him since. I get a lot of boatmen in here, and a braggin', blusterin' breed they are. Not the sort to pick a fight with."

"What's the name of the fellow that did it?"

"I dunno that either. Like I said, they come and they go. They don't often introduce themselves or leave a callin' card."

McKay's eyes hardened. "Did you report it to the sheriff or a constable?"

"Hell, no. That would just mean more trouble for me, and I don't need none of that."

"Well, then perhaps I ought to report it for you, Mr. Thorpe." McKay turned away.

Dempsey saw Thorpe reach under the bar and come up with a pistol. The army lieutenant grabbed his saber. Metal whispered against metal as the shiny blade came from the steel scabbard. With the swiftness of a rattlesnake strike, it touched Thorpe in the hollow of his throat; the pistol dropped from the bartender's fingers and clattered to the bar, and the point of the sword forced him back against the mirror where another avalanche of glasses crashed to the floor.

McKay wheeled and picked up Thorpe's pistol. He drew back the hammer, flicked the cap off the nipple with his thumbnail and poured the whiskey he'd just bought into the barrel, wetting the powder. With perfect composure, the gambler handed the weapon back to its owner. "In the future I shall not be so forgiving."

Dempsey had to grin at McKay's bravado, but beneath it all, he sensed that McKay was strung up tight and doing all he could to keep from showing it. McKay gave the lieutenant a quick glance, and without another word, he strolled toward the batwing doors, his walking stick striking the wooden floor with the cadence of a well-timed clock.

On the sidewalk outside, McKay stopped abruptly. His gray eyes were distant, and Dempsey could not read what was on his mind now. He let go of a long breath. "Thank you, Lieutenant Dempsey, for being there just now."

"You're welcome, Mr. McKay. What do you intend to do now? Inform the sheriff?"

A thin smile appeared upon the gambler's grim face. "It would do Mr. Stewart no good now, and only complicate matters for all of us, just as Thorpe said. Murder along the wharf front is as common as prayer in church pew. What is done is done. I'll tell Captain Hamilton."

Dempsey fell in step with McKay. They returned to the *Tempest Queen*, and Dempsey went off to see how the transfer was coming along and if Carr had showed up yet.

McKay went in search of the boat's master to tell him the unhappy news.

Grady Saunders gave a long, soulful whistle. "Will you look at that, Pa. Ain't she pretty?" He'd come to a halt on the boatyard road near the dock where the *Tempest Queen* was moored and was momentarily taken aback by the white, gleaming "wedding cake" sitting in the still water at the end of an extremely busy gangplank.

Deke Saunders grabbed his son by the

shirtsleeve and pulled him aside as a hand-cart pushed by a sweating soldier rumbled past and up onto the boat. "Get your head outa the clouds, boy. We're here to do a job, not to take a leisurely excursion up the Missouri on a fancied-up riverboat, and don't you forget it."

"No, sir, Pa." Grady took another step backward to clear the way for the line of men in blue hauling wooden crates upon their shoulders. The two men slipped into a break in the line of soldiers and were carried along up onto the boat. They hopped out of line once aboard, and Deke spied a sign informing all boarders that tickets to Fort Leavenworth and points between were being sold in the clerk's office up in the main cabin.

"There's where we need to go," Deke said. The two men made their way past busy soldiers, up a wide, polished staircase that forked in the middle. Deke took the right-hand branch, Grady ascended the left, and both father and son reached the boiler deck at the same time. They entered the main cabin through two of the four white doors with leaded-glass panels and grinned at their reflections upon the shiny parquet tile beneath their muddy boots as they made their way to the clerk's window, stepping almost gingerly upon the newly refinished floor.

There was a short line at the window, and Deke found himself behind a woman with a young boy squirming at her side, his hand gripped tightly in her fist.

"Here now," said Deke to the boy, dropping to his haunches, "you look like you're about as excited as a gator in a catfish pond."

The boy eyed this gaunt stranger and drew nearer to the woman's side. "I ain't never rid a riverboat afore, mister."

"*Rode,* Kenneth," she corrected, smiling at Saunders.

Deke grinned back at her, then said to the boy, "Well, I ain't never *rode* one myself, leastwise, not one so grand as this boat is."

The boy just looked at him, shuffling from foot to foot. The woman said, "He's excited because he's going to see his father, who is stationed at Fort Leavenworth. He hasn't seen him in almost a year, Reverend." The woman was young and pretty, wearing a sunbonnet with gay ribbons in it.

"Your husband is a soldier?" Deke said.

"Oh, no. Not *my* husband. I'm not married. He's my brother, and this is his son.

My sister-in-law perished in childbirth, you see." Her voice lost its lightness at the memory. "I have raised Kenneth since that tragic day. Really, the wild frontier is no place for a child, and his father sends us money and visits whenever he can."

Deke smiled and bobbed his bony head. "Of course it isn't. Well, you've a fine lookin' boy there, Miss — ?"

"Cora Mills."

"What a lovely name. And it's a blessed thing you are doing in this life, Miss Mills. You shall surely be rewarded for it in the next."

"Why, thank you, Reverend." Her cheeks reddened and she smiled prettily, and then it was her turn at the window.

When Deke looked over, he caught the gleam in Grady's eye and his hungry look as he carefully assessed the woman at the ticket window ahead of him. Deke chuckled to himself and fished through his pockets for the change he'd need to purchase deck passage for the two of them.

Chapter
Five

"I will report it to the wharf authorities," Hamilton said when McKay had finished telling the captain what he had learned. Hamilton frowned. There were many things about Stewart that Hamilton did not like. At times, Clifton Stewart could be haughty, at times prissy, but in the four months since he'd begun working aboard the *Tempest Queen*, Hamilton had seen a change come over the young man. After all, Stewart had lived nearly twenty-four pampered years on a vast plantation, with his every need instantly taken care of, either by his father's deep purse or by the slaves who were always at his call. It was going to take more than four months to outgrow all of that. Hamilton shook his head, for now Clifton Stewart would never have the chance.

He glanced at McKay. "Thank you for finding this out for me. It is sad news, indeed, and I will inform Mr. Stewart's parents as soon as we reach Baton Rouge."

"If you like, I will tell them. Clifton and

I had become friends over the months."

"I appreciate the offer, but no. As master of the *Tempest Queen* it is my duty to tell them." Hamilton drew in a breath, then letting it out slowly, he returned to the matter immediately at hand. "I better get back down there and see how Lieutenant Dempsey and his men are coming along."

"I'm certain Mr. Lansing is keeping them in line."

"No doubt." Hamilton put on his cap and the two men left the captain's cabin. Hamilton paused on the porch outside his door and drew in a lungful of river air. "I'm looking forward to being away from this place, Mr. McKay. Away to someplace where you can see the sun, and not the air."

"Good day, Captain." McKay touched his hat and strolled away, across the hurricane deck and down one of the ladders to the boiler deck below.

Hamilton went to the clerk's office to check the boarding. The list was irritably short. Belding, the clerk, said that most of the folks planning to head west on the Missouri had already booked with the packets that make the Missouri their regular trade. He thought they were fortunate to have gotten the few passengers they had.

"Well, we shall do our best, Mr. Belding." Hamilton noticed that the slender clerk's brown hair needed a comb tugged through it and that his beard could use a clipping. "Perhaps you could visit our barber before we shove off, Mr. Belding."

The clerk grinned and grabbed a handful of hair at the back of his neck. "I'll do that, sir."

"Very well, let's see if we can't add a few names to that list before tomorrow."

Hamilton left and found Dempsey down on the main deck.

"Sorry to hear about your man," Dempsey said when Hamilton came up.

"Thank you. I understand your sergeant is still missing as well."

"Yes. It looks like St. Louis has not been good to either one of us." Dempsey turned his attention suddenly to a dray that had pulled to a stop at the end of the gangplank. "We are about to bring the paymaster aboard." Twelve armed troops slipped off the dray to the pavement, and four more took up the two heavy chests. "Would you have a secure room where we could put it?"

"Humm, I've a stateroom at the rear of the boat which is used for storage. There is an outside door only."

109

"That should do nicely. There will be armed guards posted around the clock, and the back of your fine vessel should put it nicely out of the way of your other passengers."

On the next deck above, Deke Saunders and his boy stood at the railing, watching the soldiers below escort the army's payroll aboard. The troops marched up the wide stairway and went past them, into the main cabin. Deke and Grady followed the procession through the long cabin and out through the ladies' salon at the back of the boat, keeping well behind them. In a narrow hallway that led to the outside, Deke peeked around the corner as Captain Hamilton unlocked a door and stood back for the paymaster to enter. When it was all over, Hamilton handed the key to Dempsey.

Deke wheeled and hurriedly motioned Grady back out of the hallway. By time the soldiers came back through the main cabin, he and his boy were sitting at a table, seeming not to be paying any attention to the contingent of armed soldiers that came tromping back through.

"They are gonna keep armed guards at that room for certain, Pa."

"Sure they will," Deke said, running a finger under the clerical collar that itched in the heat, "but we don't have to worry 'bout that until all our boys are aboard."

"What will we do then? This boat will still be swarming with armed Federal troops."

"I'm workin' on that, boy. I'm workin' on that. We got us plenty of time yet. In the meantime, why don't you round us up a bottle of something from somewhere. It won't look proper for me to be doing it. And find us some drinkin' glasses as well. I got to keep up appearances, you know." Deke grinned.

"Sure, Pa," and Grady went off in search of the bar.

Captain Hamilton studied the open watch in his palm. Nine fifty-eight. He glanced out the pilothouse windows at the dock and the boatyard. The morning had become stifling, and the heavy, smoke-laden air did not help matters. On the high bench, his Mississippi pilot, Patton Sinclair, was lounging like a king on his throne, puffing on a green cigar, filling the pilothouse with a dense cloud of smoke. It didn't appear that Sinclair cared one whit that he had just handed over control of the

Tempest Queen to another pilot. In fact, Hamilton had the distinct impression that Sinclair was rather looking forward to wallowing about the pilothouse and watching someone else do all the work. What did he care? He was being paid two hundred and fifty dollars a month whether he stood behind the helm or not.

Sinclair's cub, young Jack Jacobs, was at Eric Jupp's elbow now. Not that the temporary pilot needed the assistance of a tyro riverboat pilot in training, but Sinclair had said the trip up the Missouri might be good experience for a cub who had already become a superb steersman. Hamilton grinned to himself, for he suspected it was just Sinclair's way of keeping the lad out of his hair while he loafed and smoked and drank.

Hamilton shut the watch's lid with a snap and buried it deep into his vest pocket so that only the fob remained exposed. "It is ten of the clock, Mr. Jupp."

"Aye, Captain." The pilot reached overhead for the bell cord that signaled down in the engine room. He gave it two jerks. In a moment the sky blackened as the fireman, on the main deck below, tossed pine knots into the boilers while Mr. Seegar, down in the engine room, pulled the levers that got the mighty steam pistons moving. The 'scape pipes hissed. The steam whistle shrilled, and all along the deck startled passengers immediately plunged their fingers into their ears. A ceiling of sooty smoke spread overhead, and fine fly ash from the belching chimneys rained down on travelers, newly painted decks, and railings as well.

The whistle sang out three times, the great bronze bell on the hurricane deck rang for the leadsmen, and in a moment the *Tempest Queen* shuddered to life and nosed slowly away from her moorings. Jupp aimed her out of the boatyard for the wide river beyond. When she had cleared the yard, the leadsmen began shouting out the river's depth, and as the bottom dropped away, Jupp spun the helm, cramped her down, and turned the *Tempest Queen* north where the mouth of the Missouri River dumped her silt-laden waters into the Mississippi.

Hamilton watched Jupp handle his boat as if he'd been born in a pilothouse. Perhaps Lieutenant Dempsey's words of praise were well founded, for Jupp seemed quite competent. Hamilton had only to assume that Jupp's partner, a barrel-chested Northerner who barely topped five feet tall and went by the name of "Little" Sam Winston, was just as competent.

Hamilton waited until Jupp had taken them out into the stream and had the *Tempest Queen* moving smartly against the strong current before clearing his throat and getting the pilot's attention. "We are running rather light, this trip, Mr. Jupp. I would like to take on as many paying fares along the way as we can."

"You want me to stop at all signals?" the pilot asked.

"So long as you believe the landing will be safe, Mr. Jupp."

The pilot glanced over, and Hamilton recognized that look of wounded pride instantly. Every pilot Hamilton had ever met knew precisely how to display it if his judgment was called into even the slightest question. "Captain, I would not make a landing that I did not judge to be safe."

"Of course not," Hamilton said neutrally. They were a proud lot, pilots were, and you had to handle them with kid gloves. An angered pilot could make a trip most unpleasant — and equally unprofitable if he so desired. Hamilton understood this not only because he'd been a boat's master for most of twenty years, but before that, he, too, had been a pilot and as proud and as boastful as any of them.

"Very well, Mr. Jupp. The *Tempest Queen* is in your hands now. I shall be about boat's business if you should happen to need me," which, of course, Hamilton knew would be a rare instance indeed. Once on the river, pilots wielded a power subordinate only to the Deity. Presidents and captains alike bent knees to a riverboat pilot upon getting out under steam. It was the law.

Hamilton made his way down to the main cabin where breakfast was being served to the few passengers who had booked staterooms. He snatched a cup of coffee off a silver service tray on his way through, wondering if the ten thousand dollar premium the army was paying to use his vessel would make up his losses. The Mississippi River was the *Tempest Queen*'s regular trade, and Hamilton could easily have filled every stateroom and taken on cargo stacked as high as the boiler deck if he had gone south.

He paused by the railing, sipping his coffee, listening to the 'scape pipes chuffing with the rhythm of a heartbeat. He squinted at the smoke overhead from the twin chimneys; it had faded from pitch black to only dirty gray now. Hamilton had instructed his firemen to burn pine knots whenever arriving or departing a town. Mountains of black smoke were what people wanted to see, and there was still a bit of showmanship in the old captain's soul.

On the main deck below, among crates of rifles, barrels of powder and whiskey, canvas-covered mounds, and the ordnance rifles, sat the soldiers balancing tin plates on their knees, seeing to their own breakfasts. Deck passage aboard the *Tempest Queen* did not include meals, although food could be had for a price from the boat's galley. Ahead, the muddy Missouri emptied into the Mississippi, and as they were fast approaching that confluence now, it seemed to Hamilton that the two rivers resisted each other, like squabbling siblings; the Missouri flowing into her larger sister, but refusing to become part of her and maintaining her darker waters for a great distance, as if insisting that she was still within her own channel.

Beneath his feet, Hamilton felt the mighty engines thumping in time with the hissing from the 'scape pipes, and he could also feel the sudden faltering of their passage as the *Tempest Queen*'s great paddles drove her up against the currents, and crosscurrents, where the two waters wrestled.

Glancing aft, the city of St. Louis slipped away beneath dingy skies. The *Tempest Queen* had entered the Missouri channel now, and where it stretched ahead of them, the heavens took on a brighter blue and a hot sun drove the morning dampness away. Hamilton inhaled the clean air, relishing it. Then he remembered the crew member he had left behind, and the sudden lift sank as his spirit plummeted. It would have been nice, at least, to have located the body. A decent burial would have been the proper way to leave Stewart, not, as Hamilton suspected, having the body tossed somewhere into the river where catfish and crayfish were even now picking his bones clean.

He shook his head sadly and handed his empty coffee cup to a passing waiter. Hooking his thumbs under his suspenders, he strode gloomily down the promenade, starting on his rounds, which were a regular morning routine for Captain Hamilton.

Standing at the bow, on the main deck, Lieutenant Dempsey was in an equally despondent mood. A lost man was not a thing to be dismissed lightly. There'd be an inquiry when he reached Fort Leavenworth. A pile of paperwork and a tangle of red tape to work his way through. But that wasn't what bothered Dempsey — in the end Carr would be labeled a deserter, even though Dempsey was certain that had not been the case. He'd sent out a squad of men the day before to scour the riverfront and another early that morning before the *Tempest Queen* had left her berth. There had been no trace of Carr. Frowning, Dempsey unconsciously balled his fist until his knuckles whitened. His brain being occupied on these weightier matters, the army lieutenant was not aware that the *Tempest Queen* had settled down to a steady, driving pace cutting easily into the Missouri's current or that the muddy water was breaking smoothly around the prow, just a few feet beyond the toes of his boots, rippling back to be beaten into froth on either side of the boat by the two mighty paddle wheels. Nor was he aware of the young woman who had strolled up onto the bow near him.

"What a lovely day to take a trip up the river."

Her words startled him out of his blind concentration. He looked over to discover the attractive woman at his side, smiling up at him, her face shaded from the sun by a white, lacy sunbonnet wrapped about with a bright, yellow ribbon and decorated with dainty red and blue flowers fashioned out of finer ribbons. In spite of the hat, she still had to shield her eyes from the morning sun with her hand. The breeze from the forward passage of the boat tugged at the ringlets that fell beneath the bonnet, and ruffled the blue dress where its hem brushed near the deck.

"I beg your pardon?"

Her widening smile punched dimples into her cheeks. "I said it is a lovely day for a boat trip up the river."

"Oh, yes, of course it is." He had not permitted his brain to dwell on such trivial things as the warm morning sun, the deep green of trees along the bank that dipped their branches to the water, or the traffic of other brightly painted boats streaming tails of gray smoke from their chimney stacks. He had been thinking about his missing man, but now this lovely woman with the golden hair and happy smile easily moved those thoughts aside. "Yes, it is quite lovely," he repeated with emerging enthusiasm.

"You are going out to Fort Leavenworth,

119

you and your men, are you not, Lieutenant?"

"We are."

"So am I. Are you stationed there?"

"No. I'm with the Quartermaster Corps. I'll see these supplies and troops safely deposited at Fort Leavenworth, and then it's back to division headquarters for a new assignment."

"You must visit a lot of forts in your job."

Dempsey had to grin at her wide-eyed awe. "Yes, I get around. I've been to most of the Western outposts in the division." She was very pretty, he decided at once, with green eyes the color of a clear emerald and smooth skin that obviously had been carefully protected from the sun.

"All that traveling must be hard on your family, Lieutenant."

"Dempsey, ma'am. Sherman Dempsey. And I don't have a family, so that has never been a problem." As he spoke he stole a glance at the finger of her left hand. To his delight, there was no wedding ring there. "And your name is?"

"Cora Mills."

"You live in St. Louis?"

"Yes, I do." She suddenly looked at the river ahead. "Have you been to Fort Leaven-

120

worth before, Lieutenant Dempsey?"

"A couple of times."

"I understand it is quite civilized."

"There is a sizable town growing up around it. Several churches. A lot of the soldiers' families are moving in."

"Really. But isn't it still Indian Territory?"

"It is; however, the military has the area well secured." He paused and then asked, "And what takes you to Fort Leavenworth, Miss Mills?"

She started to speak, but at that moment a small voice cried out, "Mamma, mamma, come look at the big paddle wheel!" A little boy ran up, grabbed her hand, and dragged her unceremoniously back from the bow of the boat.

"All right, Kenneth." Cora managed a smile at Captain Dempsey as the insistent child nearly pulled her off balance. "I'm afraid I'm off to see the paddle wheel, Lieutenant Dempsey."

Dempsey nodded his head a little stiffly, for all at once he knew exactly why Cora Mills was traveling to Fort Leavenworth. Even though she did not wear a wedding ring, there obviously was a soldier there — a special soldier to her, and to her son. He watched Cora being towed along by the excited child, and when they had disappeared, he turned back to the widening river ahead.

He grinned suddenly, thinking how quickly he'd assumed that she was unmarried and how near he'd come to saying something inappropriate, making a fool of himself. Well, his life was one of constant traveling, and as he had told himself many times before, it was unfair to burden any woman with a man who could never be at home to take care of her.

With a sobering sigh, Dempsey dismissed the encounter and shifted his thoughts back to the problem of his missing sergeant. But he found them easily turned aside, and in spite of himself, he kept seeing Cora's happy smile, her bright eyes, and with a vague discontent, most unusual for him, he abandoned the bow and strolled away with no particular destination in mind.

Chapter Six

"Watch out for your brother, Frank, you hear me?" Zerelda Samuel called after her lanky, sixteen-year-old son, who was sauntering off down the riverbank where a moment before his younger brother had rushed with a maddening recklessness that was both a product of youth and simply the younger boy's nature, which Zerelda had never been able to properly discipline.

"I will, Ma," Frank replied over his shoulder as he wedged a leather-bound volume of Shakespeare under his arm and shoved his hands into his jacket pockets.

"Don't let him get too close to the river, and don't bury your nose in that book so deep that you don't know what he's up to," Zerelda said, her hands planted sternly upon her hips, an impatient scowl upon her face.

"I will, Ma!" Frank called back again before he, too, disappeared into the trees that grew up along the waters of the Mississippi River.

She looked after him awhile, then glanced across to the buggy where her husband was unhitching the horses. "That little one will be the death of me, Reuben," but there was a faint glimmer of admiration in her compressed lips that Dr. Reuben Samuel had come to know so well in their brief four years of marriage.

Reuben unbuckled the leather straps of each harness. "He's just got spunk, Zerelda; like his mother."

Her eyes widened. "Who, me?" she asked innocently.

He chuckled and led the animals away. "I'm gonna take them to water. I'll be back in awhile."

With a final glance down the riverbank where her two sons had disappeared, Zerelda Samuel wheeled back to the buggy and lifted out a wicker basket containing their lunch. They did not often travel back to Kentucky, to visit Reuben's family, but when they did, it was always a monumental expedition, amounting to a full week's journey each way. Fortunately, there were friends and relatives scattered along the way where they could find rest from the tiring buggy ride and the hard ground where they spent many a night.

Now that they were on their way home

— already in Missouri — Zerelda was anxious to be back at their farm. But that was still almost a week away. Tonight they would have to sleep under the stars, on buggy cushions, but not tomorrow night. A smile touched her lips. Tomorrow night they'd make Laban's farm on the bank of the Missouri River and rest up there a couple days before the final, long push back to their farm in Kearney.

Zerelda spread out a blanket in the shade of a tall oak tree and prepared their lunch. In a few minutes Reuben came back with the horses and hobbled them in a patch of grass and clover. With a low groan he arched his back. His muscles were drawn taut by the hours of the straight-back buggy seat. Reuben sat on the ground, stretched his legs out, put his back to the bole of the tree, removed a pouch of tobacco from his pocket, and mechanically filled the bowl of his briar pipe.

"I wonder if Martha Davenport has had her baby yet?" he commented casually, tamping the tobacco with a forefinger.

"Martha is always two weeks late," Zerelda said, slicing a loaf of bread they had bought that morning before taking the ferry over from Illinois.

"I hope so. I promised her I'd be back in

time for the delivery." He struck a match and in a moment had the tobacco in the bowl glowing, filling the air with its pleasant odor.

"Martha has never had any problems giving birth as long as I've known her. I'm sure if you missed this one, she will do just fine anyway."

"Oh, probably." He shook out the match. "But the point is, I promised her I'd be back to help."

Zerelda glanced over. Her husband was an easygoing, gentle man, stoutly built. "You're just too dependable, Reuben. Most folks don't appreciate you like they ought to."

He chuckled and flicked the spent match away.

"Well, it is true."

"It's all part of the job."

"I wonder where the boys are," Zerelda said, changing the subject and glancing at the stand of trees.

"I hear 'em below, talking." Reuben fished a pocketknife from his vest and began methodically cleaning his fingernails. "You got to let loose of those apron strings a mite, Zerelda. You've done a good job raising them. Frank is sixteen. He is nearly a man. And Je—" His words were cut off when Frank's voice suddenly cried out from down along the river.

"Ma . . . Reuben, come quick!"

"Oh, dear Lord, Jes has fallen in the river!" Zerelda cried, leaping to her feet. Reuben was at her heels as she gathered her dress up in one hand and ran along the path the boys had followed. When they burst through the final tree cover, they saw both boys standing at the river's edge with the toes of their shoes in the water.

Frank pointed at something out in the water. "Looky there."

Zerelda breathed a sigh, whispered a prayer of thanks, and then peered at where Frank's finger was jabbing. For all the world, it looked to her to be only a snag, floating half out of the water with its spider-web of blanched roots thrust skyward. "What?" she asked, but even as she spoke the word, Reuben was tearing off his vest and putting it and his pipe in her hands. The next instant he was wading out into the water. Her confusion remained only a moment longer, and then she, too, saw the limp form of a man caught like a rag doll in the tangled roots, his upper body held out of the water, his legs down beneath it.

Reuben waded out until the water reached his chest, got hold of the snag, and slowly dragged it toward shore. Frank plunged in to help, but Zerelda caught her younger son by the collar an instant before he tried to join his brother.

"It's up over your head," she warned. "Wait here with me."

"Oh, Ma," he sighed with the exasperation of the youngest never being allowed to do the fun things that older folks get a chance at. But Zerelda held him tight, and in a minute the snag her husband was dragging had run aground and both Reuben and Frank were extricating the unconscious man from the roots and carrying him to shore.

"Is he alive?" she asked softly when they laid him out upon the muddy bank.

Reuben lifted an eyelid with a soft finger, picked up the man's wrist, and seemed to stare out into space a moment.

"Well?" Zerelda asked, this time more insistently.

"He's alive, barely." Dr. Reuben examined the crust of dried blood on the back of the man's head and frowned. "He's had a severe blow to the skull. Help me with him, Frank," Reuben said, lifting the man into his arms. "Zerelda, you go and build us a fire, then get that blanket from the buggy."

She nodded her head and shot a glance at her younger son. "Jes, you come with me."

The boy tagged along without debate while Reuben and Frank struggled under the weight of the unconscious man. Up at the buggy, Reuben removed the wet clothes and wrapped the man in the blanket. "He's mighty cold. First thing we need to do is get his temperature up."

Zerelda could see her husband naturally slipping back into his role as physician, forgetting for the moment that they were on a family outing — or even that they were alone on a country road miles from any town. St. Louis was supposed to be up north somewhere, she knew, but they had not intended to take that route. The fire blazed higher. Reuben moved the man nearer to it, and with a damp cloth he began to clean the wound.

"I wish I had my medicinals with me," he said at one point, more to himself than to Zerelda, who remained near to fetch the items he asked for. He had needle and sutures along, and he had found a salve in the bottom of his bag that he applied sparingly, but when he finished, he frowned a most unsatisfied frown and shook his head.

"We'll have to wait and see now. We

probably ought to be taking him into town where he can be tended properly."

"It's getting awful late," Frank noted, looking at the sky.

"I know. Anyway, we should not move him tonight," Reuben said. "We'll have to camp out here, it looks like. Perhaps tomorrow we can take him up to St. Louis."

"Would it be any farther taking him to Laban's farm?" Zerelda asked. "I know there is a doctor living near his place."

"I suppose it would not be any farther," Reuben said, considering this alternative plan.

Their younger boy had not said much since they had brought the stranger ashore and his stepfather had doctored him. Now he looked at his mother with wide-eyed wonderment and said, "Where do you suppose he come from?"

"No way of telling, Jes."

"Maybe he's an outlaw running from the law?"

Reuben chuckled. "You've quite an imagination, son."

"Well, he could be."

"I suppose he could. Only from the looks of him, and of his clothes, I'd say he was a laborer and nothing so exciting as an outlaw. His hands show new calluses, and even though he was in the river a long while, there is no denying that his clothes are full of soot. I'd guess he worked around locomotives or perhaps steamboats. Perhaps he fell off a passing steamer."

The boy was not wholly satisfied with this explanation, and he wandered off into the lengthening shadows, hands deep into the pockets of his overalls, kicking at a toadstool in his way.

"I'll unpack," Zerelda sighed. "I certainly had hoped we would have made more distance than we did."

Reuben frowned. "We could have hardly left the poor fellow in the water, now could we, Zerelda?"

"Oh, no. I wouldn't even suggest it!" She was startled that he would even think that. "It is only that now the going tomorrow will be that much longer, that's all."

Reuben clamped down on his pipe, thinking, then he stood and went to her side. "Here, I'll help you with that."

Frank closed his book in the fading light and set it on the front seat of the buggy. "I'd better go keep an eye on Jes," and he strolled off after his little brother.

"I still think he could be an outlaw, Frank."

The older boy tossed a stone out into the fast waters of the Mississippi and heard it plop. The river was deep out beyond the fallen tree upon which the two boys sat. "Reuben is probably right."

Jes probed the depths of a crawdad hole with the tip of a slender stick. "Who knows, he might even be a river pirate."

Frank gave a short laugh. "Hardly any of them left."

"Harvey told me last time we were there that river pirates still lure passing rafts and flatboats into shore, and they still roam the caves along the Missouri. You can ask him soon as we get to Uncle Laban's house."

"Harvey's got a bigger imagination than you. So has Uncle Laban for that matter."

"That ain't no way to talk about kin, Frank."

"Laban ain't no kin to us. He is just one of Father's friends from way back. We only call him uncle because Ma said it is polite."

Jes frowned and went back to aggravating that crawdad way down below, occasionally seeing a pincer's rise up from the black tunnel to snap at the pesky stick. "I know that." There passed a long silence, and the gloom of the coming night grew deeper. "Wonder why he got his head busted in like he done?"

"Who knows."

"Could be he was held up by high-waymen. Maybe they stole his money and dumped him in the river."

"Or it could be he tripped, hit his head, and fell off a passing steamer like Reuben says." Frank lobbed out another heavy stone and listened to it plumb the depths of the river.

The younger boy thought a moment and then suddenly said, "You know, if I was grown up, I might be a highwayman."

Frank grinned and looked over. "You don't know the first thing about robbing folks."

"Maybe I'd rob banks."

"People don't rob banks, leastwise not in broad daylight. People *burgle* banks, in the dead of night, and usually when there ain't no moon."

"Why?"

"Why what?"

"Why don't people rob banks in the day-light?"

Frank looked over, amazed. "Why, you haven't learnt a whole lot in your thirteen years, have you. People don't rob banks in the daylight because everybody will see who they are."

"You could wear a mask."

"Even if you did wear a mask, they'd shoot you down before you stepped outside the door."

"Oh" — Jes went back to teasing that crawdad — "guess I didn't think about that."

"I'd say you didn't."

Another few moments of silence, and then in a small voice meant more for his own ears than those of his older brother's, Jes said, "I bet I could figure out a way to rob a bank in daylight — if I worked on it."

"You'll get yourself a rope around your neck, too, if you work on it. Come on, it's getting dark. Let's go on back to the fire." Frank stood and started up the embankment.

"I'll be along directly."

"Don't stay too long or Ma will have a conniption."

"I won't."

"Where is your brother?" Zerelda asked when Frank came into the glow of the campfire and took a seat on a log that had been dragged over for the purpose.

"He's still down watching the river. Says he'll be up directly. How's that stranger doing?"

"His color is improving some," Reuben said, reaching for a pot on a bed of coals piled off to one side of the fire. "Want some coffee, Frank?" Reuben refilled his own cup and offered some to Zerelda. She told him she had had enough. Frank found a ceramic coffee cup in the basket and held it out for Reuben to fill.

"He's lucky we came along."

"I'd say he is. Another couple hours in that river and the cold water would have done for him what that blow to the head almost did."

"What are we gonna do with him now that we got him?"

"Your mother is inclined to tote him along with us to your Uncle Laban's place. Leave him in a doctor's care there." Reuben Samuel gave a laugh. "I think that's her way of telling us that she doesn't want to waste another day driving him north to St. Louis."

"Oh, Reuben, that's not so at all. It's just that I don't see any reason to go a whole day out of our way when taking him to Laban's place will do for him just as well."

Frank grinned, and Reuben held his peace, hiding his own amusement behind a sip of coffee.

"So, I reckon we'll just take him along. It

will be a tight fit, all of us in that one buggy, but Laban's place is not that far off. We'll be there tomorrow in the early afternoon."

Then to their surprise, the man in the blanket let out a soft groan. Frank leaped off the log. "What was that?"

Reuben set his coffee cup down and bent over the man. The night was almost full on them, with only a faint glow remaining in the western sky, but it was enough for Frank to see that the man's eyelids had fluttered, and now they opened.

"Mystie," he said. It was barely more than a breath escaping his cracked lips.

"Misty?" Frank glanced to his mother. "Is that what he said?"

Zerelda shook her head. "Maybe he can't see clearly."

"Hello," Reuben said, bending over him.

The man looked about, disoriented, and finally found Dr. Samuel's face hovering over him. He seemed to have trouble focusing, and in the end he stopped trying and his eyelids quivered closed.

"Mister, can you hear me?" Reuben urged.

The man swallowed and then again spoke softly, "Yes, I hear you. Thirsty."

136

"Zerelda, the water." Reuben put out a hand, and she passed a canteen to him. He lifted the man's head gently and poured a few drops between the parched lips.

The man gulped for the water, but Reuben gave him only a little. "Not so fast. You'll choke yourself." He lowered the bandaged head. "You've had quite a knock on the head."

"Where . . . where am I?"

"About twenty miles south of St. Louis. We found you in the river."

"River? What river?"

"Why, the Mississippi, of course."

"St. Louis?"

"That's north of here. Is that where you live?"

The man opened his eyes again, and it appeared as if he might be searching for something — a bit of lost memory, Frank suspected. "I don't know."

"You don't know where you live?" Reuben asked.

"I . . . can't remember."

"Do you remember how you got into the river, or how you got that wallop on your head?"

He struggled with that question and, after a moment, said quietly, "No."

"Hum. Well, I reckon it ain't important

137

at the moment. Tell me what your name is, mister."

The man started to speak but stopped and glanced at Reuben with a startled look. "I can't seem to remember that either."

Frank was aware of his little brother's coming up the riverbank and drawing a stop at his side. "He is awake!" Jes said softly.

Frank nodded his head.

The younger boy inched forward for a closer look.

Reuben asked, "You can't remember your own name?"

The man stammered, struggling with it, but in the end he closed his eyes and said, "I don't remember."

"Well, you've been hit pretty hard on the head. I've heard of men losing their memory from a blow like you got. Most often it returns after a day or two. In the meantime, don't you fret none. We'll get you to someplace where you can rest up. We are out here in the middle of almost nowhere tonight, but tomorrow we'll be to a place you can rest up at." Reuben thought of something and said, "When you woke up you said the word *misty*. Do you recall why?"

The man looked over. "No. I don't remember saying it."

"Well, it don't matter much, I guess. Are you hungry?"

"No. Sleepy."

"Then you go back to sleep, mister, and in the morning you might feel more like eating. And don't fret none either. You're in good hands. Nothing will happen to you while we're looking out for you. My name is Reuben Samuel, Dr. Reuben Samuel. This is my wife, Zerelda. And over there are her two fine boys, Frank and Jesse James."

Chapter
Seven

When Clifton Stewart had regained consciousness that evening, he could remember
nothing of himself or where he had been. At
that time he was still too badly dazed,
drifting in and out of a fog, to think much
about it — after all, Dr. Reuben had said his
memory would return. But when morning
came, and Stewart awoke still unable to remember even the simplest details of his past,
such as what his very name was, the problem
began to weigh heavy upon him. The dilemma of his faulty memory became more
pressing as his strength returned.

He sat propped against a tree while the
family packed up the buggy. He wanted to
help them, but standing caused his head to
whirl, and Dr. Reuben had insisted that
the proper thing for him to do was to rest.
When the horses were hitched into their
traces, Reuben gave Clifton a hand up into
the front seat beside him. Zerelda and the
two boys squeezed into the backseat, she
between them as sort of a safety zone,

Stewart figured. He knew, as he suspected she did, too, that the three of them packed in there tight as peas in a pod would shortly lead to a contest of whose elbow was more damaging if she had let the boys sit together.

Reuben got the team moving. Stewart's head spun at first as the buggy lurched forward, and for a moment he thought he might be sick. He closed his eyes, and once on their way the queasiness passed.

From the backseat Zerelda said, "We will take you to Laban Caulder's farm. It's not far from a village named Matson. Have you ever been to Matson?"

Stewart turned slowly on the seat, trying to avoid the stab of pain that exploded each time he moved his head. "Not that I can recall."

"It's a pleasant little place on the Missouri River. We'll put you in the care of the doctor there."

The day grew hot; however, they were traveling through a forest that managed to temper the sun somewhat but did little for the swarm of black flies that accompanied the buggy. Dr. Reuben puffed his pipe, and the smoke helped a little to keep the flies away, but not nearly enough. Stewart found the situation particularly annoying, for unlike the other passengers who could freely swat the pesky beasts, any sudden movement on his part only amplified the needles that jabbed his neck and prodded his brain.

As the morning drew on, he tried to recall what had happened to him. How had he gotten hurt? The effort only caused his head to ache more, and he soon abandoned that line of thinking and remained as motionless as was possible upon the jostling buggy seat, watching the green and brown of the forest pass him by on either side, smelling the humus of the forest floor.

Morning became afternoon. The Samuel family stopped near a rill of clear water to rest and to eat the remaining food in the wicker basket. Afterward, as Zerelda rinsed their few dishes in the running stream, Frank took a shotgun from the floorboards of the buggy, and he and Jesse walked out into the forest. In a little while, Stewart heard the gun boom once, far away, and when the boys returned a few minutes later, Jesse was swinging a gobbler at his side by its legs.

"Look what Frank shot us for supper tonight."

"That's a dandy-looking bird you

bagged," Reuben said.

Frank held back a smile and acted nonchalantly about the catch, but Clifton could see the boy's pride. "It wasn't anything," he said, and fetched a hunting bag from the back of the buggy that held his powder, shot, and caps. While Frank reloaded the shotgun, Jesse cleaned the bird and put it into the stream to cool it down.

Stomachs fed and backs rested, Zerelda packed the turkey Frank had shot into the wicker basket and the family piled once again into the buggy. Clifton Stewart found he could now stand up without the aid of an arm to lean on, and when he climbed up onto the buggy seat by himself, Dr. Samuel grinned around the stem of the pipe clenched between his teeth and told Stewart it appeared he was on the road to recovery.

"Now, if only I could remember who I was," Stewart said with a wry smile.

"That will come in time as well," Reuben assured him and snapped the reins.

The team pulled ahead, and in another hour the Missouri River had swung alongside the road they were following. It was still mostly hidden from sight by the thick forest, but where the trees thinned out,

Stewart had a pleasant view of the wide, brown waters. The afternoon sun glinted off its surface as if someone had scattered bits of a broken mirror out across the water, and here and there steamboats ran ahead of a trail of gray smoke, fighting the current up river or steaming smoothly down toward the Mississippi, which Stewart seemed to know lay to the east — but how could he remember a thing like that and yet not his own name? The problem nettled him, and he could come to no solution. Pondering it caused the pain inside his skull to swell, and in the end he put the problem out of mind and tried to think of nothing at all and simply enjoyed the smell of the water and trees and earth.

Ahead, the land opened up. Axes had been taken to the forest, and where mighty trees once stood, now a cluster of un- painted buildings marched down to the water's edge. A huge flatboat ahead of a little stern-wheel steamboat were moored to a rickety wharf, and a stream of gray smoke puffed lazily from the steamboat's chimneys. From the engines a cloud of white steam escaped her gage cocks.

Gage cocks? The words had come so easily, it was almost as if gage cocks were something so familiar to him that he did not have to think to put a name to them.

Dr. Reuben drew back on the reins, set the brake with his foot, and climbed down. Stewart noticed that several other wagons and buggies were parked nearby. There were horses tied to hitching rails as well, and what seemed like a large company of people lingering about, as if waiting for something to happen.

"Where are we?" Stewart asked.

Jesse said, "This is Potts Ferry. It's how we get across to Uncle Laban's farm." He was eyeing the hissing steamboat hungrily, as if the boy would like nothing better than to be allowed to get in among the mechanicals and yank a few levers, and maybe stand behind the helm in the pilot-house, which on this little boat sat down directly on the boiler deck. It had no cabins, no crew quarters, little deck space to speak of. It was designed for one purpose, and that was to push the giant raft from one side of the river to the other.

Dr. Reuben came back in a couple minutes and said, "The ferry isn't going to leave for another hour. I've paid for our passage. Why don't we all climb down and stretch our legs. There is a place to wait inside, and the proprietor said we can buy something cold to drink."

Dr. Reuben helped Zerelda off while Frank and Jesse bounded over the sides of the buggy and headed straight down to the wharf where the wheezing, weathered steamboat was moored.

"You two be careful and don't get too close," Zerelda called after them.

But they didn't appear to hear her, and Dr. Reuben grinned understandingly. "The boys will be all right, Zerelda. They just want a closer look."

"I know that, Reuben, and I know that Frank will be all right; it is that youngest of mine that I worry about. You know how wild that boy can be."

"I'll keep an eye on them," Stewart offered.

"Hum." Reuben turned a concerned eye on Stewart. "You feel like you are up to walking down there?"

"I think so. So long as I don't overdo it."

"All right. Only, if you start to feeling dizzy sit down someplace before you fall down. You have a concussion to the brain, and it will take some time for it to heal properly."

Stewart promised that he would, and he slowly made his way toward the wharf while Reuben led the horses and buggy into some shade. Reuben clasped his wife by the arm and took her up the three steps to a porch and disappeared into one of the buildings there.

Clifton Stewart was keenly aware of his frailty as he walked, but it was reassuring to be able to move about under his own power. He relished the feeling of just being alive as he stepped out onto the wharf and came up beside Frank and Jesse. He was only now beginning to understand how close a brush he had had with death. The realization made the here and now all that much more dear to him.

"Well, what do you think of this?" he said when Frank and Jesse glanced over at him. He got an odd feeling from the looks they gave him, as if they had been planning something they wanted no one else to know about. "Have you ever seen a steam engine up close before?"

The two boys exchanged looks and stifled laughs as if the question had been the most naive query they had ever heard. "Gosh, sure we have, mister," Jesse said. "Seen plenty of engines before. Bigger ones than this little old towboat. Why, one day when no one was watching I climbed up in the cab of a locomotive that had a head of steam up and everything. Sure as you're standing there, I would have taken that locomotive and gone a flying along the track if I knew what levers to pull."

"You would have?"

"Gosh, yes. That would have been more fun than the time we stole one of Uncle Laban's race horses and took it for a run along the river road."

"You steal horses?" Stewart narrowed an eye at the two boys. It was Jesse doing all the talking, but he could tell that the older, more quiet Frank was in complete agreement with his brother. "You can get in big trouble doing that, even if they do belong to relatives."

"They got to catch me first," Jesse said, pushing out his boyish chest some, as if he was in the habit of pulling off such pranks.

"Does your mother know you were fooling around locomotives?"

"Gosh, no, mister" — Jesse narrowed an eye at Stewart and his voice hardened — "and she better not hear of it either."

Stewart was caught off guard by this sudden threat in the thirteen-year-old's voice. "Well . . . well, I have no intentions of telling her," he said, determined not to let the boldness of a mere youngster ruffle him. "But you're going to get yourself in big trouble someday with that attitude."

Frank spoke up now. "Not Jesse. He can outsmart a fox — most foxes, that is, so long as he don't let his ambitions get too far ahead of him."

Stewart was amazed to hear such talk from these two boys. When they had been around their mother they wore shiny halos. Now, not five minutes out of her sight, the halo was trampled in the dirt and horns had sprouted.

Jesse started along the wharf toward the gangplank, Frank at his side.

"Hey, where are you going?" Stewart called, remembering he had promised Zerelda to keep an eye on the two boys.

Frank James spun about and narrowed an eye. "Quiet down!" His voice was a harsh whisper. "You'll bring someone down on us."

"Someone down? What are you intending to —" But before Stewart could finish, Frank and Jesse James had darted up the landing stage and were slithering along the wall that contained the engine room, and the next instant they had plunged into the dark rectangle of an open door.

"Good heavens!" Stewart cried. His view dodged about the little steamboat. No one seemed to be aboard. Regretting what he was about to do, Stewart followed Frank and Jesse onto the boat.

"What are you two up to?" he whispered.

Startled, the boys leaped back, and then seeing it was only Stewart, they turned back to ogling black machinery: gauges and levers and hissing valves.

Jesse was saying, "Harvey ain't never gonna believe that we got all the way into the engine room unless we take back some proof."

Frank glanced nervously about. Being three years older, Stewart figured the boy was aware of the trouble he'd get into if they were caught. Stewart was well aware that he, himself, had no business poking his nose into someone else's engine room and would be tossed out on his ears if caught.

"We got to take something back as proof," Jesse went on, eyeing the place purposefully now.

"Get out of there this instant! I promised your mother I'd keep an eye on you!"

Jesse ignored him and went on saying, "It don't have to be much." His eyes roamed the small engine room. "Maybe only —" He spied a wrench and grabbed it up. Inspecting it, he pointed to the name scratched into the iron handle. "There.

That ought to prove it. It says right here the name of the boat, *Lil' Sal*."

"I reckon that will do," Frank agreed.

Jesse shoved the wrench into his shirt.

"You're going to steal that?" Stewart asked.

"What do you think?" Jesse shot back.

"But . . . but you can't do that."

"Why not?"

Frank said, "Hell, mister, they ain't gonna miss a little tool like that."

"You don't go around stealing other people's property. Even if it is only a small thing."

"Aw, they can afford another," Jesse said.

"That isn't the point. You shouldn't do it!"

"Are you gonna stop me, mister? You a sheriff?"

"Well, no, but —"

"Then get out of the way —"

"Here, now, what's we got going on in there?" a gruff voice said from the passageway outside.

Stewart wheeled about, startled, and looked up . . . up . . . up at the man standing there, glaring down at him. His big belly hung over his trousers; his dirty homespun shirt was open on top revealing a mass of gray hair upon his vast, grease-streaked chest. The man wore a dirty, canvas cap upon his head, and from beneath it hung a ragged fringe of gray hair, nearly to his shoulders. He squinted at Stewart with his left eye, his right being hidden behind a patch of black leather.

"Hello," Stewart gulped.

"Hello yourself. What are you doing nosing around my boat, mister?"

"Nose . . . nosing around?" Clifton laughed shakily and said, "I am so sorry. I didn't mean to trespass, sir." Stewart put an arm over the shoulders of the two boys who had slipped out of the engine room and were standing behind him. "My . . . err . . . my nephews, Frank here, and Jesse," he placed himself slightly in front of the younger boy to hide the conspicuously unnatural bulge in Jesse's shirt "— my nephews have never seen a real steamboat before, and neither have I. I'm afraid our curiosity in your fine vessel here caused us to forget our manners."

Stewart grinned at the mountain of flesh before him, and he was vaguely startled at the long line of lies that had just come from his own mouth. It was almost as if he had heard the spiel before, or something very similar to it, and was now only parroting it. Or was lying something he did so often that it came with such a natural ease? For the life of him, he did not know which it was, but the idea that lying might be as natural as breathing was suddenly quite disturbing.

And why was he protecting these two rascallions at all? — for rascallions is what he would call them now that he'd seen how they acted when out from under their mother's watchful eye. He was under no obligation — his thoughts halted at this. He *did* owe them a debt. They had, after all, saved his life.

The big boatman's expression changed suddenly. The ice melted from his eye, the scowl flowed like honey into a pleased grin. "Well, why didn't you jest ask me, mister? I'd be right pleased to show you and your kin about *Lil' Sal*. She's named after my daughter, you know."

"No, I did not."

"Well, you jest foller me and I'll give you the big tour."

Stewart found himself being shoved along the narrow deck, with the two boys stumbling ahead of him. Whether he wanted it or not, it looked like he was going to get the *big* tour. Considering the size of the *Lil Sal*, he couldn't imagine the *big* tour taking any more than three and one-half minutes.

"By the way, my name is Emmett Potts."

Stewart felt compelled to shake the outstretched hand, but when he tried to introduce himself his brain drew a blank.

Jesse jumped in to fill the sudden void. "Hi, Mr. Potts! Gosh, it sure is nice of you to show us around this fancy boat of yours."

"Oh, she ain't fancy, not like some hereabouts on the river." He patted a peeling handrail affectionately. "But she's a good worker, and dependable as tomorrow's sunrise."

"How fast will she go?"

"Why, she'll push four miles an hour across this here river, and do it all day long."

"Gosh!" Jesse sounded truly impressed.

"We really should not take up any more of Mr. Potts's valuable time, boys," Stewart said, hoping to make the landing stage and then the safety of the wharf before Potts could tour them any farther. He eyed the bulge in Jesse's shirt and felt his heart thump a little faster.

"Nonsense, it ain't taking me away from nothin' what can't wait. Now, right up here, if you look, you'll see the pilothouse. That's where I steer *Lil' Sal* from. And right here, at your left hand, is the boiler. Nate Johnson, he's my fireman, he keeps it stoked up and burning like someplace in the eternal hereafter what we all know about." Emmett Potts winked, chuckled, and nudged them forward a step. "Now, over there you can see the steam pipe. It goes back to the engine. Err, Mr. Johnson, he's my engineer, too, he tends the engines, and I work them as well, when I ain't piloting, that is."

"How very interesting," Stewart said ineffectually. "Now, we really —"

Emmett Potts pointed a thick, hairy finger. "Look back here. See that? Know what that is?"

"The connecting rod?" Frank offered.

Potts was impressed. "Why, that's right, young man. You must have studied up."

"I think I may have read about it in a book at one time or another."

"You can read?" Potts's eyes rounded.

"A little."

"Well, someday I'm gonna learn me to read, too. Now you tell me, what does the connecting rod do?"

"It transfers the motion of the steam engine to the paddle wheel?"

"Why, I'll be — you have been studying up!"

Frank smiled thinly, and Stewart could see that he also was anxious to leave. In fact, Stewart realized suddenly, glancing at the grinning youngster, it seemed that only Jesse was getting a thrill out of lingering here, with the stolen wrench tucked not so neatly into his shirt . . . almost as if he was challenging this man to find him out.

"What are those, Mr. Potts?" Jesse pointed at a pair of rusty, black pipes sticking skyward, a few feet behind the chimneys.

"Them's the 'scape pipes, son."

"What are they for?"

"They let the steam out of the engines, and they sure do make sprightly music when we're running under a full head."

"How very interesting," Stewart said, taking Jesse by the shoulders and turning him toward the gangplank. "But now we really must be going or their parents will be getting worried."

"Yes, we better be on our way," Frank piped up. "Ma has the fits when we're away too long. You sure have a fine boat, Mr. Potts. Thank you for showing it to us."

"Well, you are quite welcome. What good manners you two boys got. I can see your folks are raising you right."

"But I want to see more," Jesse protested.

"Not now," Stewart said firmly, pushing Jesse along the deck none too gently. The boy dug in his heels, but Frank had casually taken hold of his younger brother's arm, giving him no choice in the matter.

And then, when it looked like they might make it off the boat without being found out —

Clunk!

The wrench slipped from Jesse's shirt and rang solidly upon the deck at his feet.

Chapter
Eight

"Say, what is this?" Emmett Potts narrowed his good eye at the wrench lying at Jesse's feet and lumbered forward like a big, gray bear.

Stewart's heart leaped to his throat.

The big man stopped and stared at the wrench. Stewart saw a moment of blank confusion in the older man's single eye, and he seized that moment and snatched the wrench off the deck. A wave of dizziness momentarily set him back on his heels. He grabbed at an oak keg, which fortunately was standing near him and the boy. "Now, look what you've done, Jesse," he scolded, waving the wrench. "You went and knocked that tool right off of this barrel here!"

Frank saw the direction Stewart was going and immediately joined in with, "Why don't you ever look where you are walking, Jesse?"

The confusion in Potts's eye deepened as Stewart innocently placed the wrench in the boat owner's big hand. Potts said, "Now, how did this get out here? It belongs in the engine room." The boat owner scratched his head and wrinkled his lips into an unlovely knot. After a moment he shrugged his shoulders. "Reckon I must have carried it out with me when I went off to the privy."

Stewart hid his nervousness behind a laugh. "Funny how we forget insignificant things like that," he said, hustling the boys along and off the boat.

"Yeah . . . I reckon." The knotted lips slowly straightened themselves out and fell into a crooked smile. "Well, you folks come back anytime. Happy to have you aboard." He waved them off with the wrench clutched in his fingers.

"Thank you." Stewart tightened his grip on Jesse and hauled the boy off behind the building where their buggy was parked. He set him firmly on one of the benches there in the shade. Glancing around, he dragged his sleeve across his moist forehead and said, "That was a close shave. What did you want to go and do a thing like that for, Jesse? — stealing that man's wrench like you did."

"It weren't nothing. Gosh, I almost got away with it, too. Now Harvey ain't gonna believe we got into the engine room of that boat."

"Is that what this was all about? To prove to your friend that you were able to sneak aboard?"

"Why else would I steal a greasy old wrench?"

"Why, indeed?" Stewart breathed, shaking a bit from the incident. "Well, I think your parents should hear about this."

Both boys narrowed their eyes, and the glaring looks they gave him were like razor-sharp swords, about to run him through. And at that very, ill-timed moment, Dr. Reuben Samuel and Zerelda came around the corner of the building.

Reuben grinned, seeing the three of them together. "There you are. Did you get a good look at that boat?"

Stewart swallowed hard. The boys' hot stares burned into him.

"We got us a good look, Reuben," Frank said, and shot a warning glance at Stewart.

Stewart made up his mind he was not going to be bullied by these boys, but just the same, they weren't his kids, and it wasn't his place to discipline them. "I kept an eye on them," he said, giving Frank a pointed stare in return. "I made sure they stayed out of trouble," which was the truth stripped of all the details.

Zerelda laughed lightly. "Jesse and Frank know how to stay out of trouble."

Reuben gave her a sideways glance. Stewart figured the good doctor knew more about her two boys than he was letting on. He handed the boys a brown paper bag. "Bought you some peanuts. The boat is supposed to leave in twenty minutes." He and Zerelda sat upon another bench. She set her sewing bag at her side and unfastened her sunbonnet while Reuben packed his pipe.

Stewart sat next to the two boys, caught their guarded looks at him, and could see that they were mildly relieved that he had not gone into detail about their escapade aboard the boat. He reprimanded himself for not telling Reuben and Zerelda the full truth, but then it really wasn't any of his business, and after all, the wrench had been returned — more or less.

Stewart grabbed a handful of peanuts from the bag, and it seemed to him that he had only just sat down to crack a goober between his teeth when down at the wharf a steam whistle blew. Dr. Reuben stood up.

"That's the first call to board the flatboat. I'll bring the buggy down and get it put in place; Zerelda, you and the boys can

161

stay here in the shade awhile longer. I'll be back before the ferry pulls out." He clamped the pipe between his teeth, took the horses by their halters, and walked them down to the landing.

"You boys enjoying yourselves?" Zerelda asked, lifting the bag to her lap.

"Oh, yes," Jesse said. "I think steamboats are bully, and we got to talk with the captain, too. He was real friendly."

Stewart frowned. The halos were back in place. Zerelda smiled contentedly. She removed some needlework from her sewing bag and began making careful stitches in a piece of material held in a round, wooden hoop. "I'm glad to hear that, Jesse."

If only she knew. Stewart bit his tongue and said nothing that would shatter her happy illusion.

Fifteen minutes later the steam whistle shrilled again, longer and insistent. Dr. Reuben returned, and Zerelda glanced up, smiling.

"That is the boarding whistle. Time to go."

She put her needlework away. "Come, boys," she said, shooing them ahead of her. Jesse ran down to the ferry boat, Frank strolled more leisurely, and Stewart, Zerelda, and Dr. Reuben came along behind.

"How far to Mr. Caulder's farm once on the other bank?" Stewart inquired.

Dr. Reuben removed the pipe. "Oh, not far, no more than half an hour."

"You'll like Laban Caulder," Zerelda said. "He is very quiet and thoughtful, and Bitsy, his wife, is a dear."

Stewart caught Reuben's frown an instant before he averted his face.

They boarded the flatboat where a half dozen buggies and eight or ten saddle horses shared the deck with perhaps thirty people. The whistle shrieked again, and the animals sidestepped nervously at its sound and pulled at their halter leads. On the wharf a large, gray-headed woman slid a rail into place on the flatboat and untied a thick rope from the docking post and lifted an arm in a signal to Emmett Potts, who now stood in *Lil' Sal*'s pilothouse. He yanked a bell cord, and the little paddle at the stern of the boat began to slowly turn, quickly picking up speed. Stewart felt a bump and a jolt and saw the smoke from the chimneys thicken. A fine fly ash rained down on them as the wharf slipped slowly away, and they moved out into the current. As it picked up speed, the flatboat set up a broad bow wave that broke to either side of it while, behind, the little steamer settled down to an even, powerful, thumping and hissing.

The smell of the river and the passage of the wind across Clifton Stewart's face all seemed somehow familiar, but exactly why it should remained as elusive as his own name. He determined not to worry about it just yet and instead to enjoy the ride and the sights. The river was busy with steamers and flatboats carrying freight and people east and west. The country was on the move, growing westward, and the Missouri River was her highway.

The *Lil' Sal* sounded her shrill steam whistle, and at once it was answered by a lovely, deep-throated sound that filled the wide river. Stewart became suddenly aware that the flatboat was slowing, and he heard *Lil' Sal*'s steam engines cut back some. Ahead, a huge steamboat was pushing her way powerfully up the river, her side wheels churning up a stream of froth in her wake. She gleamed in the sunlight like new-fallen snow; green handrailings bounded her decks that seemed to pile one atop the other as they climbed to the sky where gray smoke streamed from her stacks. Her beautiful whistle sounded again, swelling across the river majestically, as if announcing the presence of royalty.

The *Lil' Sal* slowed to allow the big packet right-of-way passage, and as the two boats drew near to each other, Stewart could see that her main deck was lined with soldiers and the boiler deck, above, with civilians. Some of the passengers waved as the boat passed. He waved back. The scene painted on her paddle boxes was that of dark, rolling clouds, with the sun bursting through them, its rays streaming out to touch the lettering around the curved edge of the box: *Tempest Queen.*

The shining packet pulled ahead of them, and a few moments later the ferry smacked into her bow wave and its wooden deck bumped beneath Stewart's feet. Afterward, when the water had smoothed out and *Lil' Sal*'s engines had picked up their beat again, Clifton Stewart stared long at the receding riverboat, aware of a vague discontentment gnawing away within him, and not knowing why he should suddenly feel this unhappiness. Frowning, he grabbed hold of the handrailing and put his attention ahead, on the far shore drawing nearer.

Dr. Reuben Samuel hauled back on the reins and brought the buggy to a halt in the cluttered yard. Frank and Jesse

165

bounded instantly over the side, scattering the scratching chickens across the yard even as a small woman in a pale gray dress stepped from the doorway of the little house, drying her hands upon her apron.

She was slightly built, angular of face, and she squinted at them when they climbed off the wagon. Suddenly her face beamed and a smile burst upon the scene. "Zerelda! Reuben!"

"Bitsy!" Zerelda cried back.

Bitsy hurtled down the two steps and came across the yard, arms out, searching for someone to hug. Zerelda made it there first, was squeezed energetically, and then Dr. Reuben had his turn. When they introduced Clifton Stewart, and explained his predicament, he got a hardy handshake, and a friendly welcome instead of a hug, and that was just as well with him.

"We've been expecting you, Zerelda," Bitsy Caulder said, looking her up and down and all over as if they had not seen each other in years, and as far as Stewart knew, that might be true. "I've been so excited ever since I got your letter saying you'd be by. Every day Harvey asks when you're coming."

"Where is Harvey?" Jesse asked, bounding from foot to foot.

"Now, mind your manners," Zerelda said.

"Oh, the boys are excited to see each other. Harvey is in the house."

Jesse started for the door, but Bitsy said, "I'll get him for you, Jesse. Your uncle Laban has an important visitor, and they are talking business." But before Bitsy could make good on that, a tall boy came out of the house and closed the door behind him.

"Harvey!" Jesse said, and he and Frank crowded around the boy.

Harvey was barefooted, and his clothes old and worn but clean. He had one suspender up over his shoulder, the other hanging at his side. A mop of brown hair was stuffed into a tattered straw hat and poked out around his ears. Stewart guessed his age to be somewhere between the two James brothers, even though he stood a good three inches over Frank.

"Look who has just arrived," Bitsy said.

The boy grinned, kind of shy, and said in a voice not yet fully broken into adolescence, "Howdy, Frank, Jesse."

"You've grown some since we last saw you," Frank said.

"Well, I reckon I have. You, too. And Jesse looks to be a good two hands taller than he was last year."

Jesse pulled himself up straight and grinned.

"We got us a new racehorse," Harvey said. "Want to see him?"

"Sure."

As if not a single day had passed since the last time they had seen each other, they started around to the barn. Harvey said, "And I got me a rifle for my birthday this spring."

"Gosh, for your very own?"

"Hu-huh."

"Brand-new?" Frank asked.

"Well, practically. I'll show it to you —"

Then the boys had moved around the side of the house and Stewart could no longer hear them, but as he stared after them, he caught a glimpse of silver sparkling far down beyond the trees, past a plot of land where the corn stood tall, and he heard the far-off call of a steamboat whistle, muted by the trees and distance.

"Well, let's move out of the sun," Bitsy said. They strolled around to a split-log bench on the north side of the house. Bitsy went for a pitcher of cool well water while Zerelda sat down, fanning way the August heat. Reuben said he'd had enough sitting and preferred to stand awhile and work out the kinks. Stewart remained standing, too, leaning against the corner of the house.

"She seems very nice," he commented.

"Bitsy's a dear. She's the very fiber in this family. Why, if it weren't for Bitsy, I fear —"

Dr. Reuben cleared his throat, and his quick, narrowed glance cut her words short. Zerelda smiled then and said, "Bitsy is one of my closest friends. We've known each other for fifteen years."

Stewart heard Bitsy returning. She came around the corner of the house, squinting at the ground as if uncertain of its features, carrying a tray with four glasses and a white pitcher. Dutifully, she filled the glasses and passed them out.

"Now tell me, how was your trip? How long can you stay? Your letter says you were visiting Reuben's family in Tennessee."

"Kentucky," Dr. Reuben said. He had a match to the bowl of his pipe, and when he spoke, a puff of smoke came out with his words. "Our trip was fine and uneventful, except for finding this gentleman in the river." He indicated Stewart with a glance.

"My, you are so lucky to still be alive! And that knock to your head has completely taken away your memory?" Bitsy squinted at him, smiling, and it occurred to Stewart that the downward slope of her eyes and the upward sweep of her lips formed an almost perfect oval.

"Yes, ma'am. That is true."

"And you have no notion of even what your name might be?"

"None whatsoever."

"How dreadful." The smile re-formed itself into a look of pity.

"Dr. Reuben says my memory should return in time."

"That is correct," Reuben said. "I have never personally seen a case of such total amnesia, but the occurrence is well documented. In most cases the sufferer recovers completely on his own. The time differs from case to case, of course. In some rare cases they never regain their memory. And then there are the strange cases where a second blow to the head restores the lost memory. It is a very curious phenomenon."

"Well, I do hope your senses return to you in short order, mister — oh, dear, it is so inconvenient not to have a name to call you by."

Stewart grinned at her. "Then choose one of your liking and I shall use it until my own name returns to me."

Bitsy smiled. "Now that is a good idea. Let me think. How does Ben sound? I once knew a man named Ben who looked very much like you."

"Ben, it shall be."

Bitsy seemed quite delighted with the arrangement. "This makes it all so convenient, doesn't it?"

Dr. Reuben nodded his head. "Certainly a simple solution."

"I should have thought of it," Zerelda said. "Ben. I like the sound of it."

Stewart figured that Dr. Reuben saw an opportunity in this to stretch his legs, and he said, "Well, Ben, how about we let the ladies catch up on their lives while we walk down and take a look at that new race horse Harvey mentioned — that is, if that will be all right with you two?"

"Oh, you men go on. We will have plenty of time to talk later. You must stay a couple days at least."

"We will see," Reuben said, returning the pipe to his mouth.

Stewart pushed away from the corner of the building where he had been standing and fell in step at Dr. Reuben's side, but they had only just got around to the front of the house when the sound of a door opening brought them about. Two men stepped out onto the porch. One of them, a little man not much taller than Bitsy, and at least six inches shorter than Harvey, looked at them and smiled.

"Reuben," he said, coming down the steps. "I heard you arrive just awhile ago. How are you?"

"Laban. I'm fine," Reuben said, taking his hand. "Good to see you again."

The second fellow remained on the porch, his eyes downcast, as if not wishing to be part of the introductions. He was shabbily dressed. His shirtsleeves had been cut off just below the elbows, and his trouser legs ended in frayed threads several inches above his ankles. All and all, he seemed quite disreputable. Stewart's view lowered from the tattered straw hat upon his head to the long, heavy knife at his side, and the revolver tucked in the waist of his pants — and then further to the man's feet, which to his surprise were encased in what appeared to be boots of the finest leather, shining black in the late afternoon sun as if they had seen much care. It was a striking contrast, and Stewart could not help but stare at them until he heard Reuben saying to Laban Caulder, ". . . we pulled him out of the river. He has lost his memory, and until it comes back we are calling him Ben. Bitsy chose the name."

"Good to meet you, sir." Caulder had a firm handshake, and calloused hands — like his own. Stewart wondered briefly if he was not a farmer in his other life.

The fellow on the porch came down the steps, paused near Laban, and said softly, "Th-then we can count-count on you?"

For an instant a cloud of concern came to Laban's eyes, and just as swiftly it passed and he said, "You tell old Deke I'll be there."

"To— tomorrow morning."

"I won't forget."

The man strode away and climbed atop a horse tied to a nearby tree. He reined about, dug in his heels as if he had much left to do and little time to do it in, and raced out the yard ahead of a cloud of dust. As the sound of pounding hooves receded, Laban seemed to come out of a mild trance and the smile that had been on his face returned.

"Well, where are Zerelda and Bitsy?"

"Around the side of the house. Ben and I were just going to take a gander at your new horse."

"That can wait. I want to see Zerelda," Laban said, taking both Stewart and Reuben by the arms and escorting them back.

Chapter Nine

The *Tempest Queen* was six hours out of St. Louis when a signal cannon boomed from a woodlot on the south bank of the river. Up in her pilothouse, Eric Jupp pulled the whistle cord three times to alert the shore and then rang for the leadsmen to give him the river's depth as he made the crossing and steered the big riverboat in toward the landing; a stout pier stretched conveniently out into the muddy waters. Captain Hamilton had said he wanted all passengers taken aboard. As Jupp took the boat in closer, he could see there were four men here.

At that moment Hamilton stepped through the pilothouse door and took up the spyglass from the ledge at Jupp's elbow. He studied the woodlot awhile, and when he replaced the glass on the window ledge, he was smiling. "Well, they could not have timed it any better; we are in need of taking on more fuel wood anyway, and a load of paying passengers to boot will only sweeten the deal."

Hamilton left without further comment and went down to the main deck to find his chief mate, Edward Lansing.

"Put on the steam, you crippled possums! You move like you got two left legs! Your job is to feed them boilers, not to stand around and admire the scenery. Now look at what we got here! Still a good seven cords of fuel wood left and you boys ain't hardly broke a sweat yet! You're lounging about like this was a holiday excursion! Put your sorry backs to it. Hump — hump — H-U-M-P!"

The black firemen gritted their teeth and picked up their pace, flinging the wood into the boilers double time. Lansing had worked them into a lather since shoving off from St. Louis, for fighting the current upstream took a steady head of steam, and Lansing took pride in keeping the boilers glowing cherry red so that Barney Seegar's engines had all that they needed. He didn't consider the men, only the boat. Firemen, after all, were easily replaced.

"Put your backs to it! Why, my aged mother has got more vigor than you sorry lot!"

"Mr. Lansing."

The chief mate turned away from the

blazing mouths of the eight boilers. "Captain. Things ticking away just fine down here, sir."

"So I see," Hamilton watched the glistening black backs of the firemen, the muscles beneath the sleek sable skin bulging and pumping like — like the mighty pistons that drove the *Tempest Queen* forward. "We are going in for more wood; you can give your boys a break until we make landing."

"Aye, Captain." Lansing wheeled back to his crew. "All right, take a breather, boys. We are making land to take on more wood."

Lansing didn't need to say it twice. As if someone had cut the strings on a marionette, the firemen all broke from their tasks, breathing hard and flinging sweat from their foreheads. They fell limply to any convenient resting place at hand, groaning softly, mumbling to themselves, leaning their tired backs against the stanchions, or making their way to the water barrel with its big, copper dipper.

Captain Hamilton wove through the milling crowd of deck passengers, composed mostly of men dressed in blue uniforms, and he stood at the bow as the big riverboat made the crossing and headed in toward the long pier. In the pilothouse, three stories above, the Missouri riverboat pilot maneuvered the *Tempest Queen* expertly to a landing. When she drew near enough to the pier, the men standing at her guards with coils of rope in their hands, tossed them out and then leaped from the guards to the pier and secured her there with heavy hawsers.

The larboard landing stage was manhandled into place and made fast. Hamilton strode off the boat to find the woodlot owner and strike a deal for purchase. Coming down from his little office in the main cabin, Belding, the boat's clerk, stood at the head of the landing stage to collect the fares from the four men as they came aboard.

From the handrailing, up one deck above the boiler, Lieutenant Sherman Dempsey watched the four new passengers filing aboard, disappointment showing in his face. They were only a group of local farmers, some with pistols or revolvers tucked into their belts, some carrying squirrel guns casually over their shoulders, all clad in rough homespun and wearing beards in various stages of cultivation.

The army lieutenant smelled the smoke of a cigar behind him, and when he looked over his shoulder, he discovered Dexter McKay was standing nearby, also watching the four men come aboard.

"Good afternoon, Mr. McKay."

"Afternoon, Lieutenant." McKay stepped up to the handrail. "Still thinking your lost man will show up?"

Dempsey frowned. "You are quite perceptive. I had hoped that when the shore had signaled us, it would prove to be Sergeant Carr catching up with us. But that was only wishful thinking. Turns out they are just a bunch of farmers taking a ride upriver."

McKay drew long on his cigar and let the smoke stream slowly from his lips. His thoughts seemed suddenly occupied elsewhere. He glanced down the promenade at the two men farther along who were watching with keen interest as the four new arrivals came aboard. McKay said to the lieutenant, "If I was a suspicious man, I would say that the Reverend Saunders and his boy are more than mildly curious about these arrivals as well."

Dempsey peered over at them. He saw nothing odd in the reverend's curiosity, and as far as he could tell, that was all it was. "Perhaps they are acquainted."

"Perhaps." McKay leaned his weight

onto his walking stick a moment with a faint, knowing smile upon his lips. The hot afternoon sun streaming down glinted off his neatly trimmed imperial beard as if it were beaten bronze, and his smoky, gray eyes glistened. All and all, Dempsey had the feeling that this was a man who tried always to be in perfect control of himself, no matter what the circumstances.

Suddenly McKay cleared his throat and came out of his contemplations. The point of his ebony walking stick cracked smartly upon Captain Hamilton's newly painted deck, and he said, "I suppose I should be on my way." Starting away, McKay paused and looked back at Dempsey. "Do you gamble, sir?"

The question caught the lieutenant quite off guard. Dempsey shrugged his shoulders and said, "I have been known to place a bet now and again."

McKay's smile widened. "Then perhaps you will join me this evening? In the main cabin?"

"Perhaps," Dempsey replied politely, but he had far more important thoughts on his mind than card playing.

"I will see you later, Lieutenant." With his walking stick tapping smartly, McKay strode down the promenade, passing nearby the Reverend Deke Saunders with a casual sideways glance, and then taking a ladder up, he climbed to the hurricane deck and disappeared.

Dempsey looked back at the preacher a moment, wondering what it was that McKay had noticed in the man. He saw nothing out of the usual in the man or his son and immediately dismissed them from his thoughts. On the pier below, deckhands were pouring off the boat and forming into a line to the woodlot where already — from hand to hand — four-foot lengths of firewood were beginning to make their way onto the *Tempest Queen*. As he watched the procession of wood come aboard, admiring the almost military-like preciseness with which each man carried out his task, he caught a glimpse of Cora Mills and her son approaching along the promenade.

Cora stopped at the railing by his side and peered out. "Isn't this interesting, Lieutenant?" she said, her eyes wide, her view darting along the wooden pier. "Oh, but I'm sure to a man like you who has done so much traveling, this must be all rather old stuff." She smiled pleasantly at him while the little boy in her grasp tugged impatiently to be on their way. But Cora

180

Mills stood her ground this time.

"Not at all, Mrs. Mills. It is true I have seen this before, but just the same, it never ceases to fascinate me how a bunch of rough riverboatmen can muster such coordinated activity as we see below." He had spoken rather stiffly, he realized. He didn't want to come across as a stuffed shirt. He was drawn to her, and slightly uneasy because of that, but pleased that she seemed to want to linger and talk with him. Dempsey was distrustful of his feelings toward Cora Mills — yet he knew that his feelings made no difference whatsoever and that he must remain aloof from this lovely, yellow-haired woman. Cora Mills was, after all, married.

She looked at him curiously and was about to speak when the young man standing near the preacher came over. He grabbed his slouch hat off his head and crumbled it in his long, bony fingers against his chest.

"Ma'am. I . . . I was wondering if you would want to walk with me around the boat?" He shot an anxious glance at the army lieutenant, then swiveled his gray eyes back at Cora Mills. "Since you are traveling by your lonesome, I sort of am offering to keep an eye out fer you. You don't know how rough some of these river landing and frontier towns can be."

"That is very gallant of you, Mr. Saunders. I do not think that Kenneth or I am in any peril, but if you would like to accompany us around the boat, I shan't object." Cora smiled back at Dempsey. "Perhaps we will talk later?"

"Perhaps," he said curtly. He thought he detected a bit of confusion in her deep, green eyes, but they had flashed away too quickly for him to be sure. Moving now under the insistent tug of the little boy, Cora Mills continued along the promenade.

Lieutenant Dempsey watched her walk away with the tall, gangling figure of a man at her side, and a knot the size of a fist formed in his gut. He tried to dismiss his sudden feeling of loss and anger. He had no claims on her. And neither did the reverend's bone-pile of a son, for that matter. She belonged to another man, someone stationed at Fort Leavenworth. It was unseemly to think any further on the matter! Just the same, her simple beauty, her innocent excitement over something as common as a riverboat trip up the Missouri, her endearing patience with the little boy who forever seemed to want to be someplace else — all were qualities that struck a harmonious chord with Sherman Dempsey. And now watching her stroll off in the presence of another man — even one with as little claim on her as he himself had — caused the fist in his stomach to tighten and twist.

Stepping away from the railing, Dempsey started aft along the promenade, putting his irritation aside and his mind back on his job. His saber rattled softly at his side as he walked. When he passed by Reverend Deke Saunders, he was aware that the older man had glanced at him and then quickly away.

At the back of the boat where the paymaster's gold was secured, two soldiers in shell jackets — their rifles leaning against the wall, close at hand — stood before the locked cabin door, slapping at the mosquitoes that swarmed in from the shore. They came slowly to attention as Dempsey approached.

"How are we doing back here, men?"

"We are doin' all right, sir, so long as we keep these insects from eating us alive."

"We'd be doing a whole lot better if someone would turn this here boat around so's we'd be standing in the shade, Lieutenant," the other complained.

Dempsey grinned and took a watch from a leather pouch on his saber belt. The golden lid caught the sunlight as it snapped opened, and Dempsey turned it aside to kill the glare off the glass crystal. He snapped the lid closed and put the watch away. "Another thirty-five minutes, corporal, and your replacements will be taking over."

"And that won't be thirty-five minutes too soon, sir," the first soldier said.

Dempsey laughed and continued on his rounds. When he circumvented the paddle box and stepped back out onto the promenade, Reverend Saunders's guarded glance again darted quickly away from him. Dempsey reprimanded himself for having caught a touch of McKay's suspicion. He stood there a moment, watching the firewood being brought aboard, then entered the main cabin by a side door to cross over to the starboard side of the boat and continued forward.

On the main deck at the bottom of the wide, sweeping staircase, Dempsey stepped back out of the way of the wood brigade that was quickly rebuilding the four piles of cordwood in the large space in front of the boilers and under the little cabin where the deckhands kept their war bags.

Dempsey moved through the mounds of army supplies, nodding occasionally at the soldiers bivouacked there who happened to glance up and take notice that an officer was among them. Most of his men, however, lounged comfortably in the shade, but a few had thrown off their blue blouses and were standing in the line, laughing and sweating with the crew of the *Tempest Queen*, helping with the wood coming aboard. Some men just had to keep themselves busy, Dempsey mused, grinning a bit and making a mental note to remember the faces of those soldiers lending a hand.

He had not had time to memorize all their names, but he had learned a few of them, and Private Konrad Adler — his friends just called him Eagle for some reason Dempsey had yet to figure out — a short, red-faced German from New York City, was among those with their sleeves rolled up. Dempsey had had a run-in with Adler a time or two since leaving headquarters, mostly over the soldier's drinking habits, and Dempsey considered that a mixed blessing. Adler was fierce and reckless when drunk . . . but a good officer needed to know and understand his men, even if his command over them was only as brief as this trip from Division Headquarters to Fort Leavenworth.

The matériel all seemed in order; the ordnance rifles lashed solidly to iron deck cleats with stout ropes, the small arms in their wooden crates all neatly stacked and covered with a canvas tarpaulin, kegs of gunpowder piled near the edge of the guards, far away from the boiler furnaces, and arranged to be easily pushed overboard if a situation arose that required their instant removal.

Loaded farther inboard were the casks of whiskey destined for the sutler's store. Apparently Chief Mate Lansing did not consider them as dangerous as the gunpowder, even if they did contain enough alcohol to burn like beacon fire if a spark should somehow find its way through the oaken staves.

Dempsey would have preferred to load the whiskey with the powder kegs, on the gunwales, but he knew that Lansing had to contend with the problem of keeping a big boat like the *Tempest Queen* in proper trim, and the weight of the full whiskey casks dictated that they be stacked more toward the center of the craft.

"Lieutenant?" a soft, easy-speaking Southern voice said as Dempsey made his way past a small group of soldiers.

The owner of the voice was a young corporal sitting upon the deck, leaning casually against a wooden crate with his shirt unbuttoned at the throat. He was surrounded by three friends, each equally at ease, each holding a fistful of playing cards, and upon a small box between them lay seven or eight coins.

"Yes, Corporal?" Dempsey recognized the face as one he'd seen over the course of the last week but had not yet had an opportunity to put a name to it.

"When is it we are going to reach this Jayhawker fort in Kansas?"

"I beg your pardon, Corporal? Jayhawker?"

One of the soldier's companions laughed. When he spoke, the easy, Southern drawl was thick in his voice, and almost identical to his friend's — at least to Dempsey's Northern-bred ears. "Don't you know, Lieutenant, that some folks over in Kansas have all these narrow-minded abolitionist notions. We Southern boys figure it is our God-given duty to set their thinking straight on the matter."

The four of them chuckled. It was apparent they all agreed that the transformation of the Kansas Territory, when it finally would become a state, into a slave state was their sacred duty.

"What is your name, Corporal?" Dempsey addressed the soldier who had first called to him.

"Belvedere, sir. Corporal Lemont Belvedere of St. Francisville, Louisiana."

"Well, Corporal Belvedere, I shouldn't have to remind you that your duty as a soldier is to follow the orders of your commanding officer, and that is all. Leave Kansas politics to the men and women who live there. In any event, don't look forward to having too much opportunity to worry about settling conflicting ideals at Fort Leavenworth. Most of your time, I should think, will be occupied with keeping an eye on the Sioux, and on an uneasy peace, and escorting immigrants into the Western lands — and I'm sure your commanding officer will find some very good uses for any spare moments you might have. Building roads, riding patrols, maintaining the fort, cutting firewood for those fierce Kansas winters, should keep you busy enough. But to answer your question, Corporal, barring any delays, we will arrive at Fort Leavenworth in two days."

Dempsey noticed that two other soldiers sitting nearby had overheard the conversation and were whispering between themselves. He could not tell by their expressions what they had thought of it. He only knew he did not want any conflicts over sectional differences to crop up here while these men were under his command.

"Do you two have something on your mind?" His direct question, and the challenge in his voice, seemed to take them by surprise.

They glanced at each other, then shook their heads.

"Good. See that you keep it that way."

"Yes, sir."

Dempsey shifted his view back to the four Southerners. Belvedere grinned up at him with a glint of defiance in his eyes. He pulled a card from his hand and laid it upon the box. "I don't much care for the cold, Lieutenant."

Dempsey hitched up an eyebrow. "Then, Mr. Belvedere, perhaps you should have chosen a different line of work. Good day." He walked away and heard their muffled laughs behind him. For years Dempsey had felt the tension growing in the ranks of the enlisted men and officers over the Southerners' claims that their rights were being trampled by Northern politicians. That the heavily industrialized North was now taking advantage of its economic strength to bully the South into its way of thinking was hardly deniable, but as far as Dempsey was concerned, the issue was a political one and had no place in the army. He wanted none of it among the troops he commanded. Bitter feelings were growing like a disease throughout the country, dividing it just as surely as if an invading army had come to her shores and had established a battle line. Talk of secession had slowed to a trickle for a number of years, with the South being temporarily appeased by the new and tougher laws to protect its economy, but of late the old tensions were beginning to boil to the surface again, and new talk of secession was spreading like wildfire.

How could an army fight as a unit with such sectional bitterness ripping it apart?

It couldn't!

Dempsey had refused to tolerate it among his men, weeding out the signs of the fermenting sickness wherever he came across them.

Three hours later a rifle shot rang out from the shore, and the *Tempest Queen*'s whistle answered it. The big bronze bell on her hurricane deck summoned the leadsmen to the guards, and a few moments later they began singing out the depth as Eric Jupp put the big riverboat over to collect these new passengers off the weedy bank.

Her bow nudged to a gentle stop against the muddy bottom, and the three men there did not wait for the convenience of a yawl to be lowered over the side, but plunged right in and waded out waist deep into the river, rifles, powder horns, and hunting pouches held overhead, and accepted a hand up to her guards. Shaking like wet dogs, they flung off the river, wrung it from their buckskins and linsey-woolseys, and paid their dollar and a half for deck passage fare to Mr. Belding, who had scuffled down from his cubicle, change purse in hand.

Two bells clanged below in the engine room, and Barney Seegar threw his engines into reverse, taking the *Tempest Queen* back out into deeper water and on her way west again.

Frowning into the long, afternoon shadows at her railing one deck up, Lieutenant Sherman Dempsey calculated that these delays every time some wayward farmer or trapper wanted a lift up the river were cutting deeply into his carefully calculated schedule. At this rate, it was going to add a full day to the trip!

Well, he had struck a deal with Captain Hamilton, and that agreement did include picking up passengers along the way. He had had no idea there would be so many of them.

It occurred fleetingly to Lieutenant Dempsey that the men they had taken aboard that day were all heavily armed. There must be a lot of hunters in the area, he decided, stepping away from the railing and continuing on his way down the promenade for his regular check-in on the men back there guarding the payroll.

Almost precisely above the spot where Dempsey had stood, one deck overhead on the hurricane deck, a puff of gray cigar smoke drifted out over the low railing on the gentle evening breeze.

Dexter McKay put the cigar between his lips and narrowed an eye on the three men below. Like Dempsey, McKay had noted the preponderance of weapons coming aboard that day. But unlike Dempsey, he was drawing an entirely different conclusion.

He smiled thinly around the cigar in his lips. "If I were a suspicious man," he said quietly to himself, nodding his head. His eyes shifted and his view went to the Reverend Deke Saunders, who always seemed to be somewhere nearby whenever the *Tempest Queen* put in for shore-bound passengers.

Then his view narrowed, shifted again, and riveted upon one of the men who had just come aboard. He was sitting on a crate and pouring river water from his boot. McKay looked twice to be sure.

He knew this man . . . knew him more from reputation than anything else, but they had met him briefly in a tent saloon over a roulette table one cold November night, a year ago, in a mining camp along Boulder Creek in the Kansas Territory gold camps.

Yes, McKay knew this one. The man's reputation had been so widespread, it was rumored that he had even changed his name. What was it? Charles something . . . Charles Hart? McKay wasn't certain. But name change or not, the face was the same.

McKay bit down on the cigar, and his smile broadened. What was William Clarke Quantrill up to here, on the Missouri River, coming aboard the *Tempest Queen*?

Chapter Ten

"Gosh, what did you do here, Harvey?" Jesse James exclaimed when the older boy pulled open a rough-sawn board door and waved the two James brothers inside a little room built up against the back wall of the barn. The air inside was heavy with the smell of horses, but it had a nice, cozy feeling about it — at least from Jesse's thirteen-year-old point of view. The low ceiling seemed tight enough, and on the floor of hard-packed dirt was a scrap of burlap for a carpet.

"Pa and me, we built me my own room back here. I was getting too big for the house anyway, so this is where I sleep all summer, and most the fall as well, I suspect, though I ain't tried that yet."

"Gosh, your own room?" The door crept closed under its own weight, and although there were no windows in the place, the light streaming through the gaps in the wall and door boards more than amply lit Harvey's small lodging.

Harvey grinned, pushed out his chest a

bit, and shoved over a pickle barrel that had been cut in two. "Here, have a sit," he said, plopping down on his corn-shuck mattress held off the dirt floor on a frame of willow branches and woven hemp rope. Sitting there, Harvey looked proud as a king on his throne.

Frank James straddled one of the barrel halves and stretched his long legs out. He looked admiringly around the place and then, glancing past Harvey at the wall, asked, "Is that the rifle?"

"Sure is." Harvey lifted the long piece off the pegs and ran a hand along the smooth wood of the half-stock, licking his thumb and rubbing the front sight. "It's loaded," he said, handing it across to Frank.

Frank looked it over and lifted back the hammer to see that there was a cap on the nipple. Lowering it gently back in place, he put the rifle to his shoulder and sighted along the brown, octagon barrel. "Nice heft, Harvey." He stuck his little finger into the bore. "Fifty?"

"Fifty-four. I got a bullet mold with it, and I have already made up a hundred shots."

"Lemme see . . . lemme see," Jesse chattered anxiously.

Frank put the rifle in the younger boy's reaching hands. "Take care, Jes, there's a hot cap atop the powder."

"Gosh, it's a heavy thing."

"Aw, it ain't so heavy," Harvey said as if it were nothing. He bent over, fished around in the shadows under his bed, and came up with a jug. "Have you two started drinkin' yet?"

Jesse looked up, surprised. There was a quart of whiskey in Harvey's hand. Before he could answer, he heard Frank say, "I've done a little, when Ma and Pa weren't around."

"You have?" Jesse said.

Frank looked over with worry lines deepening in his face. "You shouldn't have heard that, Jes."

"Gosh, I ain't gonna tell on you, Frank."

Harvey laughed, pulled the cork, hefted the jug into the crook of his arm, gave it a couple pats as if he knew what he was doing, and tipped it to his lips with practiced ease. He wiped his lips on his shirtsleeve and handed the jug over to Frank, who managed it with not quite the same dexterity as Harvey Caulder had.

"Ah, that's good," Frank said. "Here, you want to try a sip?"

Jesse took the jug with some dismay.

Holding it in both hands, he tasted the whiskey and immediately wrinkled his face and handed the jug back to Harvey, shaking his head as if he'd stuck it into a hornets' nest. The two older boys laughed, and Jesse grinned at himself as well. "That stuff sure got a bite to it."

"Ain't worth drinking if it don't got a stinger in its tail," Harvey said as if he knew all about corn liquor, and he took another long pull at the jug.

"Do your folks know you got that here?" Jesse asked.

"Ma don't, but Pa knows."

"Gosh, I don't think Reuben would put up with us keeping a bottle of our own around."

Frank gave a soft laugh and said, "You can bet he wouldn't."

All three chuckled, and Frank picked up the rifle again, admiring it. "I'll bet she's a real straight shooter, Harvey."

"It can pluck a clothespin off a line at fifty paces. Of course, it's the man behind the trigger what's important."

"Gosh. That would be a right handy piece to have with you in Injun territory."

"Don't know 'bout that, Jes," Harvey said, taking back the rifle and sighting along the barrel. His right eye hitched up at them, his voice lowered, and he glanced around as if to check that there was no one else in the tiny room with them. "Can you keep a secret?"

Frank allowed that he could. Jesse was too awed by Harvey's conspiratorial tones to speak, but he did manage a nod of his head.

"I don't know about Injuns, but Pa and me, we kilt us a nigger with it already."

"You did what?" Jesse felt his voice climb a mite beyond its normal range, which was still rather high for a boy anyway.

"Keep your voice down, dadgum you, Jesse," Harvey shot back, inclining his head at the barn wall, which was the back side of the room. "Someone might hear you. It's only Pa and me what knows it — and now you two. We can get into real trouble if'n that nigger's owner finds out it was us what done in his boy."

Jesse felt a chill run up his back, but just the same a small fire had been kindled in him at being made privy to such daring news. He glanced at his brother, but couldn't cipher what Frank was thinking.

Frank was studying Harvey, his hawk nose silhouetted in the filtered light, his blue eyes hidden in shadows. Jesse saw his square jaw work as he considered what he had just heard, then saw his sandy-haired head nod once. "Reckon it a good enough rifle, then," was all Frank said, and again Jesse was not able to discern the thoughts traveling through his brother's brain.

"Dang right it's a good rifle."

With the chill draining from him, Jesse said, "I'd like to have a revolver someday, or even a pistol."

Harvey grinned. "Shoot, I got a pistol, too." He dug into a wooden box for an old flintlock and passed it over to Jesse. "I only shot it once. It's a bother to keep the pan primed. Here, let me show you how it's done."

Frank said, "Sounds to me like you and your pa have some real adventures."

Harvey snapped up the pistol's frizzen and cleaned out a flash hole into the side of the barrel with a steel pick. "You don't know the half of it, Frank. Pa and me, we —" He paused and took a peek over his shoulder again, even though there was no one there. Just the same, it added a thrill to whatever it was that was coming next, and Jesse was aware that his breathing had quickened. This was bound to be something even more daring than shooting a poor Negro. Harvey continued, "— we even do some river pirating."

Jesse's eyes rounded.

"But don't go mentioning any of this to my ma. If she knew what we two do together, she'd go clean through the ceiling."

"I won't!" Jesse crossed his heart.

Harvey took a small horn of powder from the box and went on, almost apologetically, "My ma's got religion, you see. You know, it was your pa who converted her before he died. He tried to convert Pa as well, but it never took. Pa would say, 'Sinnin's too much a part of me to go giving it up now,' but he didn't mind your pa trying anyway. Never held it against him or anything. Heck, that was his job, weren't it?"

"I guess so," Jesse said.

Harvey sprinkled some fine black powder in the little depression at the rear of the barrel, then snapped the frizzen down like a lid over it. "There. That's how it's done, Jesse." He returned the pistol to the younger boy's hands and lowered his voice again. "You know that fellow that was here when you all arrived? Well, that was Harold Madden, and he's kin to Grady Saunders."

"Who is Grady Saunders?" Frank asked.

Harvey speared him with a pitiful look. "Why, he is only Deke Saunders's oldest boy, that's all!"

The name meant nothing to Jesse, and he knew it probably meant as little to Frank. Jesse asked softly, almost afraid to ask it but too eaten up with curiosity inside not to, "Who is Deke Saunders?"

Harvey nearly rocked back off the bed, and for the longest time he just stared at Jesse as if studying a dung beetle working at a month-old turd. "Why, Deke Saunders used to be one of the most famous river pirates in this here area. Pa used to run with him when he was younger, that's all."

The two James boys sat stone-still. Finally Frank picked the jug from the floor and took another sip. He handed it to Jesse, who managed a more dignified swallow this time. Frank said, "Your pa was a river pirate?"

"Sure enough. Still is. And I even done a little pirating, but there ain't much opportunity these days. It's not so easy like it was in the old days," he said as if he wore Methuselah's beard. "Nowadays you've got to have a real good lure to put a steamboat off its guard and wile it into shore. More common these days, you just board her, kill the pilot, and take her over."

With a growing sense of excitement and danger, too, Jesse sat there listening, and he could hardly believe it when he heard

Frank say softly, "I'd like to try that some-day."

Jesse looked over, startled. Frank had always been the voice of reason whenever the two of them had discussed adventures; had always played the devil's advocate when it came to such things like robbing stagecoaches or burgling banks. "You?" Jesse said.

"Well, why not? We sure aren't getting no excitement living in Kearney. I don't want to grow up a farmer, and I ain't cut out to be a preacher like Pa was, nor a doctor like Reuben. What can I do?"

"Can you go West and fight Injuns?" Jesse suggested.

Frank frowned and shrugged his shoulders. "Maybe."

The jug came around to Harvey again. He took a long pull at it, smacked his lips, satisfied, and said as if it were a common enough thing, "Well, Pa is going to pirate another riverboat tomorrow. He's gonna leave tonight."

Harvey was growing just a little too smug for Jesse's liking. Just the same, this news was about the most exciting thing he'd heard since the riverboat *Dakota* ran aground at Smith's bar that spring, and blew up her boiler trying to work her way off of it. To Jesse's dismay, when he glanced over, Frank was studying Harvey with a concentration Jesse had only noticed in his brother a time or two in the past — usually when Frank had his nose buried in a thick book.

"Was that why that fellow Madden was here?"

"Sure enough. Ma thought they was only discussing a freighting job that Pa could put his big wagon to work on, but when you all showed up and she went outside, that's when Harold Madden got down to the beans of it. He was rounding up a bunch of Deke Saunders's old boys to go and steal a riverboat filled with soldiers, and guns, and whiskey."

Jesse jaw dropped to his chest. Frank was concentrating on Harvey's every word, intent on hearing all the details, and not interrupting until Harvey had finished.

"Are you going be with your pa on this job?"

Harvey frowned and shook his head. "I wish I was, Frank, but Pa says this one is too dangerous and that I'm not old enough yet." There was no hiding his disappointment from either of the James brothers.

"How many soldiers?" Frank wanted to know.

"Harold thinks there's about fifty."

"And how many men does Saunders have?"

"Don't know that yet. Harold is hoping to get as many as he can. Fifteen or more."

Frank whistled softly. "Mighty tough odds."

"You gonna need to get rid of some of them soldiers somehow," Jesse piped up.

The two older boys looked over. "I'm open to suggestions," Harvey said.

Jesse stared blankly. "Well, I don't know, Harvey."

Another barren stretch of time marched on until finally Harvey drew in a long sigh and said, "Oh, what's the worth of pondering on it. It ain't my problem, 'cause I'm too young to go along with them."

Jesse looked down at the old flintlock pistol still in his hands. He set it down on a rickety table near Harvey's bed and said, "I'm getting hungry. Frank shot a turkey today. Maybe your ma will fix it tonight."

This brought Harvey out of his thoughts. "Yeah, maybe." He pushed the whiskey jug back under the bed, out of sight, and stood. "Listen now, you two. Not a word of what I told you to anyone. Especially Ma. Or that fellow you brought along — who is he, anyway?"

Jesse said, "Don't know his name. We found him floating in the river, caught in a snag. His head had been stoved in real good, and he can't remember even his own name. But he's all right; he covered for me and Frank when we got caught sneaking aboard the towboat. We had made it clear into the engine room."

"Naw, you didn't."

"Did too, Harvey!" Jesse looked at Frank. "See, I told you he wouldn't believe us unless we brought back something as proof."

But Frank's thoughts seemed to be somewhere else, and he did not appear to have heard Jesse's words.

Harvey pulled the door open and Jesse went outside, but Frank lingered a moment in the shadows of Harvey's room.

"When is your pa leaving, Harvey?"

"Sometime after dinner is all I know."

Jesse glanced back to see Frank's face in the shadows, expressionless as he pondered heavily on something. "What's the name of the riverboat that they are going to pirate?"

"Harold said she was called the *Tempest Queen*. Listen, not a word. On your honor?"

"We won't say anything," Frank promised.

Both older boys came out into the low, afternoon sunlight. Harvey closed the door, and the three of them started across the cluttered yard toward the little house. The grown-ups were still outside, but they had shifted their position some, following the shade around the house.

Suddenly Frank drew up. Jesse immediately recognized the look on his older brother's face. Frank had come to some sort of decision, but about what Jesse had not the faintest idea.

"Harvey."

He wheeled about. "What's wrong, Frank?"

Frank motioned him to come near, and Jesse stepped up as well. When Frank spoke his voice quavered a bit, but his blue eyes blazed, and even though Jesse had no idea what was bothering his older brother, he had caught Frank's fire as if it were an infection.

"I want to go with your pa, Harvey. I want to go with him tonight, and I want to help pirate that riverboat."

Jesse nearly toppled over backward. Frank was talking crazy, like . . . like . . . like he himself often talked! "You can't do that, Frank," Jesse said.

"Why not?"

"Well . . . well because you will get in trouble. Ma will whip you to red meat if she were to ever find out."

Frank laughed, and the derision that Jesse heard in his brother's voice stung like a green willow lash. "Look who's talking? Aren't you the little hypocrite? All you ever think about is robbing trains, or stage-coaches, and highwaymen and such."

Frank's acid remarks cut deep. Jesse felt his eyes suddenly sting, but he didn't allow his hurt to show, and he steeled his voice. "Maybe I do, but you were always the one to tell me how it was wrong, or dangerous, Frank. Now listen to you talk. You want to pirate a riverboat! If you do this, you sure enough will get yourself killed. Then what will me or Ma do? We already lost Pa, and you remember how bad that hurt. What would Ma do if you went and got shot?"

Frank winced, and his voice mellowed. "I'm not going to get killed, Jes, and be-sides, I probably wouldn't even do any robbing anyway. I just want to go along. I want to see what it feels like to pirate a steamboat." His view shifted to Harvey. "Well, what do you think? Will your pa take me along?"

Harvey considered this. "I don't rightly know, Frank. He might because you're a full two years older than me. But then again, he might not. For one thing, he wouldn't ever want your folks to find out —"

"I'd never tell them, and neither would Jesse." Frank gave his brother a glance, and slowly Jesse shook his head. "See, it won't get told by us."

"Then there is the problem of how long you all might be staying. If your folks are planning to leave tomorrow, it won't give you time to get back. Pa is driving up the river road a good piece."

"My ma and yours haven't seen each other in over a year. You know they'll want to stay together at least a few days."

Harvey pushed out his lower lip thoughtfully. "If that's so, well then I don't suppose it would hurt to ask Pa. But he might get mad that I told you about it."

"I'll come with you. I'll swear to him that I will never tell another soul."

Harvey nodded his head slowly. "All right. If your folks are planning to stay a day or two, then I'll ask him. After dinner."

Frank said, "That's all I can ask." The boys started once more for the house.

Laban Caulder grinned when Harvey came up. He was standing on the first step of the porch, and high enough to put an arm proudly about his son's shoulder. He introduced him to Stewart.

Both Jesse and Frank were surprised to discover that the man they had fished out of the Mississippi now had a name, even if it was only temporary. Ben sounded good enough, and they took to it right off as if he had never been called anything else.

Reuben was puffing his pipe, and he said, "It is too bad you have to run right off, Laban. Don't they have freight wagons in Marthasville?"

Laban laughed. "I don't know, Reuben, but when times are tough like these are, I got to take work when it comes along."

"I quite agree."

"But you will only be gone tonight and tomorrow," Bitsy said, squinting across the porch at her husband.

"I should be home by tomorrow night."

"Then why don't you take Reuben along with you for company, and while you are away, Zerelda and I can catch up on what's been happening this last year."

Laban choked as if he had suddenly inhaled a cherry pit, and Jesse grinned at his unexpected dilemma. "Err, I wouldn't want to have to put old Reuben to work, now, Bitsy," Laban stammered, "not when he and his family are traveling like they are. Why, I'm sure that once he gets home he'll have his hands full catching up with his own work."

Jesse was curious to see how this would resolve itself, but Reuben had apparently seen through Laban's lame excuse, and he said, "Oh, I wouldn't mind the work, Laban, but I've been on a wagon seat for two weeks, and if it is all the same to you, I'd just as soon spend the next few days relaxing. Maybe throw a line into the river and try for one of those catfish that you folks are famous for in these here parts."

"Harvey can show you a splendid fishing hole," Laban offered immediately, before his wife could say anything that might censor this idea.

"Well, then that's what I'd like to do." Reuben returned his pipe to his mouth, and the discussion was at an end. Jesse noticed a flutter of relief move across Laban's face . . . but then maybe not. Maybe a sigh of relief was only something Jesse had expected to see.

"I better get started on supper," Bitsy said, grabbing at the apron around her waist and wringing it in her fists. "Zerelda has brought along a nice turkey that Frank shot earlier, so I need to think of something good to do with it."

"I'll help you, Bitsy," Zerelda said, and the two women went inside.

"Now, how about that new horse?" Reuben said when the women had left.

"Ah, yes. Forgot about him. Come around to the barn and I'll show him to you." Laban stepped off the porch, and Jesse noted just how short the man really was. Jesse was nearly as tall.

Reuben gave Stewart a nod of his head. "Come along, Ben, and let's have us a look."

Stewart levered himself off the porch railing and followed them across the yard.

Frank, Jesse, and Harvey stayed behind, for they had more urgent matters to discuss, and Jesse was still wrestling with his confused feelings about Frank's joining up with Laban as the three of them strolled off into the woods and down to the wide Missouri River.

Chapter Eleven

"He'll run like the wind and keep it up all day long, hardly breaking a lather. I call him Firecracker, because that's what he reminds me of, a real four-legged explosion when he takes off."

Laban was leaning upon the top rail of his corral. He ducked under it now, and Reuben slid through the poles as well. After a moment Clifton Stewart followed. Laban advanced on the leggy chestnut stallion, talking low and gently, holding out a tempting apple that he'd picked, still a little green, from a nearby tree.

"There you go, Firecracker, take a smell. You like apples, don't you?" The stallion stood fifteen hands at the withers, and Laban's drooping felt hat rose only a few inches above that. The horse took the apple in its teeth. Laban stroked the animal a moment then grinned over to the others. "Purty, ain't he?"

"Good-looking animal, Laban," Reuben said, studying it thoughtfully, pipe clenched in his teeth, hand wrapped about its bowl. Although he attempted to look learned in matters of horseflesh, Clifton had the distinct feeling that Reuben Samuel wouldn't know a *good-looking* racehorse from crowbait.

Clifton stepped past the doctor and walked a circle around the horse with an eye for its conformation. It was, indeed, a fine-looking animal with a deep chest and wide, flaring nostrils. Leggy and slender, with a sleek rump, it looked fast and powerful. Stewart bent to feel Firecracker's cannon bone, and when he stood again, nodding his head approvingly, both Laban Caulder and Dr. Reuben were watching him curiously.

Clifton grinned. "I can believe all that you have said about him, Mr. Caulder. He has the conformation of a fine English racer — from the lines of Darley Arabian I would guess? With the proper training he might be made to pull a sulky to some fine finishes."

Laban scowled. "A sulky? He's not a trotter, Ben. He's a Thoroughbred, flat racer, and mighty good one at that."

"I would guess that he is . . . oh . . . five years old?"

Laban lifted an eyebrow. "You do know

your Thoroughbreds, Ben."

Startled, Clifton stepped away from the horse, suddenly confused. When he glanced up, Dr. Reuben was staring at him. "Is your memory returning?"

He slowly shook his head. "Not a whisper of it. And I . . . I have no idea how I know any of the things I have just said."

"For not knowing how you know it, Ben, you have managed to peg down this horse right enough. He *is* out of the line of Darley Arabian, and he *is* five years old. Firecracker is worth a good bit more money than I should have spent on a horse, but then, he is the fastest thing on four legs anywhere within a hundred miles of here, and I'm expecting him to earn back every dollar that I spent on him, and a lot more."

"I have no doubt that he will," Stewart said softly, bewildered by all this knowledge at his fingertips and distressed that he could remember nothing of how it had gotten there.

Reuben said, "You always seem to have at least one fine animal in your stables whenever we come by."

"I buy them and sell them," Laban said. "But I don't think that I will be parted with Firecracker here anytime soon."

Evening was coming on, and long shadows pushed across the yard, painting in dark tones the heaps of clutter scattered about. The three men bent through the corral rails and went back to the little house where now lamplight brightened its windowpanes. They sank into chairs on the porch and talked about the land, and the coming fall, and the crops Laban had planted out behind the house on his acreage that ran down the steep land to the Missouri River, a quarter mile to the south of them.

Darkness came over the land, and the mosquitoes grew pesky. Clifton Stewart was still troubled by the apparent knowledge he had about racehorses and his absolute lack of memory of anything beyond the moment when he awoke on the banks of the Mississippi, bundled in a blanket and under Dr. Reuben Samuel's care. As he pondered his plight, he retreated further from the conversation, for, indeed, he could think of nothing of worth to add to it. He knew little of melons or corn, and root-crop husbandry was utterly foreign to him, but what upset him most as Laban and Reuben discussed these things were the brief flashes in his mind's eye of rows and rows of fluffy white plants stretching on almost beyond sight, and the sound of something mechanical, whirling, and clunking, and scraping away in the back of his head, its identity obscured somewhere within his bruised brain.

The glow of Reuben's pipe in the darkness was like a hypnotic potion that lulled Stewart into a sleepy state where their voices merged with other voices somehow familiar, yet their identity just out of reach. For the briefest of moments the face of a beautiful woman flashed into his thoughts. Her skin was the fairest olive color he could imagine, her eyes like pearls of polished obsidian; mysterious, yet intelligent, as if her thoughts were always galloping ahead. Her hair glistened like a raven's wing catching the sunlight on a bright afternoon, and the smile he saw was as gay as Christmas morning — yet seeing it twisted a knife in his heart. Strangely out of place, though, was the fine, misty veil that drifted all around the vision, but the lovely face stood free of it, clear, and sharp . . .

Misty . . . ?

And then Bitsy called the men in for supper, and the trance was broken. Clifton pushed himself out of the creaking chair and scuffed into the house with the other two men.

The house was small, no more than a cabin; two rooms only — a bedroom that occupied one corner of it, closed off by a curtain, and a larger room where the family cooked, ate, and lived. A stout wooden table occupied the middle of the floor. A smaller table and a wooden chest were pushed up against the wall, and this was the only furniture in the place — other than a few chairs that had been conscripted into service about the table. The boys were already seated, and Laban, and Reuben, and Clifton joined them.

The table was set with plates and cups and steaming bowls that filled the air with wonderful aromas. Clifton's stomach grumbled. He could hardly wait for the women to finish up with the odds and ends of the meal. When everyone was seated, Bitsy bowed her head, blessed the food, and gave thanks for the guests, and then everyone dug in. Spoons and forks made a mighty racket against the iron, clay, and wooden bowls.

During a lull in the supper talk, Reuben said, "Ben seems to know a good deal about racehorses, Zerelda, but he still doesn't remember anything about himself."

"When I return from my trip tomorrow night, you can ride Firecracker, if you like, Ben," Laban said.

Clifton smiled. "I'm not sure I ought to. Who knows, I might have more book knowledge than actual experience. I might not prove to be the expert it appears."

Reuben said, "Riding that horse might not be a bad idea, Ben. It might kindle some memories."

Clifton looked skeptical. "Well, if you think it will help —"

"Who really knows when it comes to something as complex as the brain? What little I have read about memory loss says that the oddest thing sometimes brings it back. Riding that horse just might do it, or even another blow to the head."

Laban laughed. "Well, I can arrange for you getting a good blow to the head, Ben."

"Now watch your tongue, Laban," Bitsy scolded.

But everyone was chuckling, even Clifton.

"Captain Hamilton!"

The riverboat master drew up at the starboard paddle box and came about. Lieutenant Dempsey waved an arm at him from one of the ladder hatchways a few yards away. He mounted the hurricane deck and strode briskly over, his clipboard clutched tightly under his left arm.

"Lieutenant?" Hamilton's bushy gray eyebrows hitched up questioningly. "What can I do for you?"

The sun was low on the horizon, and Dempsey cast an eye at the darkening evening sky. All at once the *Tempest Queen* steam whistle shrilled. So unexpected was it, and nearby, that Dempsey winced and ducked his head. Three long blasts shrieked out across the water. Before Dempsey could speak, the big, bronze bell at the head of the hurricane deck, just in front of the texas, pealed, and the deep, mellow sound of it drifted out over the darkening river to an even darker shoreline.

Captain Hamilton glanced toward shore. Ahead, on the forested riverbank, a signal fire burned, and several men stood nearby it, waving their arms, only barely visible in the shadows under the trees. "Well, well, more paying customers, it seems." Hamilton's blue eyes came back to Dempsey. "Was there something you wished to speak to me about, Lieutenant?"

Down on the *Tempest Queen*'s guard, the leadsmen had jumped to the job of sounding the river, and now their calls made their way up to them, relayed along the hurricane deck by the baritone and deep base voices of the word passers.

"M-a-r-k three! Quarter-less-three! Half-twain! Half-twain! Quarter-less! M-a-r-k Twain!"

The riverboat was running near the shore, which was common practice when going upriver, for the current was not so swift on the inside, and this landing came quickly. Her bow gently nudged the soft muddy bottom on the northern bank of the Missouri River. A skiff was put over the side, and three black firemen rowed it into shore to retrieve these new passengers.

Lieutenant Dempsey said, "It is precisely these delays that I wanted to speak to you about, Captain. I know we had agreed to you picking up passengers and freight along the way, but I had no idea how frequently we would be stopping. This first day alone we have put in shore no less than seven times, sometimes for only one man, other times for half a dozen, and whole families and their wagons, and even their livestock, which you made clear to me at the start that you did not want aboard. Already the day is spent, and we have not covered nearly the distance I had calculated. Now, I have no pressing schedule to keep, mind you, so long as our landing at Fort Leavenworth is in a timely fashion. I would, however, like a reasonable estimation of our arrival time. If these stops continue, will we be looking ahead another three days . . . or four?"

"Oh, I shan't think these small delays will cost us even a full day, Lieutenant," Hamilton said with an easy smile. "But if you want something more exact to figure on, I suggest you run up and speak to the pilot. He knows this river from long experience, as you well know, for you highly recommended him."

Dempsey looked over at the pilothouse sitting atop the texas deck, but a few yards away. Eric Jupp was silhouetted behind the windows, gripping the helm now in both hands. "I don't think I need to bother Mr. Jupp at the moment, Captain Hamilton. Perhaps tomorrow, if it still appears we are moving along very much slower than I had anticipated."

"As you wish, Lieutenant." Hamilton returned his attention to the men climbing aboard. One of their number had remained on shore. He mounted his horse now and, taking up the reins of the remaining three horses there, turned away and in a moment was swallowed up by the forest.

"I suppose I shall have to go down and bid them welcome . . . later." The *Tempest Queen*'s master stepped away from the railing, and nodding his departure to Dempsey, Hamilton resumed his casual stroll around the hurricane deck. It seemed to Dempsey that the captain had very little to do once they were under steam and that it was Jupp, and his partner, "Little" Sam Winston, who wielded the real power when the boat was on the river. In port, however, Captain Hamilton regained his crown and scepter, and it was the pilots' turn to sit back and show their heels to the sky.

Dempsey was about to leave the railing himself when he noticed Reverend Deke Saunders making his way through the mounds of army matériel below. When Saunders drew near to the new arrivals, he glanced over a shoulder as if to make certain that no one was watching him and then briefly spoke to one of the men who had just come aboard. This fellow caught Dempsey's eye immediately, for he was most incongruently attired. His clothes were disreputable, his shirtsleeves ending in tattered threads, and an equally squalid straw hat was upon his head, but his feet were what riveted Dempsey's attention! They were clad in fine, black boots that shown like jet in the low sunlight. Very much like the military boots he himself wore, Dempsey thought as the two men exchanged glances and then went off in different directions.

Dempsey's eyelids came together as he remembered Dexter McKay's words. At that time he had considered McKay's suspicions unfounded. Now, he wasn't sure. Just the same, he could not see how Reverend Saunders's having acquaintances along the river made any difference in the world to the satisfactory completion of his job.

The sun touched the horizon and flared down the wide waters of the Missouri. Dempsey watched it sink out of sight, imagining its mighty fires being quenched by the river somewhere far ahead. When only a red-orange glow remained, grading to gray overhead, a thought suddenly entered his head. He frowned, and for some reason, obscure yet even to himself, he wandered off — but not without a purpose.

He was looking for Saunders's son, Grady, and he was looking for Cora Mills as well. The thought that suddenly exploded in his head and made him uneasy was that he hoped to find one or the other, but not both — at least, not together.

After supper Laban Caulder went to the barn to hitch a team of draft horses to his freight wagon. Clifton and Reuben remained on the porch, talking, while the women cleaned up the dishes. The boys were enlisted into clearing off the table, and as soon as that task was done and they were allowed to leave, they hurried outside and disappeared into the night.

Huddled together near the dark building, with the light of a lantern inside showing through the gaps in the wall, Harvey spoke softly so that his voice would not carry past the wall of the barn where his father was busy readying his wagon. "Frank, you come with me alone. It might be best if Jesse stays here. Pa's not gonna like it that I told you about him and me river pirating and such, but he'd probably take it better if'n he thinks I only talked to you about it."

Frank agreed, but Jesse figured he was being left out of an adventure he had finally come to terms with. "All right," he whispered reluctantly, "but I'm gonna stay right here and listen to what is said."

"Just don't make no noise," Harvey cautioned.

"I won't," Jesse said, still reluctant to be left behind.

Harvey and Frank went around to the big, open door, and Jesse put an eye to a gap in the wall where he could see Laban inside fitting the horses into the traces. He saw the two older boys enter and hang around the wagon, as if with nothing particular in mind to do, just wasting time. Laban asked them what they were up to, and Harvey rocked back on his heel, said "Nothing much," and casually leaned against the tall, rear wheel.

"Pa?" he said when Laban had put on the feed bags and was hauling over a heavy canvas tarpaulin that he sometimes used to cover the wagon.

"What's on your mind, boy?" Laban opened the folded tarp, examining it. "This old canvas is due for some mending real soon."

"I reckon I could do it for you," Harvey offered.

Laban glanced up, and from his hiding place outside the barn, Jesse noted the surprised look on his face. "Yes, I reckon you could, although I never thought I'd live to see the day that you'd offer to do it on your own without being asked. Now I know you got something on your mind, boy. What is it?"

Harvey shrank back under his father's sudden stare, but then he glanced over at Frank and seemed to recoup his courage. "Pa, Frank wants to come with you tonight." He blurted it out all at once.

Laban didn't move immediately, but stood as if frozen, with the tarp partly unfolded in his hands and the rest of it spread out in the bed of the wagon. Slowly his eyelids narrowed, and when he spoke, winter had come to the barn and ice crystals hung in the air.

"What is it that you have been telling Frank?"

Before Harvey could answer, Frank said, "He told me about the riverboat, and what you and others are planning to do tomorrow. I want to go along with you, Uncle Laban. I promise I'll not get in the way, and I swear I'll never mention it to anyone."

Laban ignored Frank's words. His eyes remained fixed upon his son, a tightness in his face that made Jesse think of soaked and drawn leather, or chiseled stone. "Who else did you tell, Harvey? Does Jesse know about this, too?"

"No —"

"Yes he does," Frank countered boldly. "I don't intend to lie to you, Uncle Laban. We both know about it, but Jesse wouldn't tell anybody either. I told you, no one will ever find out."

Slowly the man's eyes shifted toward Frank, and in the wavering lamplight Jesse watched them lock onto his older brother with a look of deadly warning that made Jesse's blood run cold as deep well water. He had never seen such intenseness in this man they called "Uncle" — even though no real family ties existed — not even the year he and Harvey had taken a pair of Laban's fine racehorses out in the middle of the night and ran them neck to neck along the river road.

"Whatever my boy told you, Frank, you forget right now. He was a fool to open his mouth about this, and I will deal properly with Harvey once I get back." Laban's view shifted and stabbed like war lances at his boy. Harvey shriveled beneath the stare. Laban's attention leaped back to Frank.

"Do you understand what I just said?"

"Yes, sir," Frank answered, not cowing. He was two years older than Harvey, and nearly a man himself, or so he was fond of reminding Jesse. Jesse saw that he was not going to allow himself to be as easily unnerved by Laban's threats as Harvey had been.

Laban considered him a long moment, but Frank stood tall and fearless, and there was boldness in him that Jesse had not recalled seeing before. "Then I can trust you won't speak of this again."

"I already told you that neither Jesse nor I will tell anyone."

"All right, I'll take you on your word, boy." Laban tossed the remaining portion of canvas into the bed without examining it further and began to remove the feed bags from his two horses.

"I still want to come along, Laban," Frank said. The brazen lack of the title "Uncle" rang with the dissonance of a cracked bell in the dusty barn, boldly proclaiming that Frank considered himself Laban's equal. Frank's brashness stunned Jesse. Outside the barn, he pressed his eye closer to the gap in the boards to see what would happen next.

Laban wheeled away from the feed buckets and came forward. Although a short man, he was powerfully built, with fists like knotted oak, and arms and shoulders stout as a singletree — hauling freight and hoeing acres of cropland were not sissy chores. "I reckon I didn't make myself clear, Frank, so I'll say it one more time, straight out so's you don't misunderstand me this time: The answer is no. No, you cannot come along. End of discussion! And if what was spoken here tonight should go beyond these walls, Frank, you are liable to find yourself in Glory where your Bible-thumping Pa is, long before your time."

Frank swallowed hard, but stood his ground. Jesse squirmed uncomfortably on the ground where he lay in the dark. He knew his brother well enough to never put a direct challenge like that in his path.

Man and boy considered each other, then Laban turned back to his wagon and said without looking over, "You two run off now, and stay out of trouble. I'll be along to the house directly." His voice was most amiable, as if never an unpleasant word had passed between them.

Harvey leaped immediately to the barn door and beckoned Frank to hurry with him, but Frank remained there, not moving, with the yellow lamplight highlighting his sandy hair and dancing upon the handsome, sharp features of his face. He considered Laban until the man grew uneasy under his stare and stopped his

work and looked over. Their eyes locked in
fiery combat. Then apparently having satisfied some need within himself, Frank
turned casually toward the door where
Harvey stood with white fear draining his
color. He glanced back at the wagon, and
with the ease of a man who had all at once
come to a decision, he left, but with no
hurry in his steps nor bow to his tall,
straight bearing.

Chapter Twelve

The sun had long since extinguished itself against the western horizon, and overhead a clear sky with a thin crescent moon did little to hide the stars. But the starlight was meager at best, and where the men had gathered, little of the sky was visible anyway; only a sliver of lamplight from a smoky lantern nearby caught a face here or there or picked out a movement as a hand reached across the barrel top. Voices were kept very low — all that was audible from even a short distance was the clink of glass as a whiskey bottle made its rounds; barely visible were the glowing tips of scattered cigars illuminating gaunt and bearded faces, devil-like in the dark corner of the *Tempest Queen* where Deke Saunders and his gang had come together.

Upon the barrel top that served as a table, Deke Saunders had placed his Bible, and atop the Bible, the whiskey bottle when it had finally come around to him. Two other objects occupied the barrel as well: a candle lantern with its shutter closed so that only the faintest edge of light escaped, and his Colt's navy revolver.

Faint murmurings arose from the dark corner, but when Deke raised his hands for silence, the whispering voices died away like a wave running itself out on a long, empty shore, and for a long moment only the chugging of the steam from the escape pipes overhead could be heard.

Then Deke spoke: "Anybody here don't know why I called you all together again?" When no one answered, Deke said, "Good. Then I can keep this brief." His shadowed eyes fixed upon one of the men there. "Darryl."

"Yeah, Deke?"

"You got somebody there with you I ain't never met."

"Err, yeah, I brought along a friend. He's all right, Deke. We've worked together some. He's new to the river. Only just come from out West. His name is . . . err . . . Hart. Charles Hart."

Deke studied the man. He was young, no more than twenty-two, fair of features, blonde haired. "Where you come from, Hart?"

Hart spoke with a cool detachment, as if

no man could ask him to tell more than he had a mind to. "Recently from Utah. Spent some time in the Rocky Mountain gold camps while making my way back East. I was born in Ohio."

"What do you do?"

Hart laughed quietly. "Right now, I hold up riverboats."

The men around him chuckled softly, but Saunders was not amused. "And what else do you do, Mr. Charlie Hart?"

"Charles," he corrected, his voice suddenly taut. "If I want you to call me Charlie, I'll let you know. And my past ain't none of your concern, Mr. Saunders."

Darryl said, "He's all right, Deke. Don't ride him. I'll contend by him."

Deke nodded his head. "I will keep that in mind, Darryl. All right, then to the business at hand. In case you haven't noticed, we are on a boat here what is full of booty that we can steal and sell for a big profit. The Sioux out West will pay handsomely for small arms and the guns aboard, not to mention the whiskey and other geegaws and whim-wham on its way to the trading post at Fort Leavenworth. My purpose is to steal it all."

"Mighty bold plans," one of the men muttered.

"Bold plans make for big profits," Deke came back.

"Maybe," Charles Hart said, his doubt plain in his voice.

"You don't agree, Mr. Hart?"

"In case *you* haven't noticed, this boat is swarming with soldiers, and they aren't just going to stand by and watch us carry off all of their supplies."

"That small detail has not escaped my attention, thank you, and I have figured a way to overcome the problem, but more on that later. For now I want to make clear the terms of our little partnership, and if anyone don't agree with them, then right now is the time to be parting company." Saunders looked over the shadowy crowd. Eleven men had come aboard the *Tempest Queen* for the endeavor, and he knew by Harold Madden that six others had been recruited to stand by on shore with wagons and horses to make good their getaway. Of these eleven, ten were men he had worked with before, and only the newcomer, Charles Hart, was the unknown card in his deck.

"Well, Deke, let us know what we are getting ourselves into," Waldo Hinkley, from upriver near Treloar, said impatiently.

"Only this," Saunders continued. "I plan to take over this boat, run her into shore, strip her deck clean of anything worth selling, and give it all to you boys to split up as you please. I ain't gonna take a penny from it."

An agreeable chatter made its way through the men bunched in there, rising almost above a whisper before a voice in the crowd said rather loudly, "Here now, Deke Saunders. I know you better than that. There ain't a generous bone in your body. What have you got up your sleeve? Why ain't you taking your split?"

That hammered some sense into the others, and shortly they all demanded to know what he was up to, with Hart's voice the most skeptical and insistent.

Deke quieted them, and when he had regained control of the floor, he said, "I've got my own little prize already carved out, boys, and it is this. Up above in one of the cabins is the army's payroll. That's what we are claiming as our own."

This brought about a moment of discussion among the pirates, and Clyde Horvath, an old rogue whom Deke had known since they were kids stealing canoes full of trappers' beaver pelts coming down the Missouri, said, "Who is this *we* that you mentioned, Deke?"

"Me, my boy Grady, and my nephew there, Harold."

"How much is in the payroll?" Clyde asked.

"That makes no difference to you."

"Well, I kinda see as it does," another voice came from the darkness.

"Yeah," the comment was seconded.

Darryl said, "If we are all taking the risks, then it should be split even."

There was general agreement on this point until Saunders's low, sharp retort brought silence to the crowd. "Anyone here who feels that way can leave right now. I'll get me more men who will be grateful for the generous portion I'm already offering. I planned this caper, and I'm taking my pick of the booty. Enough said. Anyone here who don't agree with that can walk away right now."

No one left, but someone did say, "Don't the army pay in script, Deke? What do you want with a lot of army script?"

"It is not script this time, but the payroll is my business. Everything else is yours, and we will all work together on it."

"All right, I reckon a sliver of the pie is better than none at all, and the pie appears big enough to split, even with you keeping the army's payroll, Deke. I'm in," Aldo said, and the others agreed to his terms as well, some reluctantly, but that didn't worry Deke Saunders, for he planned to deal swiftly and permanently with anyone who dared to double-cross him.

"There is still the problem of all these soldiers aboard," Hart reminded him.

"Yeah, how you planning to deal with them, Deke?" a man named Case Jackson wanted to know.

"I've been pondering that problem some time now, and I've come up with a plan."

"Better be a good one or I'm bowing out, Deke," another one of the pirates, Bud Patterson, said. Bud, like Clyde Horvath, was an old-timer who had gotten his start with Deke in the early years by luring trappers into shore with whiskey and women and murdering them for the beaver pelts they carried. "I'm not so fast as I once was, and dodging Federal bullets ain't my idea of a way to make a living no more."

Deke gave a short laugh. "If you dodge them bullets like you dodge hard work, Bud, there ain't nary a soldier on board this here fancy boat what's gonna nail you."

"Go on, Deke," said a low voice nearby, its owner's face hidden in the darkness, "what's your plan?"

"Come gather in a little closer, boys, and take a look." Deke shoved the Bible and whiskey aside and jammed the revolver into his belt under his black coat. "Gimme your knife, Harold."

"Su— sure thing, De— Deke." Madden passed the bowie across, and Deke parted the shutter on the candle lamp just enough to cast light upon the wooden top of the barrel. Deke scratched a wandering line into it. "This here is the Missouri River." The point of the knife poked the wood at a spot along the line. "Here is St Louie, where we started from." Farther along the line the knife stabbed again. "Here is Matson. We just passed it late this afternoon." The point of the knife marched west along the line an inch or two. "Over here a little north of the river is Treloar, and way over here is Hermann. Now, boys, if this here boat keeps on like she is going, we should make Hermann by tomorrow around noon, or a little sooner." Deke grinned into the darkness. "But I don't suspect she is a gonna keep on like she has been doing, for I plan to make our move before then."

"You still ain't said how you intend to get rid of all these soldiers," Hart said.

"Well, you just keep your britches hitched up tight, Mr. Charles Hart, and I'll explain it to you. Now, between Treloar and Hermann is a little river settlement called Catfish Landing." The knife stabbed with a finality, and Deke ground it into the wood, making a deep pit. "There ain't but about a hundred folks what live there last time I was through, and that is down from what the population was only five years ago. Twenty years ago they had a tannery there, and a growing population, but the end of the beaver trade sealed their fate, just like it done to you and me and half a hundred men who used to make a good living off of them mountain trappers."

Some of the older men there grunted and allowed that progress, and the demise of the beaver trade, had hurt them and that someone owed them a living now.

Deke went on. "I never have held much regard for the Federal army, but I have noticed this last day or two watching them that there is a bunch of them blue-soldiers what have a hankering to help out all the time whenever they get a chance. They help take on wood, they lend a hand putting the landing stage over, and help the deckhands haul on cargo or wrestle livestock into place. They are the almightiest helpful folks I did ever see." Deke chuckled. "Well, now, I figure to give them something to be helpful with. Something real important. Something that them and their commanding officer, a lieutenant named Dempsey, couldn't possibly leave alone."

"What have you got in mind, Deke?" Clyde Horvath asked.

"The way I see it, Catfish Landing is a town on its deathbed, holding onto life with weakening fingers. I intend to give it a hand up to the Hereafter. In a little bit we'll be passing a place called Growley's Wood Yard." The point of the knife stabbed at the line again. "There's a road what runs straight north from there to Marthasville, what is only a mile or so from the river." The bowie scratched a straight line and cut a little "X" at the site. "Harold has told our boys with the wagons and the horses to gather at Growley's, just below Marthasville. Tonight him and some of you boys will be getting off there. We will ask the captain to put over at Growley's Wood Yard 'cause you need to disembark. Now, I've been watching the way the captain buys wood every four to six hours. It seems likely that he plans to stop somewhere nearby there anyway, so there shouldn't be no problem convincing him that you need to be put off at Growley's."

Deke glanced up and saw that he had everyone's full attention, even that skeptic, Charles Hart. "Any questions yet?"

"Yeah, how you gonna get rid of them soldiers?" Hart demanded again.

Deke laughed softly and said, "When we put our boys off, they will mount fresh horses waiting there for them and ride ahead to Catfish Landing. The river makes a wide sweep to the south that adds thirty miles to the trip, but the river road stays north at that point, and that ought to put you far enough ahead of this here boat. But to give you an edge, I figure we can do some mischief down among the engines to slow her up some. You should make it a couple hours ahead of us, riding hard. Then all you do is keep an eye out on the river. When you see this big, white boat a coming, give out a signal for her to land. When she pulls in, you will set fire to that town. Start it in half a dozen places so as to keep everyone jumping. I can guarantee that once we make landing, it won't be two minutes, and a few carefully placed words, before every Federal troop aboard is clambering off to help fight the blazes — well, I suspect the troops guarding the gol—, err, the army's payroll, will remain aboard, but they should be easy to handle. They only post two at a time."

"So, it is gold they are carrying aboard here?" Waldo Hinkley said. "That is a mite easier to deal with than wagons loaded down with army goods."

Deke shot Waldo a narrow glance. "So what if it is? We've struck a deal. Are you going again' it?" Deke's fist tightened around the bowie knife, and its blade caught the meager candlelight as it came up.

"I reckon not, Deke," Waldo said.

"Does anyone else here have misgivings?" The knife traced a smooth arc in front of them. When no one spoke up, Deke said, "Good. Now, back to the business at hand. Once the troops are ashore, you boys get back aboard the *Tempest Queen* fast as you can. Me and Grady will pay the pilot a visit and deal with him. Bud, you and Darryl will go down to the engine room and have the engineer put the boat back out into the river. The rest of you will take the captain and passengers prisoners and make a prominent show of your rifles and other arms. I don't think the crew will make trouble with a revolver

242

pointed at their captain's skull."

"Hum, it just might work, Deke," Clyde Horvath said.

"Of course it will work! I planned it!"

"What do we do once we put back out into the river?" someone asked.

"While our boys are waiting for us at Catfish Landing, the horses and wagons will have gone farther west. Harold will be in charge of that. About ten miles beyond Catfish Landing the road follows right along the river. We will run the boat aground there and unload the goods into the waiting wagons. At that point we part company. Harold, Grady, and me will take the payroll; the rest of you can do what you like with the army goods. My advice would be to take it north into the wilds and hide it until the army tires of searching for it. Then freight it out West and sell it to the Indians."

"What do Injuns got worth trading for, Deke? They ain't got hard money," someone asked.

Saunders snorted. "They have got ways of getting money to pay for what they want, especially modern arms and whiskey. Don't worry, they will find it even if they got to steal it."

"I know where there is a cave nearby

there," Waldo said. "We used to use it years ago. The army will never find it."

"That sounds like the smart thing to do with the booty," Deke said. "So any questions?"

"Who is going to go ashore and set fire to Catfish Landing?" This was Ralph Dickerson speaking. Ralph was about thirty, compactly built, and balding. Deke knew him only in passing, for they had never worked together, but Dickerson was well spoken of among the pirate brotherhood that still plied their trade along the Missouri.

"I figure Waldo will be in charge of that. He knows the area. And you can go, too, if you want, Ralph. Then Tom Green. You know the area almost as good as Waldo, don't you, Tom?"

"I should think I do," Green said smugly.

"Let's see, that makes three. Maybe two more. How about you, Case?"

"I'll do it, Deke," Case Jackson said without hesitation.

"I want to go, too." This was Charles Hart.

Deke studied the young man. After a moment he nodded his head and said, "I reckon it will be a good test of your mettle.

All right, you go along with them, Mr. *Charles* Hart, and Waldo, you keep an eye on him. I'll want to know how he does when you get back."

Hart laughed, low and challenging. "You don't need to worry about me."

"We shall see," Deke replied. "We shall surely see." His view shifted back to the dark brood of bandits hovering near. "All right, now, let's split up before someone gets suspicious. Waldo, you go find the captain and tell him you need to get off at Growley's. Do we all know what we are gonna do now?"

He got a round of low-voiced mumbling that said they all understood.

"All right then, be off with you. Waldo, let me know once the captain has agreed to stop at Growley's. You can find me up in the main cabin. I need to buy me something to eat."

"Sure thing, Deke."

When the pirates had gone their way, Grady rubbed his sweaty palms upon his dirty shirt and said, "I think I'm gonna go and try to find me that pretty little gal what's all by herself." He laughed, and there was no mistaking his intent in the sound of it.

"Whatever you have in mind, boy, make

sure it don't interfere with what we have got planned. We have us a busy night ahead of us."

"I hope so." Grady's eyes glinted in the light of the candle lantern. "I won't do nothing to hurt our plans, Pa. I'll be careful." Grady wandered off. When they had all left but Deke, the old pirate blew out the candle lamp, finished off the whiskey, and tossed the bottle far out into the black water. Taking up his Bible, he straightened his coat, adjusted his slouch hat, and went around onto the main deck where the soldiers and other deck passengers were camped about.

In the shadows of a canvas-covered mound of boxes, a cigar brightened in the darkness. Its glowing, red tip had burned down to the man's fingers while he had waited, and now he flicked the stub out over the railing where the frothy wash from the huge paddle wheel sucked it under, immediately putting out its fire. Overhead, the chugging of the 'scape pipes had set up a one-note symphony that, unfortunately, had completely drowned out the voices of the men who had gathered in secret at the back of the boat.

He had watched as all but two of the

men strolled off, waited as Grady and Deke spoke, then Grady had also departed. Only the reverend remained, tipping the bottle to his lips, and finally he, too, finished, sending the empty bottle sailing out across the water.

When Deke Saunders left, making his way up the stairs, the man stepped from his hiding place and went to where the pirates had held their clandestine meeting. His keen eyes probed the scene for a clue of what they had been up to, but nothing of the meeting remained . . . nothing, that is, except —.

The man set aside his walking stick, removed a silver matchsafe from his inside pocket, and struck a flame. Holding it near the barrel, he frowned at the scratchings he discovered there on its top, and committed them to memory. The match burned low. He shook it out and ground it underfoot. With the frown deepening upon his face, he took up the walking stick and made his way out of the hidden alcove.

Chapter Thirteen

The *Tempest Queen* drove on into the night, her chimneys sending a shower of sparks into the air. Without too much effort, any chance onlooker might imagine that the trip was a perpetual Fourth of July celebration. Down on the main deck the red glare of the furnace fires danced eerily upon the mounded cargo and upon the faces of soldiers who had taken up residence in every available nook and cranny. The rhythm of puffing steam from the 'scape pipes and the driving splash of the paddle wheels were enough to lull a weary body to sleep. But although Lieutenant Sherman Dempsey had been up since dawn and had been around and around the huge boat more than two dozen times this day, checking on his men, the cargo in his care, and the gold locked in an end cabin and guarded at all times by two armed soldiers, and although the hour was nearing ten o'clock, he was far from weary.

Dempsey rested his elbows upon the railing with his back to the four lead-glass doors of the main cabin. The light of the crystal chandeliers inside pushed his shadow far out over the main deck below where his sleepy company of men lounged in the flickering red glow of the open furnace doors. The furnaces were buried even deeper under the deck, behind the little cabin where the firemen kept their kits, and beyond the four long rows of cordwood that were being fed into those eight fiery mouths at the furious rate of almost ten cords an hour. Inside the main cabin, a string quartet was playing a sonata, by Rossini, Dempsey thought, but he wasn't sure.

The promenade was mostly deserted. A few passengers had gathered in the main cabin, along with a phalanx of white-clad waiters in the wings, nearly stumbling over each other to be the first to a beckoning arm. The *Tempest Queen* was most assuredly overstaffed for the meager passenger list. Dempsey was certain, however, that once back on the Mississippi River — back on familiar waters, she would be overflowing her gunwales with travelers.

With a weightiness of spirit, of which he was unaccustomed, he pushed away from the railing and started for the doors of the main cabin. Just then he spied Cora Mills at the far end of the promenade where it came to an end at the larboard paddle box, back two-thirds the length of the boat. His immediate destination suddenly forgotten, and without thinking about what he was doing, Dempsey allowed his feet to veer off their set course and carry him briskly through the pale pools of light that dropped to the deck from smoky lamps stationed along the promenade's wall.

He was about to call out a greeting to Cora when she looked up from the door where she was turning her key in the lock, spied him, and gave a sudden smile. In spite of his uncertainty over engaging another man's wife, even if only in innocent conversation, and the stab of guilt that pricked his breast like a dagger when he thought of it in those terms, Dempsey's pace did not diminish.

Between him and Cora intervened a ladder rising to the next deck. As Dempsey drew near to her, a dark figure, half obscured by shadows, made his way down the steps. Before Dempsey could reached Cora, this intruder had stepped quickly over to her, and in the light of a lamp near Cora's door, Dempsey saw that it was the Reverend Deke Saunders's scrawny son, Grady.

Dempsey stopped in his tracks as if he

had walked square into a wall. Cora seemed quite happy to see Grady. Dempsey's resolve melted, and he hesitated. He had to admit to himself that he was not very dapper, and certainly not a ladies' man. In fact, he told himself, although he might be quite competent where commanding troops was concerned, where pretty young ladies were the object of his endeavors, he was . . . ungainly? Yes, that would describe him, he confessed as he stood there watching Grady chatting with Cora. Not that the younger Saunders displayed any great savoir faire, Dempsey decided, watching the two of them with a sudden envy, but Grady obviously did not lack the confidence around women that he did.

For a brief moment Dempsey's heavy spirit had vanished, but now he felt it settle back upon him, twice as burdensome as before. At least now he understood what had caused it. Promptly he turned on his heels and started away.

"Oh, Lieutenant Dempsey," Cora's voice sang out. Her words drove a spike into his boot, halting him. When he looked back she was beckoning to him. His heart leaped. At once he forgot that she was a married woman, and that Grady Saunders had intruded, and he immediately reversed his steps.

"Mrs. Mills," he said, sweeping his hat from his head.

"You wished to speak to me?" she inquired.

"I was only coming to see how you were doing. I had not seen you about earlier."

"My, how gallant," she said, smiling. "You and Mr. Saunders as well. I cannot tell you how secure I feel knowing that you two are looking out for my safety. But I must confess, I have not seen any danger about, at least nothing that would threaten me or Kenneth."

Dempsey thought he caught a note of irony in her voice, as if she somehow was more amused than flattered by their attentions. He let his suspicion pass and said, "Where is your boy?"

"I have just gotten him to bed." Her voice dropped to a hush as she took Grady and Dempsey by the arms and moved them a few paces from the door. "There, now we won't disturb him. He is so excited about seeing his father again, and about being on a riverboat, that I have had the most exacting time trying to get him quieted down and to sleep."

Dempsey noted that Grady Saunders

was not pleased with his being there. The lanky man said, "Shouldn't you ought to be seeing to your soldier boys, Lieutenant? Making sure they stay out of trouble?"

"My men avoid trouble on their own very well," he replied.

"I don't know about that. I heard some purty rough talk betwixt 'em earlier. Seems you got some good, upright Southern boys being harassed by a bunch of them narrow-minded, Northern, abolitionist troublemakers. I heard 'em bickering back and forth just awhile ago. Maybe you should go on down there and see to it that they don't cause no trouble." Grady grinned and did not try to hide the open challenge in his tone.

"My men know to keep their differences to themselves, Mr. Saunders. Philosophical disagreements have no place in fighting troops that must rely on one another."

Grady laughed. "You ain't fighting nobody at the moment, and there ain't no way to keep them phil-o-solophical differences from comin' out when you got nearly half a hundred men with nothing to do but lay about the deck of this here boat."

Inwardly, Grady had hit the nail squarely on the head, and painful as it was for Dempsey to admit it to himself, his words drove home a worry that had gnawed at him since he had discovered Lemont Belvedere and his friends discussing this very subject earlier that day. Had there been more said? — more trouble behind his back that he was not aware of? Or was Grady only groping for some excuse to be rid of him? It seemed unlikely that Saunders would have stumbled upon this very real worry by accident.

"My, my, it seems so quiet this evening," Cora interrupted, as if she sensed a battle brewing. "I have not heard a peep out of Lieutenant Dempsey's men all evening. They all are very well mannered. I think you must be mistaken, Mr. Saunders."

For a moment Grady's view remained locked in deadly combat with Dempsey's, then he looked at Cora, and as if the lieutenant were no longer present, he said, "I come down to see if you'd take a walk with me around the promenade, ma'am."

"Actually, I was hoping that Mrs. Mills would take a walk with me," Dempsey said, shocked that he had spoken so boldly in front of this lovely woman.

"I shall walk with you both," Cora said, plainly striving to avoid the conflict she must have sensed was coming, but Dempsey could see that the matter was not going to be so easily settled.

"No you won't. This soldier boy is gonna to leave. Ain't you?"

"That is unlikely, Mr. Saunders." Dempsey's reply was firm. Now that he was not contending against the fairer sex, but against another man, Dempsey was in complete control of the situation. He could see Grady's eyes suddenly cloud as the fellow considered this abrupt change in him — and Dempsey saw something else, too . . .

The lieutenant dodged instantly to his left.

Grady Saunders's knuckles had bunched into a fist at his side. The fist struck up but found only empty air where a moment before Dempsey's chin had been.

"Oh!" Cora cried.

The long swing knocked Grady momentarily off his balance, and Dempsey used it to his advantage, stepping around him and taking the gangling man by the arms, pulling them back and pinning them together. Saunders arched forward, broke the lieutenant's grip, and rounded on him.

Dempsey was a heartbeat faster, dodging aside. His own fist stabbed out and buried itself in the soft flesh beneath Grady's rib cage. The breath went out of the skinny man. He sunk to his knees, bent over, gripping himself.

"You blue-bellied bastard sonuvabitch!" Grady's bulging eyes lifted and fixed upon the lieutenant. Blind fury had replaced rage. "I'll kill you —" Grady's hand reached for the revolver tucked in his waistband, beneath the tattered ends of his shirt. Before he was able to yank it out, the hiss of steel against steel whispered in the darkness. Grady's movement froze, and his wide eyes crossed, staring at the point of Dempsey's saber a mere quarter of an inch from his nose. Slowly he backed his hand away from the six-shooter. Dempsey's blade flickered in the lamplight, plucking Grady's revolver neatly from his waistband, as if it had been an apple off a tree. The sword continued in its arc and the weapon sailed out over the dark water. The sound of its splash was swallowed up in the constant din of the larboard paddle wheel beating the river into a frothy wake.

The fight began and ended in only a handful of seconds. So quickly had it occurred that no one apparently had heard, and the promenade had remained deserted except for the three of them. The only sounds that Dempsey was aware of beyond his own breathing were the sudden exhalation as Cora released her own held breath, the constant din of steam escaping from pipes overhead, and the splashing of the paddle wheel.

"Pretty earthy language coming from a preacher's boy. I think you owe Mrs. Mills an apology."

Grady stood, shakily, still holding his gut. "I'll see you on your way to hell before this trip is over, Dempsey!"

Cora's face drained of color, and her eyes rounded like gold eagles.

Grady glanced at her but offered no apology. He scooped his fallen hat off the deck, and straightening up with some difficulty, he shambled off down the promenade, darting through the first door he came to that would take him into the main cabin.

Dempsey sheathed his saber and retrieved his own hat. "I apologize for all of this, Mrs. Mills."

"But it wasn't your fault. I would never have expected such behavior from Mr. Saunders. He is certainly not the gentleman he led me to believe he was."

Dempsey grinned and ran fingers through his hair, combing it back and settling the hat upon his head. "No, ma' am. I should say he is not."

She shivered suddenly, even though the evening was warm, and hugged herself. "To think I agreed to permit that ruffian to walk with me. It only shows how little a woman alone can trust some men."

Dempsey winced. And how little she knew of him as well. How could she know that his intentions were any more honorable — or any less despicable? And he wondered if she was suddenly thinking the same thought, only too polite to voice it. He could stand the uncertainty no longer. "You do not know me either, Mrs. Mills."

Her eyes lifted, and she suddenly smiled. "But you are an officer, and a gentleman, are you not?"

"I . . . I should like to be known as such, of course, Mrs. Mills."

"Then that is how I shall accept you, sir, until you prove differently. But now, one more point before you escort me into the main cabin where I hear that lovely music playing." She paused.

"Yes?"

"It is you who do not know *me* very well."

"How is that?"

"If you knew me, you would not continue to assume that I am a married woman, and keep calling me Mrs. Mills. It is *Miss* Mills, thank you — and, no, I have never been married, so that should answer your next question, if I am not very much mistaken. And finally, Kenneth *is* my son, but only because I have raised him since he was an infant. He is, in fact, my brother's son. My brother is a widower.

"Now that you know I am not a married woman, and that I am not being unfaithful to a husband stationed in a lonely fort on the wild frontier, would you please just call me Cora, and please escort me into the main cabin?"

Dempsey was dumbfounded. He stammered, then grinned, and when she placed her hand lightly upon his arm, the memory of the fight with Grady fled from him, and he was hardly aware of his boots touching the deck as he walked Cora Mills through the side door and into the lights and the music and the army of waiting attendants in their white coats.

"Growley's Wood Yard? Yes, I know the place. What in blazes do you want to put over there for? We running low on sticks again?" Sam Winston was saying at the very moment Dexter McKay stepped into the darkened pilothouse.

Hamilton glanced over when the door

opened and shut, then returned his attention to the pilot at the helm, and all at once Dexter McKay understood why the pilot went by the name "Little" Sam Winston. Standing there, reaching for the spokes of the big wheel, Sam Winston was barely able to peer through them out the wide pilothouse windows at the black river ahead. The cozy pilothouse had an oilskin floor covering and a comfortable leather sofa to one side where Winston's partner, Eric Jupp, snored softly. The high bench on the other side of the room was empty now, but McKay was accustomed to finding a temporarily out-of-work pilot curled up there as well. The stove was not lighted, for the night was sultry. McKay took note of all of this in a sweeping glance, and one thing more as well: Winston was standing upon an overturned peach crate.

Hamilton said, "I have some passengers that wish to be put off at Growley's Wood Yard, but we might as well take on fuelwood since we will be there already."

"It's all right by me, Captain. These passengers of yours, I suspect they would be wanting to go on to Marthasville. There ain't nothing at Growley's but a single shack and a yard filled with cut wood."

"You know better than I what is around

these parts, Mr. Winston. I don't ask my passengers why they want off. I only do my best to accommodate them." Hamilton came about and considered McKay a moment. "What are you up to tonight?"

"I'm just catching a bit of the night air, Captain. My stroll brought me here, and I decided to step in and say hello to the new pilots."

Hamilton cleared his throat. "If you are not doing anything later, perhaps we could continue with the lessons?"

"I think that will be all right, Captain." McKay opened the gold lid to his heavy watch and turned the face toward the bit of moonlight coming through the windows. "Shall we say half an hour?"

"I'll be there." Hamilton said to "Little" Sam Winston, "Thank you, and good evening, sir."

"Evening to you, Captain," Winston replied in a distracted voice, his attention upon the black water unfolding ahead of him.

Hamilton left, and McKay stepped closer to the man grasping the helm in both hands; he strained his eyes, looking ahead, past the windows. "It never fails to amaze me how you pilots can navigate a big vessel like the *Tempest Queen* through the dead of night and not run her up on a sandbar or into the shore. For the life of me, Mr. Winston, I can barely make out where shore ends and water begins."

Sam Winston looked over at McKay, then put his view back on the river. "You learn to read the water. It takes time, and a lot of practice, but you learn."

"But for the most part I cannot even see the river."

"You have to feel it as well as see it, Mr. — ?"

"McKay. Dexter McKay, at your service, sir."

"A good pilot has got to develop eyes that see what other men's can't, and a sixth sense when it's too dark or cloudy to see or when the storm is so heavy it draws a gray curtain in front of your eyes. The Missouri is a harder river to learn than the Mississippi; that's why I get paid twice as much as a Mississippi pilot."

"Is that so? Twice as much?" McKay said with genuine interest, and his hand dipped into a vest pocket for the pair of dice resting there. But he resisted his natural inclination and put his thoughts back on the real reason he had come up to the pilothouse. "Then, I reckon you know this river from one end to the other by rote."

"You got to, Mr. McKay, unless you want to end up on a bar. But I don't have to know the river clear up to its end. I generally only work the lower Missouri. Don't usually get much above Yankton, so it doesn't do me any good to keep every bar and bend fresh in my head up above that point."

"But you certainly have maps of the river, in the event you wish to traverse a portion of it that you are not familiar with, say above Yankton?"

"*Charts,* Mr. McKay. We use charts on the river, not maps. I have them, but for the most part they don't do too much good. You got to actually study the river and memorize it anew each time you travel her. She's a fickle lady, she is, and changes so quickly that any chart drawn up would be wildly inaccurate within a year."

"I see." McKay paused. "You say you have these charts? With you?"

"Sure I got 'em with me. Never use 'em though."

"I understand. You carry your charts inside your head."

Winston looked over and grinned. "That I do, just like most good pilots."

"But it would be interesting to see one — I mean for someone like me who knows nothing about piloting a riverboat on the Missouri, it might be interesting."

"You want to see one? I got 'em over there in my kit. Here, take the helm whilst I dig it out for you," and without warning Winston caught McKay by the sleeve of his jacket and hauled him over in front of the helm.

"But, I have never —"

"Just keep her pointed straight ahead. Ain't nothing dangerous in this stretch of the river so long as you don't let her drift to starboard, in which case you'll run us up into the shore."

"But —"

"I won't be a minute." Winston stepped down off the peach crate and released the helm. McKay immediately felt the river taking command, pulling at the helm as he tried to hold it firm, and true. He tightened his grip on the big wheel as if it were a living thing trying to escape. His knuckles blanched, and he felt his face draw tight as he strained to see the black water beyond the torch baskets at the bow.

Winston seemed to be in no hurry as he dragged out a leather valise from behind the high bench and began rummaging through it. As he sorted through his belongings, he said, "It ain't so bad going upriver, McKay. The current helps the rudder take a good bite of the river. But if we were heading downriver, well, that would be a different story. We'd have to be pulling a good seven knots just to stay ahead of the current, for if we did not, the boat would drift with the current."

"How interesting," McKay said, his palms beginning to sweat upon the spokes of the tall wheel. Its wide span reached nearly to his chin, and the bottom portion of the wheel disappeared into a slot in the floor near the toes of his shoes. McKay had watched pilots spin the wheel hard over and stand on the spokes where they dipped into the slot. They called that "cramping her down," and they had always made it look so easy that he had no idea it actually took *muscles* to keep the boat pointed in the direction it was supposed to go!

With nose buried in the dark valise, Winston was removing shirts, trousers, a cigar box — McKay hazarded a glance at the little pilot, then immediately riveted his attention back on the dark river ahead. His brow was growing moist beneath the band of his hat.

"She's drifting to starboard, McKay," Winston snapped, his head still down in his valise, arms flinging dark and unrecognizable items into a pile.

How could Winston know that with his head buried like an ostrich? "Starboard — err, the right?"

"Take her over five degrees."

"Five degrees? Err — what exactly does that mean?"

"Ah, here they are." Winston brought over a thick, leather-bound folio, stepped up onto his crate, and without a glance at the river, took the helm in his left hand and dragged it over to the left — the larboard? McKay always had to refer to his right and left hands when figuring starboard from larboard — most embarrassing — like a child who, just learning to cipher, counted on his fingers to determine his sums.

"Here you go. Take a look at 'em."

"Thank you, Mr. Winston." But Dexter McKay was mostly thankful that he was away from the helm and that "Little" Sam Winston was once again back in control of it.

"Don't light a lamp. It ruins my night eyes."

"I certainly will not!" McKay opened the folio and canted it to the windows where the pale moonlight fell upon the pages as he unfolded them. There, in long sheets of heavy paper, was the river laid out for him. "About where are we now, Mr. Winston?"

"Sheet three, the middle," he said as if the book were open before him and his finger upon the page. Indeed, McKay thought, the book was before him, all there in his carefully trained brain — from St. Louis up to Yankton — and probably beyond as well.

"Yes, I see it. Err — where would be Growley's Wood Yard?" He carried the folio of charts over, and Winston glanced away from the river to stab a stubby forefinger upon the page. "Oh yes, I see it." The name had been penned in flowing script above a blackened square on the north bank of the river. Above it, the span of his thumbnail, McKay found the name *Marthasville*. His eyes followed the line of the river. To the east was Matson, to the west he found the name *Hermann*, and between them the shape of the river took on the likeness of another illustration he had discovered only a few minutes earlier — scratched into the top of an oaken barrel.

There had been a mark in that scratched diagram — a prominent indentation made by the sharp point of a big knife — and it had been made to the east of what might have been the town of Hermann. Right

about —. McKay put his finger down and held the chart to the faint moonlight to read the name that lay beneath it:
Catfish Landing.

Chapter Fourteen

Deke Saunders was sitting alone at a table in the main cabin when McKay spied him and made straight for him, his walking stick tapping the polished parquet tile floor with the preciseness of a metronome.

"Good evening, Reverend Saunders."

Saunders glanced up, in his greasy fingers a chicken leg that he had nearly stripped down to the bone. His wary eyes narrowed. "Do I know you?"

"We have not been introduced. My name is Dexter McKay. Err . . . may I join you?"

Suspicion sprang to Saunders's eyes, but the old man kept it from his voice and said casually, "Have a seat, if you want." He continued to gnaw at the bone until it had been picked bare, dropped it on the china plate, and wiped his fingers upon his jacket. The white napkin with the cachet of the *Tempest Queen* embroidered in its corner remained at the side of his plate, untouched, folded as neatly as when the waiter had placed it there.

Saunders belched, dragged the back of his hand across his lips, and took a drink of water. "I ain't et all day, McKay. Can't afford but one meal a day at these fancy prices."

"Ah, but isn't that the perennial scourge of your calling, Reverend Saunders?"

"Huh?"

"The clergy, I mean. Men of the cloth never seem to have an abundance of money, do they? I suppose all of your income goes right back into your church, does it not?"

"Oh. Yeah, sure it does — what little there might be of it." Saunders explored the canyons of his gapped teeth with a dirty thumbnail. "What can I do for you, McKay?"

The gambler placed his tall, beaver hat upon the table, set his walking stick aside, and leaned forward with a sudden earnestness beaming in his face. "My good Reverend. It is not what you can do for me, but more a question of what I can do for you."

The suspicion in Saunders's eyes emigrated, and curiosity migrated to take its place. "I reckon I don't get what you are talking about, McKay."

"Allow me to explain. I have come into

an inheritance recently. My dear brother, Edmund, rest his soul, passed away quite unexpectedly last year. He was five years younger than myself, and you can not imagine the shock one experiences when a thing like this happens. I suddenly saw all too clearly my own mortality. I mean, if dear Edmund could leave this world so abruptly, well, then so could I, or even you, Reverend Saunders." McKay paused.

Saunders did not reply, but his eyes had narrowed and had fixed upon McKay.

"Well," he continued when he saw that Saunders was not about to comment, "Edmund had been quite successful in business. He owned an export company, you see, with a fleet of fine sailing ships that made regular trips across the Atlantic to deliver cotton, tobacco, and other trade goods to England and Europe. Now, I am ashamed to admit it, but I am not a business man, Reverend Saunders. When Edmund died, and I discovered to my chagrin that his business had come into my hands, I had not the foggiest notion as to how to manage such an empire . . . well, you might see how that, too, caused me to step back and examine my life as well." McKay paused, and this time he waited until Saunders felt compelled to put in a word or two.

"So, how does all of what you're saying affect me, McKay? What is it you want? I'm not a priest who can hear your confessions of the sins of a wasted life."

There was impatience in the old man's voice, and McKay grinned inwardly. He would not care to be a member of this man's flock. "Ah, but that is just the point!" McKay said, pouncing on Saunders's last words. "I *have* lived a wasted life! Now that I have sold off all of dear Edmund's assets, and I have his wealth safely banked and invested — enough to keep me secure for the rest of my days — my paltry life had taken on even less meaning! At least before, I had managed to eke out a living with my own hands — meager as it may have been. But in the days since Edmund's death, I have not lifted a finger to earn my own keep. At first I thought it would be a most enjoyable life." McKay managed to redden, and he averted his eyes, thinking that he might be missing his calling in life and that the stage was where he belonged. "I fear I have sampled many of the forbidden fruits of this world, Reverend Saunders." His eyes, suddenly burning with zeal, came back to Saunders's confused face. "But now I have seen the evil of the flesh, and the spoiled fruits of a wasted life. Without something meaningful to devote one's life to, it becomes stale and moldy, like old bread. Useless! Do you see my point?"

Saunders scratched his chin where the scraggly beginnings of a gray beard shaded the wrinkled skin. "I reckon I don't. Get to the point."

"I am ashamed to admit it, but these last months I have taken to playing cards heavily, and, sir, I am not very good at that. I have lost thousands of dollars at old sledge — not to mention faro, hazard, and the dice — since taking passage upon the *Tempest Queen*, which I now call my home. I fear that unless I change my life, I will gamble away the fortune that my brother had worked all his life to build — and perhaps damn my soul to perdition in the doing."

Saunders drummed his fingers. "Get to the point, McKay," he said, this time with insistence.

Ah, the compassion of the cloth!

"Err — well, the point is this. I have come to a crucial decision, Reverend. A crossroads, you might say."

"Go on," Saunders prodded when McKay fell silent for a long while.

The moment called for a dramatic pause, and McKay worked it for all its worth. He cleared his throat, stammered, grimaced, then glanced away from the older man's slitted stare as if embarrassed by what he was about to reveal. "I have decided to spend the rest of my days, and the remaining wealth left to me, helping other people, my dear Reverend Saunders. And I intend to begin tonight, with you."

Saunders's fingers stopped drumming, and for the length of several long heartbeats the old man said nothing. His hooded eyes appeared to have closed completely for a moment, and then as if McKay's words had finally become clear to his brain, Saunders's eyelids sprang apart and he bolted straight in the chair. "You're gonna do what with your money?"

"I am going to give it away, Reverend Saunders," McKay said gently and smiled. The words sounded noble and righteous, and McKay had really enjoyed saying them — even though the whole story was a lie black as tar. But that could not be helped. He had to learn the truth about Saunders, and he had to learn it soon. If his guess was right, he did not have much time left to him.

Desperate times require desperate means!

"I want to give you the first portion of it — err — for your church, you understand."

"To me — ? Ah, well . . . err . . . that's dam—, ah, darn right generous of you, McKay — err — how much are we talking about — huh?"

"Oh, I haven't decided that yet." He waved away the question as if the amount to be given were of trifle importance. "How much do you need, Reverend? Say, perhaps ten thousand? Huh? I will prepare a draft on my account at the Bank of St. Charles before we arrive at Fort Leavenworth."

"Need? I need . . . I need . . . I —"

"Well, I need a drink," McKay broke in, lifting an arm. He was immediately surrounded by three waiters. "A whiskey, please."

"The usual, sir?" one of the men asked.

"Yes, that fine Glenlivet that I have become so fond of? And you, Reverend? Do you occasionally indulge in spirits?" McKay chuckled. "I mean of the consumable sort, not the heavenly."

Saunders had regained his composure, and he said without stumbling over his tongue, "Certainly, I will have a drink with you. Whatever it is you ordered."

"Glenlivet for the Reverend as well."

The waiters left, and McKay said, "You will like it." A black cloud fleetingly enveloped McKay as he thought of his friend, Clifton Stewart, who had introduced him to the fine imported Scotch that had become such a passion for him in the short four months since he had adopted the *Tempest Queen* as his home. The death of Stewart had been most unexpected and shocking, and suddenly a pang of sadness was in McKay's voice. "It had been a favorite brand of a friend of mine," he said with the first shred of legitimate emotion since arriving at Saunders's table.

The drinks arrived almost immediately, but before McKay and Saunders could continue with their talk, Grady came into the main cabin by way of a side door. He stopped, glanced around as if confused, located his father, and came over, looking more disheveled, if that were possible, than the last time McKay had seen him.

"Got to talk to you, Pa," he said, stealing a sideways glance at the gambler.

"I'm busy, can't you see that, boy?" Deke Saunders shot back with explosive rage. Then he caught himself and smiled benignly at McKay.

"It can't wait, Pa."

Deke Saunders got control of his temper

and apologized for the interruption. "I reckon I need to hear what is on my boy's mind." He pushed back from the table, but McKay rose first, donning his hat and snatching up his walking stick.

Now that he had dangled the bait in front of Saunders's nose, it was time to depart and give him time to sniff at it awhile. "No, no, you remain here and finish your whiskey, Reverend Saunders. I shall be on my way. Perhaps we can talk later, hum?" McKay removed his gold Jürgensen from his vest pocket and glanced at it. "My, my, how the time passes." He shoved the watch back into his pocket. "I have a game to attend in a few minutes, so, if you will excuse me, I will bid you *adieu.*" He bowed slightly at the waist, and taking the still untouched glass of Scotch with him, he made his way across the main cabin to the door of his stateroom.

Deke Saunders impaled his son with a look that made the young man retreat a step to beyond the old man's reach. "You little fool. That man, McKay, he was pouring out his miserable heart to me and tellin' how he was gonna hand over ten thousand dollars to me! What could be more important than that?" Saunders was careful not to let his voice carry, but just the same he spat his words at Grady as if they had been poison darts.

"Well . . . well, how was I to know that, Pa?"

"The point is, you just don't go interrupting when I'm talkin' business."

"It only looked to me like you two was passing the time." He hesitated, suddenly confused. "Anyway, what for was that man gonna give you ten thousand dollars, Pa?"

"For my church."

Grady considered the old man a moment, then a glint came to his eyes, and not able to hold back a chuckle, he said, "For your *church!*"

Deke let his anger pass as well, a sly grin reshaping his twisted lips. "Yeah, don't that beat Cain. I reckon I do a respectable job of passing myself off as a preacher after all. Who knows, maybe I ought to start holding services again, givin' sermons, and passin' the plate. Except that after tomorrow we won't never be wanting for money again."

Grady's amusement vanished, his face turning serious again. "Pa, that's what I got to tell you. I had me a run-in with that high-struttin' army lieutenant just before I come in."

"You did what?" Deke came half out of his chair, caught himself, and lowered his voice to a snakelike hiss. "What the hell kind of business did you have to do with the lieutenant, anyway?"

"It — it was because of that girl," Grady whined. "Dempsey went and butted his nose in just when I was about to coax her into some dark corner of the boat."

"Damnation, boy! Your itch for gettin' into them skirts is gonna be the ruin of you . . . and me, too. Now, you tell me all that happened and don't leave anything out. Did he learn what we are about?"

"No, he don't know anything like that, Pa. Only now he's gonna have his eye on me 'cause —" Grady's voice cracked, and he did not finish.

"Because of what, boy?"

Grady dragged the toe of his boots across the polished tile floor, suddenly unable to look his father in the eye. "Because I told him I was a gonna kill him, that's why, Pa," he said reluctantly.

"You did what?"

"Well, I didn't really mean it," Grady came back defensively. "I was mad, that's all. I shouldn't have said anything, but I did. So, I figured you ought to know about it."

Deke Saunders settled back in his chair, drumming his fingers again: a rapid, impatient staccato of nail against wood that grew faster and faster as he thought this over. Finally Deke slammed his fist upon the table, rattling the glass. His knuckles whitened, and afterward he straightened up in his chair and slowly allowed his fingers to unfold.

"All right. What damage is done, is done. You were right in telling me. Now, you're sure that Dempsey don't know nothing about our plans?"

"How could he. We had words because of that girl, and then he hit me. I didn't say nothin' about taking his gold."

"Hush! Keep your voice down, boy!"

Grady glanced around, but none of the tables nearby were occupied.

"He hit you, you say?"

"That's right."

"You hit him back?"

Grady glanced at his boots again and shook his head. "It ain't like I didn't try, Pa."

Deke huffed. "A fine figure of a man you turned out to be. You make out like a struttin' bull in front of the ladies but can't even hold your own again' another man. All right, it's done and there ain't nothing we can do to change it now, but you listen here, Grady. Steer clear of that man, Dempsey, and keep your hands off that gal as well. We got too much riding on this here heist for you to go ruining it just because of the fire that burns in your loins."

Grady stiffened, eyes sparking like flint. "That ain't no way to talk to me, Pa."

"I'll talk to you any way I please —" He paused. Grady's fists had clenched at his sides. "I can see what you're thinking now, boy. I ought to warn you right off, the day you can whip me will be the day after they plant me, so don't even ponder it. Now, get out of here and make yourself scarce."

At that moment Lieutenant Dempsey and Cora Mills entered the main cabin by the same side door Grady had come through a few minutes before. Deke and Grady watched them take a table near the raised platform in the ladies' salon where four men in black coats were sawing at fiddles of various sizes and shapes.

"You better get out of here, Grady. I don't want you to provoke that man any more than you already have — at least not right yet."

Grady shot a glance at his father. It was plain that Grady had more to say about this matter, but he held his tongue and, wheeling about, marched to the front doors and out into the night.

Afterward, Deke Saunders sat brooding into the glass of whiskey McKay had bought for him. Across the room he easily heard Dempsey's deep voice and Cora Mills's light laugh drifting over the music coming from that end of the boat. Saunders could not hear the words that they spoke, but it was clear that the lieutenant was in no way alarmed and that whatever had passed between Dempsey and his boy had not alerted him to the conspiracy about to be placed into motion, right under the moonstruck lieutenant's nose.

More at ease now, Saunders sampled the whiskey for the first time. It was not to his liking. It lacked the bitter bite of the fare he was used to drinking. In fact, he decided, it was downright docile compared with the home brew common along the river. He downed it all in one large swallow, and his thoughts shifted from Grady's blunder and the crime afoot back to the matter of the ten thousand dollars that McKay wanted to hand over to him.

The fool!

Saunders grinned, self-satisfied, but then a disturbing problem suddenly reared its head and made him uneasy. How was he going to get McKay to write that draft before they sprang their trap and took the boat? This was going to take some thought. Deke Saunders wasn't about to let an opportunity like this slip away.

Perhaps an actor's life had been his true calling, but for now games of chance of all sorts were McKay's bread and butter, and he was most assuredly born to play monte. His hands and fingers moved the cards like lightning, with the precision of a fine timepiece. He could switch them in the very presence of a dozen witnesses, and never would one of the spectators detect the move being made — then, as if by magic, the left-hand card, which everyone knew was a queen, when turned over by the man on the other side of the table, would somehow have become the two, and mysteriously the queen would have moved to the middle — or to whatever other position that McKay deemed desirable.

And he had the banter down to perfection as well, never failing to draw crowds around his table, eager men willing to lay down their money. . . . Well, there had been one incident in Vicksburg, a few months back, when the crowds had been particularly difficult to attract, but that event turned out to have a perfectly logical explanation in the end, McKay recalled as he grinned into the mirror in his stateroom and shuffled the cards across the tabletop with such near-meteoric speed that even his own eyes failed to detect the switch.

He watched his reflection turn over the baby card on the right-hand side when in fact that particular card should have showed up in the middle.

The switch had been executed perfectly!

A man must truly love his work to be any good at it was his fervent belief, and McKay did love monte, willingly spending hours in front of a mirror, honing a skill that was already razor sharp.

He gathered in the cards, sipped the Glenlivet that remained in the bottom of his glass, and was about to lay them out again when a knock sounded at his stateroom door. Captain Hamilton in his blue box-cut coat with the gold braid on the sleeves was standing there when he pulled it open.

"Time for our lessons already?"

"I'm not interrupting you, am I?"

"Of course not. I was only limbering my fingers."

Hamilton gave a brief laugh. "As if they needed limbering."

McKay only smiled as he grabbed up the walking stick with the silver horse-head grip. He took a deck of Steamboat #220 playing cards from his dressing table, and he followed the captain out into the main cabin.

Most of the tables scattered about were unoccupied, and the captain had his pick of them, but McKay requested a particular chair, which faced out so that he could keep an eye on the passengers in the main cabin. Settling comfortably in it, he glanced past the captain at the man in the black frock coat sitting across the way, then back at Hamilton.

"Well, what will it be this evening?"

Hamilton stroked his carefully barbered gray beard and considered this as the light from the chandeliers overhead reflected off his bright, blue eyes. Hamilton was somewhat over sixty years old, McKay knew, but precisely how many years over had never been discussed. Four or five, he guessed, for more and more frequently the good captain had spoken of his soon retirement when he planned to sell the *Tempest Queen* and use the proceeds to build a house on a tract of land that he owned in Baton Rouge, on a hill above the Mississippi River.

Hamilton talked often about spending his later years on the front porch of that house, watching the steamboats ply the mighty river below, and perhaps even writing a book about his life on the river. His other dream was to travel: to California, to Europe, and to France, in particular, where he and his beloved Cynthia had been wed. Tragically, Cynthia and his two children had perished years ago when the Mississippi, in one of her rages, had crevassed their levies and destroyed the plantation house that her father had given them. Hamilton kept that part of his life locked safely away, but over the course of time McKay had come to know some of the sad story from the man's very lips.

"Let's keep working at poker. Poker seems to be the game becoming most popular these days."

"Very well." McKay ruffled the cards and shuffled them together with a flourish. It was music to his ears that far surpassed what the quartet in the corner was currently playing, which at the moment happened to be a lively tune from the pen of Stephen Foster, who had become wildly popular in the last dozen years or so.

McKay flung the cards out, and Hamilton collected his pile and began to methodically sort them.

Dexter McKay watched a moment, frowning, then cleared his throat.

The old captain glanced up. Hamilton was a man with only one vice. He did not smoke, drink, or chew, and McKay had never heard the man cuss, but cards . . . now there was Hamilton's Waterloo, and the irony of it was that Hamilton was so pathetically deficient at the game that even the most unskilled gambler could clean the good captain's pockets without breaking a sweat. As a friend, McKay had taken upon himself the formidable task of molding Hamilton into a competent cardplayer.

"What did I do this time?" There was a smidgen of irritation in Hamilton's voice.

McKay said patiently, "I believe I have already explained this to you, Captain."

"Oh, probably you have. At least three or four times I should imagine, Mr. McKay. But perhaps if you would repeat it once more?" Now embarrassment joined the vexation, but McKay knew that Captain Hamilton had an earnest desire to better his game, and he was, after all, a friend.

"Very well. Now listen carefully. In draw poker, an opponent of skill, such as myself, will immediately spot and learn your sorting habits, and will deduce what kind of hand you have been dealt. Take your cards, for example. You immediately put two of them together to the right. Those were the pair of jacks I dealt, were they not?"

Hamilton scowled. "How in blazes can I ever win at this game when you know every card that comes off the deck?"

"I do it for the moment only so that I might properly instruct you."

"Yes, yes, so you have said. Of course, you are correct, Mr. McKay. They were the two jacks."

"See what I mean? Now listen and try to learn this next point — it will call for you improving your memory, and I have already given you instruction in how to do that. When you play stud poker, look at the cards only as they are dealt to you, and never — I repeat — never look at them again."

"Yes, I remember now. Looking at them throughout the game gives a skilled opponent — such as yourself — precious information about my hand."

"Exactly. Let's pretend, for example, that you are playing Seven-Toed Pete. You have the ten of hearts showing, and a pair of kings turned down. Your next card up is the queen of hearts. If you check to see if one of your kings is a heart, you will tip your opponent off that your down cards are probably a pair. You will also reveal that that pair is not in queens, and that right now you are wondering if you can make a flush. Hum?" McKay hitched up an eyebrow.

Captain Hamilton shook his head, mildly bewildered, and said, "I shall never master this game."

"Of course you will, Captain. All it takes is time." That wasn't completely true, but there was no point in discouraging the captain's efforts.

"No, sir, not time, but a brain that revels in mathematical conundrums."

McKay laughed, and the game continued. After a few more plays, he noted that Reverend Deke Saunders had stood and was coming across the room. "Err, Captain Hamilton, I suspect we are about to have a guest at our table."

Hamilton looked over his shoulder, then back. "The preacher?"

"Yes. Err, I would appreciate it if you turn a deaf ear and a blind eye to what I might say or do?"

Hamilton frowned. "Here now, what have you in mind for that man, McKay?"

Saunders had almost arrived. "I don't have time to tell you just now, Captain, but

I will explain it all later." McKay glanced up and smiled. "Why, Reverend Saunders. You have solved your son's problem so quickly?"

Saunders's face remained stern, and McKay had the impression there wasn't a lighthearted bone in the man.

"It weren't nothing important. I reckon the boy never learnt his manners proper. You know, his ma died when he was only a tyke."

"Well, I am confident you are just the man to straighten the boy around — err, would you care to join us?"

"Don't mind if I do." Deke sat in one of the chairs. "Gambling away some more of your wealth again, are you, McKay?"

"The captain and I are only having a friendly game of poker. Low bets. Deal you in?"

"Sure, why not."

Hamilton's scowl had deepened, but to McKay's relief he held his tongue and said nothing that might go crosswise with what he had said — at least not yet. . . .

Chapter Fifteen

Laban Caulder climbed up on the seat of his heavy wagon, and taking up the reins, he toed off the brake. The wagon was painted bright yellow and, like the pair of matched horses that pulled it, revealed the pride Laban took in his stock and equipment.

Bitsy handed up a basket of food for the trip. "Now you be careful, Laban," she said, and from the uneasiness that Jesse heard in her voice, he wondered if she did not know more about the job ahead than she was letting on. In the darkness he could not see if the expression on her face matched the concern in her voice. Where they stood, on the porch, there was mighty little light coming through the window-panes, and even less reaching the yard where Laban was preparing to leave.

"I will be fine, Bitsy," he said with a laugh that sounded easy and friendly. But Jesse could never forget the sinister threat he had heard Laban level at Frank through the barn wall only fifteen minutes before.

Nearby, Harvey stood with his thumbs hooked under his suspenders, wearing a concerned scowl that had Jesse worried. He had never seen Harvey so sulky before.

Laban waved an arm at them. "See you folks tomorrow night." He flicked the reins, and the two draft horses pulled the wagon out of the yard. For a while, as the freighter swung away from the house toward the road, all Jesse could see was the rumpled pile of canvas in its bed. His eyes fixed upon it, and an uneasiness turned within him as he watched the blackness of the night close about the wagon.

He listened to the squeak and clank and rattle of the wagon rolling away, growing faint in the night until finally even that, too, was gone. His mother and Reuben went back into the house with Bitsy. Harvey made his way, brooding, out into the deep shadows toward his room against the back wall of the barn. Jesse remained, alone, staring out into the night until the creak of wood behind him made him look over.

It was only Ben lowering himself into a chair.

Jesse frowned, moved away from the edge of the porch, and sat in another chair next to him.

"Something bothering you, Jesse?" Clifton asked after a while.

The younger James brother glanced over. "No, Ben. I'm just thinking."

"About what?"

Jesse was about to speak his mind, but caught himself and said instead, "Oh, just about things, that's all."

Clifton Stewart rocked his chair back on its hind legs and considered him, but he didn't pursue it further, and Jesse was thankful for that. This man whom they decided to call Ben until his memory finally returned had become a comfortable companion to Jesse in the short two days since they had fished him from the Mississippi River. It didn't seem to matter to Ben that Jesse was only thirteen years old. Jesse half considered telling Ben what now pressed so heavily upon him, but even though he had proved himself a trusted confidant by covering them back on the ferry boat, Jesse didn't feel he could yet entrust everything to him.

"Your memory starting to come back, Ben?"

Stewart rocked forward and stretched his legs out across the porch. "Sometimes I think it might be. I get pictures inside my head that I am almost able to hold onto —

but not quite. I see faces all the time, and I think that if I ever once put a name to even one, it would all flood back to me."

Jesse thought about what he wanted to say next and was careful how he put it into words. "What would you do if when you remembered who you really are, it turns out you are a highwayman, or a pirate?"

Clifton laughed, but there was no ridicule in it, not as Frank sometimes did. "You do have a fanciful imagination, Jesse, and a definite interest in such things. To tell you the truth, I don't know what I would do if that turned out to be the case. But I don't think it will be. I will probably discover that I am quite normal and living a very ordinary life."

"But Uncle Laban and Reuben says you know racehorses real well. That's not exactly ordinary."

Clifton nodded his head. "Perhaps I'm a jockey?"

Jesse gave him a critical look. "You're lean enough, but aren't you too tall?"

"Hum. You might be right, Jesse."

"But maybe you own racehorses, like Uncle Laban?" Jesse said, his young face brightening.

"But that would mean I'd be a wealthy man." Clifton looked down at his grimy clothes and calloused hands. "I hardly fit the picture of a man of affluence."

"Uncle Laban ain't a rich man, leastwise not that I know of."

"That's right," Clifton said, and suddenly he was staring at the corner of the porch. Beyond it stretched the rails of Laban's corral, now streaked with pale moonlight, where Firecracker was kept.

Jesse's brain was clicking over. "Maybe you used to be rich, but you lost all your land and money in a big horse race, and now you are working as a deckhand on a steamboat, and planning to win it all back someday?"

"A steamboat? What makes you say that?"

"Reuben said your clothes were full of soot, and there aren't a whole lot of railroads this side of the Mississippi yet, so it must be steamboats."

It seemed to Jesse that Ben was distracted by a thought, but if that was so, he had dismissed it almost at once. "Huh? Oh, well, it could be that I live on the other side of the Mississippi, you know."

"Oh, yeah, guess I didn't figure it that way." Jesse leaned back in his chair to give the mystery some more thought.

"But I do like the part about me being

wealthy," Clifton said.

Jesse grinned.

Clifton stood suddenly. "Jesse, why don't you and I go down and take a look at that expensive racehorse of Laban's?"

"In the dark?"

"There is part of a moon in the sky. It might help jog my memory."

"Well, all right, if you think it might help." They went down the steps and out across the yard. At the corral they leaned upon the moon-blanched rails. From the shadows at the far side, Firecracker snorted and lifted his head with his ears cranked toward them. The horse came forward two steps and stopped.

"He is a fine-looking animal. His good breeding shows," Clifton Stewart said, and then he gave a short laugh and looked at Jesse. "And don't ask me how I know that. It's more like an instinct, and not something I can put into words." He paused thoughtfully. "But you know, Jes, I feel it's getting closer. As if my life and my past are waiting for me right around a corner, and I am about to step around it and remember everything."

The racehorse lowered its head as if dismissing them as not needful of his concern.

The sound of a door opening came from behind the barn, and a shaft of light stabbed out into the night, spearing the trees that grew near the back of the building. The light was almost immediately cut off when the door slammed shut, and then Harvey appeared around the corner, emerging from the shadows. He spied them standing there and came over.

"What are you two doing?"

"Looking at Firecracker," Jesse said.

"Oh." Harvey Caulder seemed to have a lot on his mind, and Jesse was pretty sure he knew what it was, as the lanky boy propped his boot on the bottom rail. For a long while no one spoke, and the sounds of crickets in the dark only added weight to Jesse's spirit.

"Jesse . . . Frank," Zerelda called from the porch. "Where are you boys?"

"Harvey," Bitsy shouted next, her weak voice like the screech of an owl.

The two women stepped out and peered out into the night.

"We are over here," Clifton said. At the sound of his voice both women came about. "We best get back to the house," he said to the boys.

"I reckon so," Jesse said reluctantly, and he shot a glance at Harvey, who wasn't smiling either.

Zerelda and Bitsy waited as they came across the yard. Once on the porch, Zerelda took a quick head count and asked, "Where is Frank? Have either of you three seen Frank?"

The two boys grew particularly quiet. Reuben came out the door and said, "Well, I see you have found them, Zerelda."

"All but Frank. Now, where could that boy have gotten off to?"

Reuben cupped his hands to his mouth and called out into the night, and when he received no reply, he shouted again.

Clifton said, "I saw the three of them making for the barn just as it was getting dark."

"Is that so, Harvey?" Bitsy asked her son.

"Yes, we went to the barn. Talked to Pa awhile. Afterwards Frank wandered off by himself."

Reuben said, "Well, that's like Frank. He's a loner, that one. If it were daylight, I'd say he was off reading one of his books."

"But it isn't daylight, Reuben," Zerelda said. "It's dark and I'm getting worried."

Reuben called again, but only the soft sounds of the night came back at him.

Bitsy said, "Someone should go and look

for him. It's not safe to be out in the woods or down by the river at night."

Zerelda turned to her husband. "Oh, Reuben, will you go?"

"I suppose I better."

Jesse had kept stone silent, and he had begun to inch his way toward the door of the house.

"Where are you going?" Zerelda said sharply, and Jesse instantly recognized the suspicion in his mother's tone.

"I . . . I was only going inside, Ma."

Reuben must have surmised from the timidity in Jesse's voice that something was wrong. "What's going on here, Jesse? What are you keeping back from us, and where is your brother?"

"I . . . I don't know."

"I can always tell when you lie to me, Jesse," Zerelda said. "I want the truth."

"Tell your mother the truth," Reuben said.

Bitsy was staring at her son. "You know something about it, too. Now, out with it."

Jesse and Harvey glanced at each other.

"Jesse," Reuben said again, sterner this time. "Tell us where Frank is."

"Is he all right?" Zerelda demanded.

"Frank is all right," Jesse said finally.

"Then where is he?"

"He . . . he . . ."

"Out with it, Jesse," Reuben said.

Jesse swallowed hard. It felt like sand in his throat. "He went with Uncle Laban."

"No, he didn't," Zerelda said. "We saw Laban off and Frank was not on the wagon. Besides, Laban would never take him along without asking me first! You're telling us a story again, aren't you?"

"No, it's the truth. Uncle Laban doesn't know anything about it. Frank hid under that pile of canvas in the back of his wagon."

Bitsy staggered back a step and said, "No!"

"He did, Aunt Bitsy. I swear."

"What is wrong?" Reuben said, seeing her face suddenly pale in the lamplight.

"Nothing," Bitsy said, recovering swiftly. "It is just that Laban will have so much work on his hands. I don't want Frank to be in the way."

"Frank won't get in the way," Jesse said in his brother's defense.

"Oh, dear," Zerelda moaned, but she was plainly relieved to at least know where Frank was. "Why would that boy do such a thing, and not tell us?"

"I think he was looking for an adventure," Harvey offered weakly.

"That's right. He thought it would be exciting. Sort of like stowing away on a ship," Jesse said.

Reuben considered them both narrowly. "There is more here than meets the eye," he said, but didn't press Jesse further.

"That boy is in for a licking when he gets back," Zerelda said. Her worry had suddenly turned to anger. Jesse did not envy Frank when he returned, even if he did have a splendid adventure pirating a riverboat.

Bitsy suddenly dragged Harvey into the house by his ear. The next minute Jesse's arm was snagged in his mother's tight-fingered grip, and before he could escape, he, too, was tripping along beside her, catching his feet among her skirts, and into the small house.

Jesse was far too close to this bubbling volcano for his liking. He had the sinking feeling that when the explosion finally did come, it was not only going to rain down mightily upon Frank's head, but he was not going to escape his share of Mount Zerelda's wrath either.

Somehow, Reverend Deke Saunders had managed to scrape up a handful of coins from his pockets for the poker game, and

Dexter McKay had allowed it to grow — at Captain Hamilton's expense. Then McKay began raising the stakes each hand. It had started so gradually that neither Hamilton nor Saunders noticed the pile in the middle of the table getting larger and larger.

Always, McKay allowed Saunders to win just a bit more than he would lose, and after an hour of this, Hamilton was beginning to let his frustration show.

"Drat it, McKay. You can at least allow me to win one of these hands," he said in exasperation, flinging his cards onto the table.

"You're talking to the wrong fellow," Saunders said, gleefully pulling the pile across the table and stacking the coins among his sizable winnings. "I reckon it is me what's out to teach you sorry devils how to win at poker." In the hour or so that had passed, Saunders had grown less reverend-like and more earthy.

McKay said pleasantly, "Well, this should help your church, Reverend."

Saunders glanced up quickly and re-arranged his carnivorous expression into something more solemn. "Yes, indeed, it will be a welcome blessing to my poor flock."

"The Lord works in mysterious ways," Hamilton grumbled, eyeing McKay and reaching for his cup.

"Yes, he does do that," Saunders agreed. "Why, I cannot believe my — my church's — good fortune at running into McKay."

"How's that?" Hamilton gruffed and sipped the coffee from its fine china cup with the gilded rim.

"Haven't you heard? He is giving me a sizable contribution. His brother up and died, and left him a shipping empire."

"A what?"

McKay shot the captain a glance, and Hamilton managed to turn his chuckle into a cough, which he muffled in his fist.

"Surely you remember me telling you about dear Edmund, do you not, Captain?"

"Humm. Oh, yes. Edmund. Your brother the . . . shipper? Now I remember. California, wasn't it?"

At once Saunders had a wary look in his eyes. "I thought you said he —"

McKay laughed and took a long pull at his cigar to give himself a moment to think, blowing a ring of smoke at the ceiling. "Captain Hamilton, I can see how you could have made that mistake. In actual fact, you are correct. Edmund did have some business dealings in California. However, his business was out of — err — Belhaven, North Carolina. But I know how you might have become confused, for I believe I mentioned that Edmund maintained a small branch office in San Francisco, from which he hired an agent who conducted some very limited trade with China."

Hamilton scowled and set his coffee cup down. "Oh, yes. I must have been confused," and McKay saw the fire that smoldered behind the captain's blue eyes.

Saunders was smiling again in his customary tight-lipped fashion, as if any real, heartfelt laugh might break that gaunt face into a thousand brittle pieces.

"Well, how about another hand, gentlemen?" McKay suggested, wishing to put the subject behind them.

Hamilton had had enough of the charade. McKay knew that the good captain did not approve of his escapades anyway, so he was not surprised when Hamilton stood and shoved his remaining few coins back into his pocket. "No, not tonight. I need to check up on the pilot." He looked at his watch. "They have taken their rotation by now, and I should make certain the new man at the helm knows we are to put in at Growley's Wood Yard." His bright blue eyes narrowed at McKay. "I should very much like to speak with you when you get a free moment."

McKay nodded his head. That bit about the pilots had only been an excuse to be away from there, for McKay knew that Hamilton never interfered with his pilots, even at rotation time, and never once had an appointed landing been missed. "Of course, Captain Hamilton. At your convenience."

"Humm." Hamilton strode away.

Saunders was glaring hungrily at the pile of coins at McKay's elbow.

"Err, another round, Reverend?"

"Of course. My church is in bad need of improvements, McKay."

The gambler laughed. "I trust you will not take advantage of me."

"Never," Saunders said, gathering up the deck of cards and shuffling them. "You are a gentleman, and your generosity is admirable."

"Why, I am flattered." McKay beamed, and counted his winnings in front of Saunders, a thing he never did when the play was serious, just as he never drank whiskey when facing a worthy opponent. He raised his hand for a waiter and ordered two more drinks while Saunders dealt the cards into two piles.

"You've been very successful tonight, Reverend. What do you say we raise the stakes?"

"If you think you can afford to lose more than you already have — oh, I guess I forgot, you have your brother's fortune to back you up."

"Yes, indeed, a fortune which you shall soon be sharing, Reverend Saunders." For a moment McKay thought he was going to see a genuine smile emerge to test the durability of Saunders's face.

"I suppose we ought to be talking about that," Saunders said, and the faint hopes of a smile vanished into the folds of his hard face.

"What's left to discuss, unless the sum is not satisfactory to you? I will write you a draft upon landing at Fort Leavenworth." McKay collected his cards and frowned deeply. "Dear me," he moaned softly to himself, yet loud enough that Saunders was sure to hear.

"The amount is satisfactory," Saunders said, but McKay heard a note of doubt in the preacher's voice, and he wondered if the cagey old clergyman was going to try to talk him into upping the amount.

Their drinks arrived, and the play went around, and when the dust had settled, McKay's stack of coins had grown by two inches.

Saunders was not put off by this little loss. He hardly seemed to have noticed it. He was clearly pondering another problem. This time he tried a more direct tack. "I'm afraid I have to be getting off the boat before Fort Leavenworth."

McKay pretended to concentrate on his shuffle in which he managed to drop a card anyway, and did not answer Saunders immediately.

"In fact, I will probably be disembarking as soon as tomorrow."

"There that should be sufficient," McKay said, finishing the clumsy shuffle and setting the cards down for Saunders to cut. When he had reassembled the halves of the deck, he glanced up. "What was that you were saying, Reverend?"

"I said, I'm gonna be getting off this boat before Fort Leavenworth. In fact, probably by tomorrow afternoon."

McKay tossed the cards into piles and picked up his. "Oh, I'm sorry to hear that, Reverend. I am enjoying your company so."

"I'm tickled, McKay." Saunders's growing exasperation was plain as he collected his cards.

An hour later Deke Saunders was cleaned out, and McKay felt not the slightest remorse as he gathered up his winnings and funneled them into the pockets of his gray sack coat. This man was no more a preacher than he was the heir to a shipping fortune! McKay was certain of that now. But who and what Saunders really was as yet remained unclear to him.

Deke Saunders stared for a moment at the empty spot in front of him where an hour before over a hundred dollars had accumulated.

"Well, well. It looks like my luck certainly has taken a turn for the better," McKay laughed and set his hat upon his head. "We will talk later, Reverend. There is still that matter of ten thousand dollars for your church. Good evening."

He hadn't taken two steps when Saunders growled, "Wait a minute, McKay!"

He looked back. "Sir?"

"You can't just up and walk out now. Not with every penny to my name in your pocket!"

McKay smiled innocently. "What would you have me to do? It is apparent that you have no means to win it back. As you say, I have won all the money that you have. I must admit, I am a little embarrassed at the fickleness of lady luck. But be of good cheer, Reverend Saunders. Soon I will prepare a draft for ten thousand dollars, and tonight's loss of a paltry one hundred dollars will be insignificant."

"Then write the draft now. Tonight!"

"There is more than that involved, as you well know. I must also compose a letter to my bank, to accompany the draft, or surely they would never release such a large sum. You understand, I'm sure."

"In the meantime I'm broke!"

"I see your dilemma." McKay pursed his lips and grasped the tip of his imperial beard between a finger and thumb, thinking. "Should I just return your money to you — hum?" But before Saunders could answer, he said, "No, of course not. A proud man such as yourself would surely refuse such an affront."

"Dammit, man, at least give me a chance to win it back!"

McKay was undaunted by Saunders's sudden profanity. Indeed, he had come to expect no less from the pretender. "I would of course be happy to give you every opportunity to win it back. Err, do you wish me to lend you the capital for your wager?"

"No, no. Sit back down, McKay. I got me something to wager if you will agree to take it."

"Oh?" Curious now, McKay returned to his chair while Saunders fished around inside his pocket. His hand came out, and he slammed the item down upon the table.

"There. Now that is worth a bushel of money, and don't say it ain't."

McKay picked it up, holding it to the light. At once he felt a thrill, then a grimness squeezed at his chest like a giant fist, but never for an instant did his expression flinch, nor did he allow the least hint of what he was thinking to show on his rigidly tutored face. A man of his profession was, after all, a master of his emotions at all times.

Indeed, the item was of great value, but not in terms of money — at least not to McKay. Instead, it had suddenly answered one of those questions that had been confounding McKay . . . and although he still did not know who Deke Saunders was, he now had a pretty good idea of *what* he was. . . .

Chapter Sixteen

The *Tempest Queen*'s steam whistle blew for the landing. Three long, melodious notes drifting out across the dark water, echoing among the black wall of trees along the shore. In answer to her call, a light suddenly appeared in the midst of the blackness, and then another, until the outlines of a building became clear. A man came out onto the long pier swinging a lantern in a wide arc in front of him.

The leadsmen jumped to the call of the bell and began singing out the depth of the river to the pilothouse high overhead. The heartbeat of the mighty boat changed, and the song her escape pipes were singing took on a slower, more relaxed beat as she nosed toward the pier. Down below, the sleeping main deck suddenly sprang to life as deckhands and firemen assembled for the task of carrying the fuelwood aboard and stacking it in place. Among them were Lieutenant Dempsey's men who had been roused by the commotion. Some grumbled and moved to higher ground and out of the wood brigade's way. Others hitched their suspenders up over their shoulders and went along with the boatmen to lend a hand.

From the promenade railing outside the main cabin, Lieutenant Dempsey and Cora Mills watched the pier emerge from the darkness. The giant paddle wheels reversed their direction with a sudden tumult of rushing water, and the *Tempest Queen* shuddered to a dead stop in the water. The current took her the rest of the way in until her guards gently nudged the pilings, which were wrapped in rope thick as a man's forearms.

In a moment the riverboat was lashed tight to the pier, and in the reflected light from her scores of lamps, Dempsey could see Captain Hamilton talking to the man who had come out swinging a lantern. He had watched this routine enough times to know that the captain was making arrangements with the woodyard owner to purchase the fuel that would take them another fifty miles upriver where the whole affair would have to be reenacted.

Cora was fascinated with every detail of the voyage, and she never seemed to tire of watching the same play being acted out woodyard after woodyard up the river. This whole trip had been like the opening of a book into a new world that she had only heard about but had never experienced. She drank in each facet of steamboat operations in the way a woman who had spent a week in a burning desert might drink in cool well water.

Dempsey liked that.

Cora Mills was bright, intelligent, and well read, and seemed to possess at least a rudimentary knowledge of every subject they happened to overturn in their whirlwind attempt to get to know one another.

"I know I shall never forget this trip, Lieutenant."

When she looked at him, he had the feeling that her words held hidden meanings.

"Please, call me Sherman. You will probably take many more like it in days to come."

"I hope so . . . Sherman." And again there seemed to be something cryptic in that simple statement. Or was it only wishful thinking on his part?

"Oh, look," Cora said suddenly, pointing. Dempsey was forced to pull his eyes off of her lovely face. "Aren't those some of the same men who came aboard only a few hours ago? I wonder why they are leaving so soon?"

Five men had mounted the landing stage and were trotting down to the pier. Whether among these five were some of the same men who had boarded a while ago, he had no way of telling, but he certainly wasn't about to admit that his powers of observation were any less than hers, and he said, "I believe you are correct, Miss Mills. Perhaps they are only stretching their legs."

"No, look, they are carrying their muskets and baggage with them."

"So they are."

"Most curious." She looked at him, puzzled.

Dempsey laughed. "I see you enjoy a riddle."

Her eyebrows hitched up quizzically. "Do you?"

"Yes, I suppose. Have you a riddle for me?"

But Cora did not join him in his humor. "I suddenly have an odd feeling."

"About those men?"

A faltering smile made its way to her face. "Isn't that ridiculous? I mean, they probably just needed to go this far, and that is all there is to it."

"There, the puzzle is solved." Dempsey

wanted only to peer into her lovely green eyes and not concern himself with the comings and goings of the passengers aboard the *Tempest Queen.* She had a suspicious side to her as well, he noted, and that was not all bad. He figured that it was all part of having a wildly active brain.

Her smile tipped, but she caught herself and straightened it out upon her face. When she looked back at the pier, the five men were gone. "Lieutenant Dempsey . . . I mean, Sherman, have you ever read Dickens?"

"Some."

" 'The Cricket on the Hearth'?"

"No, I don't recall having read that one."

"Oh."

"What is it?" he asked, seeing her once again succumb to some worrisome thought.

"It's — oh, it's nothing. A silly fairy tale, that's all."

"Not so silly if it has you worried."

She smiled at him brightly. "It's nothing, really. Only, have you noticed?"

"Noticed what?"

"The crickets. They have all stopped singing."

McKay had dropped in on the galley to look over the remaining slices of pie on the sideboard. The selection was particularly bountiful this night, and he had settled upon a slice of peach pie with a wonderfully flaky crust and had just completed negotiating for its removal from the sideboard with the kitchen chief, Maggie Divitt, when the *Tempest Queen* made her landing. Now, from the railing of the hurricane deck where the night wind was cool and gentle, he watched the five men make their way down the pier and into the black night that enveloped everything but the splotches of light scattered around the suddenly busy woodyard.

He knew from the charts he had examined, and from Captain Hamilton's instructions to "Little" Sam Winston earlier that evening, that this was Growley's Wood Yard, and that Marthasville was only a little distance north of the river. He knew, also, that both of these isolated spots along the Missouri had been prominently marked on Deke Saunders's crude diagram scratched into the top of the barrel.

McKay took a bite of peach pie, set it back on the plate in his left hand, and licked the sweet filling from his fingers, frowning in spite of the taste of the delicious dessert upon his tongue. What was that crafty old dodger, Saunders, up to?

The five men who had disembarked had been among those attending Saunders's clandestine meeting. McKay recognized one of them — William Quantrill. A gambler of limited abilities in McKay's estimation, and he knew that firsthand, for he had sat across a roulette table from him once in the gold camps near Boulder Creek. At that time Quantrill had been making his way east from Utah, one jump ahead of the law, trailing a string of warrants behind him; everything, it seemed, from murder to horse thievery. Even if McKay did not know who the others were, if they were half the outlaw that Quantrill was, Saunders deserved close watching. Especially in light of what McKay had just discovered. He patted his vest pocket, feeling the lump there that he had just won off the preacher.

On the pier below, Hamilton completed his negotiations for the wood with the yard owner and was making his way back aboard the *Tempest Queen*, rounding a stack of wooden crates . . . a fist flashed out. The sound of knuckles against flesh was like a thunderclap. McKay heard it clearly, even where he stood, high above the landing stage.

Hamilton flinched at the sound, and instantly stepped back. The next moment a second fist crashed somewhere in the shadows. Suddenly Lemont Belvedere backpedaled out into the open, his windmilling arms flailing the air, and right on his heels bounded the hunched shape of the stocky German named Konrad Adler — the one they called Eagle.

McKay left his pie sitting on the railing, and descending a hatch, he cut through the engine room where steam hissed and pipes creaked and out the door behind the furnaces and boilers. By the time he arrived on the scene, a crowd had already gathered around the two men. In those intervening minutes, Belvedere had shaken off his stupor from Adler's punch, and the two men were circling warily. McKay wove his way through the crowd to the front row in time to see Belvedere's fist lash out and deliver a resounding blow to the point of the German's craggy chin.

Eagle staggered back, and from a particular quarter of the circle of men came a hearty cheer. All around McKay, men were making bets and collecting money. He was pondering how he might turn a profit in this, when Eagle landed a solid punch to Belvedere's midsection, folding the Southern soldier in half. A chorus of cheers arose from the other side of the circle of soldiers and boatmen.

Back and forth this went, one end lifting a cheer to the other's groan, and then the sides would switch, and all the while, Belvedere and Eagle were slogging away at each other.

"Ten to one the Southern boy gets his nose mashed," someone said.

"By that immigrant abolitionist?" a mellow voice drawled. "No way. I'll see your bet!"

A third fellow collected the wagers while Belvedere landed a handsome wallop to Eagle's already blunt nose. Suddenly the *Tempest Queen*'s freshly painted deck was running red. Eagle came around, driving forward like a bull and jolting Belvedere's jaw so hard McKay thought for certain he had broken it.

More blood smeared beneath their dancing feet.

"Another five on the German!"

"Here gimme a piece of that."

Two fists shot up clutching money, and when no one immediately took it under their care, McKay collected it and casually deposited the wager into his pocket. A little way over two more soldiers were making wagers, and McKay dutifully deposited their money in his own pocket, too. *This may, indeed, prove profitable,* he began to think, working his way through the throng.

The crowd groaned in unison, and McKay craned his neck in time to see Eagle sprawled out in the blood. He struggled to push himself up and slipped back. Belvedere was swaying but still standing, breathless, and taunting the German to get back in the fight. Belvedere happened to step too close, and proving he was not yet out of the fight, Eagle lunged, caught the Southerner by the leg, and heaved him off his feet. Cheers erupted. The two soldiers continued to pummel each other amid the blood and the drool, able to rise no farther than to their knees.

"What is going on here?" Lieutenant Dempsey barked. He had made his way down from the promenade, and Cora Mills was close at his side as he pushed into the crowd. The soldiers moved apart for him once they knew the officer was on the scene. Dempsey halted and stared a moment at the two clashing soldiers, then he shouted, "Break it up, men!"

Belvedere threw another punch. Eagle managed to block it somehow and came back with a short jab to Belvedere's eye.

"I said break it up!"

The two weary warriors did not appear to hear, and continued throwing punches, but ineffectively now, their muscles growing soft.

The roar of a service revolver ripped through the night, and three feet of orange muzzle flame stabbed skyward, riveting everyone's attention. Only then did Eagle and Belvedere become aware of their commanding officer standing over them. Dempsey holstered his revolver and ordered the men to attention.

Unsteadily, both men rose to their feet, Eagle hunched over and disheveled, Belvedere somehow managing to pull himself up straight.

"What in heaven's name is this all about?"

Neither man answered. Belvedere was holding his jaw, and McKay was not certain the man could have spoken if he had wanted to. Eagle had a finger in his bloodied mouth, probing around as if searching for something that he had lost. *A molar, no doubt,* McKay mused.

Dempsey scowled at the two swaying wrecks and snorted angrily. "Would one of you two care to explain? Who started this?"

Eagle withdrew his finger from his mouth, spat a thick stream of sputum and blood to the deck, and wiped his lips with the back of his hand. "I started it, sir," he mumbled in a thick Germanic accent, and it sounded as if his tongue were wrapped in a wad of cotton. "That is to say, I took the first punch, sir."

"The first punch?" Dempsey shifted his view. Belvedere was still holding his jaw, working it back and forth now, testing it. It didn't seem to be broken, but just the same it wasn't working as smoothly as it had earlier that day. "Am I to assume that you provoked Private Adler into throwing the first punch, Corporal Belvedere?"

"Not 't aul! We wer't even tulkin t' 'im!"

"What is that?"

" 'e att'ked me fur no re'sen."

"Adler hit you without cause?"

Belvedere nodded his head.

Dempsey frowned, glanced back at Konrad Adler. The soldier was still feeling around inside his mouth. "Care to explain, Private?"

Adler removed his finger. "Sir, he . . . he made a comment."

"A comment? Perhaps you would elaborate on that?"

"I vould rather not, sir."

"Oh, you wouldn't? I am not asking you, I am ordering you! Tell me what happened, and no more hedging."

"Yes, sir. Vell, it is just that he vas talking vith his friends that's all."

"About what, Private?"

"About people. About people who come to this country."

"Go on?" Dempsey prodded.

" 'Vell,' says him, 'immigrants have no right to make opinions in this country.' Says him, 'If those from another country want to emancipate anyone, they should start by emancipating their own selves back to vhere they come from.' "

"And because of that you hit him?"

Adler hesitated. "No, for that, I did not hit him."

"Then why did you hit him?" Dempsey exploded.

Adler clamped his mouth down and did not answer.

"I'll tell you why Eagle hit him, Lieutenant."

Dempsey wheeled about at the sound of this new voice and discovered that it belonged to one of the soldiers who had been listening in on Belvedere and his Southern friends earlier that day when Dempsey had reprimanded them.

"He hit him because that Southern blue blood Belvedere was spouting off on states' rights. Eagle told Belvedere that he couldn't know what states' rights meant until someone invaded his country and took them away from him. When Belvedere asked what he was talking about, Eagle said that Napoleon had marched into Germany and conquered it, and that's what he meant. Belvedere laughed at this and told Eagle that Napoleon had every right to march through Germany, a country of inferior men. That the French were as far above the Germans as the whites were above the niggers. It was about at that point that Eagle slugged him."

"I see." Dempsey looked back at Adler. "So, because of a crack about your homeland, you hit him?"

Adler stiffened and looked Dempsey in the eye. "No, sir, I did not strike him for that."

"Then why in heaven's name did you hit Belvedere?"

McKay could see that Dempsey was nearing his wits' end to get to the bottom of this.

"I hit him because he is stupid. And he is French. And because he knows nothing of what he speaks or the evil and unjust

324

way his kind treats others who are different from them. I hit him because he admires Napoleon."

"Napoleon?"

"It was Napoleon's army that killed my grandmother and grandfather. It was Napoleon's soldiers that defiled my mother when she vas still but a child. I hit Corporal Belvedere because him and his kind enslave and murder men and women, and justify their behavior by proclaiming those people to be inferior." Eagle stopped to pull in a ragged breath. "It is Belvedere who is the inferior, Lieutenant. He is inferior because he does not see the suffering him and his kind bring to this world. And now I vill accept my punishment happily."

Dempsey considered the two men, bloodied and torn, and he said, "I will not reprimand either one of you this time. But if it happens again, both of you will find yourselves in the stockades at Fort Leavenworth. Whatever differences you two might have, keep them to yourselves." Dempsey glared at Belvedere. "And I don't want to hear any more of this sectional nationalism. Keep your political affairs strictly to yourself and out of my troops. Do I make myself clear?"

Belvedere nodded his head.

"The both of you are dismissed."

The crowd broke up amid a wave of discontent among the troops. McKay was making his way clear of them when a hand grasped his shoulder. Captain Hamilton turned him around. McKay grinned and said, "It is certainly comforting to know that a man like Lieutenant Dempsey is in control of these men, is it not, Captain?"

Hamilton frowned and said, "There seem to be some men here who are missing money, Mr. McKay."

"Really? How unfortunate."

"I seem to recall seeing you collecting bets, to *hold* I presume?"

McKay grinned, embarrassed, and tapped his forehead as if suddenly recalling collecting the cash. "How forgetful of me, Captain. In the excitement of the past few minutes it completely slipped my mind."

"Humm." Captain Hamilton was not smiling. He put out a hand, and McKay filled it with the money he had collected from the soldiers.

"I trust you will return it to the rightful owners? I'd hate to think someone lost money because of my forgetfulness." He smiled easily at the captain.

Hamilton said, "We need to have us a little talk, Mr. McKay. I really thought the last several months had wrought a change in you, but tonight, after witnessing your dealings with that poor preacher, Saunders, and now here — well, you know my rules concerning cheating. We had discussed them before I agreed to allow you to remain aboard my boat, if you recall?"

"I recall perfectly, Captain Hamilton, along with the percentage of my winnings which we also agreed upon at the time, and which I have faithfully paid each month to cover my passage. I can assure you that I have been true to my end of the bargain."

"After tonight I am starting to wonder."

McKay smiled smoothly. "Tonight, my dear Captain, I had a perfectly legitimate reason for doing what I did, and I think you will be quite interested in learning what I have discovered about the *poor* Reverend Saunders."

The captain's bushy gray eyebrows dipped together suspiciously.

McKay increased the width of his smile. "Now, shall we return that money? Afterwards, in the privacy of your cabin, I shall tell you all that I have discovered. And perhaps afterwards, we ought to have a talk with Lieutenant Dempsey, for this thing involves him as well."

McKay could tell he had caught the captain's attention. Hamilton pursed his lips, then nodded his head. "Very well, let's go on up to my staterooms and hear what you have to say."

Chapter Seventeen

"I think you handled those two men exactly right, Sherman. You showed both strength and compassion, and after all, are those not the traits of a strong leader?"

Her words embarrassed Dempsey, and he was thankful it was dark and that the small amount of light from the lamps along the promenade was not enough to show that his face had reddened.

"I only did what I thought was right, Cora." They passed through the shadows of one of the ladders that climbed to the hurricane deck above them and came to her door.

Cora Mills felt around for her key in the bottom of her handbag. "Thank you for an enjoyable evening, Sherman," she said, smiling up at him.

Dempsey did not want it to end, but the hour was late, and with the fuelwood now aboard, and the *Tempest Queen* once again pushing up the river, the boat had settled down to its normal operation. The soldiers had bedded down, and the fight between Belvedere and Adler seemed remote in his memory. Outside Cora Mills's stateroom door he reveled in her lovely face.

"I look forward to seeing you tomorrow, Cora."

"I shall, too." With a parting smile she turned the key in the lock, slipped inside the dark stateroom, and closed it behind her. Dempsey listened for the lock to turn inside, and knowing that she was now secure behind the solid door, he strolled back along the promenade. It was deserted at this late hour, and he was aware of his footsteps upon the deck, blending with the background din of churning water and hissing steam.

Dempsey returned to the main cabin. The quartet that had earlier entertained them had retired for the night, and the flames in the crystal chandeliers had been extinguished. Only the lamps in stanchions upon the wall remained lighted, but turned down, lending a soft ambience to the place. There really was no point in his lingering here. He went on through the cabin and out to the other side of the boat where the deck continued on behind the paddle box and checked in on the guards at the back cabin where the payroll was locked.

"All quiet?" Dempsey asked.

"Like a church, Lieutenant," one of the guards replied while the other hid a yawn behind his fist.

"Tired, Private?"

The slouching man pulled himself up to attention. "No, sir. It's just the engines, sir. They never change pace."

"Don't let the monotony put you to sleep."

"No, sir."

"Very well." Dempsey climbed a ladder up to the hurricane deck to surmount the intervening paddle box and to have a wider view of the black river ahead of the red glow of the smoky torch baskets at the bow of the boat. The texas, where the officers and crew lived, still showed lights coming through drawn curtains at several windows. On a riverboat, a certain number of officers and boatmen were always awake, no matter what the hour. Someone had to tend the engines and feed the furnaces.

Dempsey's mind was rambling, unwinding from the day. Cora Mills had left him with a pleasant glow, almost like a glass of fine wine, and as he strolled into the shadows of the upper swell of the paddle box, he was not prepared for the voice that came suddenly from the dark.

"Lieutenant."

Dempsey turned.

A fist shot out of the darkness, smacked into his chin, and spun him around on his heels. A second blow struck low, snapping him forward. Dempsey tried to raise an arm to protect himself, but they seemed to come at him from all directions, with fists flying and knees and feet kicking. In the blur of the fight, he had the notion that there were at least two men, and maybe three. But he never had the opportunity to learn exactly how many.

He tried to protect himself, unsuccessfully. His eyes went out of focus, and then he lost his footing and hit the deck hard. Their boots swung out, and it was all he could do to drag his arms up over his head as they hammered at his side, his chest. A boot smacked into his backbone. He cried out, and then he gritted his teeth against the explosion of pain, helpless to defend himself.

Hamilton lowered himself into his chair by the little desk where the daguerreotype of Cynthia smiled out at him from a worn, gilded frame. McKay remained standing at the foot of Captain Hamilton's bed, gripping his black walking stick, smiling that insufferable smile that Hamilton knew meant that the gambler had a winning card up his sleeve.

Hamilton liked McKay. It was just that he got tired of the man's always being right, even when the facts shouted against him. Hamilton did not know what story the gambler had to tell him now, but whatever it was, it would most likely be impossible to pick apart. And whether or not the tale was the truth was always a question with McKay.

"You were stringing the preacher along, McKay. You were working one of your schemes on him. I held my tongue tonight only because you had implored me to do so, but I expect to have the truth of it now."

"Of course, Captain."

"And none of your slick stories this time. Give it to me straight, without the benefit of the embellishments for which you are so fond."

McKay looked wounded. "My dear Captain Hamilton, I have always been forthright with you."

Hamilton gave a short laugh. "That's a barefaced lie, but I'll overlook it. Now, carry on."

McKay smiled serenely. "The truth is that Reverend Saunders is no more a man of God than I am. He is a charlatan and is up to no good aboard your boat, Captain. Exactly what his game is, I have not yet discovered. But, mark my word, the man is dangerous."

Hamilton scowled but did not immediately accuse McKay of outright prevarication. The charge seemed impossible, of course, but Hamilton knew McKay well enough to know that he was seldom wrong when it came to sizing up an opponent — whether it be another gambler sitting across a card table from him or a pretender wearing a clerical collar.

"You are certain of that?"

"Absolutely." McKay's confidence was annoying.

"I suppose you have some kind of proof? You have overheard something, or have seen something? Some sort of hard evidence?" Hamilton pressed.

"I have overheard nothing, Captain, and that is precisely why I placed myself in the company of Saunders, to determine his true character."

"And that is all you have to go by?"

"Of course not, Captain. Although I did not hear his words, I did witness a secret meeting between Saunders and at least a dozen men earlier this evening. Men who have been making their way aboard the *Tempest Queen* since we left St. Louis. Haven't you thought it peculiar that we have been stopping for so many small groups along the river? And that with the exception of one or two families with their wagons and horses, all of the people picked up have been men with pistols and rifled muskets?"

Hamilton had not noticed the oddity of it and was embarrassed to admit it now that McKay had pointed it out to him. "I had not given it much thought," he mumbled.

"I beg your pardon?"

Hamilton's view flashed up and narrowed. "I said I had not thought about it much."

McKay's smile remained as placid as a pool of water on a windless day. "Well, I have, Captain Hamilton, and because of that I have kept my eye on Saunders. After the secret meeting I just mentioned, I investigated a little closer and discovered a diagram scratched into the top of a barrel. I did not know what it meant at first, but my suspicions were aroused, and when I went to check them out with one of the pilots, I discovered that the diagram was actually an outline of the Missouri River, with various landmarks indicated along the way. One of those landmarks was Growley's Wood Yard, where just a few minutes ago five of the men who had met with Saunders in secret, disembarked."

"Disembarked? What kind of misdeed can they do aboard the *Tempest Queen* if they have already disembarked?"

"I haven't got it figured out yet, but Saunders and his boy, Grady, both deserve to be watched."

Hamilton thought it over and shook his head. "I think you are making something out of nothing, McKay. If you couldn't hear what they were saying, how in the devil do you know Saunders wasn't only conducting a church service, or . . . or whatever it is preachers do."

"Passing around a whiskey bottle and scratching maps into barrel tops with a bowie knife? Doesn't much sound like a church service to me."

Hamilton frowned. "It does sound suspicious, I have to admit. But still you have no hard evidence."

"If it is hard evidence you want . . ." McKay dipped into his vest pocket and came out holding a ring. He turned it to the lamplight, then dropped it into Hamilton's hand. "Take a look at this."

Hamilton peered at the circle of gold in his hand. After a moment he looked back at McKay, more confused than before. "It is a ring. An expensive ring. So, what does it mean, and how does this in any way indict Reverend Saunders?"

"Have you not seen that ring before?"

"No, not that I recall."

"Well, I have."

"Where?"

"On the finger of Sergeant Carr, that first day when he and Lieutenant Dempsey came aboard to engage the *Tempest Queen* for this trip to Fort Leavenworth. And that, I shouldn't need to remind you, was shortly before the man mysteriously turned up missing."

"How did you come by it?"

"I won it off of Saunders an hour ago, after you left the game."

Hamilton's cabin had suddenly grown silent except for the puffing 'scape pipes, muffled by the cabin walls, and the ticking of the brass clock above the desk. The captain didn't know what to make of the ring or Saunders's being in possession of it, and he was about to say so when the sound of scuffling came faintly from outside. Both men turned their heads as if able to peer through the wall. There were two or three sharp cracks and then some muffled thuds. The next instant a man cried out, but that sound ceased abruptly. McKay and Hamilton locked eyes, and as if of a single thought, they dove for the door. Being nearest to the door, McKay made it outside first onto the porch, glanced left then right, and spied the three men kicking at a figure on the deck.

"Hey!" McKay shouted, leaping over the porch railing.

"Let's get out of here!" One of the men said, and they scattered along the deck, and plunged down the ladders to the boiler deck below. McKay could not recognize them in the dark, and he did not try to pursue, drawing up instead by the downed man. He bent to examine him. Hamilton was a few moments behind, drawing up as well.

McKay said, "It's Lieutenant Dempsey."

They turned Dempsey over, and Hamilton frowned. "He has been worked over smartly."

"It appears they were trying to kill him."

Hamilton felt the pulse on Dempsey's neck. "Fortunately for the lieutenant we were nearby and drove those rascals off.

Did you see who they were?"

"It was too dark."

"Humm. Unfortunate. Let's get the lieutenant into my cabin." Between the two of them they carried Dempsey inside. Hamilton went through his stateroom into the texas and returned a moment later with a basin of water and a towel and began cleaning the blood away.

"Go and see if you can find Billy."

Dr. William Reuben, Billy to the crew, was the resident doctor who spent most of his time in the barber shop, but the barber would be closed this late in the evening, so McKay first tried Billy's cabin at the back of the texas, a couple rods toward the stern of the boat. Billy was there and sound asleep when McKay roused him. Ten minutes later, dressed and carrying his brown leather bag, Billy entered Captain Hamilton's stateroom.

"He has received a severe blow to the occipital bone," Billy said, working his way down. "His ribs are badly bruised, and there is a severe contusion on his spine." Billy glanced up. "Who did this?"

"That remains to be discovered," Hamilton said.

"Well, whoever it was —"

"They were," Hamilton corrected.

"Whoever his attackers might have been, they were playing for keeps."

"Will he be all right, Billy?" McKay asked.

"Blows to the head that render a man unconscious are hard to call. He appears strong, his breathing is regular, heartbeat steady, and he is young. But until a man comes out of something like this, it is always questionable." Billy glanced at McKay. "You should know all about concussions, Mr. McKay. It wasn't so long ago that you were lying in the lieutenant's place."

McKay frowned and nodded his head. "How vividly I remember."

Hamilton recalled the incident all too well. A disgruntled gambler had made his way aboard the *Tempest Queen* at Natchez-Under-The-Hill and had attacked McKay without warning late one night, knocking him insensible with a heavy walking stick, and then throwing him overboard. It was only through the greatest stroke of luck — something which McKay seemed well endowed with — that a fireman at the furnaces had been on hand to leap in after McKay and fish him out.

Billy said, "You remember how Mr. McKay struggled to come back from his concussion. I dare say the lieutenant will have a similar struggle, although he was not hit as hard."

"He can remain in my cabin until he regains consciousness. I suppose I ought to go down and find someone in authority among those soldiers and inform him of what has happened here."

Billy gathered up his tools and bottles and put them back into the leather bag. "I will stop in on him in the morning."

"Thank you, Doctor."

Billy nodded solemnly, frowning, as if he was not at all pleased at how little he could do here to help Dempsey, and he left.

Hamilton peered down at the unconscious form lying on his bed and reached for his cap on a hook near the door. "It's going to be a long night, I suspect, Mr. McKay." Hamilton held the door for the gambler, and locked it behind them as they departed.

"Hey! You two shouldn't be down here. You can get yourselves hurt." The chief engineer, Barney Seegar, grabbed up a rag and wiped his greasy fingers as he came through the sweltering engine room to where the two men had entered. He glanced at the old, scrawny one, then to the younger man in the tattered clothes. "This ain't no place to be poking around, 'fraid you'll have to leave," he said loudly.

"Are you Barney Seegar, the man in charge of these mighty engines, sir?"

"I am Seegar," the engineer shouted above the hiss of steam escaping through the gauge cocks and the clangor of the slamming connecting rods.

"I'm Reverend Deke Saunders, of the Missouri Synod. This here is my nephew, Harold Madden. Captain Hamilton said you'd be proud to show us around down here. We ain't never seen nothing like these great steam engines before. Very impressive."

Seegar cupped his hand behind his ear. "Come again? Saunders is your name, you say?"

"Reverend Deke Saunders."

Seegar frowned, shook his head, and hooked a finger at them. They followed him out of the engine room and onto the guards where the water rushed past less than two feet below their feet. The evening breeze coming off the river cooled their sweating brows, and the pounding of the engine room was somewhat diminished out here.

"Now, what was that you were saying?"

Seegar shouted. Years of working in the engine room of a steamboat had dulled his hearing, and he had forgotten at what volume most people spoke.

"I said I'm Reverend Saunders, and this here is my nephew, Harold. We were curious about your engines, and Captain Hamilton had said you would be pleased to show us around."

"The captain said that?" Seegar replied, too loud.

"Yep, he sure enough did. And since I don't sleep much at night, I figured this would be as good a time as any, and you probably wouldn't be too busy at this late hour."

"I'm always busy with these engines, Reverend. Got to mind them every minute. There is at least two of us down here all the time. Neglect them for a minute and you might burst a boiler or rupture a feed line. If something like that were to ever happen it could blow away half of the boat, and the escaping steam would scald the passengers like boiled crayfish."

"I reckon my nephew and me wouldn't want to take you away from such important work."

Seegar seemed to reconsider, then he said after a moment, "Oh, come along and

I'll show it to you, only don't touch nothing."

Saunders gave him a tight grin and symbolically thrust his hands into his pockets. Back inside the sweat box, their ears were suddenly ringing from the noise, and the heavy air was harder to breathe than the air outside on the guards had been.

"Over here we got the gauges that tell us how much pressure is in the feed line from the boilers to the piston," Seegar shouted. Saunders eyed the dials that were as large as a dinner plate. Everywhere he looked were hand wheels of various sizes, some painted red, others green, some hot to the touch, others only room temperature, which in itself was at least thirty degrees hotter than the outside air. The humidity was double that out on the guards.

Seegar took them under some low, fat pipes, encased in thick asbestos wrappers. At the far end of the room were a pair of iron spindles turning inside huge bronze and steel bearing cups. A man was watching over the turning shafts with a long-neck oilcan in hand, putting lubricant onto the bearings, being careful to avoid the sliding connecting rods not but a few inches from his elbows.

Metal slapped metal, pistons plunged in

their hot cylinders, and steam whistled through gauge cocks.

"Now this is where we regulate the pressure. The engines run best at 120 psi, that's pounds per square inch," Seegar was saying. "The more pressure we let into the cylinders, the faster the wheels turn. We can also change the steam's direction and reverse the rotation of the wheels."

"Interesting," Saunders said unenthusiastically.

Seegar nodded his head, grinning. To him it was obviously fascinating. "We can even turn one wheel forward while the other is turning backwards."

Saunders frowned. "Why would anyone want to do that? Seems to me you'd just turn in circles, not goin' anywhere."

"That's exactly why we do it. It allows us to turn the boat as if on a pivot, and change our direction of travel."

Seegar escorted them forward again. Saunders tried to make some sense of it, but the engine room of a steamboat was a foreign world to him. Everywhere, pipes wrapped in asbestos crisscrossed the ceiling, disappearing into shadows, and hand pulls hung down like jungle vines from the dark recesses twenty-five feet over their heads. "How do you stop them wheels from turning if you wanted to?"

"Each wheel has a brake drum operated off a lever. Then over here, this valve bleeds off the steam before it reaches the pistons. Got one on each side, for each wheel. Open it up all the way, and it will empty the pressure in the boilers in a matter of minutes."

"You don't say?" Now here was something that Saunders truly found interesting. He gave Harold a glance, and a small nod of his head, which Seegar did not see. "Well, it is all very interesting, Mr. Seegar. I thank you for taking the time to show us these engines. I am impressed."

Seegar grinned. "Happy to do it, Reverend Saunders." He dragged a greasy rag from his hip pocket and wiped his fingers again. "Hope you two enjoy the rest of your trip."

"Oh, we will. I think it is gonna be a very good journey. Come along, Harold."

Outside, away from the heat and the noise, Saunders said, "That's how we will slow them up to give our boys time to reach Catfish Landing. That valve Seegar showed us. We'll open it up and empty the steam from their tanks. It will take at least an hour to build it back up."

"Bu— but how are we gon— gon—

gonna do that with them two fellas in there?"

"Hum. That is gonna be a problem. We could just go in there and shoot them two engineers, and won't nobody hear the shots above all that racket for certain, but that might tip our hand, and we can't afford to do that just yet."

"I don't see ho— how it can be done any oth— oth— other way, Deke."

"There is always another way, Harold," Saunders said thoughtfully. "Now don't rush me. I got to give this problem some careful pondering. We will want to make it look like an accident. It is still early, and there will probably be a changing of the guard down there before the night's through. We will bide our time, Harold."

"I st— still say shoot 'em and b— b— be done with it, Deke."

Deke shifted an eye at his nephew. "It may just come to that. Come along and let's find that wanton cousin of yours."

Chapter
Eighteen

In the mist of the coming dawn, with the sun still well below the horizon, a faint pink tinge had begun to brighten the sky to the east. Laban Caulder turned his team off the river road onto a road heading north, and within ten minutes he could see the scattered buildings of Marthasville ahead, dark shapes upon a gray background growing brighter as the minutes passed. But before he reached the little hamlet, a blazing fire in a plowed field to his right drew his eye. He turned the team off the road, and the yellow wagon rattled over the uneven ground, pulling to a stop a dozen feet from the fire.

The men around the blaze stood and one came over, and in the light of the fire, Laban recognized Case Jackson.

"Reckon I found the right place," Laban said, setting the brake and wrapping the reins through the iron handhold loop on the side of the seat.

"Good to see ya, Laban," Jackson said. They shook hands.

"It has been a while."

"Four or five years. Come on over to the fire and have some coffee."

Laban swung off the wagon seat and moved into the light of the fire. Two other wagons were parked nearby, along with a small remuda of saddle horses tethered to a rope strung between two pickets.

"Harold said you would be along." This was Waldo Hinkley, one of the few men along the river Laban considered a friend. Hinkley hunched down near the fire, his wrinkled face grinning, with shadows chased by yellow flame dancing among its furrows.

"I almost didn't make it, Waldo. Had me some visitors stop by the farm just before I pulled out."

Someone put a cup of coffee into his hands.

"Is that you, Laban Caulder?"

Caulder looked over his shoulder. "Sid Balleau. I thought that rig over there looked familiar. How did you find out about this? Last I heard you were in Kansas."

Balleau was about Caulder's age, stoutly constructed like him, but taller. He sat on his haunches next to Laban, near the flames. "I was, but I come back to Missouri about a year ago. Madden found me over at Libertyville."

"F— found him in a sal— sal— saloon, drunk as an Indian," someone said, doing a passable imitation of Harold Madden.

A low rumble of laughter made its way through the band of cutthroats.

Balleau laughed, too, and nodded his head at Laban's wagon. "I should have guessed that was you pulling up. You're the only man I know who drives such a fancy rig, pulled by a pair of matched horses. You always did have a taste for fine horseflesh."

"You ought to see the stallion I have back at the farm."

"I'm afraid these old eyes couldn't take the dazzle, Laban."

Laban grinned and sipped his coffee. It tasted good after his long ride, sharpened him after the plodding of his horses and the rattling of his rig had lulled him into a light doze during the early morning hours. There were thirteen men there, including himself, and about half of them he did not know. The rest he had met a time or two on jobs like this one. He knew them about well enough to give a "howdy" to, and that was all. Of the thirteen, only Waldo Hinkley, Case Jackson, and Sid Balleau did Laban Caulder know enough to trust.

Case made the introductions, for he was the only one there who seemed to know each man. The mood around the blaze was easy and friendly, as if they had all come together to raise a barn, not to pirate a riverboat. Only one man remained aloof. The one called Charles Hart.

As the dawn's light pulled shapes from the shrinking shadows and brought color to the land, dimming the fire that was already burning low, Waldo Hinkley got their attention and went over the plans that Deke Saunders had worked out with him before he'd left the boat. When Hinkley had finished, he divided the men into two parties; one to descend upon Catfish Landing, the other to go on ahead to the place beyond the town where the road ran close to the river. The place where the *Tempest Queen* was to be run aground.

With the arrangements made, the men buried the embers of their fire and went to their horses and rigs, making ready to depart. Sid Balleau pulled his wagon around and drew up alongside Laban's rig.

"How is Bitsy?" Sid asked.

"She is doing all right. Her eyesight has gotten pitiful, and she still refuses to buy a pair of spectacles, but so long as she stays near the house she does all right."

"Did you know that Helen passed on?"

Laban paused at the harness buckle he'd been adjusting. "No. I didn't know that, Sid. When did it happen?"

"Shortly after we got to Kansas. It was one of them cold, wet winters, you know. She got an affliction in her lungs that first winter. Couldn't never seem to shake it, and she fought it with all she had, but it just got worse and worse, and wore her down. Nothing anyone could do for her made it any better. She was sick over a month before she died." Sid became silent for a moment.

"I lasted out the winter, then packed up and moved back here. I reckon I've been frequenting the saloons more than usual since then." He shrugged his shoulders, and a crooked smile emerged upon his face. "I thought that if I got back to something I knew, I wouldn't think about Helen so much. That's why I jumped at Harold's offer. I had intended to put this life behind me. That was why Helen and I moved out West in the first place. Funny how fate has a way of messing with your plans."

"I'm sorry to hear it. Bitsy will be grieved to learn of Helen's death. She was right fond of your wife, she was."

The smile on Sid's face twitched, then

firmed up. He glanced at the rumpled tarp in the back of Laban's wagon, and all at once his view narrowed. "Here, what have you got with you under that canvas, Laban? A tied-up pig?"

"Huh? What are you talking about?"

"Can't you hear that? Sounds like a snort . . . or a snore."

Laban went around to the back of the wagon and, sure enough, heard the low rumbling coming from under the tarp. He threw off the canvas in one swift motion and stood there, stone-still and staring.

Frank James snorted in his sleep, disturbed by the sudden removal of the cover, rolled over, and came suddenly awake. He sat up groggily, rubbing the sleep from his eyes, slowly growing aware of the stern company of men drawing in around him.

Laban hauled Frank James out of the back of his wagon by the scruff and set him down on the ground. The pirates closed in around the boy. "You brazen stowaway! I told you you couldn't come along!"

"Who is he, Laban?" Case Jackson asked, looking Frank up and down.

Laban worked his jaw in his anger, got a handle on it, and said, "He's one of the

James boys. His folks are visiting us. His ma and Bitsy are friends."

Frank eyed the men crowding near, and if he was frightened, he didn't show it. Now fully awake, he revealed steel-like composure and gave them a defiant look in return for their scowls and squints.

"He knows then?" Case asked. "You told him what we were about, Laban?"

"No, of course not, Case. I'd never let on to outsiders. It was my fool boy, Harvey, who opened his big mouth. He was bragging it up big about this job, and Frank here got it in his fool head that he wanted to take up river pirating. Harvey is gonna answer to a green-willow switch once I get back."

"In the meanwhile, what do we do with this kid?"

"I'm not a kid," Frank shot back. "I'm sixteen."

Someone laughed. "I say we cut the kid's throat and be done with him."

"No," Laban said. "Not that."

"Why not?" another voice called out.

"Because his folks are friends of ours, that's why not." River pirates weren't a generous lot, and Laban wished like hell that Frank had obeyed him and stayed back at the farm. He had all he could handle to keep these renegades from pouncing on the kid, and when he thought about it in his anger, he wondered why he was trying to protect him anyway.

Waldo Hinkley rubbed his chin and said, "I wasn't but fourteen the first time I kilt my first raftman coming down the river with a load of winter pelts."

Charles Hart spoke up. "It looks to me like he has got grit. He's a defiant cuss, and I like that. Give this Frank James a chance. Who knows what kind of future he'll have if we show him the ropes in a proper way."

Laban didn't like that idea, not with Frank being Zerelda's boy, and Zerelda and her new husband being straightforward folks and all, but at least the tide was turning from cutting the kid's throat. If Frank really wanted to become a pirate, he'd have brains enough to keep his mouth shut about it afterward — at least Laban hoped so.

Case Jackson thought it over some, then said, "If he wants to learn the pirating business, then I say we bring him along. And to make sure he don't blab it about afterwards, I think we ought to put young Mr. James here in the thick of it. He'll come with us to Catfish Landing." Jackson studied Frank and said, "How are you with using a pistol?"

"I can shoot all right."

"That's not what I mean. Anybody can shoot all right given half an hour's practice. What I want to know is, *will* you shoot? Will you kill?"

Frank hesitated and ran his fingers through his sandy hair, thinking it over. Laban chewed nervously on his lip. Frank's fate hung by the thread of what he would say next. "Yeah, I'd shoot to kill. If it was necessary."

"That's good enough for me," Sid Balleau said, and two or three other men agreed.

Jackson nodded his head slowly. "All right then, James, I reckon you're in, unless anybody here has any objections," he added, raising his voice.

"I still say we ought to cut his throat," someone said, but it was with a chuckle this time. No one gave the thumbs-down to the decision, and Frank was suddenly one of the pirates.

Frank let go of a long breath and then grinned. "I'll do good."

"You better 'cause I'll be keepin' my eye on you."

Hart laughed. "You're gonna be pretty

busy keeping your eye on folks, Case."
Waldo Hinkley chuckled as well. He had
been there when Saunders had instructed
Case to keep an eye on Hart.

Case didn't laugh.

Charles Hart said, "Why don't you let
me keep an eye on the kid? I'll see that he
keeps his nose clean."

"I'll keep an eye on both of you, Hart.
After all, I got two of 'em." Jackson turned
to one of the men who had brought the
saddle horses. "You got an extra mount for
James?"

"I brought enough along, Case."

Jackson said, "Go find yourself an animal to ride. We are about to leave, and I
don't wait for laggards, James. I shoot
'em."

Laban said to Case, "If Frank comes
along, he gets an equal cut of the take."

"If he pulls his weight, he'll get equals."

They mounted up and started for the
road but drew up to let a battered dray
with four woodcutters aboard pass by.
Men from Marthasville, on their way to
work at Growley's Wood Yard, Laban suspected as he held his horses in check,
waiting for the dilapidated cart to rattle
past. The four men eyed them suspi-

ciously, then went back to their talk. Case Jackson waited for them to pull ahead before moving out again.

At the junction in the road, the pirates turned west, toward Catfish Landing. Laban could see Growley's below with the river beyond. He had guessed right about the men; they had been woodcutters, and now the battered dray was parked by the woodyard shack.

The horsemen put their heels to their mounts and broke into a gallop. Almost at once the animals lunged out of sight leaving a plume of dust hanging in the air. They were pressed for time. They had to make Catfish Landing before the *Tempest Queen* passed her up. A good horse could easily outpace a laboring riverboat, for short bursts, and an hour of hard riding should put them at their destination well ahead of their target.

Laban drove his team through the settling dust with the two other rigs trailing behind them. He had an unsettled feeling about this now — now that Frank James had turned up. He tried to put the concern out of mind, but it refused to budge.

Deke Saunders had no idea how late the hour had become, but throughout the waning night and early morning, the dark shoreline had slipped past with only a scattering of lights to pierce the solid black wall along the way. Saunders had watched the stars and what was left of the moon shift positions overhead as the *Tempest Queen* took a southerly tack where the river made a long thirty-mile bend. But now the stars and moon had moved across the sky again. The boat was once more heading north, and that meant Catfish Landing would be in sight in another hour. He had to do something soon, or the whole plan would be scuttled.

"What time is it getting to be?"

"I don't know, Pa."

Deke glanced at Harold and discovered his nephew sound asleep where he sat with his back against some crates. Deke kicked the tip of Harold's new boots. The man snorted awake. "Wa— what's up?"

"You were asleep."

"It's ni— night, Deke. Sleeping is what I'm sup— sup— suppose to be doing."

The fourth man waiting in hiding with them, Bud Patterson, laughed softly and felt around inside a bulky vest pocket. Removing a steel-cased watch and tipping it toward a bit of lamplight making its way from a bulkhead nearby, he said in a low voice, "It's almost three and a half of the clock, Deke."

Deke grunted and momentarily shot a deadly glance at Harold. "Now stay awake, hear?"

Harold nodded his head, straightening up out of his slouch.

Deke went back to studying the engine room door only twenty paces away.

The four of them grew sleepy, waiting, until Deke suddenly came forward on his hands and knees and poked his nose around the boxes they had put themselves behind. His unexpected action brought them all awake. Deke remained there a moment, like a hound pointing out a bird, then pulled back quickly and said in an urgent whisper, "It looks like they just changed crews for the night. We can make our move without worrying that someone will stick their nose in."

Seegar and his striker left, and the new crew took over. Deke gave the new men a few minutes to settle into their job, and then he and the pirates moved quietly out of cover. They had worked over their plan in detail in the long hours of waiting, and each man knew what was expected of him. Moving through the shadows, they made their way to the engine-room doorway and peeked around. Patterson and Grady located the two workers, and when the engineers' backs were toward them, they made their move with pistols in hand like cudgels.

In half a minute, both engineers were unconscious. Grady and Patterson hauled them out to dump them over the guards into the river. Deke and Harold went to the valves Seegar had pointed out earlier — the ones that diverted the steam from the pistons and bled it away.

The heavy wheel was hot to the touch. Deke hitched his hands up into his sleeves, grabbed hold through the material, and strained. The valve was heavy and turned slowly at first. After two turns Deke heard the hiss of steam alter its pitch and the slap of the connecting rod change its rhythm. The machinery was slowing. He shot a glance at the doorway as he turned the valve all the way down.

Madden got his valve closed as well. Steam screamed from the diversion pipe, out a vent near the paddle wheel. The driving piston slowed, and now the connecting rod was struggling to complete one last rotation of the huge wheel. Then it stopped.

Immediately a bell nearby began jingling. The pilot's insistent signal from above would go unanswered, Deke mused, leaping past it. A panicky voice was echoing down the brass speaking tube. Deke hurried out the door where Harold was already waiting, and the two men slipped outside and away.

The four pirates came together in the dark, and as they started away, the *Tempest Queen* lurched violently sideways.

Now helpless in the water, the big boat was at once caught up in the stream's powerful current. The unexpected jolt nearly pitched them off balance. Deke grabbed for a railing to steady himself, and as he looked out over the water, he froze. He had not considered that killing the engines might whirl the boat out of control and ram them into a shoal or grind them to kindling against the dark bank, but now the current was pushing them on toward the black shoreline suddenly looming nearer and nearer.

Chapter Nineteen

Dexter McKay was wrenched from a sound sleep, tossed across his bed, and slammed into the bulkhead that divided his stateroom from the one next to it. He grappled at the bedstead, swung his legs over, and put his feet upon the floor in a half-asleep attempt to stop the lurching. The lamp was rattling in its stand on the wall. McKay shook off the lingering sleep, coming suddenly awake. Besides the boat acting as if it were in the middle of an earthquake, there was something else wrong as well — and then all at once McKay knew. The heartbeat had stopped. The regular drumming of her steam engines was missing, and so was the steady chuffing of the 'scape pipes.

The *Tempest Queen* lurched again. McKay braced himself and stood. "She's dead in the water," he said aloud in the darkness of his room; he dragged on his trousers, not bothering with his boots. McKay pulled open his stateroom door and stepped into the main cabin where all the tables and chairs had changed positions, now arranged haphazardly across the polished floor.

There was a rush of men through the salon, and overhead on the hurricane deck, muffled by the intervening decks, the bronze bell was suddenly signaling madly.

"What happened?" McKay asked, catching a rushing crewman by the sleeve.

"Don't know yet. The engines just stopped turning. We might be foundering."

"Foundering?" McKay made his way outside with the others, shoving the shirt-tail of his smallclothes into his trousers as he went. An avalanche of men was tumbling down the stairs, and McKay was swept up with them. The fall deposited him on the main deck, and he moved aside and took a moment to glance around. Soldiers were milling about, trying to keep out of the way of rushing crewmen, and everywhere men were asking what had happened — and as of yet no one seemed able to supply a satisfactory answer.

"Where is the captain?" someone was asking, and if he had gotten an answer to that, McKay did not hear it.

"The river is driving us into shore," a voice said in a panic.

McKay went forward to the bow and

shot out a hand for a cable to keep from being thrown overboard by the next lurch, which had shifted the *Tempest Queen* dangerously near to the snag-filled shoreline.

A throng of men rushed back toward the engine room, and shoving his way through the crowd was the chief engineer, Barney Seegar, shouting, "Out of my way. Give me room, men!"

McKay watched the shore running up on them, and he knew no matter how they tried, there was no way those engines were going to start turning again in time. Where he was standing, near the prow, his view swept past, then halted and came back, stopping on the two huge anchors lashed down to the deck with their iron flukes hooked over the bow.

Of course!

He began loosening the ropes that held the anchors fast to the deck. The ties fell apart, and he tried to shove the anchor overboard, but he could not do much more than budge it. Frustrated, he put his shoulders to it, bracing his feet against an iron cargo cleat. He had watched a single deckhand swing them overboard as if they weighed little, but McKay was not used to heavy work.

He strained again, wondering why the crew, supposedly trained in this type of emergency, had not thought to drop the anchors. Well, he couldn't be bothered with that, and he put his muscle to the task. Slowly the massive iron-and-timbered weight slid forward, and then it tottered on the edge, its chain preventing it from sliding into the swirling water. McKay jumped over the second anchor and got it over the edge, held aloft by its chain as well.

Now what?

The current whirled the boat around all at once, and the shore moved closer by several rods.

Aha! The capstan! McKay remembered now. The crew always raised the anchors with the capstan. It only made sense that they should be lowered by the same means. He leaped to the device, which rose up from the dark deck like the stem of a mushroom — a wheel hub without spokes. It had indexed holes all around it to receive the stout, wooden poles by which it was turned. McKay examined the capstan in the dark, oblivious to the rush of men all about him and to shouting voices. His attention was riveted on this single item now, but how did he make it work? He'd never paid much attention to the capstan. It was always the deckhands who operated it, and that was about all he could recall.

McKay inserted a shaft into one of the holes and pushed as he had observed it being down. The thing wouldn't budge. Something else needed to be done. What might that be?

The shore had swung so close that when McKay glanced up he could now make out individual trees among the solid black wall of vegetation. He shoved at the pole again, but nothing happened. There must be a lever or dog somewhere locking it in place, and immediately he began groping around in the dark for it.

All at once there was someone else there with him. Captain Hamilton appraised the situation in a glance, saw the anchors poised over the water and McKay struggling with the capstan. Hamilton lifted a lever, which had been hidden by shadows, and stomped on a pedal that arose out of the deck, which in the darkness McKay had overlooked. In a sudden rush of rattling chains springing forth from two holes in the deck, the anchors disappeared over the bow with a mighty splash. It seemed to take a long time for the chains to play out, singing madly across the gunnels, before they finally rattled to a stop.

Hamilton hauled the lever over again.

Somewhere in the dark water below her keel the anchors found the bottom and their broad flukes bit into the mud. The *Tempest Queen* shuddered and drew up tight, the chains straining under the weight of the big riverboat. Her stern came around so swiftly it left McKay's stomach behind. Then she hung there, buffeted, her bow facing up river, the strong current parting around it.

Hamilton drew in a long breath and let it out slowly. He looked down at McKay, who had collapsed, exhausted, against the jack staff, then he stared out over the water, and McKay followed his glance. The shore lay not two rods off the right side of the boat — the starboard, he decided after referring to his hands — and the overhanging branches were near enough to see their leaves through the light of the marginally brighter sky. Was it dawn already, or only the stars and waning moon? No, it was the coming dawn, glowing faintly below the horizon.

"The capstan is used to raise the anchors, Mr. McKay, not lower them," Hamilton said mildly, but the gambler detected the strain in the captain's carefully controlled voice.

McKay stood and brushed at his trousers, glanced down at his bare feet and rumpled small shirt, and frowned. "I will try to remember that — for the next time, Captain."

"The next time?" Hamilton lifted a quizzical eyebrow.

McKay grinned.

Hamilton's glance narrowed and shot past him toward the boilers where the red light of the fires in the furnaces danced along the woodpiles, and he strode off without another word. McKay tagged after, stepping gingerly in the dark. There was a crowd plugging the engine-room door when Hamilton got there, and at his gruff bark, the men parted and allowed him and McKay to enter.

"Mr. Seegar. What happened down here?"

The chief engineer was dressed rather like McKay. Trousers, smallclothes, stockings with the great toe of his left foot protruding — his hair had the rumpled look of having just come off a pillow. McKay combed his fingers through his own tousled mane. Seegar was pondering an item of machinery, his fists planted firmly upon his hips. He cast his glance over his shoulders when Hamilton's voice boomed above the low murmurings.

"Captain."

"Well? What went wrong down here?"

Seegar scratched an itch behind his ear, looking perplexed. "This is a real puzzler, Captain. As far as I can tell, there is nothing wrong with the engines."

"Confound it, man! Then why did they cut out on us so suddenly? What broke?"

Seegar pointed at the piece of machinery he'd been contemplating when they had come in. "That's just it, Captain. Nothing is broken. The engines were simply shut down. Both valves to the main feed lines of the starboard and larboard engines were shut down the pressure bled off."

"Shut off!" Hamilton exploded, the fair skin beneath the gray beard glowing. "We were moving up the river under a full head of steam. Who shut them off? And dammit man, why?"

McKay was mildly startled. In all the time he had known Captain Hamilton, he could not recall him ever once cussing.

"I don't know, Captain. The morning shift came on around four o'clock, as scheduled, and I went to bed. I was asleep almost at once, and then the next thing I knew I was being jolted out of bed."

"As was everyone else aboard the *Tem-*

pest Queen," Hamilton rumbled.

Seegar shrugged his shoulders. "I just got down here a few moments before you, Captain. I'll need a little while to figure out how this happened."

"Who was in charge?"

"It was Kelly and Dvorak."

"Where in the devil are they?"

"They weren't here when I arrived, sir." Seegar looked around. "Anyone here seen Dvorak and Kelly?"

No one had.

Hamilton barked a command at one of the crewmen nearby. "Get some men together and search the boat for those two. Bring them to me once you find them." Hamilton returned his gaze to Seegar. "The engines are all right then?"

"As far as I can tell, they are."

"How long before we can get the wheels turning again?"

"We've lost about half the pressure in the boilers. Give me twenty minutes and have Mr. Lansing's men get those furnaces glowing, and I should have you on your way again, Captain."

"Very well, see to it." Hamilton turned to leave.

"Captain?" Seegar said. "Do you think the morning crew did this on purpose?"

"One thing is for certain, those valves didn't close themselves. And now that the two of them are missing, the finger of suspicion points that way."

"Yes, sir, I reckon it does." There was doubt in Seegar's voice, but he was shrewd enough not to speak it now.

McKay left with the captain, and as they went up the stairs, the gambler said, "You don't suppose this has any connection with Lieutenant Dempsey's attack?"

"I don't see how," Hamilton said brusquely, all the while smiling and reassuring terrified passengers that all was under control and that they would be once again on their way in half an hour.

"It seems curious, that's all. I have been aboard the *Tempest Queen* over four months now, Captain Hamilton, and this is the first time any passenger has been attacked and beaten and the first time someone has tried to dash the engines. And both incidents occurred within a few hours of each other."

Hamilton stopped at the foot of one of the ladders that went up to the hurricane deck. "Let's suppose the two are related, what am I to do about it?"

McKay pursed his lips, and a scowl clouded his eyes. "I haven't figured that out yet, Captain. Only, if the two episodes are related, once you discover who laid in wait for Lieutenant Dempsey, you will have the person who almost sent the *Tempest Queen* to the bottom of this muddy river."

"Perhaps. But for the moment that still leaves us in the dark since Lieutenant Dempsey is unable to tell us who attacked him . . . and, anyway, it is only your suspicion. We have no evidence that the two events are at all related."

"No, we don't," he replied thoughtfully.

Hamilton started up the stairs when Cora Mills's voice called out.

"Captain Hamilton, please wait."

He halted and stepped off the ladder as Cora hurried down the promenade. Her hair was bunched up under a cotton net, and she was wearing a voluminous dressing gown hastily thrown on and clutched closed in the fist of her left hand. On her feet, McKay noted, were pretty, green silk slippers.

"Captain, what has happened?"

Hamilton drew in a short breath. He had answered this question a dozen times in the few minutes it had taken him to move from the engine room to this point, and McKay saw that the captain was becoming exasperated repeating himself, but he kept a businesslike tone to his voice and said, "It was some trouble with the engines, but the problem has been dealt with and we are in no danger. Our anchors are holding us safely in place and we should be under steam again in a matter of minutes."

"Oh, I am so relieved."

Hamilton nodded his head and started back up the ladder.

"Captain Hamilton."

Her words halted him again.

"I was just informed by one of the soldiers that Lieutenant Dempsey has been injured. Is that so?"

"Yes, it is true. The lieutenant has had a mishap, ma'am."

"Is he . . . is he all right?"

"He has suffered a blow to the head and is not yet conscious. The doctor has looked in on him. The lieutenant is in my quarters, resting."

Her hand flung to her mouth, and even in the dark McKay saw her face blanch. "Oh, my! How did it happen? It was not because of this most recent crisis, was it?"

"No, ma'am. He was set upon by a gang of ruffians, and we have yet to learn who they were." Hamilton glanced at McKay as he spoke to her. "We seem to have had an ill-fated night, and I am going to look into these matters."

"Might I look in on the lieutenant, Captain Hamilton?"

Hamilton was momentarily confused. "You may, but why should you concern yourself?"

She stammered, then said, "We have talked a bit, Captain, and have come to know each other. The lieutenant is a courteous gentleman, and I am concerned for him."

"Of course. But who is with your son?"

"Kenneth is still asleep. You know how soundly children sleep. He never once stirred."

"The lieutenant was unconscious when last I left him."

"I would really like to see him, Captain," she insisted graciously.

Hamilton nodded briefly. "Come on up, if you wish."

The three of them climbed up to the hurricane deck, and as they crossed it to the short, three-step ladder that would take them finally to the texas deck where Hamilton had his quarters, Lieutenant Dempsey staggered out onto the captain's porch and grabbed at a railing to keep from falling.

"Sherman!" Cora cried and ran ahead of them. By the time they arrived, she was helping the pale and weak man into one of the cane-bottom chairs on the porch.

McKay grinned and said quietly to the captain, "It appears they have gotten very well acquainted in the last day or two."

Hamilton said to Dempsey, "You need to get back in bed. You are in no condition to be out here. Mr. McKay, help me with the lieutenant."

"No. No, please. Just let me sit here a moment." He looked at Cora, smiled, then glanced up at Hamilton. "What happened?"

"You were attacked by some men —"

"No, I mean with the boat. Something jostled me awake, and that was when I discovered myself here."

"It was only some engine trouble. Nothing to concern you, Lieutenant. But seeing as you are awake, I would like to know who the men were that beset you."

"I . . . I don't remember — no, that's not entirely true, I remember the moment clearly. Someone called out my name. They had concealed themselves in the darkness alongside the paddle box. When I turned, I was struck. There were two, maybe three of them."

"There were three," McKay said. "I saw them run off."

Dempsey said, "It happened so fast I never had a chance to see who they were."

"Unfortunate," Hamilton said. "Finding those men might answer a number of questions."

"But you are all right now," Cora said, "and that is all that matters."

Captain Hamilton pulled thoughtfully at his neatly trimmed gray beard. "You have no idea at all who might have done this?"

Dempsey shrugged his shoulders. "No, none at all. I am sorry."

Cora said, "Well, it seems pretty plain to me. It must have been that Grady Saunders."

"Saunders?" Hamilton stiffened and glanced at McKay, then back. "What makes you say that, ma'am?"

"Sherman and that man, Saunders, exchanged blows last night. When Sherman knocked him to the deck, Saunders said he would get even — said he would kill Sherman."

Dempsey shook his head slowly and winced, shutting his eyes momentarily. When the pain passed, he said, "No, no, Cora. He was only angry, that's all. I'm sure he didn't mean it."

McKay saw that Cora did not agree with his assessment of the event, but she said no more about it, screwing her lips tight and looking concerned.

"I should like to have a talk with this man, Grady Saunders," Hamilton said. "Now, let's get you back into bed."

"No." Dempsey stood with some effort, gripping the railing for support. "I need to check on my men, and on the guards watching the payroll."

"Sergeant Glasser has taken over the troops in your absence, Lieutenant. He seems quite competent."

"Glasser is a good man, and well suited to the job, Captain Hamilton, but now that I am able to, I wish to oversee them."

"Sherman, do you really think you ought to?"

"Cora, I am sore, my head aches, but I am not incapacitated."

"Dr. Reuben says you might have a concussion," Hamilton said.

"Really, I am feeling much improved. These few minutes have cleared my head, and other than aches and bruised muscles, I am quite all right."

"I can't keep you here against your will, Lieutenant."

Cora said, "If you insist on this, at least

allow me to accompany you."

Dempsey smiled at her. "I would be pleased to have you accompany me, Cora. Only, shouldn't you first get dressed?"

Cora looked down at herself. In her concern over him, she had completely forgotten the dressing gown that now hung open revealing her blue, cotton nightgown. "Oh!" She grabbed the robe together and with a faltering smile said, "It won't take me but a minute to get dressed. I will be right back," and she hurried off.

The steam whistle shrilled all at once, and then a puff of steam burst from the starboard 'scape pipe. A few seconds later another billow of steam shot up out of the larboard pipe, then the starboard again sang out, and back and forth it went, faster and faster until the sound blended together in a familiar symphony.

"It looks like Mr. Seegar has the engines up," Hamilton said.

The paddle wheels had begun to turn and the *Tempest Queen* shuddered, wood groaning as she once again began to challenge the mighty Missouri.

The sky was brighter and down low in the east; the vegetation had begun to take on color. A fine mist was lifting off the river, and with the anchors hauled aboard, the shoreline slipped away as they moved out into deeper water.

"Thank you, Captain, for your concern and your aid," Dempsey said.

"You are welcome. And don't overdo it right away. If you should have a relapse, I will never hear the end of it from the boat's doctor."

Dempsey managed a grin, then moving with care, he made his way off the porch and across to the ladder.

McKay looked down at himself, wiggled his bare toes. "I suppose I ought to return to my cabin as well and do something with my appearance."

Hamilton viewed him up and down. "I'd say it's rather becoming — in a rustic sort of way."

"Thank you, Captain. But I prefer my old attire, and really, shoes are so much more comfortable than going barefooted, in spite of what passes for local customs in this part of the country."

Hamilton managed a laugh, although his heart was not in it. He had a great many things to concern him now, to occupy his thoughts. "I will see you later, Mr. McKay." He wheeled to his cabin door, then hesitated and looked over at McKay again. "Thank you for thinking of the anchors. We would have been in a bad way if you had not kept a clear head."

"Of course, Captain. You are welcome."

Hamilton entered his cabin. McKay left the porch for his own stateroom and a fresh change of clothes.

Chapter Twenty

Clifton Stewart couldn't sleep. Although he had managed to doze on and off throughout the night, something kept nudging him awake — something he could not put a finger on. But it had unsettled him just the same.

Stewart had no idea what the time was, but he felt sure that the dawn must not be far off. He had spent the night on a straw tick mattress outside on the porch, and knowing sleep was impossible now, he threw off the blanket and sat up, staring long and hard into the darkness, as if somewhere out there he might find the source of his discontent.

He rose quietly so as not to disturb the people still sleeping inside the house, pulled on his boots, went down into the yard, and stood a long time peering up into the sky. A montage of memories crackled through his brain like a ribbon of firecrackers, and then they were gone. Stewart shivered, even though the air was warm. It was so quiet out here he imagined he could hear his heart beating. Even the frogs had finally managed to find sleep.

Why can't I?

In the dark corral, Laban's sleek racehorse whinnied softly. Stewart strolled across the yard, leaned on the rail. The horse hitched his ears forward and stared back at him.

"I can almost reach out and grab hold of it," he said softly. "It is so infuriating to know that it is so close, and yet the veil remains drawn. If only I could pull back a corner of it, I am certain the past would flood back in a torrent, and I would remember everything; who I was, what I was." Stewart slammed his fist into the rail.

A movement caught the corner of his eye, and he whirled. His first thought was that Indians were sneaking up on him, but then almost at once he knew that was impossible. Indians no longer stalked this part of the country. It was 1859, after all, and the farmer and townsman had done a fair job of taking all of Missouri from the Indian.

"Who is there?" Stewart's view riveted on a pool of deep shadow beneath the wide-flung branches of a nearby apple tree.

Another movement. His breathing had quickened, and now he settled it and said, sterner this time, "I see you there. Step out and show yourself."

The figure came forth.

"Jesse?"

"It's only me, Ben."

"Why aren't you inside, asleep?"

The boy came across the shadowed ground, hands thrust deep into the pockets of a pair of overalls. When he got close enough, Stewart saw the worry lines on the boy's young face.

"What's bothering you, Jesse?"

"I don't know. I just couldn't sleep."

Stewart smiled. "I guess I can understand that. I couldn't sleep either. But I can see there is something troubling you, right?"

"No, there ain't . . . well, I don't think there is, Ben."

"I think I know what it might be."

"You do?" Jesse's eyes hitched up, and in the wan light of the night sky, the boy's eyes were round and earnest.

Stewart nodded his head. "I think you are worried about your brother Frank and what is going to happen to him once he gets back home and your mother lays into him. And I think you might be worried a little that you will be punished, too, for not telling her sooner."

"Oh." Jesse blinked and looked away.

"Did I get it wrong?"

The boy shrugged his shoulders and looked at the horse at the far end of the corral. Whatever was bothering Jesse, Clifton figured the boy wasn't ready to talk about it. Neither spoke for a few moments, and then Jesse glanced back at Stewart.

"Ben?"

"Yes?"

"Yesterday, on the ferryboat, you covered for Frank and me."

"I did — against my better judgment."

"I can trust you, can't I?"

Clifton Stewart frowned, considering the boy's worried face, hearing the tightness of his speech. In the last couple days, Clifton had not known Jesse James to be anything but bright, imaginative, and sprightly. This somber side was something unexpected. "What is it, Jesse, what's got you troubled?"

The boy made a false start, hesitated, seesawed, and finally mumbled something Stewart did not quite make out.

"You're going to have to talk plainer than that, Jesse."

"You got to promise not to tell anyone, Ben."

Stewart had an ill feeling about what was to come, and he could not give the boy the guarantee he sought after. "If Frank is in trouble, I won't promise not to tell anyone, Jesse." Stewart scrutinized the boy. Jesse was being torn in a half-dozen directions. "I think you better tell me anyway."

"All right. I just gotta get it off my chest, Ben. I promised I wouldn't tell, but I keep thinking of Frank with them pirates, and wondering if he will get himself hurt, or killed. . . ."

"Pirates? Hold up a second. Is this another one of your stories, Jesse?"

"No, honest. Uncle Laban wasn't going to Marthasville to haul freight like he told everyone. Uncle Laban is a river pirate, and him and a bunch of other men are meeting up there, and then they are going to pirate a riverboat. Harvey told me and Frank all about it." Jesse halted in his rapid-fire confession and then said, "It has always been me who wanted to have adventures and to run away with the pirates or go scouting for wild Injuns. Frank has always been the one to show me reason and try to talk sense into me when I got out of hand — like I sometimes do. I couldn't believe it when he said he wanted to go along with Uncle Laban so's he could pirate that riverboat, too."

"Pirate a riverboat?" Stewart said, hoping he had not heard what he knew he had heard.

"That's right. The boat's name is the *Tempest Queen*, Harvey says, and it is carrying army goods, and the pirates are gonna all get a split of it."

A dozen images exploded inside Stewart's head. He clasped his temples, for suddenly there was a pain like a hammer driving down upon his head.

"Are you all right, Ben?" Jesse asked, worried.

Stewart shook his head as if to dislodge the bits and pieces of the shattered picture that had formed one instant and had fled the next. Slowly the pain subsided. "Yes, I'm all right."

"What happened?"

"I . . . I'm not sure."

The creak of a door opening sang out into the night, a sliver of light reached out behind the barn, and the next moment Harvey Caulder was peeking around the corner of the barn. "Who — who is out there?"

"It's only Ben and me, Harvey."

"Jesse? Is that you? What in blazes are you doing up and about so early? It's just nearly four of the clock, I reckon." Harvey came forward a few steps, clutching something in his right hand, holding the lantern in his left, high so as not to ruin his night eyesight.

Clifton said, "Harvey, I need to talk to you."

Harvey squinted at him in the dark and said cautiously, "What about?"

"About your father, and about Frank."

"What about my father and Frank? What do you want to know about them?"

"Harvey, I told Ben," Jesse blurted. "I had to. I was being eaten up inside with worry. I wish Frank had never got it into his head to go along with your father."

"You told him! How could you, Jesse?"

"I had to."

"Don't you know what you've done? If this ever gets out, they'll hang Pa by the neck, and me, too!" Harvey was in a panic. "What am I gonna do now, what am I gonna do?" Harvey cried. Then all at once he seemed to find an answer to that question. His right hand came up, and now Clifton Stewart saw what the dark object he had been holding was. An old flintlock pistol. Harvey thumbed the hammer.

"No, don't do that!" Jesse cried and leaped for Harvey.

The hammer fell.

Stewart had a brief vision of sparks spitting from beneath the frizzen, and a vague awareness, a split second later, of the blinding muzzle flash as the timeworn piece fired, bucking in the boy's hand.

And that was the last thing that Clifton Stewart remembered.

The arc of blue-white electricity seemed to rip the sky apart, and thunder crashed all about him, shaking the river with a rumble like booming cannons, drowning out the sound of the huge paddle wheel turning so near to him that the wind whipped up its backwash and flung it into his cheeks like angry hornets. Stunned, he stood there in the rain and wind and watched, and he could do nothing to stop it. The big black man had stepped out onto the guards, dangerously near to the thrashing paddle, and without a moment's hesitation he had leaped out into the black, choppy water as far as his powerful legs would carry him.

He watched the man momentarily pulled below the waves. Then his head broke through the choppy surface, but again he was dragged down. When finally he emerged from the inky depth, his strong arms and mighty legs were driving him away from the *Tempest Queen* and into the crashing night.

He lost sight of the black man then, and still confused, he turned slowly back to the woman on the deck who was clutching the iron cargo cleat in a death grip, as if her very life depended on it.

"Why did you do that, Mystie?"

"Because I had to." A lance of blue-white light glanced off her disheveled ebony hair, showed in her wide, black eyes.

"I don't understand. He belonged to someone —"

"Now he belongs only to himself," she said, lifting her perfect chin defiantly.

Then suddenly he understood. The shock set him back on his heels. "You — you're an abolitionist?"

She nodded her head.

He was at a loss. How did one handle a revelation such as this? It so went against all he had been taught growing up in the big plantation house, surrounded by black slaves all of his life. "This can't be true, Mystie. I love you!"

"Do you really?" The edge in her voice cut deep into his heart.

"What do you mean by that?"

"Mr. McKay once asked me how honest

I could be with you," she said. "He thought that even if you knew the truth you would still love me. I did not think so."

"Truth? Mystie, what are you talking about? If you mean freeing that runaway slave, well, yes, of course I can forgive you."

She released the cargo cleat and stood, finally finding her own strength. "That's not what I mean," she said. "The truth is, I, too, was born on a plantation; one very much like your own, I should think. My father was in line to inherit it all, until he made two mistakes that my grandfather could never forgive him of. My father's first mistake was falling in love with a slave on grandfather's plantation, a mulatto. My mother."

He took an involuntary step backward, shocked.

"His second mistake was that he loved me, too," she continued, not giving him a chance to speak. "I lived the first twelve years of my life in the slave quarters. I *was* a slave in the eyes of my grandfather. On my twelfth birthday my grandfather gave me a present: I was told that I was now old enough to become a full field hand, and he put me out to do a full task of work. Finally my father could stand it no longer.

He had some money of his own, not much, but enough to buy my mother and myself from him.

"He bought us! His own family. He bought us like a man buys a horse. Got the receipt and everything for us. Then he took us up north to Illinois where he applied for and obtained our papers to prove that we were once and for all, free."

She paused, her emotions ragged, collecting her thoughts.

"I have never been back to the plantation. I have no idea whatever happened to my grandfather, and if Father knows anything, he has never spoken of it." She came finally to a stop, drawing in another ragged breath.

He slowly emerged from his shock, staring at the lovely woman with the hair like a raven's wing and clear skin as pale as his own. "You . . . you are a Negro?" he managed to say.

"About one-quarter," she answered simply, suddenly drained of her anger. "But that doesn't make any difference, does it, in the South where a single drop of Negro blood is all it takes to condemn a person to being chattel?"

He shook his head, too stunned to speak. "I . . . I cannot see you again, Miss Waters," he managed to say, choking a bit on the tears that gathered. "Good-bye." He wheeled about and rushed away.

"Clifton!" he heard her call after him, but his tears drowned out her words as he rushed blindly away.

Clifton . . .

"Ben? Ben, can you hear me, Ben?"

Clifton Stewart sat up with a bolt, his head burning, sweat streaming down his cheeks. His eyes were wet, and the taste of salt was upon his tongue.

"Thank God," a woman's voice said somewhere behind him. He looked around, startled to find himself here, and not in his stateroom aboard the *Tempest Queen* where he had fled to after leaving Mystie Waters that awful night.

"What am I . . . ," he started to say, and then he remembered.

I remember everything!

Clifton swung his feet off the bed, but Reuben Samuel's strong hand held him back.

"Whoooa. Hold up there, Ben. You need to stay put."

"But I can't." He winced at the sudden pain in his head, put a hand on his forehead, and felt the moist bandage there.

Samuel said, "You were lucky, Ben. Jesse here told us all that happened. He knocked the pistol aside just as it fired and the bullet only grazed your skull, but it knocked you out cold."

"How long have I been unconscious?"

"Only a few minutes. The shot woke us up. When we got out there, Jesse was bent over you, and Harvey there, why he was white as new flour and shaking like a leaf."

"I have to go. The *Tempest Queen* is in danger."

"What in the world are you talking about, Ben?" Zerelda Samuel said. "What is the *Tempest Queen*, and who is this Mystie Waters you keep mumbling about? You had the same name on your lips the day we took you from the river."

"I haven't time to explain. Did Jesse tell you?"

Dr. Samuel looked over at the boy standing against the wall. Harvey was in a chair, hunched over and staring at his feet. "He did not. We have been too busy getting you in here and the bleeding stopped."

Jesse stepped forward and squared his shoulders. "Uncle Laban is a river pirate. He went upriver not to haul freight, but to waylay a riverboat named the *Tempest Queen* and steal guns and such that she is carrying up to Fort Leavenworth."

There was the sound of wood creaking,

and when they looked over, Bitsy had collapsed into a chair, her face drained.

"Is this true, Bitsy?" Dr. Samuel asked.

She seemed unable to speak at first. She brushed at her eyes and said, "It could very well be true. I know Laban is always up to some sort of mischief. I try not to peer too closely into his dealings for fear I might discover what he is really about. I have lied to myself all these years, wanting to believe him a fine and honest man. But he is not. He could very well be up to what Jesse claims."

"What about Frank?" Zerelda cried, suddenly realizing the danger her son was in.

"I'm sorry," Bitsy said meekly.

"I have to stop them." Clifton tried to stand again, but Reuben held him back.

"No, Ben, you should rest. Besides, what can you do now?"

Clifton knocked away Reuben's hand and stood. "You can stop calling me Ben. My name is Clifton Stewart, and I must stop Laban and his pirates, for I work on that very steamboat. The *Tempest Queen* is also my home. I have friends aboard her, and I must do all I can to help them!"

"Your memory has returned?" Reuben asked.

"Yes."

"You will never catch up with them," Harvey said, still in the chair, but looking up now. "They were meeting at Marthasville, and that's most of twenty miles from here. Then they were going on up the river, and who knows where they might be now."

Stewart thought a moment, and all at once it came to him. "Firecracker. Atop Firecracker I can cover that distance in no time."

"Can you ride a horse like that, Ben — err, I mean Clifton?" Zerelda asked.

"Can I ride a Thoroughbred? My father raises racehorses. I used to burn up the track at the Merryville races every Sunday!"

Bitsy said sharply, "Harvey, go saddle up Firecracker. Make sure you put on that light saddle Laban uses when he races."

"Yes, Ma," the boy said, standing. As he passed Stewart, he paused, glanced at him, and said quietly, "Sorry I tried to kill you. I wasn't thinking."

"Forget it," Clifton said. He had more urgent matters to concern himself with now than the action of one frightened boy.

In five minutes the horse was saddled and brought around to the house. Clifton leaped to its back, feeling powerful muscles beneath him twitch with pent-up energy just waiting to burst forth. Firecracker knew well enough what was required of him.

"God speed you," Zerelda said as he took up the reins. "Please take care of Frank for me."

"I'll do what I can."

"Mr. Stewart," Reuben said, coming from the shadows where his wagon was parked. Firecracker strained at his bit, and Clifton held him in check, controlling the energy waiting to be unleashed. Reuben handed up a revolver. "Take this. I keep it in the wagon when we travel, but you might need it."

Clifton checked that it was loaded and that the caps were on the nipples, and he shoved it under his belt. "Thanks. I hope I don't have to use it."

Dr. Reuben stepped back, and Stewart turned Firecracker's head away from the house. Digging in his heels, Clifton was instantly launched onto the road in a furious explosion of four legs and flying mane that sent him barreling on his journey.

Six men rode down the middle of the street toward the long, rickety finger of timber at the end of town pointing out into the river. The sun was not yet high enough to clear the trees that grew up around Catfish Landing; the river was still in shadows, and mist rose from the dark water.

Waldo Hinkley reined to a halt, and the other pirates pulled in their mounts alongside him. Hinkley studied the sleepy village. A dog barked somewhere behind the unpainted houses that were slowly being consumed with vines from uncut yards. A troop of chickens out for an early stroll pecked their way around a corner onto the main street and up along the boardwalk in front of a row of weathered buildings.

Charles Hart looked the place over and grinned at Frank James, who was astride a tired sorrel at his left. "This here place is a tinderbox just waiting for a spark. Why, I'm surprised it hasn't gone up in flames already."

Hinkley turned his horse into a hitching rail and dismounted. Stretching his muscles, he kneaded the small of his back. They had covered a lot of miles, racing to beat the sun, and both men and horses were in need of a good rest. But first there was a job to do.

Hinkley said, "I had my doubts, but we made it. Old Deke was true to his word. He did figure out some way to delay that boat."

"Maybe so, but when the road swung back along the river I got a glimpse of that fancy steamboat making her way up. She ain't but a few miles behind us, and making five miles an hour, I'd wager," Dickerson said, massaging the seat of his britches and standing oddly bowlegged. "We ain't got but a few minutes, so let's not waste 'em palavering."

"We got time." Hinkley scanned the single road through Catfish Landing. "The town is coming awake, and mighty soon these stores are gonna be opening for business. I want to be done with the deed before too many more folks crawl from under their blankets." He took a canvas sack from off his saddle and, fishing around inside, brought out a fresh box of Lucifer matches. "Each of you take a handful of them," he said handing the block first to Charles Hart, who broke off a half-dozen matches from the brick and passed it next to Frank.

"Ralph, I will be wanting you and Tom Green to take the horses and go on down to the pier. Use your rifles to signal the boat when she comes into view. Case, me, Frank, and Charlie here will station ourselves throughout the town. Once we are all done, and the town is making like a funeral pyre, and everyone is rushing about to put the flames out, Tom, you take the horses and ride ahead to where the wagons will meet us."

"It is *Charles,*" Hart said tightly.

Waldo grinned. "Charles. I forgot, you're temperamental about your name."

Hart smiled thinly. "Well, it's the only one I got."

"That's a lie. Your name is no more Charles Hart than mine is President James Buchanan."

They looked over at Case Jackson who had just spoken. "What do you mean, Case?" Waldo shifted his view to Hart, then back. "What makes you say that? If his name ain't Charles Hart, what is it, and why is he keeping it from us?"

Case pushed his slouch hat to the back of his head and allowed a smile. "Darryl and me, we got ourselves oiled up yesterday afternoon with some good corn liquor. We go back a lot of years. Darryl used to live in Jefferson City, where I come from, you know. Well, we got to talking about old times, and then somehow we got on the subject of this new fellow that Darryl brought along." Case looked at the man who called himself Charles Hart. "Suppose you tell 'em your real name, Charlie."

"Well?" Waldo said. Every eye was on Hart.

Frank James had come to like this young man who was not much older than himself, and he was as curious as the others now.

"All right. Case has got it straight. My name ain't Charles Hart. I only took that name to shake the law what's been tailing me since I left Utah." His eyes were suddenly cold and intense, and when their heavy lids narrowed Frank sensed descending about the man a swift ruthlessness that up until this moment had been hidden behind the facade of his alias, Charles Hart.

"Suppose you tell us what your name really is, not that it is gonna matter much now, and this ain't really the time or place to be hashing this out, anyway." Waldo glanced down the road at the river where the first streak of sunlight had turned the water to gold. "Be quick with it, and we'll continue the discussion later."

"Quantrill. William Clarke Quantrill . . . if it really makes any difference."

It didn't to most of them. Case Jackson knew of the man's reputation only through Darryl, but Tom Green had heard of him. "From what I read in the papers," Green said, "this man, Quantrill, has raised a little hell out in the Territories."

Waldo snorted. "Deke will be interested in hearing that. We will see how good he is at hell-raising here at Catfish Landing. Now, let's get moving. Remember, when you hear Ralph and Tom signaling that riverboat, that's when you set fire to everything that will burn — and shoot anybody who tries to stop you."

Frank felt suddenly weak in the knees, and he said, "What about the folks still asleep?"

Waldo gave the boy a contemptuous leer. "What's wrong, James? Is this not exactly what you had bargained for when you decided to run off and play pirate?"

Frank stiffened, about to defend himself when Quantrill said, "I'll take him along with me. Frank will do fine. Don't worry about nothing, Waldo." Quantrill turned and strode away, and Frank found himself tagging along behind the man in spite of himself.

Chapter Twenty-One

Morning on the river — any river — was the finest time of day! Hamilton didn't even mind it that he'd been up several hours already. He had watched the coming sunrise from his porch: horizon turning from violet to pink, and finally the glory of a new day bursting across the sky, and the black water suddenly shot through with streaks of gold while its blanket of vapor melted beneath the warming air.

But even this pleasantness did not dispel the concern that had gnawed at him since the predawn near disaster. He had gone down to the galley afterward, grabbed a cup of coffee, and was making his way along the promenade, watching the bend in the river ahead, when Chief Engineer Seegar found him.

"The men have been all over the boat, Captain, and there is still no sign of them."

"Humm. This is an odd turn of events." Hamilton's bushy, gray eyebrows came together. "Dvorak has been with us over two years, and Kelly almost as long. Why would they impair the engines, putting the boat in peril, and then abandon her?"

"I know those men, Captain Hamilton. They wouldn't do that. Both are conscientious engineers and loyal to the *Tempest Queen*."

"Humm." Hamilton frowned into his cup of coffee, then looked up abruptly. "I am afraid I have to agree with you, Mr. Seegar. So, what does that leave us with?"

Seegar shrugged his shoulders. "The only other possibility is that someone else must have done it, and that means Dvorak and Kelly have come to some bad end."

"Unfortunately, you have drawn the same conclusion that I have."

Seegar was grim. "If that's the case, we are even farther away from solving this puzzle than before."

"Perhaps." Hamilton sipped his coffee, trying to pull the scattered pieces of a puzzle together and not having much luck. *Luck?* He huffed silently to himself. If McKay had been there, the gambler would most certainly have some notion or another — but whether he would be willing to expound on it was another matter. McKay always played it close to the vest. Even though at the moment Hamilton would have welcomed almost any help, he was disposed to try to work the puzzle out himself instead of consulting the gambler.

This is childish, he reprimanded himself. The most expedient means to the end of this problem was what he should be seeking. It was not that Hamilton in any way disliked McKay, for, indeed, he had become quite fond of the gambler and his peculiar ways. In truth, he had to admit to himself, he suffered from a bit of envy toward Dexter McKay, who seemed in control of every situation.

Hamilton recalled what Cora Mills had said about Lieutenant Dempsey and Grady Saunders locking horns the previous evening, and he pondered the suspicions McKay had expressed. *Were* the two incidents somehow related?

"Mr. Seegar, have you by chance seen Reverend Saunders and his boy about?"

"Saunders? Not lately. Not since I gave him and his nephew a tour of the engine room last night like you requested."

"Like I requested?"

"Yes, sir."

"Humm. Who told you that?"

"Why, it was the reverend himself."

"And you showed them through the engine room?"

"Only took him through quickly. He didn't really seem too interested. Personally, I think he was having a hard time sleeping and was only trying to fill the hours."

Hamilton gripped the green handrailing and frowned ahead at the river unfolding before them. The Missouri was not like the Mississippi. It was not nearly as broad, and the shores were mostly hung down to the water with wild, tangled growth instead of the careful manicured grounds that he was used to watching pass by on the lower Mississippi. There were no levees to speak of on this uncultivated river, and the water ran right up to the shore, creating dangerously shallow shoals at every bend.

He wanted to be done with this trip up to Fort Leavenworth. It had been an ill-fated journey from the beginning. Young Clifton Stewart had been killed, Sergeant Carr had disappeared, Lieutenant Dempsey beaten, and the *Tempest Queen* nearly dashed to pieces upon the shore because of treachery aboard . . . and the only common factor it seemed — except for Stewart's death in a barroom brawl — was the Saunderses — father and son.

"I think it is time to find the Reverend Saunders and have a talk with the man," Hamilton said.

Seegar was scowling. "You think he might of had something to do with this morning's near disaster?"

"I don't know, but every way I try to work it out, his name keeps cropping up."

"I'll go with you."

The crack of a rifle shot far ahead pulled Hamilton's gaze toward a long pier that had just come into view around the river's bend. Two men were standing there, still small in the distance. A second rifle boomed. Hamilton could see the gray puff of powder smoke rise into the air a moment before he heard the shot.

Overhead, the *Tempest Queen*'s steam whistle answered the signal.

"More passengers," Seegar commented.

Hamilton frowned. "This has been the busiest trip I can ever remember," he said, and once again another of McKay's suspicions echoed in his brain as the pilot rang the big, bronze bell for the leadsmen to begin sounding the river's bottom.

"You ever set torch to an entire town, William?"

"No, I haven't ever done anything like this," Quantrill said, and Frank heard a note of apprehension in his new friend's voice. The two of them were hunkered down inside a flimsy, abandoned shack that they had discovered right in the middle of Catfish Landing. It was cluttered with trash and yellowed newsprint left behind by its previous occupants. Its rotting wood walls were bored full of worm holes and infested with termites. A perfect tinderbox, Quantrill had said when they first peeked through the holes where windows had once been.

"What's bothering you now, William?"

Quantrill glanced over and gave Frank a grin. "This isn't exactly how I would have done it if it was up to me."

"How would you have done it?"

"The way the Sioux or the Cheyenne might. I'd have come in with torches already burning and hit Catfish Landing hard and swift. And I'd have stayed on horseback so's to make a quick getaway. I don't much care to sneak around, trying not to be seen, and then after I've set fire to the place, having to make my way — maybe even fight my way — down to the pier and get back aboard that boat."

Frank crushed a fat spider beneath his boot and spread the green smear along the floorboards. "Yeah, I sort of see what you mean."

"Yep, hit and run, that's the way I'd do

it if I was in charge."

Frank grinned. "Maybe someday you will be."

This seemed to please William Quantrill.

After a few minutes Frank said, "If you ever do strike out on your own, let me know. I'd be pleased to ride with you, William."

Quantrill nodded his head. "I'll keep you in mind, Frank. I will surely keep you in mind."

A rifle shot down by the river brought them both instantly alert. A second followed in a matter of seconds, and not long afterward the distant call of a steam whistle answered the signal.

"Guess it's time," Quantrill said, taking a match from his pocket.

Frank had a lump the size of a fist stuck in his throat, and all he could do was nod his head. Quantrill's match sputtered and flared, and somehow Frank had managed to light his own as well.

"Let's make some fire, Frank," Quantrill said, grinning and putting the match to a yellowed, crumpled ball of newsprint. . . .

Clifton Stewart lay low along Firecracker's strong back, his heels keeping up the steady pounding that had begun the very moment they had left Laban's farm and had struck the river road. Now that the sun was finally up, Clifton let the animal stretch out and run free, and the miles passed beneath its flying hooves without Firecracker yet showing any signs of tiring.

Stewart knew a good horse when he rode one, and Fire cracker was first-rate. His father had raised the finest Thoroughbreds around Baton Rouge, and Clifton had sometimes spent an entire Sunday afternoon at the Merryville races riding every animal in his father's stable, and generally to a victory. The training he had received then was paying off now. The countryside fairly fled past him, but he kept his concentration on his riding, not on sightseeing, flying past slow wagons and leisurely early morning travelers with hardly a glance, leaving them far behind him almost before they knew that something had passed them by.

Clifton had only four thoughts running through his brain: The condition of the road immediately ahead of him, the feel of the mighty dynamo pounding beneath him, an alertness for a sign indicating the Marthasville cutoff — and the vaguely disconcerting problem of what he was going to do once he did catch up with Laban Caulder and his pirate conspirators.

And underlying all of these was the dread that, even with his best efforts, he would arrive too late to help his friends!

A sign ahead marked a road he was approaching: *Marthasville!*

Stewart reined Firecracker to a stop and held him there as the horse strained to be once more set free. He recalled what Harvey had said. The pirates were only meeting here at Marthasville and then going on ahead. Should he turn to the right or maintain his course on the river road? He glanced to the south where the muddy Missouri River swirled past the pier of a woodyard. There were men at work, hauling fuelwood to be stacked and dried. On an impulse, Clifton pulled the horse about and bounded down the road toward the shack near the pier.

A woodcutter looked up, startled by the sudden appearance of Stewart and the horse with wide flaring nostrils and heaving chest.

"Have you seen a bunch of men come past here this morning, sir?"

The woodcutter set his ax aside, removed his leather gloves, and dragged a sleeve across his sweating forehead. "Been a couple people by this morning, but I don't know if they're the ones you're inquiring about."

Clifton frowned, then recalled Laban's wagon and said, "You would remember them. One of the men drove a yellow freight wagon with a matched pair of draft animals."

The woodcutter shook his head. "Sorry, I can't help you."

A lean, weathered man in patched gray britches and a coarse red shirt, wearing a new straw hat above a sharp, chiseled face, stepped out of the shack and squinted into the low morning sun at Clifton's back. "I've seen the wagon you are talking about, mister. It was up the road a little ways when me and my mates come down from Marthasville early this morning."

"Is it still there?" Clifton asked, renewed hope pulsing through him.

"Naw. They all pulled out right behind us."

Stewart's hopes sank again, but at least he knew now that he was on the right track. "Did you see which way they went?"

"Sure I did. They went west, following the river road."

Stewart glanced up at the road he had

just come off of, then back again. "How many men were there?"

"Can't rightly say. I never did count 'em. My guess is, there were right around a dozen, and three freight wagons. I did count them, and I remarked to my mates about the fancy yeller one."

"How long ago was this?"

"Oh, let me see" — he removed the hat and scratched the sparse covering beneath it — "it has to have been forty-five minutes or so."

"Thank you. You have been most helpful." Clifton wheeled the horse away from the woodcutters, burying his heels. Firecracker still had a lot of running left in him, and he plunged willingly into a head-long rush at Clifton's prodding, carrying his rider once again along the river road.

"Fire! Fire!" someone aboard the *Tempest Queen* shouted, and immediately Captain Hamilton thought a second disaster had befallen his beloved boat, but then passengers and crewmen were rushing over to the starboard railing, pointing, and the excitement rippled in the air.

In the few minutes it took the pilot to bring the *Tempest Queen* into the pier, what had begun as a dark smudge blotting the morning sky above the little river town had expanded and drifted out over the water, and now it reflected the orange and yellow light from the flames that licked hungrily at the row of wooden buildings.

The boat put into dock, and crewmen leaped off her and secured her in place, but no one from Catfish Landing seemed to care that a riverboat had tied up at their doorstep. They were too busy forming bucket brigades to attack the flames that had sprung up all over the town. Unfortunately, Catfish Landing no longer had a population large enough to cover each new eruption.

Moving through the ranks of soldiers, Grady Saunders searched for a face. He spied it among the men at the railing. Already, Grady had heard the troops talking about helping with the blaze, but they seemed to need a shove in that direction. Deke had said that might be the case, and he had figured out just what it might take.

Spying the burly soldier known as Eagle, Grady put himself near the man and said to no one in particular, but loud enough for all to hear, "Them Southern boys are fixing to put that fire out all by themselves. I heard them say they was gonna show the Northern city boys and hayseeds how folks help each other down in the South."

This got their attention like morning reveille.

"Who says that?" Eagle growled, searching the crowd for a culprit.

"Well, I think it was that soldier named Belvedere, I reckon," Grady allowed.

"He did, did he!" Eagle glanced at his friends. "Vell, boys, vhy are we just standing here?"

In a moment the word shot through the troops, and every boy born and bred north of Kentucky was scrambling over the gunnels and leaping onto the pier.

In another part of the boat, the words reached the ears of the Southern soldiers as well, and Deke Saunders was there to help fan the flames. "Why, those Northern abolitionist sons of perdition are trying to steal the glory from you fine Southern boys. To hear them talk! My word, it is surely a disgrace to just stand here while that poor town burns to the ground and the North gets the praise for trying to save it!"

Deke Saunders had had some small experience preaching fire-and-brimstone sermons, and he did not spare the ardor this time. Dissension in the country had already alienated the two groups of soldiers

415

who somehow still managed to work together but preferred the company of their own kind when off duty, and it didn't take a whole lot of persuasion on Deke's part to spur them into action.

Inside of three minutes the boat was emptied of soldiers, except for the two guards at the cabin where the gold was secured. Unlike the others, they *were* on duty, and they remained at their post.

Lieutenant Dempsey watched it all from the promenade railing. He was feeling much improved . . . especially since Cora had insisted on keeping him company. Kenneth had awakened and was with them.

"I ought to go into town with my men," he said to her.

"They may need you," she agreed. "The men are used to taking orders from you, and who better to direct them now than their commanding officer? But are you feeling up to it, Sherman?"

"I am," he said, "and you are correct, I need to be among them." He started toward the staircase. Dexter McKay intercepted him before he had gone a half-dozen steps and, with an urgent wave, hauled Dempsey into a passageway where he'd been standing, out of sight.

"Mr. McKay! What is it?" the lieutenant said, startled at the gambler's abrupt appearance. "I am in a hurry. What is on your mind?"

"You going to fight the fire with your men?"

"Yes, of course."

McKay nodded his head toward the pier where the last of Dempsey's men were dogtrotting into the burning town. "Lieutenant, I don't have time to explain, but if I have not missed my guess, I dare say you ought to remain aboard and, if possible, recall your men to the *Tempest Queen*."

Dempsey looked at McKay, then he stared back at the fiery town. Already four buildings were hopelessly engulfed, and it appeared from his vantage point that the town's people — some pulling on their clothes as they poured from their doorways, some hardly dressed at all — were concentrating their efforts on the as yet untouched buildings, tossing buckets of water being handed up from the river in a mad effort to save what was left.

"But why?"

"Yes, Mr. McKay," Cora asked, "why should he recall his men?"

"I don't have time to go into it all now.

Briefly, I have been watching Saunders and his friends —"

"This again? Mr. McKay, Reverend Saunders has become an obsession with you."

He ignored the interruption. "I think they are up to no good, Lieutenant, and I believe the reason for them being on the *Tempest Queen* is locked in a stateroom at the back of this boat."

"The gold!"

McKay nodded his head.

"That's impossible. It is guarded around the clock by two men. And besides, this boat is carrying over forty armed soldiers. How could anyone hope to steal the army's gold?"

A small, knowing smile crept to McKay's face. "Do I need to point out that presently, the two guards, and yourself are the only army aboard?"

"This is preposterous."

McKay's view shot past Dempsey to the pier below. "Is it? There. Those men coming aboard now. They are the very men who were put off last night at Growley's Wood Yard."

Dempsey glanced at the pier. "Are you certain?"

"Of course I am certain."

Cora grabbed Dempsey's arm, and her nails bit in. "Sherman, I think Mr. McKay is right. Those *are* the same men who disembarked last night."

"It is too late, I'm afraid," McKay said, frowning. "If you leave the boat now, you will never get back aboard. Quickly, come with me." McKay moved farther up the passage and into the main cabin. Reluctantly, Dempsey, Cora, and her boy followed him. They hurried through the galley where the kitchen crew gave them curious glances, and the galley chief, Maggie Divitt, stopped barking orders at a woman stirring a huge black iron soup pot and glared at them, a fist clutching a wooden spoon propped on her wide hips.

McKay tipped his hat at the galley chief, smiled, and passed on through, hurrying his companions down a narrow flight of steps. In the four months that McKay had lived aboard the *Tempest Queen* he had come to learn the layout of the big boat almost as well as he knew the dimples on the marked deck of Steamboat playing cards inside the left breast pocket of his jacket. He hurried them along another passageway, then pushed open a door and stepped inside.

Dempsey stuck his head into the

cramped room and wrinkled his nose. "The laundry room?"

"Quickly, in here."

"But it smells!"

"Yes, indeed. Horrible, isn't it? And that's why you must come quickly and shut the door after you."

Dempsey hesitated, and then as if propelled from behind, he stumbled inside and caught himself on the edge of one of the laundry baskets. At his heels marched Cora Mills and Kenneth, who had his nose pinched tightly shut.

"Now, with haste, under these sheets, and whatever you do, no matter what, keep perfectly quiet."

"But . . ." Dempsey started to protest.

Cora said, "Perhaps we ought to listen to Mr. McKay."

Dempsey, wavering, finally agreed, and shifting his saber around and out of the way, he sat down beside the gambler.

McKay pulled a sheet up over the four of them, and admonished them again to remain as still as death itself.

In the dim light that filtered through the ventilation slots in the door, and past the dingy sheet, McKay checked his little Remington .31 caliber pocket revolver. Satisfied that it was fully loaded and capped, he tucked it back into its holster under his coat.

A very large part of McKay hoped that his suspicions would be proved wrong . . . however, at the same time a very small part of him hoped they would be vindicated.

If they should prove false, he frowned wryly to himself, this little episode was going to require some difficult explaining, and he didn't want to even think of how he would do that!

Chapter
Twenty-Two

Deke Saunders waited until the last of the soldiers had bounded off the pier, and then with a grin, which might have been his first real show of satisfaction since coming aboard the *Tempest Queen*, he gave a nod of his head to his men below. From where he had placed himself, at the topmost railing up on the hurricane deck, the pirates already in place around the boat clearly saw the signal to begin, and at once parties of three and four men moved into action.

"Finally, it has begun, boy," Deke said to his son, who was standing beside him.

"Sure 'nough, Pa." A glint of mischief sparked in the younger Saunders's eyes.

Deke turned and squinted up where the morning sun stung his eyes, past the bronze bell mounted atop the texas deck, up at the pilothouse. Beyond its expanse of windows, he could see two men inside the pilothouse. "Come along, Grady, we got us a job to do as well." Deke made his way to the rear of the texas and climbed the stairs to its roof where the pilothouse was perched. Adjusting the heavy revolver in his belt beneath the black frock, the phony preacher and his son strolled casually up to the pilothouse door.

Moving swiftly, they flattened against the wall near the engine-room doorway and cautiously looked around the corner. When the engineers all had their backs to the door, Bud Patterson, Tom Green, and Harold Madden slipped into the steaming compartment, unseen.

Chief Engineer Seegar happened to glance around at that moment. Through the maze of pipes and the veil of vapor from where he was tinkering with the machines, he saw them come in. "You three don't belong in here. You might get hurt." He folded himself through the pipes and came across the room. He noticed that Harold Madden was among the three men. "Say, weren't you the man with that preacher last night?"

"Yo— yo— you got th— that — that straight, mister."

"I already gave you the tour. Now, you and your friends will have to get out of here before yo—" Seegar's words stopped abruptly, and his eyes widened. Harold

Madden's revolver was suddenly in his hand, and pointing at the engineer.

"What's the meaning of this?"

Patterson and Green rounded on Seegar's two strikers and held them at gunpoint.

"In a min-minute you will put those engines t-to runnin' backwards, hear?"

"Backwards . . . ? Reverse?" Seegar frowned. "What are you talking about?"

"You are gonna ba-ba-back this boat out of here."

"I will not."

Madden swung his revolver toward the strikers without warning and fired. One of the men buckled forward, gripping his side, and collapsed to the floor. The revolver came back around, steadying upon the engineer's chest. "Yo— you will do it."

Seegar knelt by the wounded man, then glared up at Madden. "Are you insane? What the hell do you want? Who are you?"

"I want this boat to st-start moving backwards when I gi-give the word."

Seegar quickly examined his wounded striker. "We need to get Karl to the doctor."

"You will need to get both of th-th-them to a doc-doc-doctor in a minute if you don't do exactly as I sa-say!"

The second striker went pale, fear pulling at his face as the revolver snapped around. Seegar looked up at him. "Bennington, do what you can for Karl." He said to Madden, "All right, I will do as you say."

Patterson and Green were glancing nervously at the doorway, but apparently no one had heard the shot above the constant clangor of engine-room noise. Harold said to them, "Make certain we aren't dis-disturbed."

"Right, Harold." Patterson put himself just inside the doorway, his revolver cocked and ready.

"Now, engineer, d-do what is necessary."

Seegar glanced one last time at the man writhing on the engine-room floor, and frowning, he went to the machinery. "I'll need help," he said.

Harold nodded his head at Bennington. "G— go help your boss."

When Bennington, on his knees beside Karl, hesitated, Tom Green, who was nearest to him, nudged him in the ribs with the toe of his boot. "Let that one be and go help your boss."

Bennington left Karl lying there and assumed his place at one of the starboard engines. The two engineers spun the control valves and grabbed hold of levers, and then Seegar paused and looked over at Madden, waiting for the pirate to give the word.

Armed with rifles, shotguns, pistols, revolvers, knives, and fists, the brigands swarmed through the *Tempest Queen.* Some leaped to her mooring posts and began chopping at the thick hawsers while others rounded up the crew and passengers who had not gone ashore to fight the fire and gathered them into the main cabin.

They scoured the boat from stern to bow, moving swiftly, collecting everyone they could find.

The hawsers were finally severed. The Missouri's current grabbed the mighty boat and drifted her from her berth.

Up in the pilothouse, Patton Sinclair was lounging on the high bench with his heels propped on a window ledge, enjoying his freedom from the helm, smoking a fat green cigar, blowing smoke rings at the ceiling while Eric Jupp stood by the windows staring out at the blaze eating its way through Catfish Landing.

"Too bad. I hate to see her go like this," Jupp said. "She has come to a sad end. Catfish Landing used to be quite a place.

I've put in here a handful of times in the last fifteen years, but I hear the stories from the old-time raftsmen that this place really boomed during the beaver trade."

Sinclair blew a smoke ring and watched it break apart against the pull cords and hog rings hanging down. "Well, one thing is for certain, Mr. Jupp, whether it be this muddy stream or the wide Mississippi."

Jupp looked over. "Oh? What might that be?"

"Nothing ever remains the same," Sinclair intoned philosophically.

Jupp gave a short laugh. It wasn't really a very deep thought, and he returned his attention to the more interesting drama being played out on shore. Suddenly a scowl crossed Jupp's face and he looked around — first at the pier, then at the shore, and finally at the river.

"By gads, we are adrift!"

Sinclair slammed his feet to the floor and was up immediately. In a glance he confirmed Jupp's startled exclamation. As if of a single thought, both men sprang for the door, but before they had gone two steps, it burst open and Deke Saunders stepped inside with his revolver drawn. Grady came in behind him, shutting the door.

Deke's frigid glance shifted between the two men. "Which one of you is the pilot?" he demanded.

Jupp glanced at Sinclair, then to the revolver in Saunders's hand. "We are both pilots, but at the present, I am the one at the helm."

Without a moment's hesitation the revolver hitched over and fired. Patton Sinclair lurched backward and crashed through the wall of windows, landing in a pile of shattered glass and wooden window frames outside on the roof of the texas. The weapon came back menacingly, and Jupp gulped at the smoking barrel's big bore staring him in the eyes.

"Now, mister, hop to it and get this boat moving and out of here. Be quick about it, and remember, one step out of line and you'll end up like your friend there. You are gonna take us on up the river to a place where I tell you. Now, move!"

Jupp glanced at the shattered windows, slowly coming out of his shock. Taking the wheel, still dazed by Saunders's viciousness, he pulled a signal cord that rang a bell down in the engine room, and spoke into the brass tube that sprouted from the floor.

"Mr. Seegar. I need full reverse."

Deke shoved Jupp aside and shouted into the speaking tube, "Harold? Harold? You got things under control down there?"

In a moment the reply echoed up from three decks below, "I go— go— got it all un— un— under con— con— control."

"Settle down, Harold," Deke called back. "We have the situation in hand. We are almost home free." Deke glanced at Grady. "You can handle this. I'd better go look after our interests."

"Right, Pa."

In the brief lull between the buckets being thrust into his hand with machine-like regularity, Konrad Adler paused to sling sweat from his brow. As he looked toward the river, along the line of men and women that made up the bucket brigade, his view happened upon the *Tempest Queen*, and his jaw fell open.

"Ach du lieber Gott!"

The soldier to his left glanced over at the sudden outburst. "What's wrong, Eagle?"

Adler remembered himself. Pointing, he switched back to English and said, "The boat, it is pulling away vithout us!"

The news of the riverboat's departure shot along the bucket brigade as if it were a living telegraph wire. "What's going on?" the soldier asked.

Eagle said, "I do not know. Vhy vould the lieutenant leave us behind?"

Some men started for the pier, but they drew up after a few strides when it became apparent that unless they could swim faster than the *Tempest Queen*'s steam engines could drive her up the river, it was hopeless to try to catch her.

"What are we going to do, Eagle?" his friend asked.

Eagle watched the black plume of smoke making its way up the river. Although he was only a private, the men looked to him. Adler had charisma, and strength in his character, and even his compact size spoke of power. He was decisive in whatever he did, and this was no different. Eagle shifted his view from the riverbank's smoke to the plume rising black and hot overhead. "Ve put this damn fire out! Ve vorry about getting up to Fort Leavenvorth later."

That seemed to settle it among most of the men. Some of the Belvedere contingent resented an immigrant Northerner making the decision for them, and it clearly would have set better with them if one of the sergeants had said it rather than Adler, but the facts were plain: There was nothing any one of them could do to stop the *Tempest Queen* from leaving now, and putting out the conflagration was of immediate importance.

The men re-formed the lines, and buckets of water resumed their way to the flames.

The first indication that something was amiss was the sudden bursts of steam hissing from the 'scape pipes. Then the paddle wheels began to turn, and the *Tempest Queen* halted her downriver drift as her bow came around, pointing now to the west.

"We shouldn't ought to be going anywhere, should we, Bill?" the one guard asked the other.

Bill left his post and leaned out over the railing, craning his neck to see beyond the expanse of white-painted wood that enclosed the paddle wheel. When he looked back concern was in his face. "I don't think so, our men are still ashore fighting the fire. That is most peculiar, I'd say."

"Me, too," the first guard agreed, wary now, and not sure what to think of the matter, but firming up his grip on his rifle musket just the same.

Neither soldier had much time to dwell on the problem, however, for without warning two men dropped from the roof overhead, and in the span of a single heartbeat, both soldiers lay dead at the foot of the cabin door where the paymaster's gold was locked up.

The pirates dragged the bodies aside and hurtled themselves into the door. Wood groaned, bulged, then a shadow moved across them and they glanced over.

Deke Saunders came down the last steps of the ladder with his revolver in hand. "Leave that door locked up for now."

The pirates backed off, eyeing the revolver pointing at them. "Sure thing, Deke. We was only curious to see what was inside."

"That's my business, and none of your concern. Now, I've got to get down to the main cabin and help with the passengers and crew that we've rounded up there. You two stay here, and if that door ain't still locked when I get back, you're dead men."

"This is an outrage!"

"Shut up, Captain."

Hamilton glared at the elder Saunders, who had just come into the main cabin.

Deke made his way to the raised platform where the musicians had entertained the previous evening. He looked out over the crowd of alarmed boatmen and passengers, herded together there inside the main cabin. The river pirates pressed the crowd in closer, all the while keeping their weapons at ready. There might have been fifty people here to watch, and only a dozen of them to do the watching.

"Shut up everyone and listen," Deke Saunders shouted, and when the murmuring subsided, he went on. "We've taken over this here boat. Some people have already been killed. Others will be if anyone is stupid enough to try anything against us."

"You can't get away with this," Captain Hamilton growled.

"We already have. The army is busy fighting that fire back there, and so is half your crew, Captain. What do we have left here? Galley help, some scared passengers, a few nigger firemen. What's to stop us from *getting away* with it?"

"By thunder, I will do everything in my power —"

"And you will get yourself killed for your efforts. Now shut up before I begin feeling not so generous and I tell the boys to shoot the lot of you."

A chambermaid who was standing near the stage said weakly, "What *are* you going to do to us?"

Deke leered at her, looking her up and down. "Why, if you weren't so plain . . ."

"That is uncalled for!" Hamilton raged, pushing his way through the crowd to the foot of the stage.

Deke stepped off the stage in front of Hamilton and without warning came up with a short jab to his gut. The captain groaned and buckled, standing there bent over, trying to catch his breath.

"I didn't like the tone in your voice, Captain Hamilton. In fact, I don't much like you at all." Deke yanked open the captain's blue jacket and took Hamilton's watch from his vest pocket. He stepped back up onto the platform where he could see above the crowd and raised his voice. "The next person who figures he has a complaint about the way I am handling this will get a bullet for his trouble. Any questions?"

None was voiced.

"That's better. That's more the way I like it." He looked at the watch in his hand and opened the lid, studying the dial a moment. "Now, this here is what we are going to do. I am gonna wait two minutes, and in

434

that time I want every man and woman in here to march outside. You are all gonna take a swim, and them who ain't jumped into the river by time the two minutes are up, I'm gonna have my men shoot."

Hamilton straightened up painfully and drew in a breath. "For the love of God, don't do this. The paddles will pull them under before anyone has a chance to swim away!"

Deke shrugged his shoulders. "That should be interesting to watch. They can take their chances with the paddle wheels and possible death, or they can stay here and face certain death by my men."

"At least let the passengers off behind the wheels," Hamilton implored.

"It don't matter to me which end of the boat they jump off of, so long as they are in the water in two minutes. And the time starts now."

Instant panic exploded in the room. Hamilton shouted above chaos, "Everyone! Leave by way of the ladies' salon and out the side doors to the stern of the boat! Everyone! Listen! We must depart through the back doors and onto the promenade behind the paddle wheels!"

The crowd shifted toward the rear of the main cabin, plunging into the doorways. In their frenzy they forced their way through two and three at a time. A woman screamed and fell, and they stampeded over her, heedless of her plight.

Hamilton managed to drag the woman to her feet. She was only half conscious as he scooped her up into his arms.

"One at a time!" he yelled above the torrent of panic-driven voices. "We will all make it out, but you must be calm!" Hamilton's words fell on ears stopped up by fear, and on they drove, recklessly, trampling those who had fallen beneath their feet.

"You have thirty seconds," Deke shouted. His warning only intensified their panic to be out of that place.

Some men dove out the side doors, willing to take their chances with the paddle wheels. A burly black fireman had stayed at Hamilton's side. As the last of the throng finally pulled through the doors, he said, "I's will hep yo' wit de' hurt folks, Capt'n Hamilton."

Hamilton recognized the big fireman. His name was Willis, and he reached down and collected two of the fallen men under his massive arms. Hamilton and Willis carried the injured passengers outside. Willis sat on the railing, swung his legs over, and still clutching the two unconscious men, leaped out into the frothy water churning behind the big boat.

Hamilton mounted the railing next, watching the people bobbing in the *Tempest Queen* wake like jetsam thrown overboard from a sinking ship. His heart sank at the thought of leaving his boat to these hooligans, but he didn't have time to dwell on the unfortunate turn of events. Out of the corner of his eye he saw that Deke Saunders was coming through the doorway. Without a moment to waste, he tightened his grip on the woman in his arms and stepped off the edge.

The choppy water closed over him, but in a moment he had clawed his way back to the surface, and when he had blinked the water from his eyes the *Tempest Queen* was steaming away.

From the stern railing Deke Saunders watched the small, bobbing figures recede into the distance. Case Jackson came up alongside him.

"That went easier than I thought."

Deke gave a short laugh. "I was almost hoping they wouldn't make it in time." He turned away, and they went back inside the main cabin. "How much of the crew do we have left on board?"

"There are the engineers yet, and the chief mate along with three of his firemen to keep up steam until we beach her. Then there is a pilot at the helm."

"And that is all?"

Case nodded his head.

Deke was frowning. "I didn't see that army lieutenant, did you?"

"Dempsey? No, but I reckon he's ashore fighting the fire with the rest of his men."

"Maybe. How about that fellow McKay?"

"Haven't seen him either."

Deke and Jackson went out the front doors and down the main staircase.

At the foot of the stairs, Deke stopped and looked around at the cargo stacked about. There was much more here than they would be able to unload or carry. His view stopped momentarily upon the casks of whiskey inboard near the piles of fuelwood, and then at the kegs of gunpowder lined up neatly along the guards.

"Get the men together, Case — those who ain't keeping an eye on someone, and bring them here so's I can talk to them."

"Right." Jackson went off through the mounds of matériel, and in ten minutes eight men were gathered at the bow near the anchors.

"In a little while we will be grounding this boat," Deke said to them. "When we do, we will first unload the rifles, revolvers, and artillery, and the whiskey and gunpowder. Those will bring the most money later. Whatever we have time for afterwards will be just that much gravy." He looked over the men and saw a face among them that he did not recognize. "Who are you?"

"Frank James."

"I ain't never met you, have I?"

"Nope, I don't suppose you have."

"He came along with Laban Caulder," Case Jackson said.

"Laban? Well, I reckon if you are good 'nough for Laban, you're all right by me," Deke said to him, and then, "Someone come with me. I'm gonna need help with carrying down a chest."

William Quantrill stepped forward and volunteered himself and Frank for the job.

Clifton Stewart first saw the smoke climbing into the morning sky miles back, and when he finally reached the hamlet of Catfish Landing, the fire had already been brought under control, but not before half the town lay beneath piles of glowing embers. It appeared to him, as he pulled Firecracker to a halt and looked around at the disaster, that fully one-half of the people here in Catfish Landing were wearing uniforms. He urged his horse forward again and drew up by a group of soldiers sprawled beneath a tree. Some of them were passing a ladle of water around; others were patting the sweat from their faces. Most were stretched out on the ground and breathing hard.

"Is there a fort near here?" Stewart asked.

One of the soldiers looked up. "Nope, none that I am aware of."

"Where did all of you come from?"

Another soldier, who spoke in a German accent, said, "Ve are off of the *Tempest Queen*, bound for Fort Leavenvorth. But she pulled out vithout us."

"She did what?"

Someone laughed and said, "Yeah, it don't make sense to us either. I reckon we just wait until they realize their mistake and come back for us."

Stewart frowned and said, "I don't think they will be coming back."

"Vhat do you mean?" the man with the accent said.

"What I mean is, the *Tempest Queen* has been taken over by river pirates. I only learned of their plan this morning, and I have been riding hard to stop them, but it looks like I am too late. My name is Clifton Stewart, and I work on the *Tempest Queen*."

"Pirates!" The German soldier leaped to his feet.

A soldier at his side said, "What can we do about it now, Eagle?"

"I don't know, but ve can't just sit here and try nothing!"

Stewart called, "They are going to load the army's supplies onto wagons. That means they must be planning to put the *Tempest Queen* into shore somewhere upriver."

"Ve must find horses, and veapons!" Eagle said, and the word passed swifter than the fire that had raged through Catfish Landing. The townspeople, grateful for the help the army had given to them, opened their livery stable, and from every building that still stood poured a flood of rifles and revolvers. In the heat of the excitement to find mounts and weapons, the differences that had separated the troops disappeared as they forged themselves into a single fighting force.

They had been tricked into leaving the boat, the soldiers suddenly realized, and the town of Catfish Landing had been sacrificed to the pirates' cause. Altogether, no one was particularly happy about what had been done to them.

Every available horse was saddled up, but in a town the size of Catfish Landing, that still left half the troops standing there and watching as Clifton Stewart at the head of a contingent of Federal troops pounded out onto the river road fifteen minutes later.

Chapter
Twenty-Three

A sudden commotion swept through the *Tempest Queen*; footsteps had advanced and then receded in the companionway beyond the laundry-room door, and from different directions came the voices of angry men, the cries of startled chambermaids, and more distantly, Dexter McKay heard the muffled reports from revolvers and rifles.

"I should be out there," Dempsey said softly.

Footsteps stopped outside the door just then, and a moment later it opened. The four of them huddled under the dirty pile, barely breathing until the door slammed shut again and the sound of pounding footsteps faded away.

"That was close," Cora Mills whispered.

McKay grinned at her in the dingy light where they bunched together under the sheets. "We can thank the odor of this place that it wasn't any closer."

Dempsey was frowning.

McKay said to him, "There is nothing

you could have done to stop it, Lieutenant. Your men were cleverly lured off this boat, and if I am not mistaken, in a very short time we will be putting back out into the river."

No sooner had he spoken than a low shudder shot through the *Tempest Queen* and the familiar heartbeat of her engines began pumping.

Dempsey glanced at him. "Do you mean the fire was set on purpose?"

"It was."

"You have it all figured out, don't you, Mr. McKay?"

"Not all of it, my good fellow. But enough to have known when to seek cover."

"And how long do you intend for us to remain under cover?"

McKay shrugged his shoulder, threw off the sheets, and leaned back against the laundry-room wall. "I don't believe they will bother to look in here again. And as for how long we will have to wait, well, I think we will know when the time comes for us to venture out."

"We will?" Dempsey was scowling. "Then what?"

McKay laughed softly. "You're the military man. I'll let you figure that one out."

He extracted the deck of playing cards from his inside breast pocket and casually began to cut and shuffle them. "A game anyone, hum? Euchre? Poker?"

Cora looked incredulous. "My, you are the cool one, Mr. McKay. The *Tempest Queen* is being overrun with brigands, and you want to play cards."

"Oh, no. You have it entirely wrong, Miss Mills. I play cards not because I have no trepidations. No, no, I play to keep my hands from shaking" — he flashed a winning smile at her — "and to keep my mind off of what most likely will be an unfortunate end for us all unless we are very careful."

Cora Mills put her arm around Kenneth and drew him nearer to herself. "You are not very reassuring, Mr. McKay."

"No, ma'am." McKay cleared a place on the floor and laid out three cards. "Monte, then?"

"No, I don't think so," Dempsey said, sounding disheartened. "I really ought to be out there doing *something!*"

"In time, my good fellow, in time."

Within a few minutes Catfish Landing was only a distant smudge of black smoke in the sky. Deke Saunders had the chest of

445

gold carried down from its compartment and placed on the deck near one of the landing stages. He put Harold Madden atop it, told him to stay alert, and reminded him that a third of what was inside it was his as well.

The pirates were tearing open the crates, checking on their contents, deciding what was worth taking and what was not. Some of the men had broken into a cask of whiskey, and the drinks were flowing freely.

"You best cut back on that," Deke said, stopping among them on his way up to the pilothouse, "or you'll be too drunk to unload any of it."

They raised a toast to him and continued on. Deke didn't press the point. All he cared about was the payroll, and if the others failed to take their share of the booty, well, it was no skin off of his nose. There would be three horses waiting for him, his boy, and Harold when they got to the rendezvous. They'd split the gold between them and leave the others to unload the munitions and stores. He'd done his part by arranging the robbery. It was up to them to see to it that they got away with something.

"Here, have a drink, Deke," Bud Patterson said, shoving a mug at him that had been appropriated from the boat's galley.

"Not now." Deke left them to their folly and went up to the pilothouse.

"Any trouble, Grady?"

"No, Pa. He's done what I said so far."

Deke peered ahead, through the half-shattered windows. He looked through the splintered hole at the body still sprawled atop the texas among the glass, then took the spyglass from the ledge and studied the shoreline. It was going to be close, but Deke figured that if the men who were supposed to meet them on shore did not run into trouble, the horses and wagons should be arriving at the rendezvous about now. Timing was everything, and he was cutting it close to the hide, but that couldn't be helped. Saunders was confident they'd be there.

"Someplace near here the river roads cuts in and runs right along the shore. You know the place, pilot?"

Jupp had the helm in both hands as if afraid to let go for fear that Grady or Deke would take it as aggression and plant him outside the pilothouse just as they had with Sinclair. He swallowed and ran his tongue over his dry lips. "I know the place. It's not far ahead."

447

"That's where I want you to put in."

"There is no wharf or pier to put into."

"I know that. I want you to get a good head of steam behind you and run this here boat up onto the shore just as far as she will go. Far enough to put the landing stages onto dry ground. Got that clear?"

"Yes, sir."

Deke said to Grady, "I'll spell you up here. Go down and keep Harold company. He's sitting on that gold for us, and I don't trust our friends down there any farther than I can spit."

"All right, Pa." The younger Saunders turned to leave.

"Oh, and don't let anyone talk you into sampling that John Barleycorn that they got flowing like water down there. We got to keep a clear head. Afterwards, when we are safely away, then we can celebrate."

"I understand, Pa."

Grady left, and Deke put the spyglass back on the shoreline ahead.

"The place you want, it is right around that next bend," Eric Jupp said, licking his lips nervously.

Deke put the glass down, and with his revolver steadied in Jupp's spine, he leaned against the back wall of the pilothouse to wait.

"There it is," Jupp said a few minutes later when they had come around a point of land jutting into the water.

Less than a mile ahead was the road, and waiting there, just as he had hoped, were the three freight wagons and the horses.

"Very good." Deke gave a genuine grin again — only the third or fourth since the start of this journey. "Can you get this barge moving any faster?"

Jupp called down the speaking tube. "Mr. Seegar, you there?"

Seegar's voice came up a few seconds later. "So far I am."

"I am going to need all the speed you can give me."

There was uncertainty in Seegar's voice when it echoed back from the engine room. "I'll do what I can. I hope you know what you're doing."

Jupp frowned at the brass tube that rose from the floor and opened up like a tulip. "I'm only doing what a man with a re-volver pointed at my back is demanding to be done."

"Yeah, I sort of got the same problem down here, too."

The steam venting through the 'scape pipes quickened its tempo, and the heart-beat of the *Tempest Queen* stepped up

449

like a man suddenly thrown into a foot-race. Deke Saunders grew tense. He put the barrel of his revolver into Jupp's back.

"Get her all the way into shore, mister."

"I'll do my best."

"You better pray that is good enough."

Jupp gulped and shouted into the tube, "I need more steam, Seegar."

The engineer did not reply, but beneath their feet they could feel the pounding engines pick up a notch, and now the shore-line was racing toward them.

"Something is happening," Cora Mills said all at once. Her green eyes suddenly stretched wide with fear.

"What is it, Mr. McKay?" Dempsey asked.

"It's the engines. They are running at full speed." The gambler gathered up the playing cards and returned them to his inside pocket.

Dempsey said, "Perhaps we are being chased, and the pirates are trying to outrun them."

"Perhaps," McKay said doubtfully, "or maybe something else entirely."

"Like what?"

"You asked when we would know the

time has come. I have a feeling that time is about on us —"

The room lurched beneath them, and they were thrown against the far wall. Baskets and boxes flew off the shelves and came crashing down on them. A horrible groan of wrenching timbers shot through the vessel, and then the room lifted on one side and Cora, Kenneth, Dempsey, and Dexter McKay tumbled into a heap of arms and legs, flailing at the sheets and towels.

"Oh, my!" Cora said, struggling up out of the smelly pile of laundry and pushing her suddenly loose hair back from her eyes.

"They have run into something," Dempsey said, standing and shifting his saber around and in place at his side.

"Are we going to sink?" Cora cried.

"Of course," McKay said, "that is how they are planning to do it. Lieutenant Dempsey, they have run us up onto the shore, and now they will begin to unload the army's matériel, and its gold, too." The gambler fished around the heap for his walking stick and stood up.

"We are not sinking?" Cora asked again.

McKay shook his head. "I rather think not."

Cora was relieved to at least hear that.

"They must be stopped," Dempsey said.

"Precisely," McKay said, brushing his jacket. "But I am afraid we are going to find ourselves outnumbered."

Dempsey opened the door and peered around the corner. "It is clear."

"Have you decided what we are going to do, Lieutenant?"

"First, we need to get our hands on weapons. After that I am sure something will come to mind."

"Ummm. Good plan."

"I'm coming with you," Cora said.

"No, you must stay here where it is safe," Dempsey said.

"I'm afraid the lieutenant is right," McKay agreed.

"But — ?"

"Besides, someone needs to stay here with Kenneth."

Cora saw the logic in that and slowly nodded her head. "Yes, you are right, Mr. McKay."

The two men stepped out into the companionway, closing the laundry-room door behind them. Dempsey withdrew his saber silently from its steel sheath, and McKay took a firm hold on the silver horse-head grip of his ebony walking stick. As they stole quietly up into the abandoned galley,

McKay said, "They will be occupied with unloading the spoils, I should rather think."

"Yes."

McKay stopped and looked at Dempsey. "Err, I suppose we ought to discuss what it is exactly we are planning to do once we find them."

"To do? Why, to save the army's property, of course."

"Hum . . . that's what I thought."

When McKay didn't immediately follow, Dempsey paused and said, "Well?"

"Lieutenant Dempsey, I was just thinking. Err, can't the United States Government afford to lose a few guns. I mean, is it really worth life and limb to directly confront these ruffians just to rescue them — err — do you think?"

"Sir, it is not a question of whether or not the government can afford to lose the matériel. I am an officer of the United States Army, and I must do everything in my power to stop them!" Dempsey looked at McKay sharply. "Are you afraid?"

"Afraid? My dear man, I am terrified. Aren't you?"

"Well, yes, I suppose I feel some anxiety —"

"There. See what I mean."

"I still intend to do what I can. After all,

I am responsible for the supplies reaching Fort Leavenworth."

McKay pursed his lips and thought a moment. In the abandoned galley he could hear the pirates outside, one deck below. "Yes, yes, yes. I want to stop them as well, Lieutenant. But I think it is going to require something a bit more thoughtful than getting our hands on weapons and then hoping something comes to mind."

"Do you have a better idea? I'm open to suggestions, Mr. McKay."

"Lieutenant, it has occurred to me that we each have different, but similar goals. You want to rescue the army's goods. I only want to see that Captain Hamilton's vessel is taken back from the hands of the pirates. I propose we can do both and at the same time avoid a direct confrontation — or at least postpone it."

"How?"

"How?" McKay grinned thinly. "How about stealing the *Tempest Queen* back from Deke Saunders?"

Dempsey blinked, opened his mouth to speak, but closed it before any words emerged. Then slowly a smile broke the solid line of his lips. "That's audacious, Mr. McKay."

"Yes, I rather thought so myself."

"But how do you propose to do it?"

"I think a visit to the engine room is in order."

"Mr. McKay, I need not remind you that this boat is swarming with bandits. I don't see how we can reach the engine room without being seen."

"We won't be observed if we use the back door."

"Back door? I didn't know there was one."

McKay hooked a finger at the army lieutenant and started back down the companionway they had just come along. They hurried past the laundry-room door, and at the end of the passageway was a window. McKay twisted his walking stick and withdrew the short, seventeen-inch sword secreted within it. Dempsey used his own saber, and between the two of them they removed the window from its frame and quietly set it against the wall.

McKay leaned out and looked down. Here the back of the boat dropped straight to the water below, but he could see the railing on the next deck down where the tiller and its cables were located; it was inaccessible to passengers, but the crew could get to the little deck from the galley or by a doorway in the back of the engine room.

"We need a rope of some kind," he said.

Dempsey dashed back to the laundry room and a moment later returned with an armful of sheets. They bound them together, and McKay tossed one end out the window while Dempsey secured the other end to a nearby door handle. Hooking his walking stick under his suspenders, McKay climbed out the window and lowered himself to the deck railing below. Almost immediately Lieutenant Dempsey's legs came swinging into view, and the army officer scrambled over the railing as well.

McKay tried the door to the engine room, but it had been locked from the inside. He went around the back of the boat to a wall. Beyond it sat the huge, red wheel within the paddle box. McKay stepped out onto the guards where the river swirled a few feet beneath him and swung around the edge of the wall into the paddle box, balancing himself on a timber cross brace. Dempsey was right behind him. McKay inched along the beam, grabbed a handhold against the far wall, and gave Dempsey a hand over to the catwalk that was really no more than a foot-wide ledge running between the paddle wheel and the boat's side. It was gloomy inside the paddle box. Steam hissed through one of the vent pipes down low where dark water moved beneath her keel.

"What are we doing in here?" Dempsey asked.

"There is a door just forward of the wheel."

Dempsey glanced at the narrow space between the motionless paddle wheel and boat, and frowned. "Through that?"

"It's the only way." McKay started along the catwalk. Where the huge paddle wheel sat silently on its axle shaft, he had to expel the air in his lungs, and still the battered, red paddle boards brushed his vest buttons as he sidled between them and the boat. Once past the wheel, McKay began breathing again, waiting for Dempsey to make the tight journey.

McKay pulled at the small, sliding door to the engine room. To his relief it rattled open upon its iron rollers. Inside, the engine room sounded like a den of snakes, and the temperature bordered on torrid. The gambler crept past the starboard engine and halted behind a steam pipe the thickness of a medium-size tree trunk. He spied the chief engineer across the steaming room, kneeling upon the floor near the wide door to the outside. Seegar's striker, Bennington, was nearby. McKay could not make out what on the floor was occupying their attention, but as far as he could tell, Seegar and his assistant were the only two people in the room.

"Stay here a moment until I make certain the pirates are not about," McKay said softly to the army lieutenant at his side, and moved out. When he stepped through the vaporous clouds of steam, he must have appeared as an apparition, for all at once Seegar leaped about and stared at him. A moment later he let go of his suddenly held breath.

"Mr. McKay!"

It was then that Dexter McKay saw what it was Seegar and Bennington were doing. They had been bending over a body lying in an expanding pool of blood. "Is he dead?"

"No, not yet. He is losing a lot of blood, but I don't think the bullet hit his vitals. If only we can get him to a doctor, but the scoundrels have thrown everyone overboard."

"That explains why they are no longer prowling the boat," McKay said. "Err — are we alone?"

"As soon as we ran her ashore, the villains all skedaddled. They are all busy stripping the _Tempest Queen_ of her cargo."

McKay waved an arm for Dempsey, and the lieutenant came through the vapors.

McKay said, "How much steam have we, Mr. Seegar?"

"We're carrying a full head so far — a hundred and twenty pounds. I'm letting it bleed away."

"Yes, I saw it when we came in."

"You came through the paddle box?"

"The back door was locked. Err — have we enough pressure to get the paddles turning?"

Seegar's eyebrows dipped together. "What do you have in mind, McKay?"

"Backing us off the bank and out into the middle of the river."

"And then what? Without the furnaces being stoked, we will run out of steam real fast."

"All we have to do is get back out into the current. The river will carry us away."

"We'd be adrift, and with no way to steer her from down here. Besides, the pirates will still be aboard."

"We can seal ourselves in here, can we not?"

"Well, yes, I suppose —"

"And once in the current we can reverse the paddles as needed to point the boat."

Seegar nodded his head. "Sure, and you

can steer her with an oar stuck out back, too, if you had a half-dozen men at it. But not very well," Seegar said sardonically.

McKay smiled, unruffled. "We don't need to be precise. We won't be putting her into a berth, Mr. Seegar. We only need to get her pointed in the right direction. With any luck the current will carry us back to Catfish Landing where Lieutenant Dempsey's men must surely still be waiting for us."

Seegar frowned. "Sorry, McKay. It ain't exactly been a good day down here. Your plan just might work. Only one hitch that I can see."

"What is that?"

"We might not be able to pull ourselves off this muddy shore."

McKay grinned. "The odds are intriguing, are they not? And besides, what have we to lose?"

"Our lives," Seegar said dryly, then, "but, damnation, I'm willing to give it a go! Bennington, get that main door closed, and drive a spike into it. Mr. McKay and Lieutenant, you will have to cover the windows, for that is certainly where they will attempt to get at us from."

The main door rolled shut on its iron wheels, and Bennington drove a nail

460

through it into the solid frame behind. The two engineers tackled the engines, spinning valves and pulling on levers. McKay stationed himself near the left — the larboard side of the room — while Dempsey took the starboard, standing ready with his curved saber in hand.

The mighty engines wheezed, and a spurt of steam shot up the 'scape pipe as slowly one piston slid into its cylinder. A second shot of steam burst from the 'scape pipes overhead, and then another, and the wheels began to rotate, slowly picking up speed.

It would only take a few moments for the pirates to realize what was happening, and when they did, they would be swarming down into the engine room like moths to a fire — and it wouldn't be long after that before the pirates broke through their meager defenses.

McKay crossed his fingers and, with his little Remington in hand, waited for whatever would come next.

Chapter
Twenty-Four

The sudden burst of steam brought Deke Saunders's head around. He was on shore talking with the wagon drivers, and his men had already begun to tramp down the landing stage with crates of small arms over their shoulders and to roll barrels of whiskey toward the waiting wagons when the first gray puff erupted from the 'scape pipes and shot into the blue morning sky.

"The bloody bastards are trying to escape!" Saunders drew his revolver and bounded back up onto the *Tempest Queen*. His men on shore scrambled for their weapons and pounded up the stage after him. The pirates already on board were confused by this unexpected rampage and by the thrumming of the engines coming to life again, but it took only a moment for the word to spread, and then every renegade aboard the *Tempest Queen* knew what was up. They piled in behind the furnaces with Deke Saunders and drew up where the engine-room door had been shut.

"Open it up!" Deke ordered. The men leaped to the task. When the heavy door wouldn't budge, Deke ordered it broken in, but it soon became apparent that the timbered sliding door had been well designed, and no amount of bruised shoulders was going to break it down.

The *Tempest Queen* shuddered as if coming awake from a deep sleep, and her paddle wheels began to turn, digging powerfully into the water, but her bow held fast.

Inside the engine room, Seegar was eyeing the pressure gauges dubiously and slowly shaking his head. He glanced over at McKay. "It isn't gonna work. Without the firemen to feed the furnaces, we can't keep up the pressure. We are already down to seventy pounds per square inch, and it's falling fast."

"How low can it go before the wheels stop?"

"Anything much below twenty will shut her down."

"What you're saying then is that unless we get out and push, we aren't going to get off of the mud."

"It sort of looks like that's right, McKay," Seegar said somberly. "I'm sorry it didn't work."

A bullet ripped through the door, splintering the wood. Then a second hole opened up. McKay flinched and backed out of the line of fire.

"Those crazy fools!" Seegar roared. "If a bullet should pierce one of our steam lines, we will all be scalded to death!"

Dempsey sprinted across the room to McKay. "This is not going to work. We need to draw their fire away somehow."

"I fear you are right, Lieutenant." McKay holstered his revolver under his jacket and shouted at Seegar, "Keep trying to back us off as long as the steam holds out!" and then he crawled through the machinery to the back door. But fists were already pounding it from outside. "The rogues must have discovered the makeshift rope we left dangling from the window."

"Now what?" Dempsey said.

McKay cast about the engine room, and his view settled upon the little door they had entered by. "There is another way," he said and dashed across the engine room. He pulled the door open. Just beyond it the paddle wheel splashed furiously, and water rained down in the paddle box like a spring downpour.

Dempsey eyed the huge turning wheel as McKay tapped his tall beaver hat firmly upon his head and, taking a tight hold of his walking stick, stepped out onto the narrow ledge.

"Stay back from the wheel," McKay warned above the roar of splashing water and the chill draft inside the dark wheel box. He moved as far forward as the little ledge would permit.

Dempsey stepped out behind him, staring at the menacing vanes thrashing not a foot from his right shoulder. He wiped the streaming, muddy water from his face and mouth. "Now what?" he shouted back.

McKay sidled along the ledge to the forward end of the paddle box, which was not so very far yet from the pounding wheel. One slip into the frothing, muddy water just below them and they'd be sucked up under the wheel and crushed beneath it. He grabbed an iron handhold affixed to the wall. The muddy water sloshing inside the wheel box had slicked the ledge like ice.

Dempsey pressed his spine against the wall. "How in the devil are we getting out of this mechanical hell, McKay?"

Dexter McKay inclined his head at the far wall, across the well of angry water, where a ladder was built attached to the wall of the paddle box. Through the gloom and raining brown water it was hardly distinguishable from the rest of the timbers and supporting beams inside the box. "That ladder goes up to a trapdoor on the hurricane deck, near the engine-room skylights!" he shouted above the roar of the paddle wheel. "I've seen the crew use it when working on the wheel."

Dempsey frowned at the ladder across the way, and at the span between it and them; twelve feet of crashing water and whirling death. "I hope they turn this beater off first."

"Most assuredly," McKay shouted. "Careful now. We will follow the ledge around. There are handholds and we shall be all right."

"Just get moving," Dempsey said brusquely.

McKay inched along the ledge, made the corner, caught himself when his heel slipped in the slush, and grinned. But Dempsey didn't grin back; his face was like carved stone, his expression a perfect caricature of terror as the roaring wheel, an arm's length away, slung its watery hurricanelike darts at them.

McKay made the ladder without disaster, and stepping onto it, he hooked an arm through a rung and waited for Dempsey to inch near enough to give him a hand over. "Quickly! We must hurry, Lieutenant."

The twelve feet finally covered, Dempsey braced himself against the wall and studied the small leap from the ledge to the ladder. Mustering his courage, he pushed off the ledge, but his foot slipped on the mud, and his hand missed the ladder's rung.

McKay caught Dempsey's arm an instant before the lieutenant plunged into the churning water. The weight of the falling man nearly wrenched him from the ladder. He was aware of the sound of cracking wood overhead, but now he had all he could do just to maintain the slippery arm in his grasp. Dempsey's legs dangled in the cauldron below, the suction was dragging him from McKay's grip. He clawed at the gambler with his free arm, grabbed a piece of McKay's frock coat, but everything inside the paddle box was coated with slippery muddy water, and Dempsey's grasp slipped.

McKay was losing his own grip on the lieutenant as well. Another rending of wood cracked like a rifle shot through the tempest confined within the paddle box. The ladder attached to the wall moved. McKay dug his nails into the arm still within his grasp, straining beneath Dempsey's weight and the pull of the water at his legs.

As the lieutenant grappled wildly in the air, his eyes bulged at the thrashing wheel; then the fingers of his left hand found McKay's pocket and latched on tight. He managed to pull a leg up and hook his heel onto the ledge. With the drag of the water somewhat diminished, McKay heaved up and Dempsey's other hand snagged the bottom rung of the ladder.

The lieutenant pulled himself up, gripping the ladder in both arms, panting.

"Are you all right?"

"Yes — yes, I think so," he panted. "Thanks to you, Mr. McKay."

"We don't have a moment to lose. Quickly, up the ladder."

"I'm not certain I am up to it just yet."

"Your fall nearly wrenched the thing off the wall, Lieutenant. I suggest we ascend it as quickly as we can and be out of this place before it decides to collapse beneath us."

Dread returned to Dempsey's face. He glanced at the thrashing monster a few feet away and, without further prodding, clambered up the ladder with McKay following closely behind.

The ladder ended thirty feet above the water, near the apex of the paddle wheel. A trapdoor opened onto the hurricane deck. They tumbled out into the morning sun and, breathing heavily, leaned back against the engine-room skylights. McKay was aware of his racing heart. Even in the heat of a high-stake card game, he could not remember it ever having beaten so quickly.

"I should not care to do that again."

Dempsey's face was ashen. "*You* should not care — ?"

"Think of the stories you will be able to tell your children in your old age."

"Following you around, Mr. McKay, I doubt very much that I will ever have an old age to enjoy."

A small smile moved across McKay's lips before they settled back down into a stern line.

"So, now what?"

McKay wiped his face with a damp handkerchief and, returning it to his pocket, said, "Desperate times require desperate actions — err, or perhaps a bold bluff? Come along."

Dempsey scowled unhappily and jogged after McKay.

The pirates were still at the engine-room door and trying to reach its high windows.

McKay and Dempsey made it down to the main deck unseen. The gambler could hear the steam from the 'scape pipes slowing now and the sound of unproductive splashing coming from the paddle boxes. The engines were steadily running down, as Seegar had predicted they would, and for all their efforts, the *Tempest Queen* was still caught firmly in the muddy bank of the Missouri River.

They moved among the cargo, examining the smashed crates of army goods. "What is it we are looking for, Mr. McKay?" Dempsey asked impatiently.

The gambler's view settled upon one of the cannons. "What exactly is that, Lieutenant?"

Dempsey followed the directions of McKay's nod. "It's a three-inch ordnance rifle. Why?"

"Can we load it?"

"Not without being seen, I'm afraid. We'd have to locate the shells first, then the powder canisters, and fuse. Then, if we are lucky enough to get that far, we'd have to unlash it from the deck just to aim it."

"Hum. Not very convenient," McKay muttered softly. "Fuse? You say you have fuse for that cannon?"

"Ordnance rifle, Mr. McKay. It is an

470

ordnance rifle. It has a rifled barrel. And, yes, somewhere among all this cargo is fuse."

"Show me where."

"Well, they have done a fair job of scattering it already. Let me see; it had been placed over this way." Dempsey led off in a crouch, keeping behind the cargo as best as he could. He drew up near a wooden crate and used the edge of his saber to pry up the top. "Here it is —"

McKay grabbed up a length of it. "This should do nicely."

"Should do nicely? Exactly what is it you have in mind, Mr. McKay?"

The gambler's gray eyes gleamed in the morning sunlight. "It is time to see if this Deke Saunders is holding a pat hand, or if he can be bluffed."

"Mr. McKay, this is not a game of cards."

"No, indeed not, Lieutenant; however, the principle is quite the same." McKay moved out with the bewildered lieutenant at his heels. On the guards, where the gunpowder had been stacked, he hunkered down behind some crates and extracted a silver cigar case from his pocket.

"Amazing! See, Lieutenant, they survived the dousing," he said, taking out a

471

cigar and biting the end off.

"You are a curious man."

McKay smirked around the cigar in his mouth and struck a match from his silver matchsafe, which had also come through the ordeal undampened.

Dempsey cast a wary glance at the keg of powder stacked nearby, then to the length of fuse in McKay's hand. "I am not sure I am going to like this bluff of yours, sir."

McKay sucked in and exhaled a ribbon of smoke. "Let us hope that the Reverend Saunders finds it equally appalling." Using the end of his walking stick, McKay knocked in the plug on one of the powder kegs and put the fuse into the hole. "Now to get their attention" — McKay handed Dempsey his little Remington revolver from under his coat — "that is, if the water has not reached the powder or caps."

Dempsey stared unhappily at the cigar that McKay had poised dangerously near the short fuse. Then, drawing in a breath as if to say he had resigned himself to whatever fate this brash gambler had in store for him, he thumbed back the hammer, raised the revolver in the air, and squeezed the trigger.

The Remington cracked like a big firecracker, and a few seconds later two or three curious faces appeared. They saw McKay, saw what mischief he was about, vanished, and the next instant McKay and Dempsey were facing the entire pack of renegade river men.

"Good morning, gentlemen," McKay said jovially, smiling as if he had not the least care in the universe. "Ah, Reverend Saunders, I see you are here as well? I hope to try to dissuade these pirates from their life of sin, yes?"

Saunders glared at the cigar hovering perilously near the fuse. "McKay. I should have known you'd have the gall to try something like this. You seemed too slick to be trusted right from the beginning. Has all that money you inherited from your *poor* dead brother made you simple? Or, let me make a wild guess. There ain't no money, is there?"

"I truly regret to say that there never was, Reverend."

"Then why the lie?"

"To scratch an itch."

"So, you were on to me right from the start."

"No, Reverend, not from the start. But it didn't take too long to figure out something was afoot."

"Some men can be too clever for their own good, McKay."

"True."

"What do you expect me to do? Just walk away from all this after the trouble I went to?"

"That is exactly what I expect you to do. I want you and your pirate band to simply walk away from the *Tempest Queen*, climb aboard those wagons and horses, and let me see their tails disappearing over the top of that ridge."

Saunders laughed. "McKay, you *have* gone simple. Even if you should light that fuse, my men will shoot you dead and pull it off before it reaches the powder. Face it, you've been skunked."

"I don't think so, Saunders." McKay tapped the ash from his cigar and moved it over the open hole in the top of the keg. "Now, any wagers on just how long it will be before the next hot ash falls, Reverend? Of course, there is no guarantee a spark won't fall immediately. If you do shoot me, what's to stop my cigar from plunging promptly into the powder?"

Saunders's face went taut, and eyes widened. "Now — now, McKay. What — what you're doing there is plain stupid. A spark can *fall* at any second! You'll blow us all to kingdom come!"

"Yes, it is a possibility." He covered a yawn with his hand and patted his mouth. "So, I should think you and your men will want to be leaving shortly? A good long distance away, hum? If all this powder should go off at once, no place within a hundred rods will be spared of destruction, don't you think?"

"You're willing to kill yourself just to stop us? You're crazy, McKay!"

The gambler clucked softly and shook his head. "My, my, look how long that cylinder of ash has grown in just these few moments that we have been talking about it."

"I'm gettin' outa here, Deke," one of the pirates said.

"Yeah, me, too."

"Hold up, he's got something up his sleeve," Saunders shot back.

"Maybe he does, but I ain't gonna hang around to find out what it is!"

"Everyone! Stay put!" This was Grady Saunders's voice, and it came from the deck above them. He had come from one of the side doors to the main cabin, up on the promenade deck, and as he stepped to the railing, he shoved Cora Mills and the boy ahead of him. She grabbed at one of the ceiling posts to keep from falling over it, then Grady wrapped his arm around her waist and pressed the barrel of his revolver into her temple. "Looky what I found sneaking down the companionway."

"Cora!" Dempsey cried.

"Sherman!"

"Unhand her, you rogue!"

Grady said, "McKay. Step away from there or she's a dead woman."

Dempsey was aghast. His eyes shifted toward the gambler. "You must listen to him, Mr. McKay."

This was a most unexpected turn of events, and McKay felt his gambit falling apart. His brain scampered around, reassessing the odds and what his next move should be.

"Mr. McKay, please!" Dempsey insisted. "He will murder Cora if you don't. This venture is not worth that! Let them have the cargo; let them burn this boat to the water if they like. It is not worth Cora's life!"

"Listen to him, McKay," Deke Saunders said, his eyes still frozen upon the cigar poised above the keg of gunpowder. "Put that cigar down, and I promise you we won't hurt you."

Dexter McKay laughed and said, "I

wonder if you didn't make that same promise to Sergeant Carr before you murdered him?"

Dempsey glanced at him, startled.

Saunders stammered, "Carr — ? But how — ?" Then he shut his mouth. "You are too clever for your own good, McKay. All right, go and blow us all into the Hereafter. We will only be a couple heartbeats behind that gal, anyway. Grady!"

"Yeah, Pa?"

"I'm a gonna count to three, and if McKay ain't thrown that cigar overboard by then, kill the woman."

"I will, Pa."

"One . . . Two . . ."

"All right, Saunders, you win." McKay flung the cigar far out over the water.

Deke Saunders let out a long breath and took the revolver from Dempsey's hand. He stepped back out of reach. "You two move away from them kegs," he said, waving the revolver. "Grady, bring the girl and the kid down here."

Grady pulled Cora from the railing and marched the two of them down to the main deck and shoved them alongside Dempsey. Deke studied the four of them narrowly as Dempsey drew Cora near to him and put his other arm over Kenneth's shoulder.

"What are you going to do to us?" the lieutenant said.

McKay grimaced and wished that Dempsey had not asked. It was pretty plain what Saunders had in mind for them.

Deke Saunders gave a low laugh. "I've got right appropriate plans for the four of you — well, three of you at least. But first I want to deal with McKay." He turned McKay's own revolver on the gambler. "I don't much like you, McKay. You've played me for a sucker and you've messed in my business one time too many."

Without warning or hesitation, he thumbed back the hammer and shot McKay in the chest.

Chapter
Twenty-Five

Cora let out a cry and buried her face in Sherman Dempsey's chest.

"All right, Cora, all right," the lieutenant said, trying to comfort her while staring at Dexter McKay, sprawled face down on the deck. He shifted his view back to Saunders. "I suppose we are next."

Saunders flung McKay's revolver away and yanked his own Colt's navy from his waistband. "I reckon you are, only I ain't gonna shoot you. No, that would be too quick, too easy. I'm gonna let you sweat awhile, and ponder how you was about to do me and my men in. You and your lady friend and her kid can think real hard on it, army boy, while me and my men finish what we started. Hinkley, Green, take these folks up to the bow and tie them to the jack staff. Make sure you do it good and tight. The rest of you men get busy with this stuff. Grady and Harold, move that paymaster's chest ashore."

Before the men went back to work, Deke

told them to leave three or four kegs of gunpowder where they were, and take the rest.

"How about them engineers?" Ralph Dickerson asked.

"Leave 'em be for now. They have about run out of steam, and besides, they ain't gonna be getting off of this tub alive anyway, and we got more important things to do than to worry about fishing them out."

Frank James lingered there a moment longer, staring at McKay.

"What's wrong, Frank?"

"Huh?" He looked over his shoulder at Quantrill. "Oh. I . . . I have never seen a man murdered in cold blood before."

Quantrill laughed. "It's kind of a shock the first time, but you get over it. In a while you won't even think about it. The next time gets easier, believe me."

Frank slowly nodded his head. "I reckon it's something I'll have to get used to."

"We all did at one time. You ain't no different than any one of us — now."

Frank looked up sharply. A slow realization of that one-way bridge he had just crossed came to his face. "You're right. I'm just like you and Deke and Tom Green and Case Jackson — and Laban Caulder."

Quantrill laughed again. "Come on, let's claim our share of the spoils before we get left out."

"Try again," he said, straining at the ropes that dug into his wrists.

"It's no use," Cora said, frustrated. "I can't free myself. They are so tight my fingers are starting to tingle."

"I'm scared, Mama," Kenneth said, trying not to cry, but Dempsey heard the stifled tears in the young boy's voice just the same.

Dempsey gritted his teeth against the sharp stab of tearing flesh and wrenched his wrists, but the ropes held, and finally he stopped trying and leaned his head back against the jack staff. Cora was tied to his back, and he couldn't see her face unless they both looked over their shoulders, but where their hands were secured, her fingers managed to reach and twine with his own. He knew he had fallen in love with this wonderful woman. He had not started this trip looking for someone to share his busy life with, but somehow he had found her. And now, in a short while, it would all end. . . .

I cannot allow that to happen! Dempsey silently said to himself.

With renewed vigor he bunched his fists and pulled, but the ropes only cut deeper, and a trickle of warm blood crawled down his fingers and dripped from their tips.

"How do you think they will do it, Sherman?"

Dempsey shook his head. "I don't know."

There followed a short pause, then Cora said, "I think I know how."

He looked over his shoulder. Their eyes met and she said, "They are leaving some gunpowder. I think they intend to —"

"Does it make any difference how they intend to do it?" he interrupted her, thinking of the small boy there with them, listening.

"No, I suppose not." She looked out across the water, and he went back to watching the pirates file past them and down the landing stage, bent under their loads of army goods, filling up the freight wagons on shore. They had begun to roll off the ordnance rifles now; the first of them had already been tied to the back of a fully loaded wagon and was being towed out of the way as a second wagon pulled up.

"Poor Mr. McKay," she said after a while.

"He tried to help," Dempsey said. "He could have easily stole away without being seen, but he didn't."

Suddenly Deke Saunders was standing over them. "If you had been smart, you all would have gotten off when you had the chance. McKay ought to have kept his meddling nose out of my business. You all ought to have. Where has it gotten you?"

"You'll not get away with this, Saunders. The army will hunt you down. They won't stop until they have apprehended every one of you."

Saunders laughed and reached under his black frock coat for a half-smoked cigar. "They will try, I reckon," he said, striking a match along the jack staff and putting it to the cigar's charred end. He shook out the match, took the cigar from his lips, and said, "But the army already has its hands pretty full with them Injuns out in the Territories. And considering the way Congress has castrated their budget, there ain't a whole lot of hands left to go around. Anyway, this country is sitting on a powder keg, just waiting for the right spark to come along, and I've got a feeling it ain't gonna be long before it blows sky-high. The government will have more important things to bother with than one small shipment of arms. Especially if the Republicans win into the presidency next year. Them fine Democrats won't take to that very well. I already hear talk about secession if that happens. No, if them Republicans get into office and try to emancipate all those slaves away from them fine Democrats, them Southern Whigs, and them unreconstructed Know-Nothings, there is gonna be a fight like you ain't never seen before, and this here government ain't gonna have time to worry about a small fish like me. Nosiree, they ain't."

Deke drew on the cigar and looked around the deck. "Well, seems like my boys got pretty much what they were after. Speaking about powder kegs" — Saunders studied the glowing tip of his cigar and managed a grin — "there are one or two that I need to tend to now. Good-bye, Lieutenant, Miss Mills."

Saunders left them there and made his way back to where the pirates had left the small stack of kegs. He told his men to get clear of the *Tempest Queen*. Those few still aboard her scuffled off like rats off a foundering ship.

Dempsey craned his neck after Saunders. He was aware of Cora, twisting her wrists in the ropes. Kenneth had finally succumbed to his fear and was whimpering quietly. Saunders momentarily disappeared behind some crates still left aboard, and when he sprang back into view, he was hurrying toward the landing stage.

Cora cried desperately, "Please, take Kenneth with you!"

But Saunders paused only long enough to laugh and flick his cigar at them. He ran down the stage and swung up on the horse waiting there for him.

"Let's get away from here, boys!" he shouted, galvanizing the pirates into action. Freightmen cracked their whips, and those outlaws on horseback kicked their mounts into motion.

Dempsey stared at the powder kegs. He could not see the burning fuse from his vantage point, but a telltale ribbon of smoke rising up behind the canvas-covered mound of trade goods the pirates left behind signaled the deadly clock ticking away. Quickly he calculated how long it would take for the fuse to burn down to the gunpowder. They had little more than a minute left. He gave his ropes one last burst of strength, but they held tight. All they could do now was wait.

Cora must have known, too, how little time they had left and that it was hopeless to struggle any further. She said softly to the boy, "Remember that song we used to sing when you were little and I'd put you to bed?"

Kenneth sniffed and said, "I remember."

"How did it go again?"

His small voice cracked, and then he began to sing a song about frogs and crickets. It was a lullaby Dempsey remembered his own mother singing to him.

He closed his eyes, giving one last try at the ropes as his brain silently counted down the seconds. In his mind's eye he watched the sputtering flame eating away at the length of fuse, crawling closer and closer to the gunpowder. . . .

An explosion snapped his eyelids open. But it wasn't the kegs of gunpowder as he expected. It was a rifle shot. And then another, and then the whole hillside where Saunders and his pirates were fleeing erupted into gunfire.

It was the army!

It was *his* army!

Dempsey instantly recognized his men. The one called Eagle was at the head of the column, and alongside him rode a civilian on a sleek, long-legged horse, brandishing a revolver, firing into the scattering pirate band.

As the army swept in, this civilian wheeled his horse around and fired, dropping a pirate. He took aim again, and another brigand fell. Eagle and the soldiers were curiously armed, not military regulations at all, but they fought superbly just the same, and the pirates fell beneath their charge.

Dempsey glanced over at the powder kegs, half hidden by the pile. The fuse had stopped smoking! It could mean only one thing; it had reached the powder and any second now —

The civilian wheeled again and drove his powerful horse straight for the *Tempest Queen.* It slid to a stop at the foot of the landing stage and the man leaped off, bounding up onto the boat.

"Where is everyone?"

"They've all been put off," Dempsey said, "and you must abandon her, too. The pirates had set a fuse in those kegs, and they are going to blow any second!"

The man fell to his knees and began working at the knots.

"You must save yourself!" Dempsey insisted. "The fuse has burned down. This whole boat is going to blow up any instant!"

"My dear man, I certainly hope not. It

would most ruin my clothing far beyond the abuse they have already sustained."

Dempsey heard the voice, and he could hardly believe his ears. His head flung around and his eyes expanded. "Mr. McKay!"

Dexter McKay held the short piece of cannon fuse for Dempsey to see, and casually tossed it away, brushing the dust from his clothing as he came across the deck.

Cora looked like she had seen a ghost. "But you were dead! I saw Saunders shoot you!"

McKay shook his head and smiled serenely. "That little revolver of mine is really most inadequate. I ought to buy something more robust, but anything larger would simply ruin the lines of my jacket." McKay put his hand inside his coat and pushed a finger through the little hole in the material at his breast.

"I don't understand," she said, shaking her head.

McKay removed the deck of cards that he kept there. "Fortunately, Saunders used my own revolver. If he had shot me with his Colt, I would, indeed, have been dead."

Dempsey said, "Lady Luck was on your shoulder this time."

"Lady Luck is always on Mr. McKay's

shoulder," the man working at their bindings said. The ropes fell away, and Clifton Stewart stood.

Dexter McKay stopped in his tracks, seeing him clearly for the first time, and then with an exuberant burst he cried, "Clifton!" and threw his arms about the man. Suddenly remembering his aplomb, he released him, but he continued to pump his hand with a vehemence that almost took Stewart's arm off. "We had given you up for dead."

"I almost was dead, but thanks to a family who fished me from the river, I am quite all right now — except for a bit of a headache. Tell me, what happened here?"

"It is a long story, and we will have plenty of time to tell it, but first there is the matter of these scoundrels whom the army has now in charge." McKay smiled at Dempsey, Cora, and Kenneth. "I am pleased to see that they did not hurt you. After the bullet hit me, I was stunned for a few moments, but then once I realized the deck of cards in my pocket had stopped it, I decided I could be of more use if the pirates thought me dead."

"But weren't you frightened?" Cora asked, rubbing her bruised wrists.

McKay eyed her curiously, then laughed

lightly. "Frightened? My dear lady, I was terrified!"

On the riverbank, Dempsey's men were rounding up the last of the pirates. Some had made good their escape, but most had not. Those not wounded or killed had been taken under guard. "I need to go and help my men," he said and strode down the landing stage. In a few minutes the soldiers drove the pirates up onto the boat, bound them hand and foot, and stood them along the deck in a row.

Dempsey came back aboard and said to Stewart, "My men tell me you alerted them to the real peril the boat was in. I owe you my sincere thanks, Mr. Stewart."

"I am only too happy to have been able to help out, Lieutenant."

Seegar and Bennington ventured out of the engine room, and seeing the situation now well in hand, and the army in control, they carried the wounded striker out onto the deck where he was made comfortable and his bleeding attended to by the soldiers. Jupp made his way down from the pilothouse, followed by two soldiers carrying Sinclair's body. They laid him near the six dead pirates.

Dempsey scrutinized the line of pirates standing there. He stopped at the haggard-faced old man. Saunders was cradling an arm. A bloody bandage tied near his shoulder was crimson, and a small red pool was spreading at his feet.

"Is it true? Did you murder Sergeant Carr as McKay says?"

"Sure I murdered him. He got greedy."

"Greedy?"

Saunders's face was hard, his eyes hateful. "Whose idea do you think this was in the first place?"

Dempsey knew the answer to that by the tone in Saunders's voice. "It was Carr's?"

The river pirate gave a short laugh. "His pa and me, we were working this here river when you were still in swaddling. I hadn't seen Carr in years. Then one day I get his letter laying out the deal. I said I was in, and I set it up, then got the men together. But young Carr got greedy, he did. Wanted more than the split we had worked out. So's I kilt him."

"But why would he do it?"

"He wanted to get into government. I reckon because his pa made good thieving on the Missouri, Philip figured he'd do even better thieving in Washington, and he saw the money this job would bring as a way to get there." Saunders snorted. "I didn't never tell Philip he was wasting his time. Already too much competition in government for his kind. He'd have done better sticking to what he already know'd."

Dempsey grimaced and walked on. He stopped again and looked at the boy standing there, his head bowed, shoulders stooped. "You're a mite young for this sort of thing, aren't you?"

"I'm sixteen," the boy said looking him in the eye.

"I'm sorry to say you'll be a lot older when they let you out of prison, son."

"Frank!"

Frank James looked over. "Ben? What are you doing here?"

"I was the one who brought the army."

"Why?" Frank was having difficulty keeping his voice from breaking.

"Because this boat is my home. This is where I live and work. And besides, what you and Laban did was wrong. I had to stop you." Stewart glanced at the bodies laid out on the deck. "See where it has gotten your uncle?"

Frank started to speak, choked on his words, and then cleared his throat and said, "I reckon I let some of Jesse's wild stories get to me. I should have known better."

"Yes, you should have. You have disappointed your family, Frank, but more than anyone, you have hurt Jesse. He always figured you for having more sense. He looked up to you."

Frank lowered his eyes, and his head fell back to his chest.

"Lieutenant Dempsey, might I have a word with you . . . in private?" Clifton said.

The two men walked across the deck and conferred quietly a moment. When finally they had come to an agreement, Dempsey strolled back, looking grim as he surveyed the pirates once more. He thought he had overlooked Grady Saunders, but no, he had only looked in the wrong place. Grady was stretched out with the other dead — next to a pirate wearing shiny army boots!

Carr's boots! he realized all at once.

"Get a tarp over those bodies, Corporal," Dempsey said to a soldier standing nearby. To a sergeant who had come up, he said, "Take these pirates into the main cabin and see that they are properly secured and two guards are over them at all times. Looks like we will have more than army matériel to deliver to Fort Leavenworth."

"Yes, sir. All right you sorry lot, start marching up those stairs, and I'll shoot the first one of you who steps out of line."

The pirates began to shuffle toward the wide staircase in short steps; the ropes at their ankles would allow no more than that.

Dempsey watched them being led away, then he frowned deeply and said, "Sergeant, bring that young one here to me."

Frank James was shagged out of the line and hauled over to Lieutenant Dempsey. "You have an advocate, Mr. James. You are fortunate. Mr. Stewart has pleaded your case, and I have agreed to put you in his hands. This goes against my better judgment, and my authority to do so is questionable; however, Mr. Stewart performed a great service for the United States Army, and I have agreed to grant him his request." Dempsey signaled one of his men to free the boy.

Frank said, "Thank you, mister."

Stewart took him by the shoulder and escorted him off the boat to the horses, which had been rounded up and tethered between two trees.

When they had left the boat, Cora came up to Sherman Dempsey and took his arm. "I think you did the right thing by letting that young one go. Maybe this scare will prevent him from falling into a life of crime later on in life?"

"You think so?"

"I do, Sherman."

Dempsey frowned. "Then why do I feel like I've just made the biggest blunder of them all?"

She squeezed his arm and gave him a reassuring smile that helped him put Frank James out of mind.

On the shore, the first of the passengers that had been thrown overboard were finally making their way along the river road, and Captain Hamilton was at the head of the bedraggled group. He stopped abruptly and planted his fists on his waist, looking over the scene before his eyes — the soldiers beginning to unload freight wagons, his boat run up into the muddy shore. With a burst of renewed energy, Hamilton made straight for the *Tempest Queen*'s landing stage.

"By Glory! You've managed to put the pirates down. My congratulations to you, Lieutenant, and to your soldiers."

"Thank you, Captain," Dempsey said, "but really there are others to thank. Mr. St—"

"Has my boat been damaged any?" Hamilton interrupted, his blue eyes hitching left and right and finally riveting the chief engineer. "Mr. Seegar. How did the *Tempest Queen* come through the ordeal?"

"I haven't had time to check her out, Captain. But we were fortunate to run up on mud, not into snags that might of ripped her hull. I don't think the damage is great."

Hamilton glanced at the smokestacks. "Then get the firemen to work and let's try to pull ourselves off of here."

"Most of the firemen were put over the side with the rest, Captain."

Hamilton pulled the reins in on his headlong rush to get his boat back into the river. "I suppose I am being somewhat impatient, Mr. Seegar. There is a proper order here, and the first item is seeing that all our people are safely back aboard" — he looked at Dempsey — "and that your supplies have been returned to the *Tempest Queen*." Hamilton shifted his view. "Where is Lansing?"

"I'm right here, Captain," Chief Mate Edward Lansing said from behind him. He was making his way up the landing stage, his clothes soaked, his hair plastered flat against his cheek and neck — in a soggy state very much like Captain Hamilton and all the other almost-drowned passengers and crew of the *Tempest Queen* who were currently filing aboard.

"Mr. Lansing, once your men have made

it aboard, give the lieutenant assistance with his cargo."

"Yes, sir. I'll just run up to my cabin and change clothes."

"Now, where is my pilot?" Hamilton said.

Dexter McKay said, "Mr. Jupp was about a few minutes ago, Captain. But Mr. Sinclair is dead."

This brought Hamilton's head around with a snap. "Patton — dead?"

"The soldiers carried him down from the pilothouse." McKay inclined his head at the row of legs poking out from beneath the tarpaulin the soldiers had drawn up over the dead.

Hamilton shook his head wearily. "Sinclair was a crackerjack pilot, and a fine man. I shall miss him, in spite of his arrogance."

"It was just the pilot in him, Captain," McKay said. "They are all like that."

Hamilton nodded his head. "Yes . . . yes. We have lost good men on this trip. I shall be most happy to be rid of this wretched, muddy stream."

Dempsey released his arm from Cora Mills's grip and said, "Well, I need to get about the army's business," and after giving Cora a most generous smile, he hurried down the landing stage to help his men — moving aside for a young man with a sack slung over his shoulder, making his way up it.

The young man who had stepped aboard the *Tempest Queen* wore a broadcloth jacket, a white straw hat that gleamed in the sunlight, and a broad, black leather belt to hold up his trousers. A thatch of tow hair poked out from beneath the blinding hat, and he came across the deck toward Captain Hamilton with a self-assured swagger that at once reminded McKay of someone else. He stopped, looked around the *Tempest Queen* with an eye that obviously appreciated what it saw, then he dropped the sack at his feet.

"I know this boat," he said, squinting up at the hurricane deck, then to the colors flying from the jack staff. "She's the *Tempest Queen*." His view came back to Hamilton. "Then you must be Captain William Hamilton."

"I am —"

"I have passed you by a time or two on the wide and glorious river east of here. What are you doing away up here, on the Missouri?"

"You are a boatman, sir?"

The man grinned. "I am." His chest

swelled a bit. "I'm a licensed pilot. Apprenticed on the *Paul Jones*."

"Under Mr. Bixby?"

"The very one."

"Bixby is a sharp pilot," Hamilton said.

"I've a friend by the name of Grimes, who speaks highly of you, Captain Hamilton, and of the *Tempest Queen*."

"Ah, Mr. Absalom Grimes. I know the man well. He spends most of his out-of-work time riding the high bench up in my pilothouse."

The man looked around the boat again, his view lingering on the dead men laid side by side. "What has happened here?"

"River pirates," Hamilton said briefly.

"Pirates!" The man's eyes sparked, as if a thought had just occurred to him, and then he laughed and said, "Why, when I was a boy growing old along the Mississippi, we bare-footed kids used to sneak out of church on Sunday mornings and go down to the levee to watch the riverboats passing by in their splendid grandeur, their decks all fenced and shining in the sunlight. And we used to allow between us that if we lived right, and we were good, God would permit us to be riverboatmen — or pirates!"

He laughed again, but when he saw that

none of them was in any mood to join in on his humor, he straightened his face and said, "I was just on my way down to the Mississippi. I've a berth on a boat there. I've been visiting friends near here and thought I'd walk back and paint the countryside afresh upon the canvas of my brain, but seeing as this is the *Tempest Queen*, the *Queen* of the Mississippi, I was wondering if I might ride down with your pilot?"

McKay could tell Hamilton was flattered.

Hamilton said, "You are welcome to come along, sir, but we are going upriver, to Fort Leavenworth. We won't be back to the Mississippi for another week."

"Upriver? I see. Well, it looks like I caught the bull by the wrong end again." He grinned. "I need to be back in St. Looie in three days, so I reckon these old dogs are just going to have to put up with broken-down boots and darned socks a little while longer, and carry me like the good Lord intended they should do."

Clifton Stewart came up the landing stage just then. Hamilton's view shot past the stranger, and suddenly a smile exploded across his face. "Mr. Stewart!" Hamilton roared, and McKay thought that

Hamilton was going to throw his arms around the young fellow as McKay had a few moments earlier, but instead the captain clasped his hand in both his own.

"Captain Hamilton. You do not know how happy I am to have found you, and the *Tempest Queen* again."

"It was Clifton who brought the army," McKay said.

Hamilton looked back at him. "But — but I thought you were dead!"

Stewart smiled. "I'm afraid the report of my death was an exaggeration."

"I like that," the stranger said. He licked the point of a pencil that he'd fished from his shirt pocket and began scribbling on a scrap of paper upon his knee. When he discovered them staring at him, the stranger grinned up crookedly and said, "Never know when the occasion will arise when a clever proverb will be useful." He folded the paper back into his pocket and pushed the stub of a pencil after it.

McKay smirked, but said nothing.

The man hefted his sack back over his shoulder. "Well, since you are going upriver, and I down, I reckon I ought to be on my way. Nice meeting you, Captain Hamilton. I will sound my whistle the next time our boats pass." He turned to leave, then thought of something else and said, "If you should ever need a pilot, I'd appreciate your looking me up. You have a fine boat, and I'd be pleased to have a hand on her helm someday."

"We have just lost one of our Mississippi pilots. If you did not already have a berth, I'd consider your offer, sir. I don't believe I got your name?"

"It's Clemens, sir. Samuel Clemens."

"I will keep you in mind."

"Thank you. I hope the second half of your trip is not as exciting as apparently the first half has been. Good day." Sam Clemens tramped down the landing stage and, putting his feet upon the river road, turned east.

"Amen," Captain Hamilton breathed softly. He felt his vest pocket for his watch, frowned, and asked, "Anyone have the time?"

McKay dragged out his heavy, gold Jürgensen. "It is only eight-twenty of the clock."

"Humm. Feels much later."

McKay grinned. "You're just not used to taking your exercise so early, Captain."

"If you wish to make jokes, Mr. McKay, you may leave with that not so humorous Mr. Clemens." He glanced around and raised his voice. "All right, we've a boat to run. I want to be back on the water in one hour. Let's get cracking!" Hamilton turned on his heels and marched back to the engine room.

McKay watched Cora Mills take her boy by the hand, and together they went down the landing stage to be nearer to Lieutenant Dempsey, already busy getting the army's matériel back in some sort of order, his quartermaster's training taking control again.

"Well, Mr. Stewart," McKay said, leaning upon his walking stick. "You must tell me all about your adventures of these last few days."

Stewart let out a sigh. "I daresay, you will not believe it, Mr. McKay. But you had a few adventures of your own, too."

"That young man whom you escorted off. You know him?"

"His name is Frank James. And it was he and his family who fished me out of the river and saved my life. I believe the lad was just out to fulfill some boyish dream and had the misfortune to fall in with the wrong company. He is really a well-mannered and studious lad. I had promised his distraught mother when I left that I'd do all I could to watch out for him.

Fortunately, the lieutenant was grateful enough for my timely arrival that he let him go at my appeal. I sent him back home on one of the finest horses I have ever ridden. I think Frank James and his little brother, Jesse, have had all the pirating they can stand for a while. They are good kids. I'm glad I was able to divert Frank away from a life of crime."

"He was lucky."

"And if anyone knows about luck, Mr. McKay, it is you."

Dexter McKay turned with Stewart toward the wide, curving staircase, then climbed up to the main cabin. "Oh, I don't know. It sounds to me like you have had your fair share of her blessings as well. I know it is still early, but I think we both could do with a sip of something, don't you?"

"Anything will be good, so long as it is black coffee."

Dexter McKay laughed, and hitching his ebony walking stick under his arm, they left the main deck to the soldiers bringing Dempsey's supplies back aboard.